The
Detective's
Daughter

Lesley Thomson was born in 1958 and grew up in
London. She went to Holland Park Comprehensive
and the Universities of Brighton and Sussex. Her
novel *A Kind of Vanishing* won the People's Book
Prize in 2010. Lesley combines writing with teaching
creative writing. She lives in Lewes with her partner
and is working on a new Stella Darnell mystery.

Also by Lesley Thomson

Seven Miles from Sydney
A Kind of Vanishing

LESLEY THOMSON

The
Detective's
Daughter

HEAD
of ZEUS

First published in the UK in 2013 by Head of Zeus Ltd

9 7 5 3 1 2 4 6 8

A CIP catalogue record for this book is available from
the British Library.

ISBN (HB) 9781908800244
ISBN (XTPB) 9781908800251
ISBN (E) 9781781853177

Printed in Germany.

Head of Zeus Ltd
Clerkenwell House
45-47 Clerkenwell Green
London EC1R 0HT

www.headofzeus.com

For Mel.

Acknowledgements

I have many to thank for their time and support. Several people gave thought to my research questions. I would like to offer special thanks to: Detective Superintendent Stephen Cassidy of the Metropolitan Police for his generous help. When sharing his knowledge Steve considered the context of my characters; this made his information invaluable. However, any perceived inaccuracies are all mine. Francis Pacifico of the London Underground who shared with me his experience of daily life as a driver on the District Line. Ann Laker of Transport for London for arranging the special morning I spent travelling up and down between Ealing Broadway and Upminster in Frank's cab, which confirmed my love of London's underground transit system. I spent many blissful hours in the Hammersmith and Fulham Archives journeying into the past; indeed, losing all sense of the present. Staff were helpful and informed. This is a wonderful resource: for writers, but also for residents of the borough and of London. Dr Harriet Wood for her considered help with vital medical information and for 'fact checking' the fiction. Any residual errors are mine. And to Lisa Holloway and Melanie Lockett for their forensic reading and excellent feedback.

I am extremely grateful for the loan of solitary spaces in lovely parts of the country in which to write. A big thank you to: Debra Daley; Kay and Nigel Heather; Liz and Kathryn Reed; Margaret and Ivan Roitt.

I would like to thank: Juliet Eve; Alex Geldart; Marcus Goodwin and specifically Greg Mosse.

My warm thanks goes to my agent, Philippa Brewster, who is a joy to work with; to all at Capel and Land, particularly Georgina

Capel and Romilly Must. And thanks to my editor, Laura Palmer, whose feel and commitment to the story made the editorial process such a pleasure; to the great team at Head of Zeus, particularly Becci Sharpe and Clemence Jacquinet; thanks to Richenda Todd for her gimlet-eyed copy-editing and to Jane Robertson for her all-encompassing proof-reading.

'*To walk is to lack a site.*'

'Practices of Space', Michel de Certeau

Above a pond,
An unseen filament
Of spider's floss
Suspends a slowly
Spinning leaf.

'Dark Matter'
A Responsibility to Awe, Rebecca Elson

Prologue

'Jonny!'

Kate Rokesmith heard no sound from three floors up where, insisting that his new toy come on their walk and despite her efforts to dissuade him, Jonathan had gone to fetch the steam engine from his bedroom. She took a silver cigarette case from her jacket pocket, flipped it open, snapped it shut, put it back.

Where was he?

She rearranged her scarf, welcoming the cool silk against her skin in the stuffy heat. She would have to confess that the prized engine was scratched and flecked with crustaceans best not examined. At breakfast she had appreciated her little boy's creativity when he poked Shreddies through the cab window and trickled milk down the funnel; she had made only feeble efforts to stop him. Although she had kept Jon away while the spare room was decorated, somehow plaster dust had crept in around the wheel axles and, once moistened with spoonings of milk, had set hard. At least the wheels still turned. It was not a good idea for Jon to bring the 1950s Triang steam engine to the river.

Kate had ducked out of her mother-in-law's birthday lunch on the pretext of a headache. Time had not secured either Mrs Rokesmith a toehold towards intimacy. Kate appeared to the older woman listless and entirely wrong as the spouse of an established civil engineer. Hugh Rokesmith's mother was fond of the 'idea' of her grandson, but found his full-tilt reality irksome. Outside work, Hugh shirked the role of mediator and did nothing to encourage a

1

rapprochement between his mother and his wife; Kate's decision to stay at home with Jonathan suited them all.

As soon as Hugh had driven off, Kate told her son they must have fresh air so would go to the river.

She caught her foot on a kilim spread across the spacious hall floor and stooping to smooth it hit her forehead on the marble edge of the table. Tears welled as the pain exploded and she pummelled her scalp furiously.

'Jonathan. Hurry up!'

No answer.

Once by the river, she told herself, Jonathan would abandon the engine in favour of dagger-shaped stones, snakes of rope and leaves and twigs that would end up in his duvet or stuffed in his toy-box.

His mother's systematic disposal of his treasures was to the little boy a betrayal that he could not articulate.

Kate wandered through to the dining room. It smelled of polish. They seldom entertained: she was no cook. Hugh met his clients in restaurants. The room had become his impromptu study. Papers and technical drawings were laid out on the table that she and Jonathan were under strict orders not to touch. In one corner was an upright Kemble piano that Hugh had bought Kate for her twenty-first birthday three years before. The lid was up, a book of Beethoven Sonatas open at the 'Pathétique'. This was Jonathan's favourite and his mother knew it by heart.

Standing at the instrument, Kate played the opening bars of the Adagio cantabile. Perhaps she hoped Jonathan might be lured down by the poignant melody, the notes rich and mellow in the high-ceilinged room, but he did not come.

She returned to the hall and absently tapped out the tune on the balustrade; she pictured him crouched in her wardrobe, hands clamped over his eyes, his face buried in her coat; a new game that culminated in spectacular tantrums when she would not play with him.

The tide would be coming in.

The air in the house was still. Plaster dust lingered, making her skin feel dry and papery.

'Jonathan! Last chance or I'm leaving you all alone.'

No answer.

If he were here, Hugh would have stormed upstairs to fetch him; used to assessing risk, he would assume his son was hurt or systematically damaging something. Kate craned up the stairwell to the topmost landing and met the cantankerous eyes of Brunel, the adopted stray cat. Jon wasn't there.

She peered in the oval mirror. It was spotted with silver, but she could examine the cut on her forehead, delicately dabbing at beads of blood, wincing when it stung. She had attempted to divert Jon's attention by giving him her good luck amulet, but he had been unimpressed and plonked it on the hall table.

In the suspended quiet, the tick-tock of the ancestral grandfather clock, a faithless presence in its sombre ebony case, marked time. She heard a noise from above; it would be the cat.

With the blood wiped away, the wound was faint.

'Here he is!' Jonathan Rokesmith had developed a trick of speaking about himself in the third person. Hugh said it avoided taking responsibility for his actions. Kate found it strange.

'Sweetheart, at last!'

She reached out to her son who was stumping downstairs in blue wellington boots instead of the sandals she had put him in. A graze on his knee had practically healed; the skin a livid pink against his toasty brown tan. He would have a scar, despite her attempts to stop him picking at the wound.

Sturdy, compact and red-cheeked, Jonathan Justin Rokesmith, with his choppy shock of hair, fine blond like his mother's, a kitchen-scissors fringe flicking over one eye, was charmingly oblivious that he had delayed their expedition. The four-year-old waved the illegal engine aloft, making choo-choo noises as, left foot first, he took each stair with reckless intent, sure that his mummy would catch him should he topple.

'Are you my special man?' Kate pushed her palm against Jon's chest forcing him to halt. He grinned, shying from her looming kiss. Abruptly she let him go and he stumbled before regaining balance.

As Kate and her son came out of 47 St Peter's Square, the next-door neighbour Professor Ramsay was climbing out of his vintage Rover, a car that Hugh and Jonathan coveted. He paused on the pavement to mime approval at Jonathan in his boots and billowing *He-Man and the Masters of the Universe* T-shirt, military marching down the path. Kate shrugged her shoulders in a show of helpless pride. In sunglasses, tight-fitting trousers and shirt that flattered her, she might have turned heads, but that day the streets, bleached by relentless sunshine, were deserted and there was only Mark Ramsay to appreciate her.

A world expert in Parkinson's disease, the professor was busy, so Kate did not expect conversation. His wife was less predictable; Isabel Ramsay might initiate chat, give a stern nod or appear not to see Kate at all. If it was a 'talking day' this would involve eulogies about rambles with her 'gorgeous baby Lucian'. Her stories – garnished with sentiment and bread for ducks – lacked the blood, mud and bruises of Kate's outings with Jonathan. Isabel Ramsay spoke as if her children were young; in fact Lucian, brisk in brogues and chinos, was about Kate's age and not, she thought, gorgeous. He must always have been impeccable and obedient – unlike her own child.

Hugh had once remarked that the Ramsays had been glamorous sixties people, appearing in gossip columns and throwing parties for friends in high places until some scandal. Her husband's eye for detail did not extend to humans so he could only hazard that one of the kids had got into a scrape involving a girl. Kate decided it was Lucian: the quiet ones were trouble. As Jon chattered confidentially to his toys or constructed tunnels from stones and twigs, she was grateful he had the imagination to misbehave.

'Embarking on an expedition?' Lifting a garden spade and doctor's bag from his car, Professor Ramsay addressed the boy, who knelt on the kerb coaxing a beetle into a porthole in the back of the engine's cab.

'We're going to the Bell Steps, aren't we, Jonny?' Kate, with the mother's anxiety that her son would ignore the question, replied in a cheery tone.

However, the boy announced: 'He is going to fight at a war.' Jon gravely eyed the spade.

'Splendid. We need good soldiers.' Mark Ramsay tucked the spade under his arm.

Jon snatched up his engine and struggled to his feet, causing the beetle to tumble out of the cab. It was crushed by his heel when he set off in a straight line, keeping to the kerb.

'I've a headache so cried off my ma-in-law's. A stroll should clear it,' Kate ventured, taking her eye off Jonathan.

'This is headache weather,' Mark Ramsay agreed, swinging the medicine bag as, smiling, he watched Kate set off in pursuit of her son.

She straggled along the baking street towards the church, dazzled by darts of light from flecks of quartz in the paving and oppressed by the dome of white-blue sky. At Rose Gardens North, the asphalt had softened and swollen in the intense heat. Kate felt her limbs grow leaden. She glanced back; Professor Ramsay was still by the kerb.

Too late she made an effort to steer Jonathan away from the statue of the Leaning Woman. Naked from the waist up, as the name implied, the statue leant towards the Great West Road with arms folded; her sublime pose, describing the curve in the carriageway, contrasted with the clamour of speeding traffic.

Jonathan had become attached to her. He painted sloppy powder-paint pictures of her and fashioned lumpy clay models with misshapen breasts.

'Boo!' He sprang out from behind the plinth. Kate pretended shock.

On their last visit he had been dismayed to find her actual breasts slathered with green paint and a plastic strawberry punnet dangling like a handbag from her arm and demanded Kate climb up and take it off. She had been unable to snap the nylon cord or undo the knot, but had promised that next time they would bring a knife. She had presumed he would forget and had brought no kind of cutting implement.

Jon rampaged around the statue, deaf to his mother's assurances that she would remember the knife on another walk. He slid to the ground with a despairing sob, lips pouting, grizzling: 'You said you would be-fore and you did-ent.'

Kate snatched the steam engine off him and stalked away. His yells escalated to choking screams. She made for the subway ramp and did not stop when the noise subsided into intermittent wails. Later, this scene – a little boy huddled at the foot of a statue, hugging his knees – would shock the police officer who was unable to persuade him to leave.

Kate plodded on, her sandals slapping the ground; glare bounced off the concrete slope, the tiled walls, the metal railings, all conspiring to bewilder and enervate.

She did not hear the footsteps or notice that the crying had stopped.

The engine was wrenched from her, the metal ripping a nail on her forefinger. Jonathan barrelled past, jolting her hip, and belted on into the tunnel.

'You hurt me. You idiot!'

She turned on to the lower ramp. Through the subway railings she caught a flicker by the statue, but dismissed it as a trick of the light. The turquoise tiles were closing in. A ring pull in the gutter flashed in the sun as she passed.

'Calm down, darling.' Kate tried to sound calm herself in case anyone could overhear. Jonathan had gone and she really did have a headache.

In the convex mirror at the mouth of the tunnel a figure merged into the darkness.

St Peter's church bell struck 'quarter to' as the boy galloped along the subway, toot-tooting his way, his voice hollow. The fading sound had a melancholy quality, dying away in the ceramic-lined chamber. Although it was cooler here, the air was raw with exhaust fumes and the smell of piss.

Kate emerged on to Black Lion Lane South. The jumbled sounds of a television drifted from open windows in the Ram public house where baskets of vibrantly red geraniums, leaves frazzled, hung along the frontage, the red of their petals finding echo in the red umbrellas casting shade over empty tables. A solitary pint glass stood on a window sill; it was too early for lunchtime drinkers.

Kate steered Jonathan across Hammersmith Terrace. He shook her hand off his shoulder when she prevented him running his engine over the bonnet of the Ford Anglia outside the end house. She checked her hair in its wing mirror and caught Jonathan being Worzel Gummidge, lurching crabwise down the Bell Steps.

With no boats to churn up the river, the flickering surface mirrored spindly trees lining St Paul's School playing fields on the far bank. The turrets of Hammersmith Bridge tottered as light obliterated the looping spans between the portals. If he were here, Hugh would inform them that the bridge had been designed by the man who created the London sewers and was opened by the Prince of Wales in June 1887.

She stepped gingerly over to where the wall of the gardens on Hammersmith Terrace cast a strip of shadow along the top of the beach; the shade did not afford a drop in temperature. A line of moss in the brick marked the level of high tide. Slung from iron hoops was a chain stained a lurid green by slime and weeds. Kate grasped this to steady herself on the rough ground.

On the shoreline, Jonathan Rokesmith filled the funnel of his engine with specifically chosen stones and fragments of glass. These, he explained to his invisible audience, were 'je-wels'. He liked the sound of the word and repeated it when he reached the critical part of his operation. He guided the engine into the water. This was naughty. He looked to see if his mummy was watching.

The river filled and the current increased; the engine stirred lazily in the shallow water and for a while, made of metal and weighted by stones, remained anchored in the mud amongst rubble and the debris of centuries. It dislodged itself and, lifted by the current, was swept away to catch against a stanchion at Putney Bridge and sink. Buried in the silt of the Thames it would not be found for eighty-three years.

Kate Rokesmith was dead, her body sprawled on its back in the shrinking shade. Her neck twisted, she gazed sightlessly at the river, tangled tresses of her hair fanning out over the sun-baked mud. The swelling above her eye was stark as gravity drained the blood downwards and that side of her face gradually paled.

The tide encroached, narrowing the shore below the Bell Steps, which apart from the body was deserted.

Over the following weeks people would pick over the events of this day. In the Ram, drinkers sifted the few facts, retracing the likely route of the young mother's walk from St Peter's Square to the banks of the River Thames.

Kate Rokesmith's decision to go to the river changed the lives of many. Jonathan's memories of his mother would fade to a procession of shadows and murmuring embraces less substantial than his dreams.

In Britain, the Wednesday of that week was a public holiday. For decades, inhabitants of the London Borough of Hammersmith and Fulham could describe where they were when Prince Charles married Lady Diana. The wedding overshadowed the murder two days earlier; few could recall that otherwise ordinary Monday in July 1981.

Even the smallest observation might have helped the police solve the murder of Katherine Rokesmith. In the end, it did not.

One

The Toyota took three attempts to fire and the car was out of sight by the time Terry got moving. A skilled driver, he wove through the lunchtime traffic, snatching space, overtaking to slip in two vehicles behind the car at lights on Chalker's Corner. It was indicating right. There was no right turn. Terry felt heat rise as the police officer in him wanted to pull alongside and flash his badge. The car crossed the junction but the indicator had warned him there would soon be a right turn. At Lower Richmond Road the car did indeed go right, then right again to rejoin the A316. Terry slid in behind and when it took the slip road on to the M3 congratulated himself on keeping his petrol tank full.

Terry Darnell knew he was dealing with a meticulous and observant personality, likely to notice a vehicle keeping pace, so he hung back until the M25; then he risked overtaking and keeping the vehicle in his rear-view mirror. He knew better than to underestimate his quarry: people surprise you.

Later he dropped back and tucked into the left lane with the car ahead. Luckily this was a cautious driver who would not speed; just like a woman. Just as well because Terry's ten-year-old 1.4 engine would not be tortoise to this fuel-injected hare. He increased his distance when the other car crossed into his lane.

When it took the exit, Terry didn't need to keep the car within his sights. He knew where they were going.

The hamlet had no through road and, although close to a town with a station, felt to Terry as remote as the depths of Dartmoor. It was remote in time too; iron lamp-posts had yet to shed light on a Victorian pillar box and the one street sign. Spreading oaks and forbidding acers and flint walls partially concealed substantial detached houses.

Terry watched the car go off left and continued on the bypass before he took a road to the sea and doubled back.

He let the Yaris bump along a lane treacherous with potholes and, steering it on to a secluded verge, killed the engine. If anyone came he would ask for directions to the church; that always went down well.

Terry registered his full bladder. He had not touched the flask of coffee he had made for staking out the premises; these days he wanted to piss all the time. He relieved himself behind the boot of the car. He tested his camera with shots of the tyres; feeling the tightening in his chest, he dismissed it.

The air was freezing; snow was forecast. He buttoned up his jacket. Snow would obliterate clues and hamper the simplest action. He did not find it as joyful as when Stella was little.

A weather-beaten sign pointed him towards the church and, picking his way along a rutted footpath crunchy with fallen leaves, he reached a lych gate. The intense quiet was broken by bells chiming three o'clock. Already the sky was darkening. He patted his pocket; his torch was there.

As he unlatched the gate and walked under the tiled canopy, another bout of dizziness overwhelmed him; despite what the doctor said, Terry knew it was blood sugar dropping. He had not eaten since his cornflakes that morning and these days he could not get away with it. There was no quaint village shop and he was reluctant to go into the town. It was when the perpetrator was cornered that less experienced detectives grew careless. Later he would eat the Kit Kat in the glove box with his coffee.

Terry lowered himself on to a bench within the lych gate and, resting his head back, read the laminated notices pinned opposite: flower rotas, times of services; a Wednesday coffee morning. His attention was aroused by a sign on red paper: 'If you have lost a child, or know of a child that has died, however long ago, please come and join us in remembering them.'

He wondered if anyone could come or if it was for locals only. Did it matter if your child was alive and lost only to you?

He mulled over how many parents in this backwater could have suffered such a particular bereavement. It could not amount to a large congregation. A child had gone missing in the sixties near here; the girl had never been found but, as was becoming frequent, Terry could not conjure up detail. Some poor sod was tortured by that case; worrying over minor specifics, rifling through files he knew off by heart. Terry wiped his face – his memory really was on the blink – the poor sod was called Hall and was dead. He had read that the girl's parents had also died; they would not be attending the service.

Kate Rokesmith's murderer would be brought to justice. His own torture was at an end.

Terry took the path to the church. The tower was square and tapered; each point where it slimmed was marked by a line of jutting bricks giving the impression the structure could be telescoped upon itself. On its spire a golden cockerel weathervane facing towards the sea glinted in sunshine escaping from a break in the clouds. He remembered it from the funeral; it had put him in mind of his little girl. By then fifteen and doubtless into make-up and boys, she had no time for him. It was like one of Stella's drawings which he had mounted in a scrapbook. Stella's primary school pictures were bright with colour; if only life was how she had drawn it. When he asked if he could keep the ones she did on her visits, modest about her talent, she would shrug OK. The scrapbook still gave him happiness.

He had attended the service with a colleague, a woman whom he had quite fancied. Afterwards they dropped off for a drink at a pub on the A3 where she had called her boyfriend from a phone booth by the toilets; no mobile phones in those days. So that was that. Terry told himself it was not wise to mix business with pleasure. Instead, he had not mixed it with anything. Neither of them had seen anyone suspicious at the funeral. The case was as cold as ice and Kate had only been dead six weeks.

The murderer had been there, coiffured and respectable, in the left of the photograph by a headstone, watching the coffin carried out from the church. Three decades on, Terry, knowing whom to look for, had quickly spotted the killer in the crowd.

Any hope the Rokesmith family had of privacy had been dashed by the photographers, journalists, television crews and the obligatory straggle of onlookers who packed the churchyard. They had made Terry's job harder but now he was grateful; he had the picture. It only proved the culprit's presence at the funeral, but it was a start.

It would have been easy to chat with mourners without them batting an eyelid. There was no talk of a stranger acting oddly from the would-be detectives on the ground that day. Truth be told, Terry had been more interested in his sergeant – Janet, that was her name; after all, they believed they had solved the case, so in reality were only crossing Ts.

Hugh Rokesmith, Terry had observed to Janet over a pint of Fuller's London Pride, had given a sterling performance, with the boy in his arms the perfect prop for the grieving widower. Terry had gone into the telephone booth after Janet and, with Stella's weathervane drawing on his mind, called the Barons Court flat to see if she fancied meeting when he got into London. Stella informed him she was busy.

The dizziness ebbed. Trying to recall the whereabouts of the grave, Terry stumbled over uneven ground, going anti-clockwise around the building. The word 'widdershins' popped up: he had an idea his mum had warned it was bad luck to go widdershins around a church.

For the first time since Stella was born, Terry felt that luck was on his side. He threaded between the grassy mounds, the grass was damp with winter dew, and soon the bottoms of his trousers were sodden. He was long-sighted and could see the words engraved on headstones yards away. He ignored a row of nineteenth-century vaults for the moneyed dead, the mausoleums creating gaps like the canyon-like avenues in Manhattan. Or so he imagined, he had never been there.

In this section, headstones were older: Terry made out 1814, but most inscriptions were illegible beneath greenish-yellow lichen that crept over the eroding stone. Some were broken, their pieces lost in foliage or laid on top of the grave. Those who had tended the plots were themselves long dead.

An impenetrable hedgerow of beech bounded one side of the graveyard, woven through with tendrils of ivy and clumps of holly.

Terry came upon a gate and peered through the curling metal; another hedge within meant he had to crane sideways to see a house on a lawn. It was from one of the stories he had read to Stella: a witch's house in a forest clearing, with lattice windows on the upper floor beneath gables carved with cut-out birds in flight, their shapes echoed by silhouettes of actual birds circling the stout chimneys.

Terry shrank back. Although the windows were dark, someone might be watching. On a weekday winter afternoon, a visitor to the church was rare; he would not blend in.

He stuck to a flagged path, grateful for firm ground and hastened between bushes clipped to form columns into an overgrown area with a wall, beyond which stretched away fields, brown and grey in the fading light. He crossed the grass in the gathering twilight and there it was; shaded by a larch and hidden from most sightseers: 'Katherine Rokesmith. 27th July 1981'.

Terry doubted that these days the name would mean much to anyone.

A bunch of flowers leant against the headstone. Terry's heart beat faster as he bent to examine them. Five yellow roses, their heads browning, the wrapping wrinkled from rain; he estimated they were about a week old. There was no shop label or price. He tore off a flower and dropped it in his pocket to show Stella. The grave was in good order, the grass clipped with no weeds; someone was tending it. Terry circled the plot snapping pictures: of the stone, a close-up of the roses and of the epitaph. He used flash: the merciless light highlighting the deteriorating writing. It could have been centuries old, yet some letters had no moss or lichen on them, as if whoever had begun restoration had given up or planned to return.

Suddenly the stillness was broken. The sound was slight, but Terry identified it instantly: the scrape of a shoe on gravel.

Someone was coming.

Two

Monday, 10 January 2011

A woman sat in offices on Shepherd's Bush Green integrating new clients into a cleaning schedule. It was an early morning task she enjoyed; it involved creating a list of staff, lining up availability to match time slots and applying a colour code to cells on a spreadsheet. Blue for mornings, yellow for afternoons, green for evenings and light green for late nights. She was methodical, switching between grids, extracting data from two files to populate a third. She chewed spearmint gum with her mouth shut, her jaw quietly working.

The starched white cotton shirt, sharp haircut and tailored suit trousers hinted at an authority confirmed when, having identified cleaners to cover the shifts, she tossed her gum into a waste bin and dialled the numbers on the list. She was pleasant but firm, overcoming objections or obstacles from the seventeen freelancers who worked exclusively for her. By five to nine the rota was complete and she had been at her desk three hours.

She strode through to the main office to fetch client details from signed contracts in her PA's pending tray and was startled by knocking. A policeman was gesticulating through the wire-reinforced glass door panel.

'I'm looking for Stella Darnell.'

'You've found her.'

At six foot and in her mid-forties Stella was taller and older than the officer.

While he talked she grabbed a cleaning equipment catalogue from a shelf and, resting it on a filing cabinet, scribbled busily, squeezing words into the margins and around pictures of a soft

15

banister brush with a wooden handle and a galvanized flat-top socket for a broom. 'Superintendent Darnell … coming out … Co-op … Seaford … collapsed. Ambulance in 10 mins, paramedics worked … failed revive … dead on arrival.'

Stella circled 'dead on arrival' and laid down her pen. She contemplated the banister brush. It was not necessary, but would impress fussier clients; she would ask Jackie to order one and see how it went.

A mug of tea materialized by the catalogue and, as if she hovered far above, Stella gazed down uncomprehending: she had not heard Jackie arrive. The policeman's voice, droning on like a radio announcer, was drowned out by the telephone. She counted the rings: it was answered on the seventh. Not good enough. She stipulated it should be picked up at three max.

'Clean Slate for a fresh start. Good morning, Jackie speaking, how can we help?'

The tea was scalding and sweet. Stella's own voice was reminding Jackie that she didn't take sugar and Jackie was replying slowly and patiently, explaining in words of one syllable that it was for shock.

Your father is dead.

It was not until the late afternoon, in the Royal Sussex County Hospital in Brighton, that Stella entertained the notion that she should be upset. All day she had dealt with the police, medical staff, administrators and Jackie, who treated her with practical sympathy. Everyone's response was out of proportion to Stella's so she was grateful at last to be alone.

The NHS bag containing Terry's belongings banged against a door as she emerged on to a goods road between the Cardiac Unit in a high-rise block and the shambling nineteenth-century building which housed the reception she had arrived at five hours earlier. Once a paean to Victorian endeavour, it was dwarfed by a maze of new-builds clad in steel and glass, its grandeur undermined by stuccoed pre-fabs and flaking render. She dodged a van and pushed through plastic flaps into a passage with a suspended ceiling and a flooring of epoxy quartz screed that emphasized a list to one side and gave her the impression of being on a ship.

Terence Christopher Darnell was pronounced dead at half past eight a.m. in the street where he had collapsed twenty minutes earlier. A female doctor told Stella that the probable cause was cardiac arrest but they could not be definite until they had performed a post-mortem. It was most unlikely, she had assured Stella, that 'Terence' had experienced pain.

His name is Terry.

She rarely called him Dad.

Stella frowned. She had not considered that he might have been in pain. She had also been informed, perhaps by the policeman, who was clearly both relieved and appalled by her lack of tears, that a lady coming out of the Co-op behind Detective Superintendent Darnell had said he'd toppled over like a toy soldier making no effort to save himself.

He was a toy policeman, Stella had nearly said.

She shouldered through another set of doors and found herself in a chapel; warm and dark, the quiet extreme after the bustle of the hospital.

Stella was about to leave, but arranged around an altar was a semi-circle of chairs and she slumped on to the nearest one, and dropped the NHS bag beside her.

Terence Christopher Darnell's sudden death would mean extra work at a busy time, she mused. Stella's parents had divorced when she was seven and her mother had not seen her ex-husband since Stella was old enough to visit him without being delivered or collected. Suzanne Darnell would lament that her marriage had been a wrong turning; she lived alone in West London, having made no further navigational errors. She would not help her daughter dispose of Terry and his belongings.

In Stella's business, death was a prompt for a house clearance and thorough clean in readiness for sale; Terry's death need be no different to any other, she told herself.

Although she was Terry's only child, it had surprised Stella that he had a slip of paper in his wallet naming her as his next of kin because she saw him no more than three times a year. Sitting on the hard chair, surrounded by wall plaques commemorating patrons and patients of the hospital now at peace and in a higher place, Stella dwelt on the earthly fact of the death of a man she hardly knew. His body had not looked at peace.

Two electric candles dripping with fake wax were plugged into a socket on the altar. Stella recognized the scent as one of the flower fairy ranges of Asquith & Somerset and doubted it could be on the NHS preferred supplies list. A bunch of fresh freesias drooped out of a cream plastic vase beneath a stained-glass panel of the Madonna and Child. She made a mental note to order lavender spray for Mrs Ramsay in St Peter's Square. On her last visit, there had been a stale odour; she suspected the old lady of smoking, although she claimed to have given up.

This led her to think about her other clients and, getting out her phone, she scrolled through her messages. Jackie had signed up someone responding to the advert in the local paper and had trialled a new cleaner in the office after Stella had left for Sussex. The woman had not passed, but Jackie wanted to know if she should hire her anyway. Stella tutted at this, the noise distinct in the silence; rapidly her fingers busied on the keypad as she instructed Jackie *not* to take on someone who had failed the cleaning test. As Stella dreaded, her business could not carry on without her being there.

Paul had texted, wanting to see her. She had not told him about Terry, nor did she want to. He would be hoping that over a bottle of wine he could persuade her to let him move in.

Jesus, pale and chipped upon the Cross, gazed down at her with blank eyes as she typed: *Let's call it a day. We know it's not working. Stella.*

She hesitated before adding an 'x', but then, just before she pressed 'send', she deleted the kiss. She did not love Paul – whatever love was – and it was better to be honest. She watched the envelope icon tumble into infinity to become a dot, and insisted to herself she was doing Paul a favour; he could find someone who loved him.

Having mustered up the wherewithal to release herself from a relationship about which she had been ambivalent for too long, Stella tackled the NHS bag. Each item was in a sealed packet, which did not stop a sour reek of sweat escaping, sickly and clinging. Her stomach coiled. She extracted the leather wallet with delicate fingers – the crackle of plastic was loud in the chapel; she had given it to Terry for his fiftieth birthday over fifteen years ago. She had asked the shop to have his initials embossed in silver: 'TD', forgetting about 'Christopher'. The letters had rubbed away to the merest indentation. Terry had folded up the birthday wrapping paper, smoothing it flat on his coffee table, and let slip how his colleagues nicknamed him 'Top Cat'. Stella had been infuriated, although she could not have said why. The policeman in her office had momentarily stepped out of role to exclaim that Terry was a 'top man' but if this was meant to console her, it had landed wide.

The clothes he was wearing had been folded and placed together. His dark grey suit was from Marks & Spencer's Autograph range: the jacket had a tear under the shoulder; a blue cotton shirt striped with brown was also torn with loose threads trailing where the paramedics had ripped away the buttons. Applying the method of fixing the age of a tree, salt rings under the arms indicated to Stella that Terry had worn it for two days. Little though she saw him, she knew Terry ironed his shirts and kept his hair washed. On the few occasions that she kissed him – in greeting, or on departure – his chin was smooth and scented with Gillette Series Aftershave Splash Cool Wave, his hair smelling of Boots anti-dandruff men's shampoo. He would not wear anything more than once. She looked up and caught Jesus looking at her balefully. She considered that the detective, whom her mother insisted was happier with tagged corpses and evidence bags than with his family, was now a collection of belongings sealed in plastic and backed up by a sheaf of paperwork. Terry would have hated such an end.

Stella passed over underpants, shoes, a T-shirt and balled-up socks and stuffed them all back in the bag, inhaling deep the chapel's flower fairy scent.

The nurse who had taken her to see Terry's body must have been on some training course about dealing with bereaved relatives. She was keen that Stella should banish timidity in the presence of her dead father.

Stella had noted his greasy hair was brushed the wrong way and the stubble on his chin was white. A stained tooth was visible between stiffened lips. She had not seen Terry lying down since she was a child. He was naked under the sheet, draped loosely over the gurney.

'It's OK to touch him,' the nurse had whispered encouragingly.

Stella pretended not to hear. Keeping her hands in her pockets, she nodded in confirmation like an actor in a police procedural drama and muttered: 'Yes, that's him.'

Identification was not an issue; the hospital had his driving licence. She refused the offer of 'time alone with your dad', thinking what was the point? At the nurses' station, she caught sight of Terry's name on a form: 'Certification of Life Extinct'.

Beneath these words she scanned his admission notes. Words floated free of their sentences as she read, her brain fighting to dismiss meaning: 'Attempted to resuscitate. Police called. Date of death Monday 10 January 2011. Last seen alive, Broad Street, Seaford, 8.25 a.m. today. Means of identification: personal papers – driving licence, bank cards. No suspicious circumstances.'

A doctor had signed his or her name and underneath the signature had printed more legibly: 'May he rest in peace.'

The chapel door banged and a wheezy man in a fluorescent jerkin that showed off his beer gut pattered in, sighing.

Stella drew her jacket around her and tipped Terry's Accurist watch into her palm. She put her hand through its heavy bracelet and snapped shut the clasp. Her wrist looked childlike and the watch slid up her arm, cold against her skin. It would need links taken out to fit. Terry kept it three minutes fast for punctuality, a tip

Stella followed. In the same bag was his wedding ring. Her mother had thrown her own in the bin. Stella presumed Terry wore it to make women think he was married, just as Suzanne's ringless finger signalled she was unattached. Stella had retrieved her mother's ring from a wad of damp tea bags. She now had both rings.

There was no spare underwear or toothbrush and this confirmed her growing suspicion that Terry had not expected to be away overnight. What was he doing in Sussex?

The last bag was labelled 'Contents of pockets' and comprised a half-eaten packet of chewing gum, £7.80 in change, a scratch card with a winning prize of ten pounds and the head of a yellow rose. She took the flower out of the bag; it had no scent and was browning. She did not think Terry liked flowers. She found his keys.

Stella knelt up on the chair, leaning over the kitchen table, and worked her way through each key.

'Daddy has lots of doors.' She began to chatter on and bang went his chance to have a read of the paper. Propped on her elbows, she questioned him about each one like a detective. When she behaved like a grown-up, going all serious, he had to try not to laugh.

He started by answering promptly, as if it was a quiz, but after a while had to admit he got fed up; it had been a long night and he needed his bed.

'Do you lock up murderers and throw away the key?'

He snatched the bunch off her.

'Where'd you get that from?'

'You know where.' In came her mother. Suzanne has to have a go.

Game over.

Stella dangled the keys from her forefinger. When she was twenty-one Terry handed her his door keys; in case of emergency, he had explained. He had cancelled her birthday dinner that year to attend a fatal stabbing on the White City estate. Her mother said giving her his keys was his idea of a rite of passage and that would be her lot. Once she was over eighteen, Stella had told herself she had no need of a father.

Two months ago, suspecting an intruder, Terry had heightened the back garden wall with a trellis and changed the locks; he had not given Stella the new keys.

Now she had them and had inherited the doors they unlocked: she had unrestricted entry to Terry's abandoned life. She brushed the leather Triumph fob with her thumb.

Where was his car?

The stained-glass window had become opaque; it must be dark outside. The man had gone. She could not remember what car Terry drove: the Triumph Herald had long ago packed up on him. The police officer had relayed an offer of help from Terry's colleagues at Hammersmith Police Station, which she had refused. She would not ask anything of the police.

Terry's wallet bulged with papers: receipts, loyalty cards, the driving licence and sixty-five pounds in twenties and a five. He was one coffee away from a free drink at Caffè Nero; she had presumed greasy spoon cafés were more him. She struck lucky: a receipt from a filling station in Seaford. She peered at the faint blue ink and worked out that Terry had bought petrol at sixteen minutes to eight that morning.

Stella had never driven Terry; if they went anywhere together it was in his car. When she passed her test – first time – her mother had told her that Terry did not trust women drivers.

At the bottom of the bag two glistening ham rolls nestled in a Co-op carrier; the doughy bread mummified in cling film had been flattened by a can of Coke. Her stomach heaved: Terry had bought them just before he died.

At London Zoo, Terry had treated his little daughter to a bottle of Coke. Stella hated drinks with bubbles but at the giraffe house she had upset him by calling him 'Terry' as her mum did, instead of 'Dad', so she sucked dutifully on the pink straw, willing the level to creep down, the bubbles exploding in her throat. They waited on the westbound District line platform of Earls Court station to go the one stop to her new home in Barons Court and Stella got a feeling in her tummy. She swallowed a rush of saliva and stayed stock still.

The train clattered in, doors swished, a voice boomed and when people pushed behind her Stella threw up over shoes and legs. Brown foaming liquid chased along the carriage floor. The train was taken out of service and it was her fault.

She had retreated to the new bedroom, with no toys and a stain on the ceiling. Before being sick she had planned to say 'Thank you for having me, Daddy' to make it all better. In Stella's memory her parents' voices conflated with the policeman who had mutely reprimanded her lack of emotion: *'What were you thinking of? You don't know your own daughter. She hates fizzy drinks.'*

You don't care about your father.

The NHS bag bulged with bald indicators of a life. Stella did not think of Terry Darnell filed in a steel drawer in the hospital mortuary, but as following her out of the hospital warning her to mind her own business.

Jackie had told Stella that Seaford was a seaside town twelve miles east of Brighton; she took the coast road recommended by her satnav. A notice announced Seaford was twinned with Bönningstedt in Germany. She swung past the station over a mini-roundabout, took a left then a right on to a street with Barclays Bank on one side and a Pound shop on the other. She was in a ghost town: no cars; no pedestrians on the shop-lit pavements. A crisp packet broke free from the shelter of a lamp-post to spin and skitter along the camber like tumbleweed. A church clock tolled nine as Stella stopped the van outside a disused Woolworths store and turning off the engine became aware of a creaking like a rocking chair. She got out: further along the street the metal sign for a men's clothes shop swung back and forth; the place unsettled her.

Jackie had said Terry died at a difficult time of the year: right after Christmas. Stella did not see what that had to do with anything; she had not spent a Christmas with Terry since she was seven.

The Co-op had closed an hour ago. Stella guessed that it must have looked the same when Terry arrived early that morning; the shelves restocked with packets, jars, bottles, their labels stark in the low security lighting. Rows of shopping trolleys were corralled next to the fruit and vegetable section, ready for the next day. Terry would not have used a trolley for so few items; he had not touched them. Opposite, she read 'Sweet Moments' on the fascia of a handmade-chocolate shop; perhaps these were the last words that Terry had seen.

If Stella expected to find a clue to the drama that had taken place in the doorway twelve hours earlier, she was disappointed. The two-storey shop buildings, block paving, tang of disinfectant and yellow plastic 'wet floor' hazard cone near the tills yielded nothing. It could have been any Co-op store in any town.

She stepped back from the store to where the pavement extended into the road for a pedestrian crossing delineated by ridges. Terry had told her that gold studs on the stones marked the boundary between private land and the public walkway, or had he? An outlet next to the supermarket was to let; unopened mail piled up on the door mat.

Terry had arrived here early that morning; he must have stayed the night somewhere but, since he hadn't even taken his toothbrush, Stella was sure he had not planned to. Where had he stayed?

She was staring at a snatch of white. She bent down: a piece of paper had wedged between the bars of a drain cover. She extracted it and in the low security light of the Co-op doorway unpeeled it, careful not to tear along the fold. It was a newspaper photograph, photocopied on a skew, cutting off some of the image. A footprint had transferred the surface of the pavement like a brass rubbing so she struggled to read the caption: *To th   ma   or Mr   say launches Charb   new vi   all.*

The black and grey pixels comprised a group of people, their features bleached out in sunlight. There was a figure in the foreground who might be a woman, but a splodge of dirt blotted her face. Triangular shapes crossed the top of the frame. The only unmistakable element of the photograph was a church. The angle of the shot made it appear to be balanced on the woman's head and the time on its clock was midday. Although there was nothing about the cutting to connect it with Terry, Stella slipped it into her pocket.

She heard the beeping of a reversing vehicle and scanned the street; it was empty. She hurried back to the van and saw that a light was flashing on an automatic teller in the wall of a building society on the other side of the road. At the end of the street a stretch limousine rolled by, a gaggle of young women in orange afro wigs hanging out of the windows bawling Robbie Williams' 'Angels'; the raucous sound faded into the night. The beeps stopped and the light in the cash machine went out. She approached it: a twenty-pound note lay in the cash tray.

Stella retrieved the note; brand new, it crackled when she folded it into her coat pocket with the cutting. She saw a 'P' for a car park and, jumping into the van, slung it left down a narrow road with a terrace of cottages on one side and a building with a castellated roof silhouetted against the sky on the other. Ahead of her was the car park. Four cars were dotted around the asphalted space and again Stella tried to recall the car Terry had owned.

She felt about among Terry's things and at the bottom of the bag found his keys. When she pressed the remote button on the fat plastic head there was no response. She extended her arc and hazard lights to her right flashed twice.

The blue Toyota Yaris had a parking penalty clamped to its windscreen by a wiper; Stella ripped out the ticket in yet another plastic bag and, nerving herself, got in the driver's seat. She caught a whiff of vanilla deodorizer and saw with approval that Terry had plugged an air purifier into the cigarette lighter socket. The car started first time. She cruised around the area until she found a residential street with no parking restrictions. Before getting out she gave the car a brief check, searching for a clue to why

Terry had been in Seaford. She found nothing but a Kit Kat wrapper and a half-drunk flask of coffee that had rolled under the front seat and concluded that the vehicle would need valeting before she sold it.

Only when she had locked the car did Stella notice that Terry had, after all, paid and displayed; a ticket face up on the dashboard was valid until eight fifteen that morning.

Terry had died fifteen minutes after the expiry time.

Half an hour later, Stella was speeding along the M23. Her rear-view mirror reflecting the empty motorway was a black rectangle. Earlier there had been tail-lights ahead, which were snuffed out when the driver rounded a bend and had not reappeared. She adjusted her phone in its cradle on the dashboard.

Where was Terry's mobile phone?

She rumbled on to the hard shoulder and, releasing the seat belt, scrabbled through the NHS bag on the front seat. There was a shuffling in the back of the van. Stella froze. She had not adhered to her own rule of looking in the interior if she left the van. It was easy to hide amongst the buckets and spare overalls. She heard the shuffling again, then a thump, and she spun around.

A bag of dishwasher salt granules lay on the carpeted floor. Many clients included appliance maintenance in their contract and someone had stacked the bags on the racks without securing them. Another was about to go; Stella clambered through the seats and caught it. She stowed the salt where it belonged, on the bottom shelf in a plastic container.

She checked the central locking and remembered why she had stopped. One thing Stella did know about Terry was that he always kept his mobile phone with him. Yet it was not in the NHS bag nor in his car, although there was a phone charger in the glove box.

The keyboard on her BlackBerry was fiddly in the feeble light but eventually she selected 'Dad'. She clenched her teeth, waiting for it to connect: some part of her expecting Terry to answer.

The ringing briefly fell in step with the click-click of her hazard lights. She was about to hang up when it stopped.

'Who's that?' Stella almost said: *Dad, is that you?*

Who's that? a woman responded.

'No, who are you?' Stella demanded.

No, who are you? It was her echo.

The line deadened with an almost imperceptible change in quality; a cessation of sound as if someone had replaced a receiver.

The screen said 'Call duration twelve seconds'. Stella selected 'Dialled numbers'. 'Dad' was top of the list with 'Clean Slate' underneath: her last two calls.

She pressed 'redial'.

This time the answering service cut in and Terry's voice invited the caller to leave as much information as they liked. Even in retirement he was encouraging witnesses to come forward with evidence, available any time of the day or night.

Stella had always told herself that if she called, Terry would be too busy to talk.

Her voice hesitant, she asked whoever had the phone to ring her to arrange collection.

Maybe Terry had dropped his phone when he collapsed and it had been stolen by kids. Thinking that she had called the wrong number, she went into 'Dialled numbers' again: the word 'Dad' lost meaning the longer she stared at it.

Stella caught her reflection in the side window, the dark rendering it high contrast: lumpy hair, her eyes lost in their sockets and her mouth a grim pencil line. She ran the window down to erase herself and was hit by cold wood-smoked air. Beyond the carriageway ragged trees were outlined against the sodium-pink sky of a town. A light blinked through the branches, moving, vanishing, then appearing closer and she heard a long low whistle.

She looked in her wing mirror and saw that a car was parked on the hard shoulder twenty yards away with its lights off. It hadn't been there when she had pulled off the road. She tilted the wing mirror, but it was too dark to tell if there was anyone inside. She did not want to wait to find out; she started the engine and gunned the van out into the middle lane. Fixing her seat belt, she accelerated to seventy. Careful of petrol consumption and after all a policeman's daughter, Stella did not speed.

By the time the lights of London twinkled ahead, she was clear: Terry's death was a task to be ticked off and then she would move on.

She easily negotiated the tight gap between bollards on Hammersmith Bridge, but instead of joining the Great West Road to go to her flat in Brentford, she crossed a deserted Hammersmith Broadway and headed for the office.

Shattered from the day but exulted at the prospect of working, Stella paid little attention to headlights that stayed behind her all the way to Shepherd's Bush Green.

Three

> *'Now the day is over,*
> *Night is drawing nigh,*
> *Shadows of the evening*
> *Steal across the sky.'*

Jack sang softly while he strolled through the subway and up the ramp. At the statue he paused under cover of the hedge and the bells pealed again, this time counting the hour. The church clock was a minute fast – not that when he was walking he cared about measuring time. On his journeys he noted only slipshod work, wanton neglect and deliberate damage; he counted dented cars, skirting scatterings of windscreen glass glittering on kerbstones and squashed smouldering cigarette butts tossed in gutters. Jack took trouble on behalf of those who did not bother.

The sound of the bells reverberated in his ear. Sundays were the worst, Jack confided to the statue of the Leaning Woman; the chimes and changes upset him more than horns, or roadside drilling, which at least had purpose. Blood had trickled down his neck, warm at first, drying to a crust. He had been instructed not to tell and, good at keeping secrets, told no one. He cupped a hand over his ear – the cold made it worse – but the ache was too deep.

In the lamplight breaking through the tree branches, the statue stretched her arms out to him.

Today's journey had been simple; the route on the page was like two circles attached by a straight line and Jack ended up where he had started: on Church Road in Northolt in the London Borough of Ealing. From there it was no distance across Western Avenue to the Underground station, a building dating from 1948. After clicking through the route on Google Street View he scribbled the year on page fifty-three in his street atlas. On Street View, he plotted anything of potential interest in the *A–Z* before embarking on the actual journey. The five and three of fifty-three added together equalled eight and the numbers 1948 added up to twenty-two which in turn equalled four. Four and eight made twelve which made three. If this was a sign, Jack did not know what it signified.

He had chosen the middle carriage in the train. Northolt was on the Central line so he was unlikely to know anyone, and if he did, he was ready with a plausible excuse.

He made the journeys in strict page order during the day. At night, his favoured time was reserved for walking the city without a map, when he was reliant on a future Host to lead the way. As he passed each house, he saw which blinds were drawn, which curtains pulled or shutters swung across. People were careless, and left gaps. He slowed down when a possible Host stopped at his gate, dawdling to get out his door key. Most did not have the forethought to have it ready as Jack always did; if they did this he would know they did not after all have a mind like his own. However, they might offer him a warm and friendly home while he looked for the True Host.

If the man entertained suspicions – those with minds like his own were men – Jack walked on head-down, his efficient step intended to allay their suspicions; he was just a man going about his business.

He marvelled that people set store by burglar alarms or a steel-plated doors with double mortice locks and then left doors on the latch to pop out to dump newspapers and cans in the recycling bin or to whisk a dog around the block for a last walk. He tut-tutted at the welcome of keys beneath doormats, secreted under ivy or tucked inside plant pots. Those who made him truly at home left him a key dangling from a string on the inside of the front door.

He would wait beneath a sill out of sight of the street or in the recess of a bay window while lights went on and later were extinguished. He was soothed by the muffled jumble of music and voices within, confident that soon he would join them. If the person lived alone, he would have liked to reassure them that soon they would have company.

Jack regretted that these relationships, however meaningful, had to be short. He called the unwitting residents Hosts, preferring to think of himself not as a guest or cuckoo in the nest but as belonging.

Only those with minds like his own knew a person can be randomly chosen by another and such a mind is alert for that eventuality. Like the man sipping coffee in the window of a café, or the man wired to an MP3 player on a Tube escalator who did not acknowledge Jack when he made room for him, or the fussy middle-aged man on the towpath. When certain inhabitants of London slotted their security chains into place before going to bed, they were unaware they had a visitor.

People were oblivious. How often solitary dog walkers, children playing, joggers – those types who strayed off paths and were out at odd times – reported nearly missing a body, assuming it to be a pile of clothes or rubbish. Sometimes, even in a city, the dead lie undiscovered – buried in snow, on wastelands, in alleyways – for weeks.

The presence of water does untold damage to a crime scene.

For those killers intending the corpse as a gift, like a cat with a bird, he presumed this was a disappointment. For professionals with a mind like his own, those who did not crave cheap adulation, measured time mattered only briefly: every second was good because vital clues were eroded and destroyed. Jack understood how valuable was the currency used to buy or kill time.

He was disappointed how few had minds like his own and was meticulous in eliminating each one.

He slipped a roll-up out of a slim silver case and in the shelter of his coat lit it. He palmed it and, hiding the glowing tip, stepped from behind the hedge on to the pavement. At Rose Gardens North he checked but the Toyota Yaris was still missing, the house in darkness. He continued into St Peter's Square. Restless and alert though the old lady was, she must be asleep by now.

Jack's choice of Host was not always random.

Four

January 1985

A tufty man called a Head Master squeezed his shoulder, bunching his blazer and pinching his skin, before pushing him into a steamy room of staring faces. Jonathan did not like to be touched and squirmed out of his grip. The faces fuzzed and zoomed before him, until a round pudgy one came into focus and Jonathan landed in a chair beside him. A woman's voice called this boy Simon. Later he found out that the boy's other name was 'Stumpy', the same as the brother of Pigling Bland who was taken off in a wheelbarrow. The voice whispered that Simon knew the ropes and would look after him. He did not need rope and waited for his daddy to say so.

The chair had rough edges which scratched the backs of his legs. He was told to sit right up to the table. He looked to see where Daddy was sitting.

He had gone.

Jonathan tried to get up but the Simon boy was in the way. The name 'Justin' was on the blackboard and the voice, which he saw belonged to an old woman, told the boys to greet the new boy:

'He-llo, Just-in,' they chanted in straggling unison.

Jonathan said nothing because he was not Justin. This mistake made him hopeful he was in the wrong place and that soon his daddy would come for him. Anyway, the boy who *was* Justin would want his chair back. He tentatively raised his hand to explain this but the Simon boy grabbed his wrist with nails as sharp as Brunel's claws and left four marks like smiles on his skin. Surreptitiously – or the boy might see – he licked them. They

33

tasted of pocket money, which was no comfort. If he tried to leave again the Simon boy would make more smiles.

The teacher said she was Miss Thoroughgood. Jonathan imagined the name as a great nodding daisy with splaying petals. He associated names of things and people with colours, creating disparate groups according to their hue. After this, his first day at boarding school, the process would also work in reverse: white daisies would evoke the overweight woman in her late fifties who had been his form teacher, and lower his mood.

Miss Thoroughgood wrote her name on the blackboard in squeaky letters. The other boys already knew it so they watched him, snorting behind their hands and pulling faces while the teacher had her back to the class. The name – being long – went on and on and he blushed, growing hot as he tried to copy it on the cover of the exercise book on his desk. His fingers slid down his pencil and, scared to look up, he made up the rest.

Thorpettitoes.

The name of the mother of the eight little pigs in *The Tale of Pigling Bland*. Jonathan felt a dull foreboding in his tummy and to make it go away he imagined the birthday cake his mummy had made. Open mouths around the table ready to gobble him up. He screwed up his eyes.

The other boys had already been at the preparatory school in the Sussex countryside for a term. The little boy understood, more or less, that it would be better for all concerned that he come here. The headmaster had said he was 'the spitting image of his lovely mother and going to be tall like his father'. These facts were important to Jonathan: such are the facts and phrases small children overhear and collect to form an incoherent reality.

Another fact: he was not Justin and, certain of this at least, Jonathan believed that once he explained the Daisy-Lady would let him go home.

Forty-five minutes went by. The seven-year-old was proficient at reading the time and no longer talked of big or little hands. Justin did not come and nor did his father.

The lady said it was Morning Break. This he knew about: he sang it with his mummy:

Morning has broken,
Like the first morning,
Blackbird has spoken,
Like the first bird.

The teacher told the boys to form a crocodile. Now the mistake would come to light; Jonathan sprang up and tucked his chair in.

'File out two by two,' Thorpettitoes demanded shrilly.

Jonathan was bewildered. Other boys jostled, and shoving him into line the boy called Simon took his hand. *'Now Pigling Bland, son Pigling Bland, you must go to market. Take your brother Alexander by the hand. Mind your Sunday clothes, and remember to blow your nose.'*

Miss Thoroughgood, presuming insurrection, commanded that at the end of break, at the first whistle they must be still as statues and at the second whistle, walk sensibly to the classroom.

Jonathan gazed disconsolately at colourless sky through a window above a map of the world stuck with drawing pins. Fact: he knew the names of eleven countries. The boys were shouting; the teacher was at the head of the crocodile.

The daisies in the garden reached his shoulder and were gold in the middle before they disappeared. His daddy said they were spreading and that grass was less trouble to maintain so he did not mention that his mummy had planted them or that he did not like green grass however little trouble it was to maintain.

Crocodiles were green and slid secretly underwater after their prey. The classroom door bashed him when the boy in front let it go. He held it for a boy with a runny nose who stepped on his heel, pulling off his shoe. The boy did not say sorry. Jonathan bent to do up his laces.

'We are going to be last.' Simon squeezed his fingers tight.

The playground was behind the neo-Gothic mansion and a

trek from the classroom. The twenty boys crocodiled across a quadrangle of cobblestones. It was a flaw in the conversion from private house to institution that the cloakroom could only be reached by a circuitous route involving going outside without coats. The boys' pinched faces were whipped by a harsh wind off the South Downs that swirled leaves and twigs around their grey-socked legs. They were not allowed to run.

Jonathan turned his ankle on the wet cobbles; his new shoes cut into his shins and rubbed the back of his heels. He longed to break free from Simon's grip. An oblong of dry stones lay where his daddy's car had been.

'We eat here.' Simon waved his other hand at a hall with a fireplace the size of a doorway. A table stretched away and high above were rafters.

'I won't be here,' Jonathan informed him confidently.

'Yes you will.'

Half of Simon's finger was missing. Jonathan wrenched his hand away, revolted by what was not there, but Simon recaptured him and held him fast.

'Don't do that again.'

He concentrated instead on the ceiling beams. His daddy had told him about the principle of the Action of Forces. Fact: builders put a short distance between each beam to keep the load to a minimum. Jonathan would tell the boys this. He was startled by a clacking like bullets and saw the lady who had been nice when they arrived behind the counter. She was busy with her typing and did not see him this time.

The boys barged through a green baize door that closed by itself.

They clattered along a tiled passage with a vaulted ceiling, their voices deafening him. One boy exclaimed in disgust at the greasy cooking smell, the others imitated him until the teacher silenced them. There was no daylight and Jonathan pretended they were in a dungeon, the walls hung with chains. It was not hard.

The cloakroom smelled of cheese and the coats hung like

roosting birds from giant hooks. Simon led him to one labelled 'Justin'. Jonathan said nothing because he recognized his own coat.

They were on a stretch of grey asphalt with a gravel path around it and on one side a sloping grassy bank with a beech hedge with leaves of burnt umber: Jonathan's favourite colour.

The Daisy teacher was chatting to a lady with a chin like the moon and Jonathan wondered if they were talking about him because suddenly they looked at him. He smiled but they did not smile back, and he took heart from this: perhaps his wish had come true and he was invisible.

Simon let him go and ran off to join in a game of football. Beyond the hedge, Jonathan saw hills speckled with frost and splodged with dark patches for woods. He trailed around the pitch gravitating towards a female blackbird hopping along the hedge with a stick the same length as herself in her beak. His mummy had called him Pig Wig for eating too much cake and he said that Pig Wig was a girl and the cake was his. The blackbird flew away over the hills. Pigling Bland and Pig Wig escaped from Thomas Piperson. Jonathan could be Pigling Bland *and* Pig Wig; that way he would not be alone. He wished for wings, but nothing happened because he had run out of wishes.

A football slammed into his chest. Jonathan kept upright and pretended he was fine, tripping over the ball at his feet. The boys were waiting for him to kick it back into the game but he could not breathe and his inaction decided even the kinder ones that the new pupil was after all an enemy:

'Sissy.'

'Four-eyes.'

He snatched at his spectacles but Simon threw them into the air. Eventually he discovered them in the grass. Mummy did not know about his new spectacles. He escaped up the slope to a flower bed with no flowers. He identified rosemary, lavender and rhododendron bushes and then found a gate in the hedge and, beyond, a muddy path with brambles that twisted out of sight. He gripped the top and fitted his foot into a space in the metal but then stopped. He would be quickly captured; now was not the time.

Jonathan returned to the flower bed where he found a spider completing a web strung between a seeding thistle, fluffy like sheep's wool, and a tall cane. He counted the threads that connected the spans. There were ten on one segment, nineteen on another and twelve on a third. The number would relate to the stress on each section between its points of suspension. He nudged the thistle with his sore hand and the web trembled, making the spider stop its work. His daddy told him that spiders were natural engineers; their intricate structures of viscous material were wind- and water-resistant so that although the web oscillates in difficult conditions it remains intact. If there were boys here, he could explain: 'You let out a thread until it floats and finds a petal or a wall or this wood. It is sticky so it will catch and hold, then you run along the line giving out more thread to make it strong. Once you have your baseline, it's easy.'

He had lots of facts, he promised his audience: his birthday is on 15 March and he once had a hedgehog cake with lolly sticks for spikes. He has a train set with signals and a tunnel and his daddy builds bridges. His daddy was here but he has gone. This was not, Jonathan considered, strictly speaking a fact.

Then he thought that perhaps it was.

He scraped at the soil with a stick. A beetle made its way over the crinkly terrain of a leaf; tumbling, it tipped over, righted itself and scurried on. Jonathan captured it.

'A spider can eat its own weight in food. This beetle is, as you see, nearly the size of the spider so will last it a long time. Fact: spiders can survive up to a year without eating.'

He held the beetle in his loosely clenched fist. Some children could not bear this, girls especially, he informed the boys. They thought him particularly brave when he told them that the six beetle legs tickled inside his hand but he did not care. He flicked the beetle at the web. It was heavy and fell short. Jonathan had not expected this and the flow of his lecture faltered. He tried again, bringing it closer and watched with satisfaction when the black casing opened and the whirring wings caught on the last span. The beetle tried to break free and only became more entangled. Jonathan, hugged his knees and breathing deeply, commented: 'If it had not panicked it might be alive. This behaviour is common in humans.'

The spider moved inexorably towards its prey along the threads, landings and staircases, up-down-along-up-down-across. Jonathan's new trousers were tight over his legs and made his skin prickle. His hand hurt only when he pressed the marks. The spider began work on the insect and soon its beetle-shape was lost in a silken bag like a well-disguised present. The spider crouched on top of the lump.

'It's sucking out the blood.' Jonathan remarked airily.

'He's a nutcase, now he's talking to himself.'

Jonathan pitched face forward on to the soil. His glasses ground into his eye sockets and he was pulled over on to his back. Simon bounced on his stomach, thrashing the air with the thistle stalk as if he was a riding a horse. Strands of cobweb floated around them. The beetle lay amongst the mulch of rotting leaves. The spider was dead.

Jonathan heard the whistle but did not obey the rule about being a statue; instead he limped away over the grass. The second whistle shrieked and he dreamed of flying over the hills and far away.

'You are my prisoner.'

Simon tied his arms behind the goalpost. Jonathan interlocked his fingers and thought of his mummy.

'Hold tight. Look right and left and right again.'

'You are going to burn to death on the stake. Stay there while I get matches.' Simon banged Jonathan's head against the post.

'We have to go in,' Jonathan gasped.

'You will die.'

A fact.

A cold weather front was heading in from the English Channel and the sky darkened, colours muted to greys and greens. In the silence of the empty playground the little boy listened for his father's car, positive he would know it because of what his father called the dodgy exhaust.

Miss Thoroughgood was on the cusp of retirement. She had little appetite for exercising authority and had not counted in her charges, so she failed to see that the new boy was missing.

The wind ballooned the goal netting and rattled the beech hedge; it stripped the last leaves off the horse-chestnut tree and sent them swirling across the pitch. A thickening blanket of cloud descended. A master glanced out of the staffroom window and spotted a kid cutting lessons.

'Hey you, young man! Get inside or I'll serve you detention.'

'*What's that, young sirs? Stole a pig? Where are your licences?*'

Jonathan made a final wish and, wriggling, found that he was not tied up; he raised his leg and took a step. He could walk. He was free. He looked at the stake to which he had been tied and saw that there was no rope. A warmth was travelling down the inside of his thighs, like a flame licking, the material darker where the heat had spread. He ran along the path, his arms stiff like a tin soldier, his wool trousers chafing his inner thigh and the warmth turned to ice.

He flung open a door marked 'Toilets', smashing it against the wall, and skidded to a stop by the urinals. He fumbled with his fly although there was no point. When he twisted on the tap over the sink a deluge of water spattered up over his face, down his jacket and the front of his trousers. He was wet everywhere. Jonathan had enough presence of mind to see that this was useful. He raced through the smelly dungeon, pushed on the green door in the hall, ducked his head as he passed the high desk and burst out into the freezing entrance, all the time alert for an ambush.

He thought he had been away for a very long time but the crocodile was only outside the classroom door.

'Justin! What did I say about two whistles? You're soaking!'

'I washed my hands after the playground.' He was hoarse.

He threaded his way between the desks to the chair that was not his chair. The boy called Simon gestured with his stumpy finger and Jonathan looked down at the sodden fabric; he had forgotten to do up his flies.

'Mummy's boy wet himself!'

Jonathan sat up straight, waiting for Justin to come to claim his seat. He told himself that he could easily survive for a year without eating.

Five

Isabel Ramsay was preparing for bed.

She could feel a draught, standing by the sink in the kitchen. She decided that the cleaner had left a window open. The girls got hot vacuuming or polishing and ignoring her advice about wearing layers, opened windows and wasted precious heat. Except her present cleaner was careful, not like her daughters, who left clutter without a thought for others.

She shuffled through to the dining room where there was enough light from the kitchen to see that the curtain on one of the long windows was not properly drawn. That explained it.

The heavy gold brocade was topped with a plain pelmet. The catches on the window sashes had been screwed down years ago, because the balcony, adorned with railings matching the one above, was an ideal place for a burglar to hide. Eleanor had told her this was one of her hideouts; she had spied on dinner parties through the glass because in those days they never pulled the curtains and everything was open for all to see.

A silhouette with wild hair glared at her through the pane. Isabel's hand fluttered out and she managed to steady herself on a glazing bar. After a while, with slow deliberation she smeared her palm down the glass. She made a mental note of its position and then wiped the damp of the condensation on her skirt. Eleanor should have been in bed hours ago. She flapped the curtain across and blotted out her youngest daughter.

Good, the radiator was off. The cleaners turned it on, flagrantly flouting her assurance that they would soon warm up if they put their backs into it. Her new cleaner was not like that, she reminded herself.

Isabel preferred the dining room in the evening, lit by silver candelabras and flames leaping in the grate: her Queendom. In the chill dawn it was hard-edged and mundane. When she cleaned, Lizzie crashed and banged; sweeping ash on to newspaper and grumbling about her knees, her sciatica or her sister in New Zealand.

Someone had placed a vase of lilies in the fireplace. Not Lizzie, she was dead. Isabel was certain that she had been to her funeral, or was that the Howland woman? Howland, that was her name; it had been eluding her for the last week. Anyway, someone's suffering was over and they were at peace, just whose suffering Isabel could not at this moment put her finger on. She pictured the lane from the church in Sussex. However, the past got intertwined and she might have been thinking of the bloody village hall thingy. There were no mobile telephones to explain to Mark or the damned police that she was delayed by nonsense. She had assumed that, like the song, she had all the time in the world to put it right. Perhaps after all she had – the days crawled on and on.

Disjointed recollections floated through the old woman's consciousness like frayed threads while she stooped and pulled the lilies out of the vase by their heads, catching the unwieldy stems on the rim. The vase hit the fender and exploded into tiny pieces over the hearth. She flapped her hands helplessly: it was one of a pair belonging to her husband's mother. Isabel pushed some of the china with the pointy toe of her Chinese slipper, only Gina would consider it precious.

An identical vase on the mantelpiece still held flowers. The old woman pushed it along the ledge, the lilies smearing the wall in its wake. Toppling off the edge, the vase took the carriage clock with it; the glass on the face made a pretty sprinkling sound above the metallic crash when the brass casing hit the tiled hearth. The clock was a prized possession of the Hanging Judge. Mark, ever his dutiful son, had made it her job to keep it wound. It was face up; the time was right except the second hand was not moving.

Isabel flopped the dying lilies on to the tablecloth, scattering fine powder from their stamens over the fabric. Once upon a time this would have been a disaster.

Someone protected the oval table with a template of felt overlaid with a midnight-blue damask cloth. Isabel could hear Eleanor under there, scribbling away in her notebook; their every word, every action recorded. She steadied herself and the table groaned under her weight. There were too many spectres in the house for her liking; she would talk to the cleaner about it. Wednesdays and Fridays were her days. Friday was Isabel's favourite day: it was the day Mark sent her flowers when they were courting.

She scrabbled at the tablecloth and hauled it off. It was heavier than she expected and she tottered backwards. Beneath was a walnut surface mapped with blobs of wax, scratches and ringed with wine-glass stains. The table sat fifteen but there were only ten high-backed chairs. Isabel lowered herself into a carver at one end. The wine was rich red in the candle flame. Around the room her guests' complexions were suffused with bonhomie, summer skin tanned and glowing. They watched her raise a glass to her lips in silent toast before they drank. Mark was on his fifth Scotch. That tousled hair keeping him boyish, he reached too close to fill a girl's glass. Deep bass exclamations and guffaws of laughter spliced with women's flittering interjections fell silent when Isabel signalled for a hush to find out if anyone wanted more to eat or drink.

The night is young.

She floated on a desultory tide of sexual appreciation, tossing her head to deliver perfect smoke rings to the ceiling, her skin alive to the knowledge that more than one pair of eyes glittered with desire for her.

The draught stiffened her bones and the clink of cutlery and glass faded to stillness. Isabel Ramsay stared uncomprehending at empty chairs, the denuded table and broken china strewn over the floorboards.

She drew her shawl around her. Gina said she should wear thick cardigans; really meaning she was too old for bare shoulders.

Gina had always been old. The door of the Viennese wall clock had swung open and struggling to her feet she slammed it shut, lacking the courage to rip it off the wall. The fastening was bent and it opened again when the mechanism struck the quarter with a whirr. Gina warned her that unless it was fixed it would lose value; the girl price-tagged everything.

The shaft of light from the hall eclipsed for a moment.

She caught her foot on the bundled tablecloth on her way to the kitchen for her water. The tobacco smoke was fainter. If she told her children, they would take action: sack the cleaner; call the police; bring up the question of shunting her to a home.

She mounted the stairs, the ache at the base of her skull now focused on one place like an accusing finger; she dipped her head in a fruitless effort to avoid the prodding sensation. In each hand she clasped a tumbler of water, the last two glasses from a wedding present of eight. Soon they too would be gone. Gina reprimanded her for not holding on to the banister, more bothered about the Waterford crystal than her mother's safety. As an incomplete set, the glasses had no resale value, Isabel told her daughter; she didn't tell Gina about her falls. Last week Isabel had stumbled on to the landing throwing wine in a spray over the carpet; the stain was still there. She would add it to the cleaning list.

Eleanor said all the kids avoided the fifth stair when they crept in from parties. Isabel had never noticed that it creaked. Eleanor had remarked in her particular way that 'Dad knew'.

Isabel caught her foot in a tear in the carpet. It had been laid in the spring of 1968. Gina wanted to sort out a replacement; Jon could get Axminster at trade price. Mark or someone had refused. Mark probably, keen to accept nothing from his son-in-law.

Falling was nothing to do with age, Isabel told the children, it could happen to any of you.

When she reached the top landing, the lights went out. Power cut. Another one. She had to depend on light slanting in from the windows to find her bedside table and avoid spilling water on the plastic radio from Gina and Jon. She forgot and switched on the anglepoise, and then left it; at least she would know when the electricity came on.

Mark's bedside cabinet needed sorting: she moved his spectacles case and in the poor light shifted his ever-growing pile of books for space to put his glass. The smell of beeswax reminded her to talk to the cleaner about something.

The bells struck ten or eleven or twelve, she had lost count, she told Hall or whatever he called himself. She shuffled to the window wrapping her shawl around her and peered down.

Unlike many London squares, the park opposite belonged to the council. The land had been purchased in 1915 to stop a proposed development of houses. When the Ramsays moved to St Peter's Square in 1957, a team of keepers based in a hut at one end had tended the plants and bushes and swept up leaves and litter. They also kept an eye on unattended children. Now the upkeep of the lawns and paths was outsourced to a private company and residents added plants of their choosing to immaculate beds. The keepers' hut, its windows and door sealed with metal panels, had lost definition beneath a chaos of graffiti.

The lone call of a song thrush in the horse-chestnut tree was amplified in the darkness.

Mark's arm encircled her. Isabel shifted. He lifted her breast, as if testing its weight. Like a television programme she was not enjoying, Isabel snapped off the picture.

Footsteps came from the church, a chock-chock on the pavement accompanied by a lighter pattering; Isabel tapped her feet in their twinkling slippers in time to the sound and hurriedly smoothed down her hair, flattening a hand over her stomach. Her cotton shawl emphasized bony shoulder blades and a tall spare frame on which a linen skirt exposed still shapely calves and ankles.

The village hall shindig was crammed in to make way for the big day; so much that was petty and pointless had repercussions. What's more, the bloody place went to rack and ruin; it was all a waste.

A woman with a pushchair and a boy clutching its handle scurried into the pool of lamplight and out again. The lights of other houses winked through the swaying branches. Isabel rubbed her mouth ruminatively: when there was a power cut, surely everything went out?

She batted Mark's pillow to make an indentation for his head. She held his latest paperback up to the orange lamplight and squinted at the title: *Our Mutual Friend* by Charles Dickens. Mark abhorred fiction and stuck to the truth. She fanned the pages and a shape floated on to the duvet. Patting about on the fabric she found a half-smoked cigarette and sniffed it. The smell made her happy for a fraction of time. She tried to slip the stub back in the book but gave up and climbed into bed, letting it drop to the floor.

Isabel lay on her back, her body so slight that the bed appeared empty. Although she told her cleaner that she was a light sleeper, she did not stir when, some time later, the fifth stair creaked.

Six

A telephone rang from somewhere beyond the waiting room. Stella skimmed the *Daily Mail* she had taken from the pile of newspapers and brochures on the smoked-glass table, pondering how the old-fashioned bell was at odds with the modern techniques of dentistry boasted of in the glossy marketing.

It was her phone. She rummaged for it in her rucksack and hastened to the conservatory at the end of the waiting room.

'Stella, are you there?'

'Speaking.'

'No, I mean are you at the dentist?' It was Jackie, her personal assistant.

'Yes I'm here,' she hissed into the handset, stirring toothbrushes displayed in a cane basket on the window sill that resembled the gift sets with soap and baubles of bubble bath nestling in straw she received every Christmas from clients who saw no irony in giving soap to a cleaning company.

'You'll feel better.' With less conviction Jackie added: 'Good luck.'

At nine that morning Jackie had found Stella at her desk dosed with painkillers that had not masked the hammering in her jaw and, without consulting her, sourced a dentist online and booked the first appointment of the day.

Stella had not divulged her fear of the whining drill, the scraping of metal on ivory and the electric shocks of exposed nerves. Or her revulsion of latex-coated fingers poking around her mouth; never would she admit to feelings or failings.

The pain had started when she got home from her visit to the office last night. On top of Terry's death, toothache was the last straw; she had ignored it, replied to her emails and designed and priced an oven-cleaning package. The throbbing increased and she decided to stipulate to the undertakers that the funeral would be basic: no cars, no flowers, no music. No mourners.

In the morning Jackie handed her the address of the surgery on a Clean Slate compliment slip and, snatching the keys for a spare van, gave Stella twenty minutes to get to Kew.

Stella had no intention of going; she would pretend Mrs Ramsay had called and asked her to come a day early. Yet obeying the satnav's peremptory directions and driving along untypically clear roads to 'reach her destination' – a tree-lined street of detached Edwardian villas off the South Circular – she had arrived with five minutes to spare and a pain that was robbing her of her senses.

She had slotted the van into a tight space outside the surgery, crunched over a gravel sweep, circumventing a huge four-by-four car to steps between plinths, each supporting a stone eagle with outspread wings. A brass plaque on one, smeared with dried polish, read: 'Dr S. A. I. Challoner. Dentist'. Nursing her jaw, Stella had pushed open one of two studded doors and gone inside.

She returned to her seat and took refuge in the newspaper.

Her phone rang again: Paul had called her at home and so far today had sent five texts. She switched off the handset.

'You must be Stella.'

Stella looked up from an article about the curse of the Kennedy dynasty to see a resurrected Ted Kennedy: a middle-aged man with ebullient greying hair in a pristine white coat, piercing blue eyes and a smile of perfect teeth. He spoke as if her presence was a happy discovery and put out his hand. Stella rose.

'I am Ivan.' He kept her hand for the right amount of time in a grip that was firm but did not crush.

When he gently shut the door to his surgery, all extraneous noise ceased.

The richly decorated room reminded Stella of the sitting rooms of many of her clients. Floor-to-ceiling shelving of hardback books: Austen, Dickens, Eliot, Homer and Trollope were – she was gratified to see – in alphabetical order. The opulent décor of rich ochres: yellow, terracotta, deep oranges contrasted with the midnight blue of Mrs Ramsay's tablecloth. All this demoted the harsh white dental equipment to ornamental rather than the main activity of the room. Stella's dread diminished and she waved at the bookshelf indicating *Wuthering Heights*.

'Good story.' She dared risk no more; she had only skimmed it at school.

'Don't you love it?' Dr Challoner was examining his instruments, laying them out on a long marble-topped table with lion-paw legs.

'I wouldn't go that … Yes, I do.'

'It was my wife's favourite too.'

This stopped Stella from adding that she'd been annoyed by all the bad weather and had given up before the end. As Dr Challoner guided her to the chair, she kept to herself that she did not see the point of fiction and, lying back, became aware of the faint notes of a piano.

Although Stella knew little about classical music, she recognized it. Mrs Ramsay had put it on every day; the music was depressing and Stella thought it could not be good for her. Mrs Ramsay said the music came from the walls, which was the sort of illogical remark that had led Stella to suspect she was going mad. On her last visit, Mrs Ramsay, behaving as if in the scene she was describing, had rhapsodized over some bird – 'Don't look up, you will blind yourself' – hovering above the ruins of a village and had cautioned: 'Sssssh! See the children playing. Keep an eye on what they are doing.'

Stella had been compelled to reply that she could not see anyone. Mrs Ramsay had pointed out that the top of the cistern needed a wipe, which it did not.

Stella had taken over Mrs Ramsay's cleaning two years ago when one of her staff was frightened by the old lady pretending to be a celebrity at an opening ceremony and forcing her to hold up a length of parcel tape that she snipped with a pair of pinking shears.

Mr Challoner clipped a plastic bib into place around Stella's neck and adjusted wrap-around sunglasses on her nose. He elevated her into position and Stella allowed herself to relax.

As he stood over her, a lock of his hair slid over eyebrows so defined Stella wondered whether he plucked them. She could not identify his aftershave: a mix of musk and incense cut with juniper berries and spicy pepper and calculated that veins criss-crossing the backs of his hands put him in his mid-fifties while his translucent complexion and prominent cheekbones made him seem younger.

'My nurse is off sick. It is she who runs this tight ship, so do bear with me.' He snapped on surgical gloves with a magician's flourish.

'I like this music.' Stella regretted speaking. It opened possibilities of a discussion in which she would have nothing to say.

'When my son was small this was his favourite, he made my wife play it every bedtime. One gets sentimental once they grow up. If music had been more accessible in Proust's time, he might have experienced it as a vehicle of transcendence instead of a morsel of sponge cake.' He gave a quick smile.

Stella opened wide to avoid responding and her jaw clicked the way Terry's did; her calm evaporated.

'I'm transported to his bedroom, tidying his toys, reading Beatrix Potter or some such to him. Raise your hand at any time during the procedure if you want to rest and rinse. Creeping out, I would have to stop and gaze at him, his face deceptively angelic in the glow of the nightlight, he hated the dark.' Dr Challoner appeared distracted; then he shrugged and picked up a sickle probe from his tray.

Stella imagined a father who read his child stories, held her hand in the street and sat her on his knee to ask about her day at school. Bright light warmed her face when Mr Challoner repositioned the lamp; she closed her eyes.

It was over.

Mr Challoner was keying details of his treatment into a computer. Stella tottered against the chair as she tidied her hair and tugged at her clothes. The bib lay on the counter.

She had a gum infection under her lower left second bicuspid for which he scribbled a prescription for antibiotics, reassuring her that, apart from a spot of plaque and decay behind her top left incisor revealed by the X-ray, her teeth were good. With his hygienist on holiday he had performed a clean and polish. He would see her again for the filling which he made sound like a treat in store.

He delivered Stella to his receptionist and with a slight bow bade her goodbye.

Outside it occurred to Stella coming out of the reception, that the wall where the surgery had been was blank. She put this crazy impression down to the lidocaine numbing one side of her face; it turned the visit into a not unpleasant dream.

She stuck to the speed limit on Chiswick Bridge thinking about the little boy tucked in by his father. Terry could not have named her favourite music. Her phone's ringtone was amplified through the speakers and propelled her into the present.

Jackie had left a voicemail about Mrs Ramsay, although crackling made the message unintelligible, Stella guessed Mrs Ramsay wanted her. When doing costing analyses Stella never built in the extra attentions she gave some clients regardless of their business worth. Such efforts, she had explained to Terry, were key to her success.

Stella did not reflect that the extra touches were because she cared about Mrs Ramsay. Page two of her staff handbook warned cleaners of the dangers of mixing emotion with business: *You are one side of the dustpan and brush; the client is on the other.*

Stella resolved to start on Terry's house that afternoon. The pain in her mouth had gone and as her van rumbled over the rickety Hogarth flyover the cloud lifted. She angled the visor to cut out low sunlight and estimated, based on years of experience, that clearing his possessions need take no time at all.

A police car and a van marked 'Scientific Support Branch' were parked outside Mrs Ramsay's house. The back doors of the van were open and inside Stella could see the same blue plastic slide-out containers that she used for storing cleaning equipment in her vehicles. She drew in behind, wrenching up the handbrake to the furthest notch.

Blue police boundary tape, rattling in the breeze, had been tied across the gateway of Mrs Ramsay's house and a policeman blocked the path.

'Sorry, madam, you can't pass this point.'

Stella looked over the officer's shoulder to the shadowy hall. A lookalike Terry in a crumpled grey suit, balanced on his haunches, was inspecting her shampooed rug. A woman in scene-of-crime overalls sprinkled powder along the dining-room window sash bars which Stella had treated only last week and now would have to do again. The detective came out on to the porch, speaking into his phone.

It was not Terry.

As he kicked his heels, stamping on the mat and smacking dirt off his trousers, she caught the words '… place is a tip…'

'I'm going to have to ask you to move on, madam.'

'I'm here to see Mrs Ramsay. We handle her cleaning.'

The constable folded his arms. 'Not any more. Mrs Ramsay died in the night.'

Seven

May 1985

The engine hurtled too fast into the tunnel; he should have applied the brakes sooner. Everything went into slow motion. His tummy churned, his tongue was a dead thing and when he tried to shout the sounds were lost in yawning blackness. Beakers of tea and coffee, books and bags slid gracefully off tables. Suitcases tumbled out of netted racks and blocked gangways as ceilings and floors changed places. He was alive to noises only experts would identify: cogs loosening, axles shearing off, metal grinding and snarling. The engine was swallowed up by the hole in the hillside.

The urgency in the air was intoxicating, yet the engineer in him worried that the collision and consequent vibration would weaken the tunnel roof and expose mistakes. The driver's cab should survive, he calculated as the engine roared out the other side dragging carnage in its wake like tins tied to a wedding car. The second carriage had telescoped into the first. Too late he blew his whistle: this was the best part and he had looked forward to it but his ribs hurt as if splinters of glass had lacerated his organs and his nostrils filled with the stench of rotting roots and claggy soil. The train careered off the track and came to rest beside a watering can.

Jonathan had been proud of his tunnel, excavated into a mound of topsoil; it was high and wide enough for the rolling stock. He surveyed the damage: there were cracks around the opening which would develop into critical fissures and fatally undermine the structure if not repaired.

'You went too fast.' Jonathan dared to be cross with Simon. He rubbed his hand on his shorts leaving a bloody stain; he had been biting his thumb. Someone would be displeased with him; at this moment, dazed by the incident, Jonathan could not remember who that would be.

'You're a scaredy-cat, Justin.' Simon was matter of fact.

Justin, for that had been his name for four months now, shuffled his feet to alleviate pins and needles. Simon sat with his legs apart; there was a graze on his knee from football. Justin's legs were skinny and pale; his football shorts flapped around his thighs, like a skirt, Simon said.

Simon says: Justin's a girl.

Simon says: Justin's a weirdo.

Simon's willy lolled in the depths of his shorts; everything about him was bigger. Justin concentrated on the tunnel in case Simon caught him staring and called him names. He was fretting about the incident, and wanted to be alone to inspect his train.

The kitchen garden had been a secret but, falling into a routine of going there instead of the playground, Justin grew careless and Simon had seen him. He sneaked up when Justin was doing the opening ceremony for his new cut and cover railway tunnel behind the greenhouse.

'Can I have a turn?' Justin should not have to ask for a go with his own train.

'Unfortunately you cannot. I need to perform more test runs.' Simon was imitating him. He knew nothing about engineering or trains, Justin fumed.

Simon shoved the engine along flattened soil that Justin had weeded and designated a 'sand drag' – intended to prevent a catastrophe such as this. He had not taken human error into account because he did not make mistakes. He would have liked to have installed a Moorgate control but lacked the tools. There were no actual rails; he had constructed the track along a section of earth he had punched flat with a brick. Justin dreamed of real tracks raised on ballast. Simon was pressing down on the engine's tank until it sank into the mulch at the foothills of the compost heap.

'Stop doing that with your mouth.'

'I wasn't.'

'You were. I don't want to have to get cross with you.' Simon put on a girl's voice. Justin did not talk like that, but did not point this out. Simon tried to shift the engine, but soil had clogged its wheels and it was mired.

Justin sifted soft earth; he must wash his nails before supper or Miss Thoroughgood would tell him off. She was leaving at the end of term so everyone was supposed to treat her nicely. Simon's nails, all nine of them, were clean. Justin turned so that Simon would not see his mouth twitching.

He had developed a sniff accompanied by a flick of his fringe to distract attention from the tic that had begun after he started at boarding school. He also gnawed at the skin around his thumbnail. Simon called him 'the Vampire', which made no sense to Justin as he did not suck blood. Some of the younger boys called him this out of windows or from around corners.

'There's nowhere for the passengers to get out.'

Simon was right; he had not built a station. The tunnel had been complicated: he had worked out the strength of the roof, the width of the tunnel – half as much as its length – drawing and revising diagrams in his notebook after prep but had forgotten about alighting and disembarking.

Had there been other boys, he would have explained how he'd embedded struts made from ice-lolly sticks in the walls. He fixed them with roofing felt made from folded toilet paper layered with leaves and twigs and overlaid with a mortar of earth and some sand he had found by the shed.

I added water from the tap that I carried in this paint tin.

Mortar, he would inform them, dries as hard as concrete. He would run a road over the tunnel or perhaps lay a park with a statue, but Simon must be got rid of first.

Simon had warned that if he told on him Justin would be in trouble for messing up the vegetable patch and trespassing. He explained it was for this bad behaviour that Justin had been sent away.

'I will kill you and bury your body so that no one will ever find you and then your flesh will be eaten and your bones will crumble.' Simon stuck the hand with the half-finger inside Justin's shorts. 'I'll say you escaped again.' At first he was gentle, but then he squeezed and Justin felt sick. Simon's fist struggled like an animal beneath the school regulation material.

'Message understood?' Simon pulled away.

Justin blinked back tears.

Simon never spoke of his random attacks and afterwards they both behaved as if nothing had happened. Justin had an oblique idea that Simon's behaviour was sanctioned by a higher authority so did not believe he could stop it.

A storm roared about his ears, whipping soil and stones into the air that stung his cheeks. He dashed water from his face, ducking from the paint tin, and clasped his hands over his head. He opened his eyes. Simon had reduced his tunnel to clumps of earth, wads of discoloured paper stuck with splinters of wood and scattered with onions, carrots and wild garlic.

The small boy remained on the raised vegetable bed, a statue save for jerks of his head. He wore an expression of quiet despair.

At last he retrieved the engine from the far side of the bed and wiped sand and soil from the funnel and cylinder with toilet paper. He pushed a loose wheel into place and cleared slathers of wet earth from the carriage windows; the smiling people were gone. He peered in: passengers were sprawled on the floor, or wedged between seats.

Justin's face was wet; Simon liked it when he cried. He looked around and saw he was alone, which made him uneasy.

He imagined writing to his mummy, putting the case for her to fetch him; she would not think he was a coward – except maybe she would. Perhaps he was.

The boy trailed up the path, past the greenhouse, to the gate to a bridle path that led to the road. He knew this because he had tried to escape. So much freedom just beyond his grasp.

To the little boy, the walled kitchen garden had a quiet of its own, its once richly planted beds now populated by rabbits, only one corner tended on occasional visits by an elderly gardener.

He heard an irregular clinking, persistent and distinct like a Morse code message. A dog lead hung from a washing-line post, the frayed strap weathered to a soft pink. In the breeze the clasp, oscillating like a pendulum, tapped out Jonathan Justin Rokesmith's plot of revenge on the parched and knotted wood.

Eight

The light flickered and the lamp-post emitted an insistent buzz. At half past ten the Great West Road was still busy, headlights sweeping over the bollards stopping access to Rose Gardens North, their shadows in continual flux. Neither the buzzing nor the traffic penetrated a mantle of silence in the cul-de-sac.

In the 1950s the arterial road cut a swathe through West London, and all that was left of Rose Gardens was a row of six Victorian labourers' cottages. The six new lanes extended to London Airport. The council, perhaps in bureaucratic penance for the demolition of the ivy-clad dwellings and burgeoning orchards bounded by hawthorn hedgerows, designated a patch of leftover land for recreational purposes. Bushes and infant cherry trees dotted newly sown grass (no dogs or balls allowed) in scant imitation of the orchards. Benches – each dedicated to a worthy councillor – were placed strategically in the shadow of the church. Each spring the trees offered a pink spray canopy, their colour offsetting the miles of tarmac. Soon the road claimed its first fatality: an eighty-one-year-old woman, her body memory obeying a vanished map, walked along Black Lion Lane as if the new road were not there and died instantly. Central railings were installed to discourage further deaths.

Time passed: the bushes grew into a forbidding shrubbery, tree trunks thickened, weeds ruptured the paths, frost forced the cracks apart to become potholes for rainwater and rubbish. In response to a residents' petition, the benches – a magnet for drunks and suspicious-looking men – were removed. In the gleam of moonlight the plunging branches of the grand old sycamore provoked nameless dread in scurrying passers by; the paths were abandoned for a muddied track short-cutting over the grass to the subway. Set back from the Great West Road, shrouded from the pavement and St Peter's Church by encroaching foliage, the little park was no longer a place to linger.

Stella could have come to Terry's house at any time; assuming her to be grieving, Jackie did not expect her to be at work, but she was loath to meet Terry's neighbours so she waited until it was dark. On her return from Mrs Ramsay's she had found Jackie interrogating the revised rota. Michelle's son had broken his arm, Felicia had resigned to work privately, Maxine's brother had been in a car accident so she had gone to Manchester and Shelley was already doing the workload of two: they had a staffing crisis. Stella took all the shifts. A drawback of success was that she did less cleaning so, despite her high-calibre team, she relished any chance to do the work herself.

After two hours of vacuuming, polishing and mopping in the offices of a financial advice company by Hammersmith Underground station, she had stepped out on to the Broadway and, zipping up her windproof jacket against a bitter wind, driven to the house where she had spent the first seven years of her life. It was another job, she repeated to herself; Terry was another client.

She caught a movement in bushes across the road and peered through the windows of her van, ready to drive off. There was no one.

The lamp-post came to life and orange light dulled the colours of the parked cars to muddy brown and made gaunt shadows that quivered on the camber. Stella scanned the shrubbery again and wrongly assumed that a lumpish shape in the undergrowth was a bush.

She kept close to a privet that Terry had let grow tall – presumably to block a view into his living room – and unlatched the gate. Immediately she tripped on a hard object and her key-ring torch revealed a cast-iron shoe scraper: a painted squirrel nibbling on a nut in the middle of the crazy paving. She carried it to the front door, using the toe of her steel-capped boot to edge it into line with the tiled step. Stella fished in her jacket for his keys, too preoccupied by the enormity of her task – she had never been to Terry's house uninvited – to consider why the scraper was on the path in the first place.

The lamp-post went on and light picked out recently repointed brickwork and newly painted sashes. Stella guessed that Terry had done the work; he would not trust others. It was probably such stubbornness that had killed him.

In 1981, the year Margaret Thatcher's Conservative government increased police pay, Terry worked more overtime than usual and was able to buy the corner house that he and Stella's mother had rented after their marriage in 1966.

Many of Clean Slate's clients lived in this part of Hammersmith: lawyers, judges, actors, journalists; ambitious professionals with no time or inclination to scrub or dust. The area was more openly opulent than it had been in the late sixties during Stella's time there, when a mix of ramshackle upper-middle classes and working people like Terry had resided more comfortably side by side. Nowadays a policeman would be unusual; Stella guessed that Terry had not socialized with his neighbours so would not be missed.

Terry Darnell had cared little about social class; a detective, he could enter any home and poke about under baths, stairs and floorboards with impunity. He could delve into the recesses of all manner of lives and expose the unspeakable. Stella too, unimpressed by her clients' status, applied astringents and detergents, wielded brushes and mops, listening without comment or judgement to dilemmas and dramas not dissimilar to those investigated by her father.

However, as Stella stared up at the drawn bedroom curtains and tightly slatted blinds, she found the notion of a shared experience with Terry untenable.

She ran the soles of her boots over the scraper and shook loose his mortice key, which turned easily in the lock. She was not so lucky with the Yale; it would not budge. Used to the idiosyncrasies of locks she inserted her gloved fingers into the letterbox, the flap mouse-trapping them, and eased the door back and forth while manipulating the torque with the key. She detected the correct position in the cylinder, the tumblers released, the plug rotated and the door opened.

Dry leaves were crushed underfoot behind her.

Stella left the door ajar, the key in the lock, and rushed to the gate. Wind tore through the hedge, smacking at her jacket, shaking chimes hung in next door's porch that set off a tinkling discord of notes.

She put her staff through a drill for entering empty premises. The handbook instructed vigilance; keep the key at all times. *Do not leave the door open even to go out to the bins: a burglar needs only seconds to slip inside.*

Besides her van, four cars were ranged along the nearside kerb; the bays by the bushes were empty. A gust sent leaves and a squashed milk carton racing along the gutter and somewhere a can clattered and bounced on tarmac. The lamp went out and the carton was subsumed into velvet blackness. Stella concluded that leaves and twigs scraping and sweeping on stone could sound like shuffling soles. She was uptight and letting her imagination run riot, she told herself.

In the hall she skidded on a heap of mail-order catalogues in plastic wrappers silted up on the brush mat and had to kick them out of the way to shut the door.

Upstairs a clock ticked and from the kitchen came the drip-drip of a tap. The air was cold but lacked the stale atmosphere she would have expected of a place shut up and unoccupied even for a couple of days. She identified Lavender and Vanilla from Glade's Relaxing Moments Collection, which she reserved for middle-range clients prior to a sale or new letting to lend a positive impression to the most tired or drab of interiors and reinforce the conviction that Clean Slate did a thorough job. Terry fitted this 'average' profile; most of her clients in this district preferred a less synthetic scent.

Unwilling to attract attention with lights, she twisted on the miniature Maglite attached to her key ring.

Always carry a torch in case the lights fail.

Phantoms shivered and re-formed when she levelled the beam around the hall. An old man flinching and jerking morphed into a coat stand draped with jackets, the telephone table was an arching cat that evaporated as the newel post, a slip of a cartoon character, rose to attention and then swooped up the stairs. Stella picked her way over the catalogues and along the passage to the kitchen.

Something had triggered the security light; Stella leant over the sink but could see no one beneath the window sill and decided it was branches of a forsythia bush waving in the wind. She turned to the room; pale appliances and worktops were clinical in the vibrant light.

There were none of the items that often take up kitchen surfaces: coffee-makers, toasters, cooking implements stuffed upright into ceramic pots, cutting boards harbouring germs; she guessed that little cooking or eating took place and recalled the Coke and two bacon rolls in the Co-op bag. Terry grabbed his food on the run; it was fuel only. She closed off the dripping tap, comforted by a whiff of bleach from the plughole.

On recent visits to Terry, Stella had seldom gone beyond the front room but remained on the sofa, drinking tea. They both knew that the sooner she finished it the sooner she could leave.

The American-style fridge with an ice dispenser dwarfed a reproduction country pine dresser that Stella remembered from her childhood. Ever the opportunist, Terry had snapped it up with a double bed, the kitchen table and her bedroom wardrobe from a man doing a house clearance next door to the scene of one of his crimes. Her mother told friends the cherry-stained pine was the tipping point to divorce, although much of the pine, darker with age, filled her small flat in Barons Court.

The dresser was stacked with white crockery; plates propped up like blank faces in the unremitting light. In Stella's day the cupboard had been a dumping ground for household odds and ends: a basket of pegs, her mother's cookery books, chipped cups and plates that her mum got second-hand, not caring if they matched, light bulbs, candles, lengths of cables and trinkets from Christmas crackers.

The fridge, its defrosting cycle complete, shuddered to meditative quiet. Stella was surprised to be greeted by beer and bottles of wine on racks and in the vegetable storage area. She had not thought of Terry as a drinker; whenever she saw him he was about to go on duty or was already working. In a pub he would nurse the same shandy all evening. Three eggs wobbled in a compartment along the top of the door; the only other food was jars of pickled onions, a lump of cheddar and a foil dish of half-eaten shop-bought shepherd's pie. Terry would not have left food in the fridge if he'd been planning be go away. The drawers of the freezer were packed with more shepherd's pies. Her mother was sure that Terry would disapprove of her recent decision to be a vegetarian; he disliked vegetarians, she said. Stella doubted Terry cared what her mother ate. Disliking waste, Stella would take his shepherd's pies home. It felt like stealing; discouraged, she abandoned the idea.

A subtle drop in temperature came not from the fridge but elsewhere in the house.

Along the passage she made out the two panes of glass in the front door: oblongs suspended in darkness. The front door was shut. Above, a floorboard groaned; the house was adjusting to her presence.

She returned to the kitchen. Lit by the halogen beacon the garden was a stage set awaiting performers. Terry must have recently swept because only a sprinkling of leaves were strewn in the flower beds. A plastic picnic table with rainwater collecting in a dip was in the middle on the patio. Matching chairs had been tipped against it in the way Stella would have put them, to keep birds from soiling the seats. Clean Slate offered pressure-washing of paths and garden furniture in a 'Get Ready for Spring' package. She would hose down the paving and turn over the soil; the furniture could go.

She had never sat with Terry drinking a beer in the sunshine at the table, telling him about her latest contracts while he related his latest cases.

The security lamp went out. Stella groped for her Maglite.

He was watching.

Spangles of light floated before her. The torch's battery was failing; the beam wavered to a watery yellow.

She was distracted by the acrid smell of kettle descaler from beneath the sink and bent to investigate. She had searched for a plunger in this cupboard, vast to a child, sent by Terry when the bathroom sink blocked. Stella dismissed the hazy memory.

Stella Darnell judged a person by their cleaning cupboard. Those who stashed materials on shelves, penning stray bottles into plastic boxes, folding dusters, chamois, dishcloths, scourers in stacks and hung up the dustpan and brush, rarely paid invoices on time and picked holes in the service. If she opened a cupboard and the contents spilled on to the floor she could expect to make the place her own and never chase payment.

Terry's cleaning store was one of the tidiest Stella had seen.

A bowl, a dessertspoon and a mug were placed in a line on the draining board: Terry's last breakfast. He had eaten cereal and drunk coffee. His six-foot-one-inch frame had briskly crossed the kitchen, leather soles clicking on the tiles, and with swift economic motions he had scooped the inside of the bowl and the mug with the soapy scourer, sluicing each item under the hot tap, careless of scalding already roughened skin. With a fling he had shaken excess water off his hands, drying them with a flapping cloth poked into a rubber holder suctioned on the side of the fridge.

Terry had left unaware that he was walking out of his house for the last time.

The tea towel was dry. Terry had been gone two days. Why was he in Seaford?

Take deep breaths. That's it. In. Out. In. Out. Keep your eyes on the horizon. Once you get your sea legs, you'll be right as rain.

He could not loosen her grip on the handrail as a force-nine gale tossed the ferry like one of her bath toys. Passengers were being sick on the deck above and the wind spattered them with flecks of vomit. He would break her tiny fingers if he tried to prise them off the rail. Her bird shoulders rose and fell as she obeyed his instructions. The little thing was quaking; he hugged her close.

Stella nudged the bowl, the spoon and then the mug an inch from their original positions so that Terry was not the last person to have touched them; she had wiped him away. She would crate the crockery for charity. She could not lose the impression that Terry was just out of her vision, monitoring her.

She aimed the torch behind the living-room door, darkness folding in behind her. Nothing. Despite her fleece-lined anorak, Stella felt cold. She would not turn on the radiators; Terry was sparing with central heating, she was sure she had always been cold when she visited.

She appreciated the clean lines and the metal sheen of the brushed chrome coal-effect fire flush with the chimney breast. When it was new, she had mistaken it for a television. She remembered Terry's missing mobile phone and raked light under the sofa and armchair.

She was on the floor when the lamp-post came to life projecting a silhouette of the swaying hedge on to the venetian blinds. Stella shivered. With forensic care she lifted cushions and then knelt on the sofa, shining the torch down the back. Her nose close to the fabric, she could smell Terry's aftershave; he sat here to watch television.

The lamp-post went off and at the same time a bluff of wind shook the windows, its moan rising to a whine before dying away.

The air freshener was in a double socket by the gas fire. She pulled it out. As she had guessed, the cartridge was empty. Terry was too meticulous to leave a used one plugged in: further proof that he had not planned to go away, that something had made him change his mind. Something was wrong.

Stella hurried back to the hall and trod the stairs with a creeping disquiet, zigzagging the torchlight ahead. The draught was stronger here and she stopped on the landing and confirmed again that she had shut the front door.

Terry's toothbrush and razor poked out of a tumbler on the bathroom sink. She slid them to the other end of the glass shelf, but then admitting that Terry would hate to find them moved – she didn't like Paul interfering with her things – restored them to their original positions. Every object was an emissary for Terry; he had her surrounded. Stella's efforts to dispel her sense that any minute her father would appear and ask her what she was doing there were futile. She straightened the towel on the rail, although it was already straight.

Terry's bedroom was four steps up from the bathroom landing, facing the street. When she had come to Terry's for his 'access weekends' this door was always shut. She stayed in her bedroom until he called her for breakfast. Her old bedroom was on the left; she would leave it until last. Stella feared her heart would crash out of her chest when she put out a hand to open his door.

On her way to the bathroom the door had been ajar, now it was shut. Stella retreated to the lower landing and leant cautiously over the banister; stretching right over she could make out only a section of the front door. The failing beam did not reach the hall but she could distinguish the catalogues on the hall table and tried to remember placing them there. She must have put down the torch to gather them up and square them off or the pile would slither off. Her memory was getting worse.

She returned to the bedroom door, the swish-swishing of her anorak loud in her ear, and this time the door was open although she had not turned the handle. Of course the draught had shifted the door ajar. Stella let herself breathe.

The bedroom windows were locked and fitted with limiters; there was nothing Terry did not know about security. Stella swept the beam over bare walls, his bed with a melamine unit of shelves built around it and a pine wardrobe with matching chest of drawers on which sat Terry's washbag, his father's ivory-backed hairbrush with no handle and an almost empty bottle of Gillette aftershave. Stella gave him aftershave for birthdays and Christmas.

The expanse of ironed grey duvet was broken by light blue pyjamas shop-folded on a pillow. Stella did not touch them; from feet away she could smell Terry's hair product.

The three wardrobe mirrors displayed her in crude triptych, a bulky figure in her anorak, her sharp features as granite in the unflattering light.

She disconnected another used air freshener behind the bedside cabinet. A radio alarm with huge digits was next to a lamp, and a torch with a luminous casing. It worked, so she swapped it with her own.

A '1' was flashing on an LCD screen in the telephone base.

Terry had a message.

When she lifted the receiver its screen activated to blue. She pressed 'play'. A female robotic voice with an American accent announced a voicemail had been left at three minutes past ten on Sunday, 9 January 2011, the day before Terry had died.

After a signal there was silence. Stella presumed it was a predictive dialled sales call that automatically cut when the recipient did not answer but nevertheless hit 'replay'. This time when she played the message she distinguished what sounded like a gurgling spring; listening to it again she learnt nothing more.

She had forgotten 1471; she could find out the number of the caller.

She punched in the digits and another recorded voice stated 'You were called at 10.03 p.m. on the ninth of January ...' She patted her pockets for a pen while stilted tones enunciated each number; giving up she pressed 'three' to connect and a chirpy set of notes indicated the number dialling. She counted the rings: one, two, three, before a long beep and the line cut off.

Air shifted in the room and Terry's aftershave irritated her nostrils; stifling a sneeze, she saw that the bedroom door was shut. She dropped the torch and the light dipped crazily over the wall. It stopped, pointing at the mirror, the splash of light obliterating her reflection. She raked her hands through her hair; she must stay on it, she told herself. Her fingers numb with cold she tried again: 'This is Terence Darnell, I'm sorry I can't take your call right now, but if—'

Stella hurled the receiver; it bounced on the duvet, making a dent in the cotton, the voice chippering through the earpiece. The last number to dial the house had been Terry's mobile phone. He had rung to get his calls.

When she was little, it had been the usher gliding up to their seats in the cinema with a slip of paper containing a message to attend a case, or a shambling man in a pub or a café, or a staccato voice on his radio relaying cryptic information that cut their time together short. As technology progressed this came via his pager, or the phone beside his cutlery, while they waited for food they would not stay to eat.

Stella examined the telephone base. In the last year Terry's breathing had grown worse, he sucked in as he inhaled; the few times he'd called she'd heard it down the phone; every sentence seeming an effort, as if talking to her was a chore. Yet there was no sound on the recording.

The date was wrong.

While the time was right, it read nearly midnight and was three minutes fast – the date stated it was the tenth of January; it was one day slow. This meant that what the machine called the ninth was actually the tenth. Terry could not have called his answer machine: by three minutes past ten he had been dead about twelve hours.

The solution was obvious: whoever had used his mobile did not know Terry was dead and had tried to contact him to return the phone.

A tiny siren was coming through the receiver; the line was still open. She retrieved the handset and in a measured voice left her name and Clean Slate's number, hoping that Terry's battery would live long enough for the person to get in touch.

Stella remembered that this was the second message she had left and her relief dwindled. Someone had called but had not left a message; surely, had they wanted to return the phone they would have done so.

It did not make sense.

She went to the door.

It would not open. She rattled the handle. The door was locked. She was going mad.

The torch died. She flailed at the door; in the pitch black she lost her bearings and fell backwards catching the bed. Her bowel muscles contracted and she clenched her buttocks. She breathed deeply and after a bit the smell of washing detergent grounded her. She needed to pull herself together, she berated herself.

At that moment a spear of orange light cut across the door. The lamp-post had come on and was shining through a crack in the curtains.

She found the fluorescent torch – a yellow shimmering stick – at her feet, but it didn't work. The lamplight went off. She grasped again at the doorknob, wrenching it, and this time the door opened. The cold air made her shiver and her teeth chatter. She clenched her jaw, furious at losing her nerve. It was obvious that the handle needed oiling; it was a knack, that was all. As for the door being shut, she had closed it herself when she came in to stop the draught. Terry was dead, she had seen his body, he was not here.

She had to rely on her failing key-ring torch to get across the landing to her bedroom. This room overlooked back gardens in St Peter's Square and below, in the garden adjoining Terry's at the end of a winding slate path, she could make out a summerhouse. This was familiar, although she had not seen it from this angle before and not at night. She was looking into Mrs Ramsay's garden.

She had forgotten how close to Terry Mrs Ramsay lived. When she came to her house she approached from King Street and, intent on work, could forget his proximity. She had been round the corner from Terry many times in the last two years; never once had she thought about him. Her favourite client and her father occupied different worlds.

There was a shriek: hollow and agonized. Stella clutched at the window sash, her heart pumping. A bark answered, rougher and less distinct than a dog's, and a fox bounded along the path and leapt on to Mrs Ramsay's garden table, snuffling to and fro, its eyes flashing, before it melted into the undergrowth by the wall. Stella tried to regain equilibrium; never had it seemed so easy to have a heart attack.

The old lady fretted that children played hide and seek in her garden, concealing themselves under the table, in the bushes or the summerhouse. She accused Stella of not believing her but seemed mollified when Stella offered to scrub down the table, remove the bird shit and treat the wood. Stella had not invoiced her.

Mrs Ramsay had been wrong: Stella had believed her. The daughter of a detective, she was aware that the improbable was probable and had scanned the garden for signs of intruders – scuff marks, sweet wrappers, footprints in the soil – but found nothing. She wished now she could reassure Mrs Ramsay that it was a fox.

She found a silver pen on the window sill. Stella could not decipher the inscription in the poor light but could explain why it was there: Terry would have been scribbling notes at the desk and got up to check what had activated the security lamp. The patio not being visible from here, he would have gone downstairs to investigate and, fearless, crept along the passage to the kitchen and opened the back door.

She trained the torch on the door as if Terry might be about to return from the kitchen – panting and irritable – to switch off the lamp and go to bed, leaving the chair by the window as it was now, with his pen on the sill.

The torchlight flickered, grew brighter, then dimmed and died.

Stella felt about for the desk lamp, her breath uneven. It was angled downwards but after the comparative dark, the light dazzled her. A stapler, a plastic clock, a Nescafé jar jammed with pens and pencils and a pile of magazines shrank to prosaic normality.

On the shelves where Stella's few books had been were books on forensics, biographies of police officers, true crime paperbacks: the Moors Murders, the Kray twins, Harold Shipman and a copy of the Police and Criminal Evidence Act. A computer with a flat screen monitor sat on top of a blotter in a mock-leather holder. Terry would have used a computer at work, but Stella was surprised that he owned one, thinking him uncomfortable with new technology. The magazines were editions of *The Job,* the Metropolitan Police in-house publication. She sat down at the desk, which tilted as she leant upon it. By her elbow was a blank sheet of headed notepaper created on a computer unlike Clean Slate's embossed letterhead on vellum. Colin Peterson offered 'Quality rendering and screeding'. Scribbled at the bottom was: '17/6 – 21/7, spare room'. Stella fizzed with betrayal: Terry had not mentioned he was having her bedroom decorated. She folded the paper and wedged it under the leg of the desk to stop it wobbling.

The room did need a make-over: it was still the pink that Terry had chosen for the daughter he had wanted but not got. Red carpet tiles were shiny with ingrained dirt and scored with indentations from the chair wheels. She finger-tested the desk and found no dust. Methodically she repositioned the objects as if making last-minute adjustments for a party. It did not lessen the impression that Terry was in the house or that she should not be there handling his possessions.

On one wall, a laminated London street map replaced her poster of John Travolta in *Grease*. Stella knocked over the pen jar trying to see if there was anything written on the red and black wire-bound calendar above his desk. January was blank. She flicked through, searching for a clue as to why he was in Seaford. Nothing. January was blank. Terry had no life.

For the next hour she was busy: pulling out drawers, emptying files and collecting bank and pension statements, utility bills, the documents needed for probate. The shredder ground on as she fed it with out-of-date MOT certificates, insurance schedules for cars Terry had sold or part-exchanged, receipts, payslips for the last forty years. She stuffed instruction leaflets for cassette recorders, kettles, even a bread-maker, into a rubbish sack along with the police magazines. Despite her hurry, she was methodical about recycling and confidentiality. Soon the shredder bin overflowed, stalling the motor. She wasted time picking concertinaed strips from the teeth with the penknife blade on her key ring but it would not start.

In the last desk drawer, in a manila envelope, was a photocopy of Terry's will, confirming Stella as sole beneficiary of his estate. This discovery should not have been a shock – her father had no other children and she was his next of kin – yet it was.

In the silence of the shredder she heard her mobile phone beeping and pulled it out of her pocket. A voicemail: the person who had Terry's phone. She connected to the message service with clumsy fingers, tapping her feet while the automatic voice listed options, unable to circumvent the preamble. At last there was the beep signalling the message, followed by a jumble of white sound. She caught Paul's voice: 'I am outside.'

Stella rushed out on to the landing and, opening Terry's bedroom door, she ran to the window and lifted a slat in the blinds. The wind had died and the road was quiet; there was no one there. The message had been left half an hour before. Paul had given up and gone home.

In Terry's office she sat down, stretched out her legs and stared at the ceiling while her heartbeat returned to normal.

The ceiling wanted decorating, the plaster was cracked, the white paint had gone a nicotine yellow – although Terry had given up smoking when Stella was five – and on the loft hatch it was flaking off. She had forgotten the attic. Above her a square of yellow bled around the edges of the ill-fitting flap.

The attic light was on.

He took away her beaker of water. She would not drink it because of drowned birds in the tank even when he told her he had run it from the kitchen tap. She whispered that there was a murderer in the attic. He assured her it was his job to capture all bad people and there were none here. It was their game. 'My daddy catches bad people.' This time she would not play and was quiet. She did not believe him. He could not catch all bad people. In that instant he felt his world collapse.

Stella flicked off the light and stamped out on to the landing. Closing and opening the door loudly she inched back to the study out of the sightline of the trap door from which lines of light cast a glow on the paraphernalia spread over the carpet.

Whoever was up there was calling her bluff in return. Stella, fighting the urge to run, pulled on the attic doorknob releasing a ball-catch. Chill air drifted through the aperture, a scattering of grit smattered her face and she was smothered by soft fabric. Stifling a shout she crashed against the desk, knocking the lamp. The bulb smashed. She snatched at the material, her eyes smarting, and pulled it away: she choked on dust and coughed violently.

Stella made out a green fleece strung with cobwebs on the carpet tiles, spot-lit by the shaft of light. She picked it up and shook it. It had a logo for an alarm company embroidered on the breast, the 'A' of 'Abacus' forming the pitched roof of a house, the 'S' eliding with 'Security'.

Through the hatch she could see roof beams, lagged with glass fibre felt and, at the apex, a light bulb hanging from a cord.

Against her better judgement she hauled down the ladder and, grabbing the hole punch, reached up and smashed the hole punch against the bedroom ceiling, intending to flush out whoever was there. Silence.

The next time she risked going all the way up, her body tensed for an attack; she ventured on to boarding which sprang but held her weight. Except for a few boxes the loft was empty, and there was nowhere to hide in the chimney recesses or under the eaves. Then she saw the source of the draught: the skylight was tilted open. She levered it down with a bang and shut out the low-level scrawl of the A40; only her breathing was audible. She pulled herself together: Terry had forgotten to close the window and turn off the light.

A dented Revelation suitcase lay on its side out of the path of the retracting ladder. Stella recognized it: she had bounced on its lid to help lock it for their last ever summer holiday. While her mum assembled clothes, a first-aid kit, washing things, Stella had furtively explored the pockets with elastic tops, played with the straps and stroked the silky lining within which she discovered grains of sand and broken shells; vestiges of other holidays. Terry strode ahead to the bus stop, holding the case lightly as if it were empty, while her mother let the gap widen, apparently to keep pace with Stella – except when Stella had tried to catch up with Terry, her mum had tugged her arm. Stella had invested all her hopes in the pinch of sand. Terry had promised that they would make a castle with a moat but she did not remember that they had. Home again, she had crawled inside the case and shut the lid but no one had come to find her.

Behind the suitcase was a carton which had held twenty boxes of Kellogg's Coco Pops. Stella pulled open the flaps.

A row of three plump-cheeked faces framed with stiff nylon hairstyles and sightless eyes stared out. Terry had kept her dolls. One doll cried when the string in her back was tugged; the cord cut into Stella's fingers and she hated the sound of crying. Another doll wet herself when water was poured into a hole in her head. As a bed-wetter herself, she hated this feature even more. Beneath the dolls was a skipping rope, a bundle of dolls' clothes, a plastic stove and a matching washing machine. Tucked in too was a uniform for playing nurses, a plastic stethoscope, a pack of cards with the Tower of London on the back and an unopened bag of marbles with a price label of ten new pence from the post office in King Street.

Terry would bring the box into the living room after she had arrived, accompanied by a small suitcase all of her own. She would give up her coat and perch on the settee, unsure what was expected of her. The toys were never there already or they would have been easier to ignore. Instead she had to feign interest as the box was ceremoniously placed at her feet. She would listlessly stir the contents, keeping her back to Terry. He would be reading a newspaper but really watching to see if she liked her toys. So, paralysed with hopelessness and dogged by the dim conviction she would fail, but not sure how or at what, Stella had determinedly dressed and undressed the dolls, rolled marbles along the carpet and put them in the washing machine or the oven and taken them out. Later she would report to her mother that Terry had read to her, asked her about school and taken her along the towpath to collect nature. Her mother never believed her.

By the adjoining wall was a shelf unit packed with file boxes. Stella read the title printed on every box: *Katherine Rokesmith 27 July 1981.*

There were twenty-three file boxes each tied with a ribbon. As Stella hauled down the first in the series from the left-hand side of the top shelf she kicked something. It was a camp stool. It meant that Terry had spent time here. She unfolded it, and squatting with a box at her feet, eased off the lid. The inside was crammed with papers. Stella felt a wave of nausea.

Terry had stolen the paperwork of a murder case.

She flipped through the contents, the dank papery smell making her sneeze. Terry had not stolen the documentation, he had copied it: photographs, newspaper cuttings, index cards laid two to a page, the details of every person who had come forward with information, however trivial. One woman had found the wrapping for a packet of Polos in the gutter by the Ram public house; another reported her husband; two teenaged girls had seen the victim walking with her boy along Hammersmith Terrace three weeks before the day of the murder. Many pages were blotted with actual as well as photocopied mug rings and smears of grease. Every page had an MIR number in the right corner and was in strict order.

Stella did not need telling that MIR stood for Major Incident Room, the basis of an indexing system and where the police conducted every murder investigation. At Hammersmith Police

Station this room was the Braybrook Suite. Terry had taken her there.

Cold penetrated her bones and her feet were numb but she lifted out a few sheets stapled together: the Interim Report by Detective Inspector Darnell. In that instant Stella understood why Terry had the boxes.

The Rokesmith case had never been solved.

While the suitcase and the toy-box on the other side of the attic were coated in grey dust, the boxes were clean. Stella saw what had made her sneeze: a canister of Mr Sheen furniture polish stood in the shadow of the shelves, a folded duster beside it. She frowned: a damp cloth would have done better. The bulb flickered and she looked up expecting Terry.

'Go and make us a cup of tea, there's a love. Leave that to me.'

She snapped into work mode, hauling down the next box in the sequence and lugging the two over to the hatchway; her boots thumped on the boards despite her efforts to take light steps. She did not want next-door to hear, nor did she want to fall through the floor.

Two flights down the front door closed.

She clasped the boxes, ice-cold sweat trickling out of her armpits, and backed behind the chimney. The hatch door was down, the ladder was out; she would be found. She patted her pockets for her phone. She had taken off her anorak and draped it over the desk chair and her phone was in the pocket.

The church clock struck four, the sound muffled. If she shouted for help she might not be heard through the thick fire wall. She crept to the skylight and eased it up. A spattering of freezing rain drenched her face. Wiping her eyes she saw that the creeping blue light of dawn gave definition to Mrs Ramsay's summerhouse. A bird twittered, answered by another, then another; the dawn chorus had begun. She could not climb out on to the sloping roof.

Below her the house was quiet and Stella dared to peer down into the study. Shredded paper had sprung out of the bin and trailed over the carpet tiles.

Stella hurled herself down the ladder and reached back for the two file boxes. There was no one on the landing, and now there was enough light to see without a torch. Terry's bedroom door was closed. Her mind was playing games with her.

She took the stairs two at a time and in the hall skidded on the catalogues on the mat, falling heavily on one knee; keeping hold of the boxes and ignoring pain shooting up her thigh, she grabbed at a coat hanging from hooks by the door and got to her feet.

She was staring at Terry. Tired, cheekbones gaunt, hair limp, his jacket crumpled; dead staring eyes that would not stay shut as he lay on the gurney. He held something under each arm and put a hand to his mouth, as if caught in the act. The fingers were cold against her lips. She pushed back her hair; he did the same. She gasped and his mouth opened. She had never seen him frightened before; then a sharp gleam of dawn sunlight penetrated the panes in the front door, highlighting dust on the mirror.

Stella wrenched open the door, slamming it behind her and blundered out to the gate.

A coach roared along the Great West Road, its sleeping occupants slumped against the glass. Only when she had clambered into the van and set the central locking did she register that she had the box files. She threw them on to the passenger seat and started the engine, flooring the accelerator and careering out of the street and down St Peter's Square.

If Stella had checked the rear-view mirror when she turned out of Terry's road she would have seen a figure under the cherry trees walking in the direction of the river where, thirty years before, Katherine Rokesmith had been found murdered. An hour later, when she was out of the shower, dressed and leaving for the office, Stella discovered she had left Terry's keys in his house.

Nine

September 1985

Justin moved as swiftly as he dared in the deathly quiet library, slipped into the furthest aisle between the bookshelves and raced to the end where there was the door to the basement. Simon followed him into the library seconds later and, flanked by oak cabinets and creaky carousels of catalogue cards, scanned the wood-panelled room.

Simon was not as careful as his prey and allowed the door to slam behind him. The librarian, a placid woman with blurred, creamy features that had earned her the sobriquet of 'the Oyster' from the boys, paused from wiping a book with votive diligence to frown from her podium, signalling *silence* with her linen pad.

Justin tripped over a stool on casters, which spun along the aisle. He grimaced, sure he had given away his position, but Simon had wrongly anticipated him and was checking the Reading Corner by the inglenook fireplace which, with a semi-circle of high-backed leather winged armchairs, was an obvious hiding place.

When Margaret Lockett died in 1939, aged eighty-one, she left Marchant Manor to her trust to found and administrate a boarding school for the children of families connected with her father's passion: the railway. Sir Stephen Lockett had died fifty years before his daughter, an early supplier of toilet systems; he had increased his fortune through shrewd investment in Britain's developing rail network and his obsession with the likes of sanitary engineers J. G. Jennings and Thomas Twyford extended to structural pioneers such as Gustave Eiffel, Isambard Kingdom Brunel and Thomas Bouch. This apparently innocuous interest was to prove fatal.

On the night of 28 December 1879, Sir Stephen boarded a train to cross the Firth of Forth by the new Tay Bridge: a lattice-grid construction, then the longest bridge in the world. Queen Victoria had made the inaugural journey six months before. He did not let the storm already buffeting his carriage dampen his spirits and treated with boyish excitement the flickering gas lamps and loose window catch that let rain spatter on to his pocket book and soak his coat. Even when the train lurched upwards, pressing him into his seat, he did not panic. Only when he heard a crack that his understanding of sewer construction told him was the sound of inflexible cast-iron fracturing did Sir Stephen appreciate the gravity of his situation. Tall pilings crumbled, girders buckled and in moments the bridge collapsed like one of Stephen Lockett's wooden models, although this time he could not revise calculations and start again. The train plunged into the river A rush of water engulfing him, he thought of a toilet flushing but the thought had no time to develop. Over seventy passengers drowned; Lockett's body was one of those never recovered, nourishing school lore that his waterlogged ghost roamed the night-time corridors of Marchant Manor. On stormy days he shook casements and caused power cuts. Boys claimed to have caught a whiff of his cigar in the library that had been his smoking room.

Six years after the Tay Bridge disaster Thomas Twyford invented the Unites, a one-piece, free-standing toilet set on a pedestal base and Margaret Lockett doubled the turnover of her father's business living as a recluse amongst his railway relics with only his marble bust for company.

Sir Stephen Lockett's book collection, typical of a rich man without literary interest, was housed in shelves lining the walls protected by grilles and glass doors. Classics of the day: *The Dictionary of National Biography*, the 1870 edition of the *Encyclopaedia Britannica*, and the complete works of Scott, Dickens, Collins and Thackeray were bound in matching calfskin and embossed with Lockett's off-the-peg crest. Boys could only borrow items with permission of the Oyster and read them in situ wearing a pair of silk white gloves. The only boy in Marchant Manor School's present intake prepared to suffer this ignominy was now cowering in the Geography section.

When Justin poured over first-edition biographies on contemporary engineers and deciphered cumbersome treatises on new building materials or the effects of aerodynamic forces, he could convince himself that he was the son Sir Stephen had longed for. The musty tomes containing pictures and technical descriptions of masonry, key stones, deck spans, flying buttresses and stanchions impervious to collisions or waves were spellbinding. The eight-year-old guided his finger along dense print, traced diagrams of spans and suspensions, marvelling at sepia images, bold etchings and sentimental paintings of railway scenes, tunnels, bridges and viaducts, towers and lighthouses, and concocted stories to tell his mummy.

Most boys preferred the light airy refectory in the new wing. Justin would sit alone at one of the slate-grey Formica-topped tables, out of sight of the door, to write his letters, watched over by Sir Stephen Lockett.

He kept still in the Geography aisle, knowing he could no longer seek refuge here now that his tormentor had found it.

Daylight was fading. Only the insidious groan of the wind off the sea broke the enforced silence. Any minute Simon would discover him. The copy of *The Boyhood of Raleigh* by John Everett Millais glinted in its gesso-gilt frame. A barefoot man seen from behind sat on a log dressed in crimson pantaloons pointing to the sea across a stone wall. The gypsy – Justin supposed this because of the earring – had the rapt attention of two boys. Justin believed the boy hugging his stockinged legs was Simon and the other sprawling on his tummy was himself; good friends, the boys listened to stories of the old man's adventures on the high seas. The picture gave him hope that Simon would one day like him.

Even before the house became a school it had rivalled the Brighton Pavilion's thirty lavatories with twenty-five: a high number of flush lavatories for a dwelling of its size. Sir Stephen Lockett had installed three in the library alone.

Simon was waiting for him outside one of these. Justin shrank back against a door marked 'Private' set at the end of the bookcases. When the librarian fetched him books from the Lockett catalogue stored in the cellars he had noted that she did not need a key. He leaned on the door; it opened.

Luckily someone was in the toilet; of course Simon supposed it was him and he would wait patiently outside, like a spider before sucking the life out of the fly. He was twirling a pencil, his stub finger as nimble as the rest, the pencil danced along his knuckles. Fact: Simon knew nothing about spiders.

Justin heard whoever was inside the toilet pull the chain and under cover of the lavatory's thunderous flush, he stepped through the door by the bookcase and closed it behind him.

A bulb in a bracket cast tremulous light on uneven stone steps. Gingerly Justin descended and at the bottom found a switch and extinguished the bulb on the stairs in favour of a brighter light in the room. He listened for footsteps above but heard only the hissing of the cistern filling and wastewater sluicing along the soil pipe.

The cellar room used to be a scullery; it was now the librarian's lair, full of broken-spined books and dusty stationery. Cobwebs furred with dust hung from the joists like miniature hammocks and in front of a mean grate were a chair and table. Sheets of paper backed with cellophane, scissors, a scalpel and a pot of rubber solution glue were arranged on the Formica surface.

Justin would enjoy helping the librarian cover and mend books, he imagined. Across the table was a metal yardstick. He looked at the book being repaired: *The Lion, the Witch and the Wardrobe* by C. S. Lewis. Most people liked Lucy best. Justin preferred Edmund and given the chance would betray Simon to the White Witch for a lump of Turkish Delight.

He was being observed by a man with a flowing mane of hair and a thick beard. Stephen Lockett's marble bust had been banished to the cellars to make room for a colour photocopier. Justin stroked his cheek, disappointed to find it chill and unyielding.

Justin had gambled on there being another exit and behind a wooden screen of Chinese silk much nibbled by moths he found an archway to a tiled passage. Piling three hefty volumes on the table he climbed up, teetering, to unscrew the ceiling bulb and everything went dark. He managed to jump off the table and land on the floor without hurting himself. Simon had triggered events early.

After some minutes he began to fear he had overestimated him: Simon had not found the cellar door and had left the library, presuming Justin had given him the slip. Justin was disappointed because he was ready for Simon.

A slant of light lit the steps. Justin ducked behind the screen. The elongated shadow of an old man projected on to the bricks, shoulders bowed, head bent, his feet faltering at each step. It was the ghost of Sir Stephen. Justin was not frightened; he longed to meet him.

The figure turned and became Simon.

Justin drew out the blind cord and pulled it taut in readiness, letting it slacken and then tightening it. It was the ideal weapon and he handled it expertly.

Ten

Wednesday, 12 January 2011

Stella emerged out of Shepherd's Bush Tube station rush hour into sunshine. Dew sparkled on the green. Red buses, blue cars, white vans and yellow salt bins cheered the soulless roundabout and the wipe-clean walls of the new nation-size shopping centre. At this time of the morning – just before seven – the rhythm of the neighbourhood was apparent. In the dry cleaner's the owner, a woman in her fifties, dressed as if going somewhere special in pressed trouser suits with razor-sharp lapels, waved to Stella, a ticket between her teeth as she heaved clothes on hangers along racks. Stella stepped aside for a gangly young man arranging goods on the pavement outside the Pound and Penny shop. Already towers of storage boxes, swing bins and washing baskets dwarfed stacking stools and brushes stuffed handle-first into a tub. A list of wares was stuck crookedly on to the window, a crease in the laminate obliterating letters: 'Garde ware ,gift, partywar, pet upplies snaks statnery swets, toilries', which every morning irritated Stella.

The Polish mini-mart below Clean Slate's office had been open an hour already; two men were erecting the sloping display using crates draped with fake grass, while another unloaded fruit and vegetables from a ten-year-old van. Stella noted the number plate. As a rule she did not trust the owner of a commercial vehicle over five years old. She threaded past the men into the shop and from the back of the chiller cabinet extracted a litre of semi-skimmed milk with the most recent sell-by date. Dariusz Adomek was on the till behind a high counter further shielded from muggers by chewing gum display stands and a Lotto machine. Stella handed up a five-pound note.

'How's business. Good?' He ran the sensor over the barcode and passed back the milk.

'Good, yes. You?'

'Mustn't grumble.' In a Polish accent the cliché gained new life.

Dariusz Adomek had taken on a lease with the same landlord, and this slender commonality was grounds enough for mutual co-operation. He swiped change out of the drawer and poured the coins into Stella's palm.

They had the same interchange every morning, developing on it only when Stella was looking for cleaners or Adomek had heard of a new client. No one he recommended – a relative or contact recently arrived from Poland – had let Stella down, the staff turning up for work and the clients paying invoices on time. In return Clean Slate cleaned the mini-market at a discount and Stella helped Adomek with Inland Revenue forms and had Jackie compose and type letters.

Clean Slate occupied two clumsily converted rooms over the mini-mart and a mobile phone shop. Facing south across the green, the late Victorian building was prone to damp, with cracks in ceilings and mould behind filing cabinets. It was hard to heat in the winter, keep cool in the summer and keep clean all the year round.

Stella tucked the milk carton under an arm to fit the mortice in the ground-floor door before seeing that the door was on the latch. It was well before nine. The insurance brokerage on the top floor – which employed a rival cleaning company – had ignored her latest memo.

She headed up the dingy stairs, trying, as she did every day, to ignore the brown linoleum that sent a discouraging message to prospective clients. The landlord refused to decorate the common parts. The tawdry sixties-meets-seventies décor accounted for the low rent for premises in what had become a prime location. Clean Slate had the turnover to afford plush offices with straight walls and air conditioning but an office move would interrupt the hectic routine. Each year, ignoring her accountant's advice, Stella, nervous of over-stretching her business, put it off. Each day, as she avoided the dirt-engrained banister, she worked her way through the same train of thought and by the time she was at her desk other issues had taken priority, which today was how she could retrieve his keys from her dead father's house without breaking a window, smashing a lock or Jackie finding out.

A man was outside peering around the sign on her office door. 'What are you doing?'

He came towards her, a looming bulk in the cramped passage. Stella grasped the milk, fleetingly aware that dashing a Tetra Pak in his face would not save her.

She had forgotten Paul.

'Come on, Stella. We can work this out and make a go of it.' He backed off when Stella, head down, whipped both her hands up to avoid his touch. 'I've been calling and texting you,' he added plaintively.

'How did you get in here?'

'The door was unlocked. You want to watch that, anyone could wander in.'

Anyone had.

'You're seeing someone.' Paul was blocking the doorway. 'Who is it? That fuckwit Pole you were talking to?'

'No, it isn't.' Stella regretted taking the bait and giving him a toehold. 'It's none of your business who I see. Are you spying on me? You left that message last night when I was at Terry's.'

'It *is* my business if you're messing me about.' He rubbed under his chin with the back of his hand, a gesture that had once attracted Stella. 'I have the right to come to your flat. Terry who? Was that the bloke with the flash Beemer? Don't lie.'

'So you weren't outside when … Oh never mind. Look, I said it's over, end of.' Stella tried to step around Paul but he remained in the way.

'This place is all you care about.' He thumped the wire-reinforced glass.

'My father is dead.' Stella unwittingly jettisoned the standard splitting-up script for a different kind of drama.

'What do you mean? Your dad's died?' Paul put out a hand and tentatively brushed her sleeve and when she did not react, read it as a good sign and slid his fingers down to her hand.

'Yes he has. Not that you asked,' Stella retorted, aware of the flagrant illogicality. She shoved past Paul and scratched her key in the lock. 'I don't want a scene, please, Paul?' She tripped the alarm and had ten seconds to deactivate it. Once inside, her tone softened: 'This is hard enough without you making it worse.'

'I'll call later, yeah?' Paul drifted along the landing, obviously cowed by the immensity of Stella's loss. 'You'll get through this. I'm there for you. My dad died too. I am beside you on this.' He retreated downstairs.

Stella punched in the alarm code, relieved that Jackie had not been there because she would feel sorry for him. Jackie believed that what Stella needed was the love of a good man; Paul, with his pleasant if unremarkable looks and kind nature drenched in Boss aftershave, was her latest vision of Stella's Mr Right.

Forcing Paul from her mind, Stella thought how a locksmith would be expensive and attract attention but the probate papers were in her old bedroom; she should tackle them soon.

She had an hour and a half before Jackie would prop the door back and flip the 'Open' sign around, and the administrative assistant, an eager woman of twenty-two, would set to making coffee for the three of them. This was Stella's favourite part of the day; the world was clean and tidy and there was all to play for. But this morning, despite the sunshine, she was in an unfamiliar landscape stalked by the demons of Terry and Paul.

If a potential customer faltered on the lino-covered staircase, their mood would lift on entering the bright, immaculate office, with shelves of storage boxes and catalogues. A bank of filing cabinets with primary colour-coded drawers would reassure them that this was a place where promises were kept, contracts adhered to and even the most complex of tasks expedited. The laminated pages of the Staff Handbook – beside the water cooler for continual reference – counselled: *Avoid clutter: nothing without legs, apart from waste bins and filing cabinets, must touch the floor. Keep equipment on shelves and cupboards and box in cables and wiring.*

Computers in black casings were in standby mode, the Clean Slate logo floating about the screens like a fish in a tank, the 'L's in each word expressed by two sweeping brushes. Against the wall was a trestle table on which was a drinks fridge with a see-through door and a tray of white cups, saucers and plates. Three plastic storage jars from the Pound and Penny shop displayed tea bags, instant coffee and sugar. A silver jug kettle reflected the room in concave.

There was a stain on the carpet. Stella bent down and it disappeared: it was the shadow of a hole-punch by the photocopier.

While she was at ground level, she could not resist checking the floor: no bits, no fluff. She spied two paper clips and an elastic band beneath the radiator, and with her nose inches from the pile she could see no grooves made by the vacuum brush. She sniffed and was mollified by an uplifting aroma of lemon. *Six out of ten.* New cleaners did the 'home shift' before she let them loose on clients. This one had answered a perpetual advert on the website, had not come recommended by Adomek and offered only lukewarm references.

She was about to turn on the photocopier – it took ten minutes to warm up – but this was the assistant's task and Jackie was insistent she would forget her routine if Stella kept doing her job. Stella switched it on.

Two wood-veneer-topped desks, striped with bars of winter sunlight through Venetian blinds, were pushed together by the window. Creating symmetry were three-decker filing trays on each desk, marked 'in', 'out' and 'pending'. Stella's door was propped open with a foot-high cement lion Jackie had presented to Stella on her forty-fourth birthday last August. If she had minded that Stella had not taken it home, she had not said. Perhaps she understood that Stella's home was the office. She only closed her door for client meetings, which were rare; decisions were made by telephone or at what Jackie persisted in calling the 'scene of grime'.

Stella's room was a third of the main office, partitioned by a clumsy stud wall that abutted the window frame and vibrated whenever a Tube train rumbled below, causing framed certificates and awards for best cleaning company to slide askew on their strings. Stella straightened them before placing her rucksack on the visitor's chair and pulling her laptop and Filofax from it.

She had painted the walls white herself. The only colour was Clean Slate's new green and light blue logo emblazoned on blocks of sticky notes, box files, company literature and the printers' complimentary mouse mat. A spray of Clean Slate branded roller-ball pens were arranged in a papier maché pen pot, the blue and red William Morris design a gift from a client who did occasionally visit the office. Stella judged the pattern fussy, should the contract end, the pen pot would go.

She consulted her calendar – a replica of the one in Terry's study – and was relieved that she had only one appointment: a cinema in Richmond. She switched on her computer and angled the slats in the blinds to allow in a soft light.

The calendar reminded Stella about the door keys. She toyed with the notion of abandoning the house; so what if everything was stolen? If only when people died everything to do with them vanished too. If only when relationships ended the other person just went away.

A bus with Marble Arch on its destination panel inched past the window, giving the room a temporary rosy glow.

Whatever he said, Paul must have trailed her last night and, not realising that the house belonged to Terry, assumed as he always did that she was having an affair. She wished she had thought of this while he was there; it would have calmed him down. Briskly she returned to the main office where the answer machine signalled messages with subdued pips. About to press 'play', she decided to get a coffee first. There was no kitchen so she ran up to the toilets on the next floor to fill the kettle.

She could deal with Paul.

The toilets were shared with the insurance broker and with both genders which meant that the seat was generally up. The landlord cleaned the room to keep overheads down and this meant that paper dispensers were rarely filled and the roller towel, grey with overuse, spooled on to the vinyl flooring of pallid lemon-coloured flowers. There were gaps under the doors so Stella only used the toilet if she was alone. She left the kettle on the sink and went into the nearest cubicle and, loath to touch it, tipped the seat with one finger. It fell on to the porcelain with a crash. This action was unnecessary for she never sat on a public lavatory, but hovered inches above.

She sipped her coffee as the answer machine clicked into gear. Transcribing calls was the assistant's job, but Stella prepared to scribble details in the daybook in writing that no one could read.

'I would like to speak with Miss Stella Darnell.' Stella knew the type; a client who would find fault before the cleaning had begun. The woman paused after each sentence as if she intended Stella to respond. 'This is Gina Cross, Isabel Ramsay's daughter. You were her cleaner.' Stella jabbed at the page with her pen. Ye-es, so? She drew a box around the name, and made it three-dimensional.

'I want you to clear out my mother's house once we have removed valuables. My number is…' Stella was not good with numerals and had to replay the voicemail to note them in the right order.

The next three callers were a supplier and Wendy, the first cleaner to join Clean Slate, calling in sick for the first time, compounding the staffing issue. The final message was a client wanting an extra session. She left the machine off; she would answer any calls: people never tried again if they got a voice message. Clean Slate was open for business.

She copied Gina Cross's details on a sticky note and, armed with her coffee, went to her room. Mrs Ramsay always gave the impression that Gina, Lucian and Eleanor lived with her.

Unlike many of Stella's clients, Mrs Ramsay never boasted about her children's careers. She tssk-tssked while she stirred clutter on her kitchen table in search of her paper knife with which she opened her junk mail as if it were eagerly awaited correspondence. If she couldn't find the knife, she complained that one of her kids had it. Perusing each catalogue or leaflet, concocting her first drink at a few minutes past eleven each morning, splashing gin into her glass, tossing in ice cubes and dribbling in tonic, Mrs Ramsay would rail that it was her three monsters who wrecked the house, causing her to mislay things and then accusing her of absent-mindedness or senility. Her children and their friends played hide and seek all over the house day and night, creeping up and down the stairs. Stirring the liquid with the handle of a spoon, Mrs Ramsay would make Stella promise not to tell Gina, of whose disapproval she appeared afraid. Hearing Gina Cross demand that she call her 'ASAP', Stella understood why.

After several sessions of cleaning for Mrs Ramsay, Stella noticed she repeated the same stories, and some incidents involved Stella, as when the freezer thawed because 'Eleanor' had unplugged it. Another version had Gina as the culprit and Mrs Ramsay would, she informed Stella, make her daughter clean up her own mess and pay for the damage from her pocket money. Children must be taught a lesson or they got away with murder.

One day Stella was collared in the street by a distressed woman who accused Mrs Ramsay of taking her cat and calling it Crawford. Stella went inside and removed the cat, which was moulting, from the top of the boiler in the kitchen. She said nothing when she handed over the pliant orange and white animal. She remained non-committal, while the woman, now addressing her pet, divulged that the Ramsay children had not visited their mother since the year 2000.

Later that day Mrs Ramsay confided to Stella that she had found Crawford the cat dead in Elly's room. He was curled up on her bed and she had assumed him asleep, but when she touched him he was 'as cold and hard as a hat. Cats and dogs are harbingers of evil.' She had decided they should stop for a coffee to get over the unpleasantness.

It did not surprise Stella that with their mother dead, her offspring were fronting up to claim their inheritance. Such behaviour, about which she made no judgements, was not unusual.

She punched in the telephone number.

'Gina-Ware, for fantastic plastic, yes?'

Stella sat up. She had called one of her suppliers. The catalogue was in front of her on the desk because yesterday she had been weighing up their sale offer on 36-litre mop buckets with heavy-duty wringers.

'I'm sorry, wrong number.'

She rang the number on the sticky note and the same voice answered.

Gina-Ware. Mrs Ramsay had said her son-in-law, whom she dubbed Jon-the-footrest, owned a business specializing in durable plastic products, including footrests. Gina-ware was everywhere: Jackie had the deluxe footrest for her back.

'Hello, Stella Darnell speaking. Clean Slate. You called us about a house clearance?'

'I'm driving. I answered because our call centre has gone down. Meet me at the house to agree a price so you can get going.'

Stella was about to offer condolences and explain that she did not give instant estimates and would quote only after scoping the job when the line went dead.

For the next hour she worked through emails, signed her way through letters Jackie had left and calculated two outstanding quotes. With half an hour before the others would arrive, she got her rucksack from the chair and dragged out the Rokesmith box files she had fled with the night before. She set them on the desk, keeping the label away from the door, and went to fetch the shredder.

Stella remembered the murder of Katherine Rokesmith. There had been a storm of publicity, but now only a few aged under forty would know details without prompting. Many other shocking events had occurred since to occupy the public's imagination.

Terry Darnell had the afternoon off so invited his fourteen-year-old daughter to central London to see the rehearsal of the wedding of Charles and Diana. Colleagues detailed on special duty would assure them a prime position and afterwards he would take her to a restaurant – pizza or a hamburger, whatever she liked. Stella was nonchalant, saying she didn't believe in royalty. She had never been out for a meal with Terry and the idea made her nervous about waiters waiting and lots of cutlery. Up until then they'd had fish and chips, or Terry had microwaved shepherd's pie with tinned peas. Even this was an ordeal for the teenager who did not like chewing and swallowing in front of others. In preparation, Stella had ironed new jeans, chosen a skimpy top and planned to wear lipstick, which would 'show him'.

Early that morning he had rung the flat to outline the tight schedule: she must be in the foyer of Hammersmith Police Station at eight in the morning. They would travel up to town with officers going on duty, which meant, he promised, that she got a ride in a panda. Her mother warned that if she was late, Terry would go without her. She would describe any arrangement with Terry in terms of the threat of what would happen if Stella fell short. An hour before she was to leave, Stella was touching up her make-up when her mother barged into her bedroom:

'He's not coming. He's got a murder. You look like a tart.'

Katherine Rokesmith 27th July 1981.

Stella tipped papers out of the first box on to her desk. The photocopies were crinkled as if they had got wet; others were creased; all had been well thumbed. She flicked through and saw that Terry had underlined text and scrawled illegible notes in the margins.

Terry had told Stella that in the 1980s, every item in an inquiry was listed in an Action File containing a grid of numbers ticked off as they were assigned to a document. Each 'event': a witness statement, a sighting, any minor observation, got an MIR reference. In 1981 the initial recording of data was done by hand; Stella had adapted part of the process for her business.

She intended to destroy the files before Jackie and the assistant arrived so did not have long. Shredding was another of the admin assistant's duties and Stella did not want to explain what she was doing; she positioned the shredder between the desk and her chair and slid the switch to 'on'. The motor made a terrible churning sound, but closing the door was out of the question. She straightened the first pages and glanced at the top sheet.

It was a long shot of a scene bathed in summer sunshine. A trellis ran along a retaining wall; to the right of the image was a flight of steps. A mooring chain was slung along the brickwork from iron hoops. Stella recognized the location: the Bell Steps led from Hammersmith Terrace to the River Thames. One day in the summer holidays when she was about ten, she had ridden her bike there. She had struggled along the shoreline all the way to an island called the Chiswick Eyot. The wheels stuck in the soft mud and, dismounting, she'd had to drag the bike and had bent the mudguard so that it caught on the back tyre, slowing her down. She had barely made it to the road before the tide came in.

At Chiswick Mall a man shouted that 'another five minutes and she would have drowned'. He ran towards her and she threw herself on to her bike, pedalling furiously away, slowed by the mudguard. She dared not confess to Terry that she had gone to the island without checking the tide. She hid the bike behind the dustbins where his recycling bins now offered better cover. He must have found it for on another visit Stella discovered it in the back garden under a tarpaulin, cleaned and with the mudguard straightened. Terry said nothing: a more effective punishment than a telling off.

Years after the murder, Stella had speculated that the man who had chased her was Kate Rokesmith's killer.

The sunshine made mirrors of pools stranded in the mud. Were it not for the police tape, the Scene of Crime team – spacemen in their forensic garb – standing, crouching and kneeling on the shore, the body would have been easy to miss; from this angle it blended with the ground.

He plucked Stella out of the mud. Her wellingtons sank deeper into the sludge so it looked as if she had combusted, leaving her boots behind. He laughed at this and hoisted her on to his shoulders, tipping her forward to see them. He meant to make her laugh but she started crying.

'Don't they look silly, Stell!' he coaxed. 'What an adventure, we'll have hot chocolate when we get in.'

She gripped his neck between her legs and snatched at his hair. This hurt, but he did not say. He balanced her precariously and bent down for her boots. They made a sucking sound when he pulled them out. She cried all the way back.

There were eight pictures, according to Terry's numbering. She spread them on the desk, oblivious of the deafening shredder.

The original images had been black and white and the copies were high contrast making the images stark. At one remove from reality they straddled a line between fact and art. The rest of the photographs were close-ups of a woman in her twenties wearing a patterned shirt and the calf-length, side-zip slacks popular in the eighties; her feet were bare. Her hair, wet from the incoming tide, trailed in rat's tails over her face. Heightened contrast had bleached her features to a mask. One eye was slightly open and her parted lips showed perfect teeth. Puffiness in her face did not disguise that when she was alive Katherine Rokesmith had been beautiful. The final picture, a close-up of the victim's throat, showed a line around it like a necklace; a chain or a thong. Stella knew enough about forensics to recognize the mark left by a ligature.

It was not public knowledge that Katherine Rokesmith had been strangled: the police had kept the means of her death back from the media. Until now Stella, like everyone else, had not known the cause of death.

Terry had known all along.

Thirty years had passed since Katherine Rokesmith, known to her friends, family and the tabloids as 'Kate', was found floating in

95

shallow water of the Thames one Monday afternoon in July 1981. Until now Stella had never considered Kate a real person whose life was brutally terminated. During the investigation, she, like the public, had seen the photograph that would come to define Kate Rokesmith: a woman in a black and white chequered wool coat, standing on a kerbstone at the Notting Hill Carnival, a baby boy in her arms, both looking in the same direction. They were laughing, their faces two-thirds turned towards the camera revealed them as mother and son. The picture told the story.

The media would use this iconic image over the ensuing decades when anniversaries of the murder rolled around, or more rarely if a new lead emerged. Terry had not taken his daughter to Buckingham Palace that Monday and over the following months, if she saw him it was on the television behind a clutch of microphones appealing for witnesses or giving an update on the case.

'The public can be assured that myself and my team will leave no stone unturned in our search for whoever murdered Katherine. We will bring them to justice.'

For a few weeks her father's fame had been compensation: impressing her school friends was more satisfying than stilted visits to Wimpy bars and the cinema with him. As detective inspector, Terry had been in charge of the day-to-day running of the case. Kids at school brought in cuttings from newspapers for Stella to get him to sign and instead of doing her homework she sat late into the night faking his signature and composing elaborate answers to questions about the case that she gleaned from the press. The only time she did see Terry, he refused to talk about the murder.

One day Stella overstretched herself and told girls in the year above her that the police had a suspect: a serial killer who had killed loads of times. He was a local man, divorced with children at the school. One of the girls refused to leave the house and told her parents who told the Head who told Stella's mother who grounded Stella. After this, interest in her detective father waned and life returned to normal.

When she saw him on television, her mother would say that Detective Inspector Darnell was more interested in Kate Rokesmith than in his own daughter. Stella grew to hate the dead woman: her dad had never left any stones unturned for her.

After some weeks, her curfew over, daubed with red lipstick Stella embarked on what became a regular pilgrimage. She journeyed on the Tube from Barons Court one stop to the Wimpy on Hammersmith Broadway and sat with a view of the door, making a milkshake last an hour, watching passers-by. Later she patrolled Shepherd's Bush Road past the police station. She played games with herself: she was not hoping to see Terry, she was just out and about. Once she saw him run out of the main entrance and get into a plain police car that sped off, the siren diminishing. He had not seen her. After that Stella gave up her beat.

That September she lost her virginity at a party in a Kennington tower block, shoplifted perfume from Selfridges and spent evenings, when her mother was out at her latest evening class, smoking out of her bedroom window and listening to Spandau Ballet all night long. She was not a policeman's daughter; Terry Darnell and Kate Rokesmith were welcome to each other.

Beneath the photograph, Stella found an article from the *Daily Mirror* dated Tuesday, 28 July 1981.

The body of a 24-year-old mum was found by the Thames near Hammersmith Bridge yesterday by a man walking his dog. Police suspect that her four-year-old son was with tragic Kate Rokesmith when she was attacked in broad daylight. It is not known if the brutal murder of the brunette beauty, her future as full of promise as Lady Di, took place yards from the pub or if her body was brought there. Police hope that little Jonathan Rokesmith will identify his mother's killer. Detective Inspector Darnell refused to confirm if a weapon had been found. Kate, married to engineer Hugh Rokesmith, 35, who has built bridges in countries as far apart as China, the Middle

East and Germany, lived in nearby fashionable St Peter's Square. Mr Rokesmith told police he was at his mother's in Twickenham at the time of the murder. His son had complained of feeling unwell so his wife had decided to keep him at home. D. I. Darnell said that the 'hot weather that day had considerable impact on the success of forensic analysis to determine timings'.

Under a photograph of Terry at a table reading from a statement, grey suit bunched at the biceps, were the words: *Det. Insp. Terry Darnell assured the public that police are meticulously following up numerous lines of inquiry.*

Stella absently turned off the shredder, the abrupt quiet highlighting a developing headache, and continued to read. Another newspaper article, this time in the *Daily Mail*, described how police decided that Jonathan Rokesmith had left the river after his mother was attacked or she would have noticed him missing and run after him. Perhaps he tried to get help, but then the article speculated he might have feared he too would be hurt because he had not gone to the Ram, an obvious place to raise the alarm even for a four-year-old. No one had seen a boy and if he had stopped at the pub, the woman reporter stated, he might have saved his mother's life. Instead he had crossed the Great West Road, possibly, the reporter Lucy May speculated, going home. Whatever the truth, Jonathan Rokesmith had got no further than the statue, where he was found sitting an hour after the discovery of his mother's body. Masters also put forward a theory she claimed the police were considering: that the killer himself (no one supposed a woman would commit such a murder) had taken the boy but, worried he would attract attention, abandoned him. Terry had underlined the last sentence in shaky biro. Stella wondered if he gave this theory mileage.

After the murder, despite lengthy psychiatric examinations, Jonathan Rokesmith had not uttered a word; whatever had happened, the experience was locked inside him. Hugh Rokesmith moved abroad. Stella leant over her desk and, firing up her laptop, brought up Google. She found only one reference to Hugh Rokesmith: he had died nearly four years ago of cancer of the oesophagus and his son, like Kate Rokesmith's murderer, had vanished without trace.

Stella read that exhaustive inquiries had failed to unearth a firm sighting of anyone acting suspiciously that day. There were only two witnesses who had seen Kate in the last moments of her life: a neighbour and of course the boy.

A reconstruction a week after the murder yielded no fresh information apart from the usual bunch of cranks who, in a bid for attention, claimed responsibility or that they were material witnesses.

Stella knew the sort; alive to any attention, they were often scrupulously clean and tidy. Occasionally such types asked Clean Slate for a quote, which they deconstructed item by item, pointing out the advantages of their own methods of maintaining the 'hygienic imperative' as one man had put it.

The dog owner had been interviewed. The spaniel – one reporter irrelevantly included that his name was Homer – had alerted his owner to the body which in another few minutes would have been submerged and drifted downstream or sunk, the article stated. Three decades on, with the murder unsolved, it might as well have, Stella reckoned.

Stella recognized Terry's handwriting on papers headed General Registry Docket: 'I respectfully submit that this file is put away. 27th March 1983.' The case had been filed twenty months to the day of the murder.

The dog owner, a Charles Jenkins, aged fifty-six, had gone to the Ram to ring the police. This baffled Stella until she recalled that in 1981 the mobile phone was not in general use. Partial footprints had been discovered on the shore, their 'chaotic positioning' initially attributed to a struggle with the assailant, until it was established that Jenkins had returned with an excited retinue of drinkers who splashed up and down the shrinking beach, their detective skills boosted by alcohol, in search of a weapon before being 'removed' by a constable, who sealed the already contaminated scene. The incoming tide had washed away any hard evidence.

Kate Rokesmith had been strangled with a length of material, perhaps twine found in rubbish on the beach. The murder had been only months before DNA was discovered, but later tests on Katherine Rokesmith's clothing had revealed nothing. Stella found a submission from Terry three years after the file had been put away, suggesting an exhumation of the body to perform a DNA examination of any matter behind her fingernails, but a medical expert had stated that nothing about the state of the victim's hands suggested she had put up a struggle so the expense had been spared.

It seemed to Stella that use of a readily available weapon pointed to an impulse crime, making it unlikely that the victim knew her killer. The man may have seen Katherine Rokesmith and followed her, or maybe he had stalked her for days and plucked up the courage to chat her up. When she rejected his advances, he had attacked her. This idea was confirmed by Terry a few pages on: '... he had perhaps only intended to molest Mrs Rokesmith, considering her easy prey, but with a toddler in tow she could not escape.' The sentence implied the boy hampered her and Stella imagined this was Terry's opinion. There was no sign of sexual assault and a psychiatrist's report stated: 'Something about Mrs Rokesmith could have reminded the perpetrator of a mother figure and evoked in him a long-held rejection that sent him into a childlike rage. The boy remained unharmed because he was a bystander with no role in the culprit's inner drama.' Stella could guess Terry's reaction to this idea and agreed with him that the reason for not killing the boy was simple: Jonathan Rokesmith had run away.

Her theory that the killer had been watching Kate's house was demoted to 'unlikely' a few pages later; there had been no sightings of strangers in the vicinity in the days before the murder.

The pathologist's report said that the gravitational effects on blood would have helped determine the time frame within which death had occurred. The body had lain in baking sun for some time so had a high temperature. It had shifted and turned on the pull of the tide, all of this meaning that the pathologist could only give the time of death a two-hour window.

In the end everything hinged on the testimony of the neighbour who had seen Kate just before midday.

The office door opened. It was ten to nine. Stella hastily stuffed the papers into the box and gulped the cooling coffee, cursing that she could not put the shredder back without Jackie seeing.

'You're early,' she called out gaily, shoving the boxes into her rucksack and kicking it under her desk.

She smelled stale tobacco smoke. Neither Jackie nor the assistant smoked.

A man stood in the main office, his hand raised to the door panel as if he was about to knock upon it. Later it would occur to Stella that the gesture came after she appeared; but by then it did not matter.

'I'm looking for Stella Darnell.'

'You've found her.' It was the policeman all over again. Fleetingly Stella thought that this time her mother had died. She was polite; a shabbily dressed man could be a premier client. 'Can I help?'

'I saw your ad.'

Stella thought fast. She could hit him with the cement lion but by the time she got a grip on it he would have reached her. A pair of scissors lay in the box beside the photocopier, but he might suspect if she pretended to use them for an innocuous task; he would know the tricks. Would she lose her life because she was concerned to be polite to a killer? She could not placate him; perhaps that was Katherine Rokesmith's mistake, she tried to humour her killer instead of running and screaming as loud as she could. But then she had a 'toddler in tow'.

The man was speaking; patiently he repeated: 'The advert on your website?' He pushed his hair off his forehead. 'For the cleaner?

Your door was open.' His pleasant, assured manner was at odds with his dishevelled appearance.

This man, with bags under his eyes and lank hair, looked as exhausted as she felt and Stella doubted he could wield a pressure washer or a vacuum and was about to explain that the position had been filled, when he crouched down. Stella sidled towards the scissors, stealing a glance at the clock: six and a half minutes to nine. She had to keep him talking until Jackie arrived.

He crawled under Jackie's desk and reappeared cupping a five-pence piece and string of shredded paper as if they were live creatures. Stella had not spotted them; she did notice that his fingernails were clean and filed. He dropped the paper into the bin and placed the coin in Jackie's desk tidy.

'I have time in the day.' He was businesslike. 'I can give you references.'

Stella pushed an application form towards him, hiding her trembling hands. After last night she was easily rattled and anxious that he should not see he had scared her. He gripped the pen in his left hand, bunched into a fist, like a boy for whom writing was a new activity, and filled it in. She told him she would be in touch if they needed him, resolving, as she shut the door behind him, that 'they' never would be in touch.

She was stowing the shredder on the shelf in the main office when there was a rap on the glass. She stayed where she was, her legs too weak to move. He was back. She had latched the door when she let him out so he could only mouth at her through the glass, holding up something that glinted in the sunlight now filling the room.

Two minutes to nine; Jackie was never late. Stella risked opening the door, too alarmed to speak.

'I found these on the stairs. Weird that I didn't see them on the way up. I wondered if they were yours? I guess not, as you must have keys or how would … anyway … as there's no one else here but you …'

The man handed her Terry's keys.

Stella remained by the desk, his completed form in one hand, the keys in the other, listening to his footsteps receding on the stairs. At the thud of the street door she sank into the admin assistant's chair.

If she had dropped the keys on the stairs she would have heard them fall and Paul would have seen them; he always found things she had lost or mislaid. Had they been in her pocket all along? If Paul had seen the man enter the building his suspicions that she was having an affair would be confirmed. Had Paul somehow stolen the keys? Her forehead pulsed with the conflict of possibilities, all of which were surely impossible. She must have dropped them.

She read the man's application, grimacing at the block capitals slanting backwards and crammed together as he had run out of space.

Jack Harmon.

The name rang a bell but, while Stella was trying to think why it did, there was another knock on the door and she leapt out of the chair and scooted out of sight.

'Stella!'

It was Jackie. The snib was down so her key would not work. Shakily crossing the room, Stella released the catch and her PA flew past her and grabbed the nearest telephone. Stella had not heard it ringing. She had got up too quickly and leant against the table by the tea things, letting the dizziness subside.

'Clean Slate for a fresh start. Good morning, Jackie speaking, how can we help?' Jackie cocked her head to hold the receiver and, snapping on a ballpoint, swept a pad of sticky notes towards her over the desk.

'Sorry, who is this?' She steadied the pad. 'Gina? How are you spelling that, please?'

Stella signalled and Jackie passed her the phone: the voice was speaking when she put it to her ear: '… no point in coming. The police in their wisdom think my mother was murdered.'

Eleven

The bed was unmade. He sniffed the sheet: fresh laundered Egyptian cotton. He wished she would keep the bedroom in order. But as soon as she smiled he could not be cross any more. Wet from the shower, he towelled himself dry, covering himself as best he could for he was modest about his body. Drawing a comb through his hair he assured her that he belonged entirely to her, whatever she did or had done.

She liked that. 'I don't even belong to myself!'

When he examined her features, he saw their son in her generous mouth, full lips parted over faultless teeth. The scarf suited her elegant neck. On his way out he smoothed the sheets, tucking them in tight, hotel-style.

He was consumed by her and in this he was lucky; not many men felt this way about their loved ones. Most people lived half-lives servicing long-dead relationships, paying mortgages, mowing lawns, marking anniversaries; lives of drudgery that were merely endured. He was sure of her. She would never leave. He kept her secrets; he kept her safe.

He stopped in the doorway of the boy's room. He wandered in and flicked through the heavy pages of his own stamp collection, which was laid out on the table like an exhibit. He tipped a model Spitfire suspended from the ceiling: it revolved until the momentum died. On the bookshelf he blew dust off the line of intricately painted medieval knights and the Sherman and Panther tanks, strategically positioned between the Hardy Boys books and the encyclopaedias.

He had been about to get in the shower when there was a knock at the door. They were not expecting anyone; he pulled the curtains when he got home to discourage visitors. He refused to answer, but she had made him. He agreed that the caller would have seen the landing light – why draw attention to themselves? He donned a bathrobe, cool and slinky, that reached to his calves, which she had said made him look like a transvestite. He did not like it when she teased him. She teased more when he told her this.

A potato-faced woman out of a Grimms' fairy tale with black braids and a ghastly lipstick, in an embroidered gingham apron, had been about to give up. He pulled himself together. She was not a figment of some childhood fable. Her skin appeared golden in the setting sun. Beside her was a gruff daughter, an overweight teenager with a missing incisor. The mother thrust a bouquet of heather wrapped in foil at him. Superstitious, he had bought the heather before she could finish her sales spiel.

The kitchen was chilly after the hot shower. He had stopped her taking sugar; she liked lemon in Earl Grey now. He had taught her so much.

He lingered by the sink, waiting for the kettle to boil, contemplating the rooks roosting in the chestnut trees. The birds had been there for at least sixty years; his father remembered them when he was a boy. One day his own son would stand here and observe the same scene.

When he had stepped out of the shower she had knelt before him; she knew exactly what to do.

She could make him feel like a king.

The winter sun dipped behind the trees while he sipped Earl Grey and watched the rooks.

Twelve

Stella was unlocking her front door when she heard her mobile phone. No other flat on her floor was occupied, so, faint though the ringing was, it broke the hermetically sealed quiet.

'Private call'.

It had switched to voicemail. In the living room she switched on the light and sank on to the sofa, the protective plastic squelching while she waited for the message to come through.

The only client with this number was Mrs Ramsay and she was dead.

Mrs Ramsay rang at least twice a day: to amend her task list, or request that Stella bring a particular cleaning agent. Stella had not returned Mrs Ramsay's last call, made on Monday when Stella was at the hospital. In the scrambled message she had caught the words 'want a talk' and was sure what the 'talk' would involve – Mrs Ramsay would be gearing up for her annual clean. In the three years that she had employed Clean Slate, Mrs Ramsay had commissioned two days of cleaning in addition to her bi-weekly sessions. The fuss for these days was, Stella suspected, on a par with the parties Mrs Ramsay had hosted in her youth. She would fill spiral pads with prioritized lists and with the vigorous precision of a house-search insist Stella unscrew the cover on the water tank and clean behind the bath panel. Stella lifted floorboards in Eleanor's room and vacuumed between joists and under the eaves; she tidied the garden shed and the summerhouse and disinfected the drains. Clean Slate did not offer deep cleaning as a standard package but, to Jackie's dismay, Stella never charged Mrs Ramsay more than the basic rate.

Leaning on the sofa's plasticized arm, Stella yawned. She had not told Jackie how much she relished the forensic operation: covering every inch of the property, routing out hidden horrors like bloated frogs in watering cans, the dead mouse with its head protruding from a hole in a crate as if in the stocks. Now Mrs Ramsay's overhaul would never take place.

Her phone beeped: Stella listened to the voice message.

Mr Challoner's receptionist had reserved his last appointment the next evening. Stella quelled disappointment that Ivan Challoner had not called himself and selected 'ring back'. In case he, like she, listened to his answer machine, she injected warmth into her confirmation that she would be at the surgery for five thirty tomorrow.

She jotted the time in her Filofax, which she'd received from Terry on her eighteenth birthday, along with a police application form which her mother had torn up. Twenty-seven years later, shiny with use, its corners curling, the address pages and dividers dark with thumbing, Stella was lost without it. This was not sentimentality: if an object continued to be functional, why replace it? She took care of her possessions, wiping her dining-room table with tea-tree oil, buffing it with a glass cleaning cloth, flicking a duster over her hi-fi equipment. Everything in Stella's flat was new or looked new.

Stella was the first resident to put down a deposit, choosing the corner apartment in the riverside development in Brentford, aptly named Thamesbank Heights, after a hasty viewing of a model in the site's marketing suite. She justified her speedy purchase to Terry in her head, countering objections that her mother said he would make, the main one being that Stella would get her fingers burned when what was obviously a scam fell through. By the time the venture did collapse, building was almost complete so only the developer's fingers felt heat as the bank foreclosed on the loan. Stella moved in on her forty-fourth birthday, refusing help from Terry, who, being retired, said he had time on his hands.

The flat was on the fourth of five floors, so there was not a great climb if the lift broke. It offered a view over the Thames and south-west London, but Stella had not bought it for the scenery. With triple glazing, toughened security doors and CCTV, it was secure with minimal heat loss. Situated on the south side of the block, facing the river, it provided her with total privacy.

Even as the paint in the lobby was drying, the recession was in full swing and six months on only 35 per cent of the dwellings had been sold. The under-populated estate had an air of futuristic unreality, residents moving like avatars in an online game over the manicured landscape bounded by a ha-ha and dotted with benches on which no one sat. Scraps of paper, crisp packets and cartons marred the perfection promised in the marketing literature and wind harassed infant acacia trees that would not, the saleswoman had assured Stella, block out light or compromise foundations.

Stella negotiated the shallow pit in front of the main door; filled with hard core and rubbish, it awaited marble to make it a step. Few footsteps other than Stella's echoed in the quartz-tiled lobby or crunched the gravel paths winding discreetly to housed bins and garages with automatic doors. Seldom was the stillness interrupted by the ping of the lift and the swish of its door. Stella monitored the dirt on the chrome fittings and bluish-tinted glass of row upon row of desolate balconies in front of curtainless windows, their panes stuck with 'For Sale' tape. Only the show flat balcony was furnished: sporting a faded consortium-branded umbrella spiked into a patio table that smacked in the breeze like a flag of surrender. The timer for the exterior lighting was awry; lights embedded in path borders and perched on poles in the car park came on at seven in the morning and went off seven at night. The managing agent had not returned Stella's call about this or the erratic cleaning service. Stella did not want the contract; she would not be paid.

She resented meeting anyone in the mirrored lift with its motion-activated polycarbonate light fittings which, the brochure had extolled, 'offered greater durability', or crossing the pinkish forecourt of crumb-rubber, 'designed to protect from injury and increase comfort'. She did not need neighbours. In her head she told Terry she had got a bargain.

Every night, when she closed her front door, which blocked draughts and extraneous noise, she derived satisfaction from the sensible proportion of the rooms, the sleek woodwork and steel fittings. She understood Mrs Ramsay's need to peer behind pipes and beneath stairs, tighten window catches and to sterilize what no one would see. In so big a house, it was impossible to keep tabs. Had she lived there, Stella too would have had to cover all bases. Her flat in Thameside Heights – she never called it home – required little monitoring and no bother to keep clean.

She put the two Rokesmith case files on the table and flicked them with a damp cloth, which did not rid them of the odour of Terry's loft. She'd have another go at shredding at the office; a bit each day would see it sorted.

It was time for supper. Stella had a strict schedule and supper was at seven, washing up by half past, emails or other work until ten, then bed. She began by going into the galley kitchen to prepare food. The kitchen had been designed for a busy person with little time and little appetite for entertaining. The shiny appliances snugly wall-mounted with none of the gaps and nooks that so exercised Mrs Ramsay suited Stella perfectly. Right angles abounded – no wavering lines or bulges in the plaster to frustrate the eye or darken the mood, all handles and dials clicked flush to surfaces. The washer-drier, slim-line dishwasher and the eye-level combination microwave above the fan-assisted oven were white squares on a chessboard of the 'Absolute Black' granite worktop and floor tiles. Stella had taken her pick of materials from a choice too generous to be profitable. If she found herself chopping, slicing and stirring, she calmed herself with the prospect of the scrubbing, brushing and wiping to follow. She keyed in defrosting, cooking times and extra drain and spin cycles and found to solace in the sheen of a newly mopped floor.

Since Terry's death Stella had done no cleaning in her flat.

She pulled a toad in the hole from the freezer – noticing it was the same brand as Terry's shepherd's pies – and set the time for three minutes on high, and while it revolved on the plate, mused at the wasteland below intended as a child-free zone of contemplation. The centrepiece, a Yogic Om in coloured concrete, was to have included bronze plaques with meditative texts: Christian and Buddhist. Bindweed strangled the casing of a Sony Trinitron television and slabs of brickwork – the foundations of the old electroplating works – nestled amidst thistles and towering buddleia and nettles, fractured by their roots. Stella had no time for contemplation with or without children; what irked her was a job half complete.

She was startled by the door buzzer. No one but Jackie and Paul knew where she lived. She trod softly down the carpeted hall, an unnecessary precaution for no one could hear her four floors up, and pressed the intercom panel: a video screen flickered to life, the camera trained on the front doors. There was no one. Then she saw a shadow to the side of the screen: someone was outside the range of the lens. Rationally she was confident that with the lobby doors of reinforced glass, held fast with solid locks, she was safe. With few residents there was little chance anyone would let in a stranger who claimed to have a parcel or lost their key. Her own door had a five-lever lock and the frame was reinforced with a London Bar. Nevertheless she rolled her shoulders, quelling a mounting panic.

Whoever it was knew she was in. Stella checked the intercom to be sure the volume was muted and heard rapid breathing. It was her own.

The shadow had gone. She stepped up to the monitor to be certain – maybe she had imagined it. She squinted through the eyehole in the door: corridor and a strip of blue carpet tapered to the end window.

Had someone been let in? In the kitchen the microwave pinged; her supper was ready. Already it was past seven, she was running late; she turned off the entry camera and hurried back to the living room.

Her mobile phone was flashing with a text from Paul.

I am outside.

The same message as when she was at Terry's house the night before. She grabbed her keys from the dining-room table and went into her study, with a desk on which was a laptop docking station, a dictionary and a lamp. On the walls were a calendar and a map of London. She plugged the phone into a socket by the desk and laid the keys next to it so she didn't forget them in the morning. Stella had many such tricks and ruses to ensure she met deadlines and objectives.

She shut both the study and living-room doors so that she would not hear the phone or see it light up with a call or a text. Finally she switched off the ringer on her main line, congratulating herself for not yielding to Paul's pleading and giving him a key to her flat. He could not get to her now.

She munched her way through the toad in the hole, many minutes behind schedule, and eyed the rusting barbed wire spiralling along the perimeter of the demolished works. Through the gloom, between the coils of wire, was the hulk of a low-slung barge moored beneath her window. Paul had wanted them to live on a barge on the Thames. Stella had said it would be impossible to keep clean, but that was not the real reason; she knew now it was because Kate Rokesmith was murdered by the river.

Through the air vent came the rhythmic slapping of water against the wall. Somewhere over the river a flock of geese honked, the noise eerily plaintive as they made their way upstream to Barnes.

'You can tell they're geese because they're flying in that "V" pattern, see?'

Stella followed the line of his finger.

111

'No one knows why they do it. Maybe it gives them better visibility. Every bird has a clear view with nothing in front. They keep together – it's nicer than flying alone. Birds and animals are sociable creatures. Like you and me.'

Paul would presume she was watching him from the study; he would imagine she cared. Stella chewed, slicing the sausage, cutting the batter into squares, forking each mouthful precisely. She wished Paul could be more like her and understand it was over.

Terry had never been to her flat. She dismissed this thought.

After washing up her plate and speedily wiping down the tops she had caught up with herself, but instead of looking at her emails she pulled out the chair at the head of the dining table – bought because the room required one, she did not have guests – and tipped the papers from the first box on to the glass. Before shredding it would do no harm to check what Terry had taken trouble to keep. She set aside what she had read at her office. A couple of sheets floated to the floor: one was an interview with an 'internationally acclaimed medium' in the *Sydney Morning Herald* – the case had gained international coverage – who divined that 'the murderer spends time dressed in white beneath the ground beside a bubbling fountain'. Stella could not understand why such crackpots were given attention.

She turned to a clean page in the note section of her Filofax and testing her new Clean-Slate ballpoint, out of habit, made notes as she read.

The other piece of paper on the floor was page two of a transcribed interview. She licked a finger and flicked through the pile, but could not find page one. She was about to put the sheet aside, thinking that she would come across the rest in another box, when the name 'Ramsay' caught her eye.

'… you confirm that you saw Katherine Rokesmith leaving her house with her son at eleven forty-five on the twenty-seventh of July?'

'I told you.'

'How can you be sure of the time?'

'The church clock struck the quarter as I was getting out of the car. I notice these things, ever since… My children say I have a good eye. Ear in this case.' [Laughs.]

'Did you engage in conversation with Mrs Rokesmith?'

'She was in a hurry. I waved.'

'How did you know she was in a hurry?'

'I didn't. I meant, *I* was in a hurry, I was late home so… anyway… we didn't speak.'

'So Mrs Rokesmith wasn't in a hurry?'

'I couldn't say. Aren't we all?' [Laughs.]

'How did Mrs Rokesmith seem to you?'

'She looked lovely, such a stunning girl. Reminded me of me as a… anyway, I'd been at our place in Sussex. I was shattered. I had to open the new village hall – a silly shindig shoved in to make way for this wedding. Frankly, Sergeant Hall…'

'Darnell. Detective Inspector Darnell.'

'I'm muddling you up. Victoria sponges are all the same: one has to keep one's wits about one at these frightful barneys so as not to offend. I was desperate to get up to town and have a small drink and put my feet up. So, yes, I *was* in a hurry. The whole thing is bloody and of course now I wish I had stopped to talk.'

'Did you see the boy?'

'Isn't he a poppet! I think I did.'

'You are not sure?'

'Yes. I did see him.'

'Did you speak to him?'

'I waved. He waved. At least he may have. I'm hopeless at this, when you have to trawl back it's so diff... It was just another day.'

[Interview with Isabel Ramsay ends 10.01 a.m. 29 July 1981.]

Mrs Ramsay had initialled each section of the transcribed speech with bold loops of the pen. Stella knew her handwriting; despite her apparent frailty she pressed hard, indenting the paper. Her voice came off the page: Mrs Ramsay in her sitting room clinking a gin and tonic, a pen substituting the cigarette held up by her shoulder.

Stella laid down the statement. It was extraordinary that Mrs Ramsay was the last person to see Kate Rokesmith alive. Terry had interviewed her client years before she had known of her existence. Mrs Ramsay was a key witness in the Rokesmith murder and had never told her. Stella could not ask what she had thought of Terry or how much she remembered of Katherine Rokesmith because, unbelievably, Mrs Ramsay too was dead.

Stella had lost the only client whose cleaning had been a challenge: she would never deep-clean for Mrs Ramsay again.

Busily, using the edge of a box lid, Stella ruled columns in her notes: one for a description of the event, one for the date and one for the file number. The night wore on; fortified with coffee, she filled the columns with neat script. At 3 a.m. she rested her head on the plastic-covered sofa intending to close her eyes for a moment, and fell into a dreamless sleep.

The river flowed sluggishly past the solitary block of flats, its opaque surface absorbing the ghostly squares of light from Stella's living room and kitchen. At the front, sightless windows reflected a car in one of the visitors' spaces. Had the estate lights been working it might have been possible to see if someone was sitting at the wheel.

Thirteen

Jack stepped on the crack in the paving. He blamed the man in the car waiting at the zebra. For a moment their eyes locked and Jack thought here was a man like himself, at home in the night-time streets. The darkness was his friend; like Jack he had nothing to fear.

Jack had stared at him – or where the man's face should be because when the car trickled closer, its headlights dazzled Jack – and this was his first mistake. He should have paused to get his bearings, instead he took a step and that's when he stepped on the crack.

He knew the walk to Earls Court off by heart and should not have been gulled into the stupid error. Every paving stone was part of his plan but the car made his concentration slip and with it his boot.

A crack was not a real line but his dictum covered gaps between paving slabs, edges and boundaries of objects and buildings, so had to include cracks. He stared down, teetering on a high wire; in the light of the lamp-post the paving slab was a map of London, the crack being the river and the fissures and runnels rat-runs. He was hot with shame: the driver would know the extent of his mistake. The car had gone.

Night, when most of London was asleep, was Jack's best time of day. At the end of the rush hour, faces made way for lines: pipes and guttering, eaves and roof slopes, wavy lines of bunched cable and stubby lines of the sleepers beneath his cab. The line in the pavement straddled life and death and by trying to see the car driver he had tempted mortality.

If Jack's colleagues liked him, and this was an overstatement, it was because he was prepared to do the 'Dead Late' shift that finished after midnight. Most drivers hated the endless tunnel hours, claiming the silence and continual darkness killed their social lives and their ability to be polite. Jack drew comfort from the overarching brickwork with its mutely held secrets of over a century and a half; he resented having to come above ground.

He had a social life.

The street was silent; once grand houses sunk to shabby hotels with plastic signage clamped to crumbling stucco. They highlighted the banality of his blunder. This awareness thrilled up his leg, making his heart flutter like a bat trapped in his chest. His instinct was to jump off, but he refused to side-step – literally – his responsibility. He remained on the line, taking in the significance. He must learn from his mistake; he made few, so such opportunities were rare.

The driver was out of sight so he would put him out of mind. Jack hugged into his coat and, walking, tried to retrieve his rhythm, relieved that at this late hour no one else had witnessed his transgression.

A young man slouched in the portico of a hotel, the firefly glow of his cigarette giving him away. There were no security cameras here; it was a blind spot. Jack wove between the parked cars, taking care to avoid splits in the camber and the lines of the drain grille. He flicked up a cigarette from the packet he carried for these eventualities; he preferred roll-ups.

Jack wore a pleasant smile. His polished brogue mounting the bottom step, he asked for a light.

Fourteen

The WPC on 'scene guard' behind the 'Do Not Cross' police tape impassively eyed a woman in trousers that showed off a flat stomach stepping out of a cleaners' van. Her loafers were polished to within an inch of their life and she was, the officer reckoned, too smartly dressed for a cleaner. She was the boss come to collect her winnings, or in this case, cut her losses. She obviously knew the wisdom of running a spotless Peugeot Partner slapped with company details rather than a Lexus or Merc that advertised to customers that she knew how to spend their money. The officer allowed a sliver of respect for the woman, who like herself looked to be early forties. She raised her eyebrows in enquiry, ready to state it was 'no entry' whatever Ms Clean Slate said.

A car glided to a stop at the kerb and the passenger door swung out, clipping the woman's natty leather rucksack, but she did not break her stride. The WPC recognized the detective inspector's Volvo. Doing up his jacket, he bounded out of the passenger seat like Action Man and, just a fraction too late, she raised the tape to let him pass.

'All right, sir?' Of course he did not reply.

'Are you in charge here?' the woman called after him.

'Contact our communications people. You know the score, no press.' D. I. Cashman rapped on the front door, studying his shoes while he waited for it to open. The police officer did not move, underlining his authority.

'Do I look like a journalist?' The front door remaining closed, Cashman had to acknowledge her. 'I cleaned for Mrs Ramsay.' The woman fidgeted with branches on the straggling hedge, ripping off leaves. 'Stella Darnell. Clean Slate.' She gestured a thumb at her van. 'Maybe you knew Detective Superintendent Darnell?'

There was a beat.

'Terry? Terry bloody Darnell?'

Stella took in the female police constable with a slight nod and played a never-used card: 'He was my father.'

'You know what?' The detective was coming down the steps. 'Your dad taught me more than I've forgotten.' He jumped the last two. 'It's a hellish thing. I was *totally* gutted.' Panting, he gave her a clumsy handshake across the hedge. 'Martin Cashman, Detective Inspector.' He hesitated. Maybe like Terry he was happier with the evidence-bag aspect of death than with cups of sugary tea and a few well-chosen words.

Stella saw that he was the Terry look-alike of the day before, dressed in a serviceable Marks & Spencer's suit, like the one she had put into the dry cleaner's below her office in readiness for charity. He had Terry's mousy hair combed in a side parting, tipping over his collar; it was, Stella knew, due a cut that he would not make time for. In his pudgy vein-flecked features were the beginnings of Terry's double chin and his slight paunch had loosened his shirt from his waistband. He hastened to tuck it in, emitting a tang of Gillette aftershave. In no time at all, Stella reflected coolly, the doppelgänger effect would be complete.

With a look to the WPC, Detective Inspector Cashman beckoned Stella through.

Fixing the tape back into place, the officer observed Stella Darnell stalk up the steps as if she owned the place, and grudgingly envied how she had the boss eating out of her hand.

'He rang me last week… he was on form, cracking jokes. Still on the job!' The front door had been opened and upstairs Stella could hear voices, heavy footsteps and guffaws of laughter. Instinctively she was annoyed; Mrs Ramsay did not encourage visitors.

'I was sure retirement would get to him. Some can't hack having no reason to stress. Mad, isn't it? We've had blokes doing the conga on the Friday and a couple of months later I'm listening to a eulogy at their...' With scene-changing swiftness he wiped his hand over his face and made a show of shuffling his shoes on Mrs Ramsay's doormat. Stella did the same.

Mrs Ramsay would have been distressed to see her dilapidated but pristine hall a mess. Gone was the ratty rug that skidded and chalk marks outlined the stains it had hidden. The acrid smell of ninhydrin, used to lift latent prints, extinguished the lavender fragrance Stella encouraged Mrs Ramsay to spray throughout the house and a dusting of fingerprint powder greyed the coiled end of the balustrade polished so recently.

'Those were there already.' Stella indicated the stains.

'Our guys said that.' He loosened the knot on his tie as if she was depriving him of breath, as Terry did when she challenged him.

Sensing advantage Stella pressed the point home: 'I couldn't get rid of them. Mrs Ramsay didn't know what they were.' She cast around. The rug slumped drunkenly in plastic wrapping beside the antler hat stand, which was also in the wrong place.

'Blood, SOCO think. Forensics'll confirm.' He rubbed his hands together vigorously and stepped over the marks to the stairs. 'You didn't do the cleaning yourself? Big shot these days, your old man says – said.'

Stella detected sarcasm.

His shirt – blue cotton with pencil-thin brown stripes – was identical to the one Terry was wearing when he died.

'Sky's the limit,' he told her and kissed her forehead. In his best shirt, he waved her off through the gates, tracing a big rainbow arc with a sweep of his arm to egg her on but she did not look back, already Miss Independent. He stayed until she had gone. It would be three whole hours until dinnertime. He had promised to be in exactly the same place when she came out. They were going to have sandwiches in the park as her reward for being such a brave girl.

The detective's brogues could do with a buff, but like Terry he would blend into a crowd. Terry's death was a detail; there were more detectives where he came from. One day D. I. Cashman too would be substituted; maybe by the woman at the gate. Stella roused herself.

'No actually, I did handle this. Mrs Ramsay was particular and I knew her ways.'

Sunlight slanted in through the landing window at the turn in the staircase, highlighting nineteenth-century *Punch* cartoons framed in gold wood hung in step formation. Glittering particles of dust flittering in the light reminded Stella of how Mrs Ramsay would snatch at them, opening her fist like a child to examine her empty palms. She had once found Mrs Ramsay vacuuming the air, she waved the nozzle like a fire fighter putting out a blaze. Mrs Ramsay kept her curtains shut to avoid seeing what she could not remove or wipe away and was fond of saying that what was out of sight was not out of mind.

'When did you come here last?'

The hall was as chill as a church. Mrs Ramsay did not heat rooms she only passed through. Her skeletal frame clad in fraying layers of fluttering silk, cotton and cashmere, she claimed not to feel the cold.

'Last Friday for three hours. I finish at one. Sometimes I have a cup of tea, but I had a meeting in Chelsea at one thirty so had to rush.' Mrs Ramsay had been hovering by the hat stand, flapping an overcoat, smoothing the fabric. She was annoyed Stella could not stay and Stella had half expected her to bar the way. A mad notion in retrospect, but lately her behaviour had been more erratic. Busying herself rummaging in the pockets of the coat, she did not say goodbye.

The coat was not there now. At the time Stella had supposed it belonged to Mr Ramsay; his wife seemed unable to accept he was dead and like she did the rest of her family behaved as if he had just left the room.

'Did the old lady seem anxious or unwell?'

'She was always anxious; no worse than usual.' Stella reacted to the term 'old lady'; it did not describe Mrs Ramsay.

'OK.' He pulled out a notebook that was bagging his jacket and drew a pen from his breast pocket. 'Why was she anxious?'

Decades after she had left Terry, Suzanne Darnell still complained about how he never dressed for an occasion and the careless way he treated his clothes, although her own were neglected, with several blouses on one hanger and trousers, or slacks as she called them, bundled up with no regard for the crease.

'Oh, no reason.' Stella did not need the police asking awkward questions. 'Older people get anxious, and depressed, it goes with the territory.' She tossed generalizations at him like birdseed. 'She had to know when I was coming so she could be ready, her routine kept her going. Nothing odd about that.' Except Mrs Ramsay was not like the other pensioners Stella worked for. Stella pictured the last list dashed down in the bold and rounded script, her handwriting was not shaky or tiny; Mrs Ramsay had never seemed old.

She sniffed tobacco smoke, someone had smoked a cigarette; she wanted to order them all to leave.

Despite being an ex-smoker, Terry too hated the smell of cigarettes.

She returned to the open doorway and looked out at a splaying tree in the Square. The trunk was so thick that two people could not hold hands around its circumference. Wind in the night had stripped the last of the leaves, leaving branches stark and uncompromising against the sky. She could not remember what time of year the lawns would be dotted with conkers, shining as if soaked in oil; unless kids had got in before the park opened and taken them all.

'Put your jeans on over your pyjamas. Here, wear my jumper, that's it. Do up your shoelaces good and tight. We won't talk until we're clear of the house, keep close by me.' She cocked her head so he could whisper into her ear. It felt soft against his lips. If she was afraid she did not let on, clutching his hand she

scurried beside him to the Square. It was bitter; he was glad he had made her wrap up. He climbed the gate first then made her fit her boot on to the foothold between the bars. He had forgotten her mittens and worried about the icy metal. He nearly shouted with joy when she hauled herself up like a boy, rolling over the top and scrabbling with her boots for the horizontal bar. She peered into the pitch black beyond the torchlight. She was so excited. He knew then that his plan would work.

Until now it had not occurred to Stella that Isabel Ramsay's disconnected remarks, her fanciful stories, were more than eccentricity. What she had told the detective about her being anxious was true: she had been on edge. When Stella left, the bolts were shot home and she would hear the security chain while she was still on the path. When the water pipes had banged and hooted Mrs Ramsay had said it was the little boy again. Stella remembered that it was the youngest child, Eleanor, whose antics had annoyed her mother, but did not correct her. By the time she was in her van and ready to drive off, Mrs Ramsay would be peeping through a gap in the dining room curtains and Stella would wave. Mrs Ramsay did not move, her face, like a ghost's in the reflection, indistinguishable from the sky. Stella could not say any of this to the detective.

'Did the old lady get on with her family?' D.I. Cashman gave a business-like sniff, his pen poised. 'I've got here: husband was a doctor, dead over ten years, three kids…'

'I never met her children. We try not to come when there are visitors. Clients prefer their guests to see the effects of our work, not trip over a brush or slip on a wet floor. You're better off asking them.'

It was not lost on Stella that having access to the house and the trust of the frail owner, she was technically a suspect. She would not be charmed or intimidated: never would she compromise client confidentiality, especially for the police. Cashman had so far treated her as 'one of our own' and was putting up with her unhelpful responses because she was his ex-boss's daughter.

She had not made the connection that Mrs Ramsay had not seen her family for nearly as long as Professor Ramsay had been dead. She did not say that each time she came, she tidied up two water glasses by the bed both emptied: CID were not interested in ghosts.

Nor did she mention Mrs Ramsay's obsession with finding her children's dolls' house and how she had led Stella through the rooms, warning her to a avoid a creaky stair, getting over-excited as she described an 'incy-wincy' bedspread she had embroidered for the main bedroom in the dolls' house. Although she gave the impression that it was Eleanor who was keen to have the house found, Stella guessed from the way she chattered on about the dolls and the 'exquisite little furniture' that the house had belonged to Mrs Ramsay herself. Stella's parents could not have talked so intricately about her toys.

They had searched the children's bedrooms. Mrs Ramsay had shaken a fist at Eleanor's gloss-black ceiling and blood-red skirtings, like the rooms of some teenage offspring of Stella's clients. Stella ignored her fretful hints to extend Clean Slate's services to painting and decorating; their core business was to clean.

The rooms in the Ramsay's basement were a holding bay for discarded objects. A cylinder and an upright vacuum, its bag stiff and cracking with age, telephone directories and newspapers from the sixties were heaped on a single-sized bed. There was no dolls' house.

Like her own bedroom in Barons Court, no room had any toys; perhaps like Stella's mother, Mrs Ramsay had given them to charity without asking her children's permission.

Mrs Ramsay had stipulated that Stella must not touch any of this or her daughter would never learn. It did not need a detective to work out that the bedrooms had been abandoned long ago.

Mrs Ramsay's behaviour had worsened in the last month, she had lost all sense of time. Stella kept this to herself while D.I. Cashman scribbled a concluding point in his notebook with a stab of his pen and went into the dining room.

They were hit by a cloying odour: dead flowers, their stalks limp, were scattered over the tablecloth, a stain spread into the midnight blue material was not unlike diluted blood.

The detective's mobile phone rang and raising his hand he stepped out to the hall to answer it.

Oxi-clean was the only agent that removed lily stains from fabrics; supermarket stain-devils never worked as well. Isabel Ramsay frequently got stamen stains on her clothes and when Stella told her she had a means of eradicating them she had been rewarded with one of Mrs Ramsay's rare smiles.

She had put the granules out on her desk in the office to bring with her on her next visit. Jackie had accused Stella of liking to please Mrs Ramsay and she denied it, saying she was merely doing her job.

Mrs Ramsay's one pleasure was the arrival each Friday of a bouquet of lilies. Stella felt vaguely guilty that she did not buy her own mum flowers; her mother griped that Terry had never given her flowers.

At the 10 a.m. knock, Mrs Ramsay hastened to the door, patting her hair, smoothing her stomach, and would affect surprise and coquettish delight at the sight of the courier, a leather-clad man. He never lingered over her exclamations and kept on his helmet. When he had gone, Mrs Ramsay, her face a hectic flush, spent the next hour arranging the white flowers which for Stella spelled funerals. She would shuffle through to the dining-room table, the vase precarious in her bony hands, stamens staining her blouse, murmuring: 'Such a sweet thing, so kind, he always was a poppet. My guests adore flowers – men especially, despite what they say.'

Ignoring Stella's offer of help she would lower the vase, top-heavy with blooms, into the grate. This was the stage in the procedure when she got another cloud of pollen on her clothes and became distracted, her mood dampened. Stella would spend rest of the morning trying to cheer her up because she did not like to leave Mrs Ramsay feeling low.

The detective was still on the phone. Stella went over to one of the windows, and inspected the fingerprint dust on the pelmets. One morning, while cleaning these, she had overheard Mrs Ramsay on the kitchen phone complaining about the lilies. This had struck her as an unreasonable response to a present, even for Mrs Ramsay who, although exacting, had scrupulous manners. Stella had dropped the cloth when she got it.

Mrs Ramsay had sent the bouquet to herself.

On her final visit, Mrs Ramsay had told Stella that until her forties she had preferred white roses.

'I grow them in my private garden. No one knows about them. Ah, how those intoxicating blousy blooms become one's friends!'

'What made you prefer lilies?'

'Nothing lasts forever.' Mrs Ramsay had looked at Stella as if she were a stranger with no business asking her anything and, fluttering her hands, pointed out a smudge of grease under the cooker hood.

'A load of china was broken and a clock, look at that casing, it's got to be worth a few bob. I'm thinking she must have tried to defend herself.' Cashman had finished his call and was bending by the fireplace where Stella saw broken pieces of both Mrs Ramsay's vases in the grate amongst glass and the smashed carriage clock that used to be on the mantelpiece.

'Did you leave those flowers on the table?' Stupid question: the police would have moved nothing.

'We don't touch anything. The intruder must have dumped them there.'

Stella smoothed a wrinkle in the cloth without him seeing. The lilies smelled stronger as a through draught picked up the scent. She turned to see who had come in, but there was no one.

'I think she did this herself.' Stella saw it all. Mrs Ramsay would have had one of her tempers. She had not grown old gracefully; her increasing frailty frustrated her.

'Wouldn't she have it cleared up?'

'She'd fallen a couple of times so wouldn't have risked it. She knew I would do it.'

'Bit of a duchess, was she!' He sniffed.

'It's what she pays me for.' She did not say that Mrs Ramsay would have left the mess for Lizzie, the live-in help, nor that Mrs Jackson – the next-door neighbour with the stolen cat – had told her that Lizzie dated from her mother-in-law's era and had been dead for thirty years. It was Lizzie's name at the top of the lists that Mrs Ramsay left for Stella.

'The noise may have alerted her. Perhaps the intruder intended it as a weapon,' Cashman suggested.

'I'd go for that poker,' Stella returned. 'Where did he break in?'

'Ah, well, that's where it's good you're here. There's no sign of forced entry. Mrs Ramsay either knew her visitor and was happy to open the door, or – more likely, given it was night – they let themselves in with a key.'

Stella saw where this was going.

'I don't employ murderers, Detective Inspector.'

'Course you don't, but we know things can get out of hand. Might she have upset one of your people? Who worked here before you took over?' His face reddened as he ploughed on. 'Did they have a grudge, or got greedy? There are valuable artefacts here.'

Stupid, then, to destroy them.

'I got to know how Mrs Ramsay liked things done, sometimes it's easier than training up staff.' Stella resorted to sales patter. 'We tailor our processes according to the customer. I pay my staff properly; they don't look for ways to make up a shortfall. If I remember rightly the girl washed the floor in the wrong order of tasks then walked on it before it was dry. Easily done, some clients don't mind, some do. It was ages ago.'

'We'll have to talk to her.'

'By all means, bear in mind it'll be an overseas call. She returned to Elblag three months ago.'

'Is that a prison?' He shot her a quick grin.

'Small town in Poland, population about sixty thousand.'

'Terry said you were good.' Cashman whistled. 'Look, Stella, you know from your dad we have to be thorough. Could I get you to print off the names of everyone who cleaned here, just to eliminate prints and establish motives?'

'Doubt you'll find many prints besides mine. I too am thorough.' Stella knew it gained nothing to antagonize Martin Cashman; she should be co-operative. She used to tell herself to comply with Terry; if she chatted properly she could leave his house and wouldn't have to see him until Christmas. Terry would be thinking the same thing.

'Where did you find her?' Stella became the policeman's daughter. Cashman, like Terry, would work from a mix of preconceptions and prejudices.

'On the bedroom floor, staring at the ceiling like she'd been scared out of her wits. Her phone was off the hook, indicating she went to use it and he got to her first.'

He was resting his foot on the low tubular radiator beneath the sill. Stella stopped herself demanding he remove it; she had cleaned the cast-iron columns last week.

'See this?'

A hand print deteriorated to a smear as it travelled down the glass. Through the pane she saw the policewoman talking to someone but couldn't see who it was.

'She was trying to bang on the glass to attract attention, and her assailant dragged her off.'

Stella had seen such a mark many times.

'It's a test. For me.'

'A what?'

'If this was here at the end of a session, Mrs Ramsay complained.' Stella flushed. There had not been a trap like this for weeks and she had presumed that Mrs Ramsay had concluded that with Stella she had met her match. She had begun bringing in glasses of fruit juice halfway through the shift and boiling a kettle for coffee before Stella had finished. Instead of the instant coffee reserved for 'tradesmen', Stella was given ground, strong without sugar, just how she liked it.

She should never have rested on her laurels. Page seven of the

Clean Slate handbook warned: *Do not at any point imagine the client is your friend; it will compromise your work.*

Mrs Ramsay had never trusted her.

'I thought we had it tough.' Cashman sucked his pen and, at home in this house that was not his, flung wide the connecting doors to the kitchen.

Fixed to the wall beside the broom cupboard was a Bakelite telephone, its fabric cord draped across a 1968 calendar that Mrs Ramsay kept because it celebrated her best decade. It was always open on June, with a picture of a red telephone box in swinging London's King's Road. Stella could imagine the young Isabel Ramsay, toting a cigarette as she barked orders down the phone to the florist, the grocer, the Harrods' van driver, amidst plumes of blue smoke. Even in her seventies, Mrs Ramsay reminded Stella of the pre-assassination Jackie Kennedy. Jackie 'O' featured on the calendar's August page in a black and white chequered jacket and sunglasses.

Mrs Ramsay said this had been a happy family home; soon it would be dismantled and the mementoes of a lifetime scuttled into rubbish bags and supermarket boxes.

'We've contacted the eldest daughter. She was hazy about when she last saw her mother,' Cashman said.

Stella did not remember when she had last seen Terry.

'I spoke to her yesterday.' She regretted the words as soon she had uttered them. He did not need to know Gina Cross had asked her to clear the house.

'Why was that?'

'She told me about Mrs Ramsay's death.' This was not true; Stella kept her voice level. She had to hope that the officer on scene guard on Tuesday had not said Stella had been unaware of Mrs Ramsay's death until she came to the house.

Cashman appeared to change tack.

'Did Mrs Ramsay mention they were mixed up in the Alice Howland case back in the day?' Mistaking Stella's blank expression for ignorance rather than determination to make no more careless slips, he was encouraged to continue: 'A girl went missing. One of those investigations that chews away at you, though most of the guys must be pushing up the proverbials.' He trailed off.

'I keep a distance from my clients' personal lives.' Stella spoke into the silence and asked: 'What makes you think Mrs Ramsay was killed?' The evidence for murder was circumstantial and flimsy.

'She had bruises on her leg, her shoulder and her right arm.'

He lounged against the sink that Stella had given a proper going over with ceramic cleaner. It was holding up well.

'As I said, she had falls. She told me to keep them secret. I moved things to reduce hazards, but she put them back. She was hard to help. I tried to get her to see the doctor for her dizzy spells.'

'Did she go?'

'She never went out, don't think she had house calls.'

'One of the neighbours said she nicked their cat. A Mrs Jackson, know her?'

'Yes and I wouldn't go that far. Mrs Ramsay liked animals and made friends with them, that was all.' As soon as she said this, Stella was convinced it was untrue; Mrs Ramsay did not like animals.

She had imprisoned Mrs Jackson's cat in Eleanor's old room, not, Stella was sure, because she cared about it, but to punish the creature. A punishment really intended for the youngest daughter who had left her room in a mess.

'She was claustrophobic?'

'Agoraphobic. Possibly.'

'The autopsy will give us more on the bruising.' He shut the book and crammed it in his jacket pocket.

Stella wanted the police gone from the house so tossed him a red herring: 'She got headaches. Sometimes she spent all day in bed.'

Cashman wasn't listening. Interview over.

'Terry would've wrapped this up in a jiffy.' He gave a tight smile. Stella bridled at the mention of Terry. She doubted he would have had a clue. Unlike any phone messages she left for him, he would have returned Martin Cashman's call and played at detective; in fact he had called him last week.

'You don't think this is murder?'

'Not for me to say.' Stella shrugged. 'I can't see who would have wanted to murder her and I can't see anything missing, only broken.'

Through the kitchen window she noticed the door to the summerhouse hanging open. The catch needed mending. It was an item on her list of surprises for Mrs Ramsay.

'You'd have a better idea than the daughter about what's different. Do you mind if we pop upstairs and you cast your eye?'

Other than rumpled blankets – Mrs Ramsay had never taken to a duvet – Stella reported the bedroom unchanged. A twisted sheet trailing over the bedspread was proof only that Mrs Ramsay slept badly, tossing and turning, getting up and roaming the house or going to the toilet. The water glasses were in their places beside the bed; one with a lipstick stain on its rim was half empty. The SOCO team had not reached the top floor so Cashman should not have brought her here.

He trusted her.

Stella took care where she put her feet, and folded her arms to stop herself touching anything. This was for show; her fingerprints would be everywhere.

Here, where she spent many hours reading or lying in the dark with a migraine, Mrs Ramsay's absence was more noticeable. Stella avoided magazines on the floor by Mrs Ramsay's side of the bed and read the title of a book on the bedside cabinet. *Emma*. Mrs Ramsay shunned books with deaths in them and as a safeguard flicked to see who was still alive in the last chapter. She had said Jane Austen suited her perfectly.

Stella pictured Mrs Ramsay propped up against plump duck-down pillows, penning another list to Lizzie.

She walked around to Mark Ramsay's side. His staged presence, including the empty water glass, had given her the creeps but she did not share this with the waiting detective. The glass was full and a paperback edition of *Our Mutual Friend* by Charles Dickens, with two dog-eared copies of *The Lancet* from June and May 1999, lay beside it. The books changed each time she came.

'Did she have a partner?' The detective was straining to keep irony out of the enquiry; his equal opportunity training a straw loosely clutched. Terry never had that trouble, to him all people were equal and no one mattered more than someone else, including his family.

'She never got over her husband's passing.' There was something on the floor by the bed. Casually dropping her car keys Stella went as if to retrieve them.

It was squashed filter of a roll-up cigarette. Stella scooped it up with her keys.

'Terry mentioned the old lady when he phoned, weird.'

Stella's stomach flipped. Irrationally she fumed that Terry discussed her clients with anyone and she crossed the room to where two sash windows looked out on to the Square and tried to control her temper.

Two children straggled along a path in the park: the little boy wobbled on a bicycle pushed by an older girl. The bike jack-knifed and he tumbled on to the verge. Stella could hear his cries. The girl propped the bike against a bench and hauled the boy to his feet and the wailing subsided as she straightened him out.

'Why did he mention Mrs Ramsay?'

'She was a witness in a murder.' Cashman was by the door. 'I was a raw recruit in Bermondsey then. The Old Kent Road was another land to a West End boy!' He was chatty, suddenly affecting a stronger London accent. 'Your dad asked me to get hold of her statement. Anything for Tel, I said, no trouble.'

It was the statement that Stella had read last night. She made a mental note to look for the missing page.

'Why did he want it?' Mrs Ramsay had never mentioned Katherine Rokesmith. Nor had she mentioned Terry, although the name Darnell might have rung a bell.

Cashman continued: 'Didn't he tell you? He said he was going to ring you.'

'No.' Cashman had got that wrong. Terry only rang her on birthdays and Christmas.

'This was about them next door, in the eighties.' He gestured at the wall. 'The old lady – she wasn't old then – gave us our only solid sighting of the victim. She saw Kate Rokesmith setting off for the river.' She could smell Cashman's hair, his aftershave, his skin. If she shut her eyes it would be Terry.

'Katherine Rokesmith?' Her mouth was dry.

'You got it. It's down to your Mrs Ramsay that we got a time on the killing.' He said 'we' although he was at a different station at the time. Like Terry, he spoke as if he and the police were one.

Mrs Ramsay must have watched children in the square, as Stella was now doing. The girl had taken the bike and was pedalling off, the boy, probably her brother, was unable to keep up. Mrs Ramsay would have tapped her fingers on the sill, mouthing encouragement or admonishment. Did she mistake them for her own? She had crowed to Stella that she had always known what her children were up to, the parties they attended, the forbidden late nights they imagined they got away with but had not because the fifth stair creaking gave them away.

She was always telling stories – why had she never mentioned Katherine Rokesmith?

Stella looked down. The woman police officer was still talking; from here she could see it was a man, probably a journalist. This was how stories leaked, hacks feigning idle chat with bored coppers.

It was Paul.

He glanced up and Stella stepped back, colliding against D. I. Cashman, who had come up behind her. She did not want him asking Paul questions and hurried out of the room to distract him. A door in Mrs Ramsay's garden opened on to the Great West Road. Stella had a key but could not think of a reason to give Cashman for leaving that way. Paul would have seen her van; he had followed her.

He was turning into a stalker.

On the landing, she hesitated. Cashman went into the sitting room, jangling his keys like an estate agent showing round a client. There were six more stairs and on the fifth stair, as Mrs Ramsay said, the wood creaked when she put her weight on it. With the house busy, vacuum going, radio on, it would be easy to miss. At night it would be loud.

'Let me know about the funeral. We'll give him the send-off he deserves.' Cashman puffed out his cheeks. The sitting room was crowded with SOCOs, so they walked down to the front door. Shaking hands he added: 'I can't get my head around it.'

'Why was Terry ringing me?' Stella was furious with herself for asking.

Already the detective's mind was elsewhere; she knew those darting looks of distraction when Terry switched to bluff humour and fiddled with his watch strap.

'To talk to his daughter? Hey, maybe he wanted a cleaner!'

Stella took the steps outside so fast that the police officer barely managed to lift the tape in time and was in her van before she remembered Paul. There was no sign of him. Trying to sound nonchalant, she called out: 'What did that man want?'

'Directions.'

'I thought I knew him, that's all.' Stella shrugged. 'Saying that, I meet a lot of people.' She started the ignition. The officer was lying, but she couldn't argue.

'I'm sure you do,' the WPC muttered.

Stella drove round to Rose Gardens North, determinedly avoiding looking at Terry's, and uncurling her fingers examined the cigarette stub in her palm. One end was crushed as if extinguished against a hard surface. The tobacco had a distinctive smell – familiar, although she could not think why; she avoided smokers.

She tipped the butt into a plastic bag and poked it into a compartment in her rucksack. It was proof that Mrs Ramsay had started smoking again, although that didn't matter now. Her phone rang.

'Your teeth must have made an impression on that dentist,' Jackie said gaily. 'He wants a weekly clean of the flat above his surgery. The catch is, he wants us this afternoon and the rota's full. We're fresh out of staff.'

'Did you tell him that?'

'What do you take me for? I said I'd talk with you.'

She imagined Ivan Challoner in his immaculate surgery, music drifting from between books that had nothing to do with dentistry. The memory of the sweet mix of scents and fragrances eclipsed the sticky odour of Mrs Ramsay's cigarette butt. Stella had never looked forward to a filling before.

The dental surgery would be a nice piece of work, high standards and with interesting objects to wipe down and buff up for an appreciative client. But she did not want to go there as Mr Challoner's cleaner.

'Shall I add him to the waiting list?' Jackie repeated.

Stella adjusted the seat belt. She was meant to limit her cleaning sessions. First law of running a business: leave time to get more business. Dust and dirt wait for no one. Second law: learn to delegate. Being unable to see the bigger picture or take the long view had been Terry's problem. Her mother said he saw only what was under his nose.

You're just like Terry.

Stella made a snap decision: 'Get hold of that man who came in earlier – Jack Harmon was his name – his form's in thingy's in-tray.'

'Beverly. You don't like the newbies going into the field without a home run. I'm sure I could persuade Wendy although it's her day off.'

'She's seeing her dad in the home. Get *Beverly* to chase up references.'

'I'll do it myself.'

Crossing Chiswick roundabout on her way to a client in Sheen, a hearse with no coffin passed Stella, probably returning from Mortlake Crematorium. She absorbed the detective's words about giving Terry a 'send-off'. Funerals were a waste of money and Terry hated fuss; she should have said.

The police constable had not told Stella Darnell how she had boasted to the chatty neighbour that she was at Detective

Superintendent Darnell's leaving do or that his local was the Ram. Generally pissed off, she let the man know the daughter was in the house. He said he had to be somewhere but asked her to send Stella, as he called her, his condolences and he would see her later. She had been a tad indiscreet, but he had said he was a friend of the family.

When Stella Darnell had asked about him in a tone implying she had better keep her mouth shut, the officer decided not to relay his message. Later she resolved to make this good with a note to Stella dropped in D. Supt. Darnell's letter box when she came off duty since she didn't have her address.

When her shift ended, the WPC was exhausted from hours of standing in the cold and her goodwill, such as it was, having evaporated, she went straight home.

Fifteen

Thursday, 13 January 2011

The countdown began when Jack brought his train up to the buffers at Ealing Broadway. He had a break of seven minutes and thirty seconds before his last run to Barking, after which he would return to Earls Court and his journey would be over. He had agreed to do a day shift, despite it following so closely on his previous shift, because he never knew when he might have to ask a favour. Driving in the light was an experience he did not want too often. However, the coming night was his own and he celebrated this with hot milk from the coffee stand. Despite the odd choice of drink, the woman serving did not look at him throughout the transaction. She would not remember him: his driver's uniform was an ideal form of anonymity.

The motor refused to respond; the train had become a clunky weight that would not do his bidding. He reported in over the transmitter, feeling the pricking at the back of his neck: the train breaking down was another sign. Swiftly he headed through the carriages, ushering passengers to the south platform to wait for the replacement train, avoiding conversation. He, as staff, would ride in the cab with the driver, a custom Jack disliked but had to respect or it drew attention. The incoming train would drop him to the depot; he was now a relief driver. This was not a relief – it meant he had no set number: no sign.

The next train pulled in punctually at 2.58 and 30 seconds. He checked the set number: 236, trying not to think too hard or his mind would go blank. He had the impulse to walk away to evade

136

fate. But fate comes in many guises and there could be no escape if he did not know in which direction was 'away'.

He knew the young driver; he had recently qualified and, once they were in the cab and the train moving, the man became rigid with tension, gripping the handle, skin taut over knuckles like lumps of gristle. He performed each motion like an automaton. If he carried on like this he would be exhausted, but at least it meant he did not attempt conversation. Two years ago Jack had been made a trainer, so he was used to the terror the novice drivers endured, terror he had not experienced; driving a train through dark tunnels with hundreds of people at his mercy came naturally to him. As soon as he had settled into the swivel seat, manoeuvred the levers, depressed buttons and powered the train into the tunnel, Jack was at home; the Underground was his ultimate Host.

Jack sat on the right-hand side of the cab, his shoulder bag at his feet, and took sips of the milk.

Despite the chill afternoon, he asked if he could have his door open. He did not like sharing a confined space with another human being and since he was not driving he could properly contemplate the cables, the gantries and glinting rails of the other tracks. It was against regulations for the doors to remain open while the train was in motion but Jack could endure the driver's increased discomfort.

The train clattered up from Turnham Green station, where no one disembarked and no one alighted. In the distance Stamford Brook was like the stations Jack had saved up for with his pocket money: compact and transportable, with a tessellated roof canopy over each platform, a toy awaiting its part in the game.

He drank the last of the milk and at the same moment his phone vibrated. He didn't recognize the number but did get the last three digits: 236.

The train's set number.

Jack was so astonished that despite the driver he pressed the green button.

'Hi there, this is Jackie speaking from Clean Slate – for a fresh start. It's short notice, but one of our clients needs a cleaner at 4.30 this afternoon. We hoped you could do it.'

He knew about a fresh start. Jack turned to the open doorway to avoid the driver hearing: 'Don't you need references? Ms Darnell said something about a trial run in the office.'

'We will follow them up in due course. We trust you. On paper you fit and this is an emergency. Call it the trial.' 'Jackie Speaking' gave a tinkly laugh indicating she did not trust him.

A Piccadilly line train was speeding towards them from Ravenscourt Park; these trains to Heathrow, as frequent as the planes in the sky above, went like bullets on this section of track because after Hammersmith the stations were District line only.

Jack smiled: after all, he had not miscalculated Stella Darnell. He squashed the cup in his hand. The driver was slowing too soon; Stamford Brook was way ahead. He stopped himself from saying so; he was not a trainer now.

He was also right about the manager at Clean Slate: her confidence in him lasted until she got off the line. Jack had bought a tranche of telephone numbers off the internet and, applying a different ringtone to each, routed the numbers given on his references to his mobile. All he had to do was remember the referee meant to answer. When Clean Slate appeared on the LCD screen the ringtone was a man whose house Jack had for a while thought of as home. He was tempted to turn it off, but it would only mean calling back later.

'Nick Jarvis?' He kept his voice low although the driver, now in a flop sweat, was watching the station approaching as if it were a mortal enemy.

It was rather a shame the driver wasn't listening, Jack was proud of how well he brought Nick Jarvis to life with a faithful rendition of the harassed accountant's clipped speech. Time is money. Nick's reference was to the point, and not effusive. Yes, Harmon had done a decent enough job, didn't know he'd been given as referee, but yes, could recommend him.

Jack let the second call divert to answer machine. He did not want to risk Jackie picking up any similarity in his imitations; she struck him as sharp and the driver's increasing hesitancy was beginning to get on his nerves.

Over the transmitter, a voice crackled that the next westbound District train was at West Kensington. The controller reported that it would terminate at Richmond because they were suspending the Ealing Broadway service until Jack's broken-down train could be shunted to the Acton depot. The eastbound District train and the westbound Piccadilly train would reach Stamford Brook together; he loved these moments, except this train was too slow: the driver, nervous of overshooting the platform, was applying the brake early.

Jack lifted his bag from the floor and ducked under its strap, adjusting it over his chest like a child's satchel, fastener facing in; he could not risk it being snatched or rifled by pickpockets. Along with the private notes which no one must see, he could not bear to think of his possessions – his purse, his notebook, his pen – lost in the world, effectively orphaned; even the idea made him desolate.

The Piccadilly train was upon them, its ca-clunk-ca-clunk loud through the open door. They were crawling, which meant he could see in its windows: the passengers were shop dummies. Tourists bound for Heathrow, late commuters asleep or reading free newspapers were plugged into headphones; people noticed little. His driver jerked the brake and their train jolted to a halt three feet short of the platform's end. A reportable offence.

'Take it right up.' Jack was calm. 'Get your passengers off, we don't want them pitching on to the line.'

The man worked his mouth as if in rapid and silent conversation. Jack covered the hand with his own and manipulated the stick, nursing the train the necessary inches until they were fully berthed.

'I'm getting off here. You'll be OK?'

The driver nodded grimly, fixing on the platform monitor by his open door.

Jack stepped past him. He would recommend him for more training; in the meantime he wouldn't kill anyone.

On his way to Shepherd's Bush Green to meet Jackie Makepeace, as Mike Thorpe of ABC Design and Print, Jack rang her and explained in a breathy, walking-down-the-street manner that he was on his way to a client, but could confirm that Jack was a great cleaner and all-round brilliant guy. He could follow up with a written testimony in the studio tomorrow. Jackie told Mike this was not necessary. Sold.

Jack pulled up the collar of his overcoat; forecasters were saying the wind came directly from Russia.

It was extraordinary how trusting people were. It gave people like him freedom.

Sixteen

Stella was thirty minutes early, so, parking the van in the street along from the dental surgery, she hauled out the batch of papers she had shovelled into her bag before leaving for work. Twisting sideways she stacked them on the passenger seat.

She wolfed down a sweaty cheese sandwich she had forgotten about at lunchtime and read that the pathologist said a fresh swelling with broken skin above the victim's right eye was consistent with a glancing blow from a sharp instrument. Katherine Rokesmith may have sustained another wound at the base of her skull when she fell. Any bloodstains that might have spattered on ground were washed away by the tide.

Terry must have carried this document about with him: the folds on the photocopy were deep, the paper spotted with grease, no doubt from one of the beef burgers he bolted on the run. This attitude to food had infuriated her mother, whose elaborate cooking made no more impression on him than a bag of chips. She complained that, like Stella, he put ketchup on everything. Stella balled up the sandwich cellophane and stuffed it in the carrier bag behind her seat. The handbook stipulated that staff must not eat in Clean Slate vehicles.

Stella had Googled the murder and found over a thousand links to articles and books, newspaper investigations, a Wikipedia page and more than one documentary which pieced together what was known of that day. Each new exploration took a run at the story, galloping confidently towards the murder with new snippets

141

of trivia and hearsay. Over the years minor players – a man in the Ram pub, a taxi driver dropping a fare in nearby British Grove – were added to the police's General Register, dates meticulously recorded. The 'red tops' re-ran photos and inflated vague possibility to within an inch of fact. Inevitably any piece or programme ended with the inexorable fact of the unsolved murder; an intrinsic point of anti-climax. Katherine Rokesmith's murder remained a mystery and her killer at large.

During a search of the Rokesmiths' house, Stella read, traces of blood were discovered on a hall table. Possible evidence of a fight: had Hugh Rokesmith argued with his wife before going to his mother's? Cashman had said that Kate was seen later by Mrs Ramsay but nevertheless Hugh Rokesmith, who had left his mother's to get champagne during the 'murder window', was questioned at Hammersmith Police Station. This fact provoked violence: a window in his house was broken and his car was keyed so the police moved him and his son to a safe house. As senior officer on the investigation, Terry would have known its whereabouts, Stella supposed.

She wondered again why Mrs Ramsay had never mentioned giving evidence about her neighbour. She could not ask her and, thinking at a tangent, mused how already she missed her daily phone calls.

Hugh Rokesmith had not fulfilled the public's expectations of a man whose wife was murdered, nor had he cut a tragic figure. He had been pushy and arrogant, his behaviour that day open to more than one interpretation, although officially he was not a suspect.

In a paragraph free of punctuation, Terry had noted: '…a woman would be capable of the strength required to apply a ligature to compress the neck for a period of approximately fifteen seconds so ensuring death ensues.' Nowhere else had Stella found references to the theory of a female killer; she presumed it had been dropped. Her mother said Terry did not consider women capable of much; perhaps he made an exception for murder.

It was another quarter of an hour before she was due for her filling. The van was cooling down; Stella zipped up her anorak.

The police had interviewed several suspects, all released without charge. In the office that morning Stella had jotted down their names and bare details and scanning the contents list in Terry's Closing Report had seen that the interview transcripts were in box number six. She would have to go back to Terry's house. Detectives had suspected a rapist recently released from Wormwood Scrubs prison who had bought a sausage roll from a bakery on King Street at nine thirty, which put him in the vicinity. These days CCTV would have sealed his alibi.

Twenty-eight-year-old Colin Peterson had completed decoration of the Rokesmiths' spare room two weeks before the murder. Forensic tests were conducted on his tools and his clothes; his dustbins were sifted, the rubbish taken away for examination. The press camped outside his bedsit and, it seemed, interviewed everyone the sandy-haired man with the pock-marked face had ever known. An ex-partner confided to *The Sun* that Peterson had 'a wacky sense of humour and a bit of a temper on him'. Then a winning betting slip was found wedged behind the windscreen in his very untidy van – there was a picture of the dashboard in the file – confirming that at the time of the murder he had, as he claimed, been at Doncaster racecourse.

Ringing the bell at ten past twelve on the Monday, the grocer's delivery boy had received no answer from the Rokesmith home, and a florist's assistant bringing flowers next door to Number 48 St Peter's Square at eleven thirty had also got no answer, nor returned to the shop straight away. Stella wondered if in those days Mrs Ramsay's flowers had been from a genuine admirer and noted that the day of delivery was Monday not Friday. Maybe she received flowers from other admirers then too? Both young men's alibis were established and were crossed off the shrinking list of suspects. As the last person to see Kate alive, Mrs Ramsay could be a suspect, but so far there was no mention of this in the files. Stella scribbled in her notes; everything should be explored, however unlikely.

Katherine Rokesmith's murder case had been overtaken by one of the major royal events of the century and with a dearth of information, languished and all but vanished into criminal history.

In 1981 the house that overlooked the beach where Katherine Rokesmith's body was found belonged to a widow: Mrs Clarissa Glyde, aged fifty-nine. Her daughter Sarah (twenty-one) lived in the basement flat working as a potter from a studio in the back garden. Mr Glyde had died of cancer six years earlier. Sarah Glyde had a dentist's appointment at the time of the murder and had only returned to the house in the late afternoon after going to an address off Fulham Broadway where she met a woman to discuss a commission for tiles. On 27 July Mrs Glyde had been at the family's cottage in Sussex, so had seen nothing. Detective Sergeant Janet Barton interviewed the women on the morning of 30 July. A handwritten account of her interview was stapled to signed statements.

> I was shown into a room on the second floor, with one window facing on to a 150-foot garden. A single-storey workroom approximately twenty yards long partially blocks a view of the river and the length of the plot makes it impossible to see the site where the body was found.
>
> Pots and plates were stacked on sills, shelves and around the settee along with books and magazines. The daughter said she played music while she works so would not have heard anything had she been there. Nor had she in the days before. [see SG statement – page 2 MIR 349.]

Neither woman had known Katherine Rokesmith by sight, although when shown a picture of the boy the older woman said he looked familiar. Barton had asked to see the upper floors and established that from the bathroom it was not possible to see where the body was found. An adjacent room was locked and they could not produce a key.

The studio doors opened on to a patio on the south side and only by leaning far over the garden wall was the beach was visible. The garden next door had a trellis and in 1981 the house had been up for sale and was unoccupied. Both women had alibis: the Sussex village vicar had had coffee with Mrs Glyde while Miss Glyde's dentist confirmed her midday appointment. Not keen to read about dentists, Stella skipped over this bit. In five minutes she would be having a filling.

Chaotic houses were only temporarily satisfying, in between sessions the mess would return. Stella insisted on direct debits as payment could be equally erratic. She might have refused the contract had the Glydes approached her or taken Jackie's advice and charged a premium. The house-to-house inquiries had provided nothing useful: of the few at home, no one had heard or seen a thing.

At one of several sessions with a psychotherapist, Jonathan Rokesmith had ignored the cars and dolls with which it was hoped he would construct a narrative.

[J. J. Rokesmith, 13 September 1981]

Sunshine flooded the room making the wool rug a livid red. Dolls lay scattered there, some face down; others were on their sides, their limbs twisted. These positions were not significant; Jonathan tossed them there before going into the garden. The six adults did not move or speak; however, his absence allowed them relief in tension. The detective sat with his head in his hands, massaging his temples. In this, the last session, Jonathan had still not acknowledged that he had heard the detective speaking to him. Father was impatient; on arrival he announced he had to move an appointment to be there. He said these sessions are no help. The police do little to disguise that they consider Father a suspect although I have explained that Jonathan understands more than he lets us know.

Every minute that Jonathan is in the garden frustrates the adults because nothing can be achieved while he remains absent.

Today Jonathan came upon the pieces of green crayon that I had retrieved from the bin where he had thrown them during his previous session. He expended effort snapping these fragments into smaller bits and took them to the garden. When he goes there it is to a bed of tall white daisies where he sifts sand from the sandpit through his fingers becoming a sand clock measuring time. Today, before doing this, he buried the crayon in the sand and covered the 'grave' with twigs and leaves torn from daisy stems. He pushed a stone into the sand to mark the spot.

Stella was reminded of her paralysis as, in the glare of adult expectation, she had confronted the dolls in Terry's toy box.

The little boy wet the bed. Stella shifted in her seat, remembering the warmth shot through with horror when she awoke in pressing darkness to cooling reality. Her mother had caught her trying to wash her sheets in the bathroom basin and still reminded Stella of this. Jonathan's every move was recorded: he had wet the bed thirty-one times in the six weeks after Katherine Rokesmith was murdered. Stella did not do the maths but this was practically every night.

A man was heading down the street on the other pavement. Stella shrank down in the seat and shielded her face with her hand. It was Paul. He would see the van. At the last minute she clambered into the back and crawled to the back windows, which were glazed with one-way glass.

Paul's steps were erratic; he appeared drunk. He was walking as a child might, leaping and teetering on the paving as if playing hopscotch. It was not Paul; it was Jack Harmon.

Was he following her too? Surely Jackie would not have told him where she was; she was a stickler for confidentiality. It dawned on her: Harmon had been cleaning the dentist's. She flung herself on to the front seat and pulled at the door handle, intending to ask him how it had gone but then changed her mind. In a minute she would get feedback from the client. She watched in her off-side wing mirror until his bobbing figure was out of sight.

She had knocked the Rokesmith papers off the seat, so, gathering them up, she stacked them together, impatient with herself for getting flustered. Since Terry's death she had been a bag of nerves and more than ever Stella wished she could see Mrs Ramsay; a list of exacting tasks in strict running order would settle her.

Newspaper reports and witness statements from neighbours and her husband's elderly mother described Katherine Rokesmith as fun-loving and a wonderful mother with no enemies. If someone had stalked her, he had lit on a moment when he was sure he would get away with it. Stella popped a pellet of extra-strong gum in her mouth and, although unwilling to agree with Terry, concluded that it was obvious; everyone had known it at the time: Hugh Rokesmith had murdered his wife and his mother had given him an alibi.

She retraced Jack Harmon's steps. Feeling more light-hearted, she resolved that tomorrow she really would shred the case papers and clear out Terry's house.

Seventeen

Thursday, 13 January 2011

It was two months since the Host forgot to take his keys from his front-door lock and Jack had withdrawn them and sneaked along the hall. Ideally he would have used them to get another set cut, but if his Host realized where he had left them, he would change the locks. The man had been in the kitchen preparing the evening meal, his back to him, the radio blaring. Jack had shut the front door before the man noticed a draught; if he saw Jack, the keys would be his alibi. The man had been chopping onions, which made his eyes water; he kept stopping to pat them with kitchen towel, unaware that he had a guest.

The man with a mind like his own had been on the path through the graveyard. Although it was the quickest way to and from the high road, in the winter no ordinary mortal would risk the unlit secluded route. Jack's elation was akin to love as he had kept pace with the man who trotted between headstones, past the church to the gate. There was little of the grown-up about him; he was like an earnest schoolboy who makes few friends and whose silence unnerves and annoys.

He had since found out the man's name was Michael Hamilton and he was the practice manager at a local doctor's surgery. He quickly impressed Jack with his terse efficiency and ruthless disregard for the patients: the perfect Host. Jack had not imagined Michael in a relationship and was appalled to discover that he lived with a solicitor called Ellen. But by then he had adopted Michael as his Host; besides, as the weeks passed Jack found that to all intents and purposes Michael was on his own.

Logically, if he had a mind like Jack's Michael ought to have been aware of Jack in his house, but he was not. After several weeks of being an invisible guest, curled up in the cosy box room listening to birds squabbling in the gutter outside, faced with facts, Jack had to admit that Michael was not the True Host. By then he had 'met' Ellen and had another reason to stay; she made him feel at home.

From downstairs came the Chopin Nocturne, the B-flat minor, Opus 9/1. He knew it well and whispered in time:

'This is the safety-catch, which is always released
With an easy flick of the thumb.'

Jack's fluid ten-key-stretch and steady hand-to-eye coordination would have handled any nocturne, but he was tone deaf. Under his touch piano keys remained cold ivory, their action stilted. Yet when he picked out 'Three Blind Mice' with one finger on Ellen's Bechstein Baby Grand and sang haltingly to the laborious tune he could appreciate the lyrics. *See. How they. Run. See. How they. Run.*

In the moonlight Jack examined his hands and fancied, not for the first time, that if he added a lick of nail varnish and with the fine gold band on his finger, his hands might belong to a woman. He could be anyone.

Jack's associations and memories hung like fine cobwebs in the corners of the room, enhancing the sense it was his home. He kept the light low so that they would not see it under the door if they came upstairs, although they rarely did until bedtime. In his room there was a single bed, a chest of drawers and a built-in wardrobe with louvred doors; all he needed when he visited. There were actual cobwebs which he had missed last week. The couple would never be customers of Clean Slate; they set aside Saturday mornings to clean: Ellen as a penance and Michael to punish Ellen. Jack cleaned his own room, which was on Ellen's task list, because when she was in here, she texted her lover.

Stella Darnell would applaud their cleaning cupboard packed

with instruments for every activity – window-cleaning, shoe-shining, polishing – all in labelled compartments. Ellen did not know he covered for her because she was too overwrought to notice dust. As he had expected, Michael slipped in when she was playing the piano; he sniffed for polish and inspected the carpet. Thanks to Jack's efforts, he found nothing. Ellen had no idea that Michael tracked everything she did, waiting to catch her out: she owed her life to Jack's protection.

It was half past eight and they were doing what they did on what they called 'school nights'. Ellen was in the garden room playing Beethoven and Chopin from memory. Jack now had a key to the garden and the back gate; he came and went as he pleased when they were out.

In the sitting room Michael Hamilton was slumped in his armchair by the fireplace, perfectly still except when he lifted a glass of wine to thin, pursed lips while a loud television programme competed successfully with the piano. Michael did not like Ellen and tried to blot her out.

Jack pulled his *London A–Z Street Atlas* from underneath the mattress and sat up on the bed. The cleaning session was a perfect end to a perfect day. He had worked his way around the dentist's flat feeling that finally events were going his way.

Tonight, he was not driving a train and according to page sixty-six of the *A–Z* would be in Dagenham. This journey was out of sync. He was much further on in the *A–Z*. Months ago he had accidentally turned two pages at once. The pages had taken him to East London, Barking, Homerton and East Ham. This area was relatively unfamiliar, although of course he had been to East London countless times in his Upminster or Barking train. Jack would have preferred to take the main line to Rainham rather than use the District line to avoid Underground staff recognizing him. But he had no choice; the pen line on the page began at Dagenham East and he was obedient; he was alert for signs. The book, which he had found years ago on a train, was defaced with routes in ballpoint on every page; they were a sign.

The page's marked-out route formed a loop that took in Ballards Road, Rainham Road and New Road with a tail at one end trailing to down to Rainham station. He fished his laptop out of his satchel and fired up Google Street View. Jack 'walked' his journeys online before embarking on them in 'real life'; his ghost self familiarizing himself with the journey.

He placed the Street View icon – an orange figure – on the Underground station and moments later a picture filled the screen. The sky in the scene was grey, the street shrouded in a premature dusk. As Jack mouse-clicked along the road to the station, the sun came out, heightening the colour of an orange windscreen-repair van – the model identical to the Clean Slate fleet – being tailed by a red lorry which blocked his view of the station. He clicked on down Ballards Road, hoping to see around it, which of course he could not as this was not real life. His street atlas was dated 1995, but on Street View he found office units and streets that in the atlas were depicted as blank space. The A13, which in his book had an estimated completion date of 1996, was finished; his A–Z charted the past. When he walked its designated routes he walked in the past; or as far back as 1995. He took scant comfort that sprawling car compounds were still there sixteen years after his map was published. He brought up the satellite version – from the air, the metallic hinterlands of cars and coaches appeared as ploughed fields where once, long before his A–Z, there had been marshes.

Sparrows skittered on the sill behind him. Jack told himself that he could lean out and crush them in his fist. The drone of a car engine did not distract him as he clicked the cursor behind a black estate car up Rainham Road. In the next click the car vanished and he had the road to himself. He spotted a police car parked on a grass verge almost concealed by bushes and glimpsed the wrist watch of a phantom officer in the passenger seat raising raised an arm to his face. Tomorrow he must look out for the car and skirt this part of road. He clicked back to the station, the sun disappeared and once more black cloud descended.

Outside Dagenham East station, the red lorry was still there. Jack shut the machine and slipped it back in his bag.

Stella Darnell had let Jack work for her; he had jumped the biggest hurdle but it meant he could not justify staying with Ellen and Michael any longer and must prepare his next move. This was sad: he had enjoyed his days here. He had grown to know their habits, their likes and dislikes. When the couple were at work he and the spiteful Burmese cat had the house to themselves.

At night Ellen shut the curtains in the garden room to keep the next day's light off the piano. Unless Jack was already upstairs, he had to freeze on the patio until they had gone to sleep and he could creep in. Tonight after finishing at the dentist he slipped in only minutes before Michael.

The couple had been together for twenty-two years and their dynamic was set fast; Michael wielded absolute supremacy, forcing Ellen to sneak around the edges for slivers of freedom. Like many couples they could have married, if only to cement the emptiness, yet neither of them had the heart even to do this.

Jack swung open a louvred door and retrieved the tin he kept hidden behind their photograph albums – Michael's proof of a good life led – and a tower of shoeboxes bulging with tape cassettes rendered defunct as audio technology outpaced them. The other door had jammed shut, which was Jack's first clue that the house was in limbo. Like Isabel Ramsay's, the soffits were peeling and cracked; loose drainpipes shivered on gusty days and clogged gutters groaned with the weight of mouldy leaves.

His tin held his trophies: cut-out figures from newspapers, magazines and clothing catalogues, purloined plastic solders, foreign coins, pressed flowers and a spirit level – apparently innocent boyhood treasures. He had added curling passport pictures and photographs prised from albums bound with an elastic band. Some evenings, feeling despondent, he would deal them out in a game of Happy Families. Their faces populated his dreams like the faces on platforms before he took his train into a tunnel and they were snuffed out.

Even a detective would have difficulty drawing a conclusion about Jack from his biscuit-tin collection. A teaspoon – borrowed, he never stole – from a woman who had poisoned her cat. She used it to stir her bedtime cocoa, a ritual she followed regardless of events. She no longer needed it. Nestling in the bowl of the spoon was a springy bundle of hair gathered from a brush. One morning each year he sniffed the brittle clump to strengthen his resolve. He did so now as his courage waned; it was painful to leave his Hosts. He lifted the top from a miniature oak box and counted three milk teeth; relics from a childhood not his own. Jack was their guardian. Every object held a snatch of life. He tilted the box to the light. At the bottom of the tin lay two postcards, one showed Hammersmith Bridge from the Barnes end and the other was a longer shot of the bridge with pontoons and a sailing yacht in the foreground. The address side of the cards were blank; on the left of each, scrawled in swift turquoise italics, were the words '11 a.m.'

In a matchbox, a cabbage-white butterfly rested on a bed of cotton wool. Jack had *borrowed* the butterfly from Nat, the set designer, whose flat had hung with crucifixes, masks woven of small-boned creatures and the heads of animals hunted by irrepressible Victorians. The man's collection of medical monstrosities in their stoppered jars had given Jack hope. He had gazed at the cirrhotic liver, the tiny amputated limbs and the pallid foetuses floating in formaldehyde and been sure this was the man with the mind like his own. The flat was kept dark and cold to preserve his Host's artefacts; his flirtations with mortality a celebration of life.

One night after Nat had gone out – Jack did not like it when his Hosts abandoned him – he found an ornamental cage on the dining-room table. Within its delicate structure were a hundred cabbage whites on white branches or clinging to the bars, their wings folded. Many lay dead on the floor of the cage, a carpet of soft petals. Nat had procured them for an interior scene with no colour meant to depict a lost past. Jack had since seen the film in the cinema. In the film the butterflies were still alive and he had wanted to snatch at the screen – as he had seen old Isabel Ramsay catch dust particles – and save them. He could not tell which butterfly was the one now in his box of trophies.

He had been certain of success when he'd spotted Nat on the Goldhawk Road at two in the morning retrieving a dead cat from the gutter and dropping it into a bag. A few days later Jack came across a poster like a Wild West bill stuck to a lamp-post that appealed for the safe return of a much-loved pet,dead or alive. Jack grew excited about Nat and supposed the feeling – his senses heightened to appreciate beauty in all he saw – was like being in love. He had found a like mind; happily he accepted Nat's unknowing hospitality.

But, brushing the butterfly's wing, Jack recalled how after a week he had struck up conversation with Nat in the basement bar he frequented after work. Like himself, Nat had few friends. He ordered the same drink as Nat – people are at ease with those like themselves – and sat nearby. It was Nat who spoke first and soon he was rabbiting on about himself, never noticing that Jack offered nothing in return. Nat had been born in Chiswick, he knew the area well; everything fitted. Jack ordered them both a second glass and raised a toast. When the barman snapped up the empties Jack nodded him a thanks, but Nat ignored him. Jack frowned. Despite it fitting the profile, he disliked impoliteness.

The bar was filling up and they had to shout to be heard. An hour and four drinks later Jack received a blow. Nat had moved to Sydney the day John Lennon was shot in December 1980. The Australian film industry was taking off and he got constant work, only returning to Chiswick when his mother died in 1991. Jack's mouth filled with sand, and the room spun. Nat had wasted his time. With the flip of a coin, what had passed for love switched to hate and blindly he made his way to the flat and packed up his things. When he shut the front door and set off to look for a new Host Jack's tin of trophies included the white butterfly.

He regretted that their parting was so abrupt he never said a proper goodbye to his Hosts.

This was three months ago and now Nat's flat – free of effigies and corpses – was occupied by a new tenant. Jack still had a key, but it was no longer home.

He would despair that the rest of his life might be constructed of blind alleys and false alarms; of treachery and disappointment. Ellen's piano music drifting up from downstairs had brought him solace and so he had stayed.

He lifted out his latest acquisition: a rounded lump of green glass an inch in diameter, its flawless surface twinkled like a jewel. Minute droplets of air suspended in its centre completed its perfection. Isabel Ramsay had passed it on to him. It was a shame that their time together had been cut short.

The wardrobe contained Ellen's summer clothes. Stale perfume pricked his nostrils. Maintaining the illusion of one life while leading another was onerous and Ellen was lying to her lover as well as to Michael, citing traffic jams and complex clients as causes of delay; she was a solicitor, so truth was there to be managed not upheld.

Michael had only to cook, clean and garden, book holidays and pour wine to bind Ellen into domestic expectations and stipulations as a spider wraps up a fly. Theirs was a charnel house whose lines and shapes Ellen tried to blur with glasses of red wine and clouds of cigarette smoke before sinking into numbed sleep strictly on her side of the bed. Michael was a shell in which the sound of the sea was revealed as the thud of blood pounding which will one day stop.

Jack sang softly to himself:

A time to be born and a time to die...

The piano music had stopped; Ellen would come upstairs to check for texts. He clambered into the wardrobe. The change was fractional; someone had added the tartan anorak with frayed elasticated cuffs and a rip in the hood that should be on a hook in the porch. Who had brought it here? He examined the anorak's stiffened fabric and found Ellen's flip phone was in the pocket. She kept her phone on her so there must have been a development for her to have hidden it here. Any minute she would come in. He shifted until he was concealed amongst the clothes.

The message icon was flashing.

'Miss u. Can we mt Snsbrys CrPk. Usual time. For 5min?

The text had just been sent. Ellen had put the phone on silent; he had yet to see her make a mistake. For the first time it occurred to him that only a particular kind of mind could retain such varying levels of being. But he was looking for a man.

A time to kill and a time to heal...

The phone's Inbox was empty. Ellen left nothing that might implicate her and had dubbed the man 'Dentist'. Michael knew the name of their dentist and could check the number in her address book and see it did not match. In one of the coincidences that made life so good Jack had seen that their dentist was Ivan Challoner.

So far Michael had not got hold of Ellen's phone, but it was a matter of time. Placid and patient Michael Hamilton would one day wield the claw hammer he stored in the toolbox under the stairs. Unless Jack could stop him. Most of the time he liked to blend into his Hosts' households; sometimes, like now, he must intervene and bring matters to a head.

Jack could not play the piano, but his texting was dexterous and swift. *I'm going to leave. Ring on main line in 5. Ellen xxxxxxx.* Jack pressed 'reply'.

He dropped the handset back into the anorak pocket as the bathroom pipes swished. Right on cue, the main-line telephone clanged throughout the house. Ellen burst into the room, making for the cupboard. Jack hugged his knees. If she pushed aside her anorak and looked behind the boxes it would be over.

She gasped. She had seen that the text had been opened.

Jack nearly cried out. Michael was standing in the doorway. He had not heard him come up the stairs and Ellen had not heard him either. She jumped when he spoke.

'Phone call for you.' His voice grated; he was holding out the receiver.

He knew.

'Say I'll call back.' Ellen slammed the wardrobe door, stuffing her phone into her back pocket.

'Why?' Michael allowed himself a tinge of irony.

'Oh, OK, pass it.'

Through the coats Jack could see Michael's fish stare and his cheeks pink and puffy from wine. He handed Ellen the phone and moved aside for her. He was looking at the louvred cupboard doors.

He knew Jack was there.

'Hello? What? What are you doing ringing … no, I don't need any. I don't take sales calls.'

Silence.

'Who was that?'

Ellen elbowed past him. 'Double-glazing.'

'He asked for you by name.' Michael spoke softy, remaining where he was.

'I must be on a list.'

'We have the telephone preference service. You should report it.' For some reason tonight Michael was pushing it. Jack felt sick.

The piano resumed.

Michael walked over and shut the cupboard door properly, slipping the catch into place. Jack could see him, looking about the room, before he too returned downstairs.

Jack felt his own phone vibrating. He did not recognize the number.

'Hello?' He cupped his hand over the mouthpiece.

'Stella Darnell.'

Stella Darnell. Her voice was tremulous; she must be on her way somewhere; working even when she was walking. She would hate dead time.

'Can I call you back?' he whispered. 'I'm on a train.'

'That's better, I can hear you now.' She was irritable, as if it was Jack's responsibility to be audible. 'It's just to say you've passed the probation.' She was pausing for him to be pleased. Jack had to work out how to lift the catch on the cupboard door from the inside before Michael returned.

'Mr Challoner wants you to clean every week. Come into the

office tomorrow to sign a contract and collect your schedule.' Stella did not ask if he was free. Jack liked that about her.

Through the receiver came the chimes of bells; he would know them anywhere. There was background chatter: a pub, he guessed; there were three near St Peter's Church.

He knew where Stella was and why she was there. Jack pushed at the wardrobe door and it gave way with a crack. He had broken the lock.

'*Thank you for having me,*' he whispered to his Hosts, stowing his trophy tin in his bag.

He was almost disappointed not to find Michael on the landing.

The piano filled the gaps between speech blaring from the television. Both doors were shut; light bleeding beneath them allowed him to creep to the understairs cupboard. He opened the flap on the concertina tool box. The claw hammer was heavy and split a couple of stitches in his coat when he crammed it into his pocket.

The front door made no sound – he had oiled the hinges – and he stepped outside. It was snowing and he kept to the edge of the path although flakes were falling fast and soon all sign of him would be erased. On the street, he paused to look back at the house that had been a home, its windows gold squares of welcoming light then strode away humming:

A time to plant and a time to uproot what is planted.

Jack disliked goodbyes.

Eighteen

Thursday, 13 January 2011

They were alone. The chilly receptionist, a woman in her late fifties, had gone for the night and in a casual tone Ivan Challoner invited Stella up to his flat for a drink. They were, he said, both off-duty.

That afternoon Stella had hired a recruit without vetting him to clean a space she had not seen; it would be sensible, she told herself, to inspect Jack Harmon's work, so she broke the handbook rule of not socializing with clients, and accepted.

She would not call him 'Ivan', despite his invitation to do so; she did not forget that clients were not friends however well she got on with them. If Terry had taught her anything it was to keep her distance. Mrs Ramsay had been no exception, she had assured Jackie.

As they mounted polished wood stairs, Stella tried again to identify Challoner's aftershave but could not. While he fetched drinks, she dabbed the surface and underside of a coffee table, traced her forefinger along the picture and dado rails, the skirtings and the rim of the door. Quickly she inspected behind the sofa: there was not a fibre, crumb or hair. With short dog-like sniffs she detected beeswax and tea tree. She did not imagine Ivan Challoner allowed dirt to accumulate. It was obvious that every object had its place: the gilt-framed mirror replicated a jade figurine of a winged horse set on the centre of the tall boy and on the walls paintings and etchings were positioned beneath discreet down-lights. Jack Harmon's skill had been to maintain this elegant precision.

Jack was the best cleaner Stella had ever hired and she reminded herself not to tell him this.

An unlit chandelier hung from a rose plaster moulding, droplets of glass trembling in the light of two Chinese table lamps. Stella disliked dim lighting: it hid bacteria and stains; however, tonight she was soothed by the crimson velvet curtains pooling to the carpet eliminating the hum of the South Circular. As in Challoner's surgery, the world beyond was far away. She sank among silk cushions on a sumptuous sofa and forgot about Paul. Her gaze took in dark green walls, plump plaster cherubs plucking mandolins or clasping single blooms emerging from the shadows. She forgot Terry too.

Rousing herself she got up and peered at a painting of fuzzy blocks. A label on the frame named the artist as a Mark Rothko, which meant nothing to Stella for whom art was a trap for grime and germs. The rectangles of mauves and black did not justify the beautifully polished frame although the indistinct shapes found echo in her throbbing jaw as the painkiller loosened its grip. As she retreated to the sofa once more she knew she would avoid offering comment on anything in the room. She was wise enough not to pretend expertise, and anyway, Clean Slate's handbook forbade staff to remark on a client's premises beyond a non-committal: 'This is nice'. *Cleaners are*, it instructed, *Agents of Change. A client does not want Clean Slate operatives to apply judgement, taste or prejudice while in their home or office. Cleaners are visitors. Do not forget that clients are our Hosts.*

No client wanted his or her life filtered through the wielder of a steam cleaner or carpet sweeper. Stella confined her assessment to how much a place cost to clean. Estimating the complexity of the work required to keep Ivan Challoner's plush sitting room intact, she fretted she had undercharged.

Ivan Challoner reappeared bearing a tray clinking with an array of glasses, bowls of pretzels and olives and a dusty bottle of Sancerre in a silver ice-bucket. He twisted out the cork, flourishing the bottle-opener like a practised barman. He held the bottle by its base and poured equal measures into sparkling glasses; then he proffered crackers that smelled of fresh baked bread and tasted deliciously of herbs and garlic. Stella was hungry but, anxious not to reek of garlic, had only one.

Ivan Challoner folded his long frame into an armchair facing the fire and crossed his legs at the ankles, displaying a glimpse of white skin beneath creased trousers. His shoes were polished like a police officer's. Stella drank the cool wine and deliberated whether a conversation opener would be to ask if he cleaned them himself.

Their conversation was in fact easy and flowing, any silences comfortable, as they swapped views on running a business, acknowledging the truth of the cliché that it was hard to find reliable staff. Nevertheless Stella was scrupulous in letting Challoner know that she succeeded. She snapped up the chance to assure him that circumstances allowing, he would have the same cleaner each session. He had remarked that he would be with patients when Mr Harmon called so would not meet him. Stella faltered: naturally he would not concern himself with cleaning. Perhaps Challoner sensed her discomfort for he added: 'However, it is reassuring to hear this. My receptionist was terribly taken with how your people bring their own vacuum cleaner. It saves battling with the temperament of our equipment.'

Placated, Stella remained vigilant; clients who kept a distance from the process tended to be disappointed and were not worth the nuisance they would become.

She gathered his children had grown up in this house when he mentioned a son's friend had been hit by a car outside the gate. There were no wedding or graduation photographs, which Stella guessed he would consider vulgar.

Challoner wore a thin gold ring better suited to a woman. She concluded he was a widower and that the ring must have been his wife's, which explained his reserved manner; it was grief. She had seen it in other male clients who had lost their partners. There were two kinds of grieving man. The first sort grew beards and lived in squalor and Clean Slate only encountered them when a busybody friend or relation hired them to restore order. She liked these jobs. The difference made was stark: month-old dishes were washed, carpets shampooed, sheets laundered and put back on beds in rooms light with air freshener within which the clean-shaven client could begin again. Stella used a rota of staff for these types because they were liable to propose marriage to anyone who ranged into their orbit. The other sort were more businesslike, demanding a seamless existence in which the hole made by the absent partner was filled by a continuation of the cleaning routine. They must step on shiny vinyl or varnished floorboards without disruption or distraction, barely aware of their loss. Armed with an anti-static cloth or a stringent stain remover, Stella believed that with her team she nullified death's impact.

Ivan Challoner was in the second group. Jack Harmon had maintained the order to the standards of his wife. Stella could not bear to think how he had managed until Jack's visit.

Set in a recess was a nightlight that had been burning when she came into the room. She had not seen Ivan Challoner light the candle. Jack Harmon must have done it. She felt a flicker of unease.

Ivan Challoner proposed a toast to Clean Slate and clinked glasses. He made a remark about Harmon being as 'elusive as the original' which Stella did not understand. Flames flared in the grate, sending sparks up the chimney; the room smelled of burning chestnut. In the pause as they drank, pockets of gas hissed and popped.

Stella was reluctant to return to the freezing streets.

Thick flakes were quickly settling by the time she gingerly made her way down the path. She struggled to her van, feathery shapes floating and spinning around her.

Fortified by the wine – she had kept to one glass – and once more lulled by Ivan Challoner's unruffled presence, Stella felt courage enough to attempt Terry's house. If she stuck at it, she reckoned she could complete it in a week. From Kew, she could be there in twenty minutes.

When she pulled into Rose Gardens North, the streetlight was out and the weather had deteriorated further. Butterfly flakes swirling against the windscreen disorientated her and she shielded her eyes from flurries that stung her cheeks, balking at going inside even for shelter. She could not face Terry's grey suits and starched shirts, the toe-to-toe shoes worn with the uneven tread that had given him back trouble.

There were footprints on the path.

Stella jumped back in the van and, skidding at the corner, parked it in a space out of view on the north side of Black Lion Lane. She would go to the Ram; it was Terry's local and in her mind was the illogical notion that her father would be there and she could give him back his keys.

Snow overlaid every horizontal surface casting a translucent light. Like death it was a leveller; time telescoped, changes and distinctions were lost under a white shroud. The footprints outside Terry's house must be the postman's, the one person who after death continued to visit. She hurried on, keeping away from the graveyard where black headstones trimmed with white recalled the gloomy rectangles in Ivan Challoner's painting.

A tangle of boxwood and holly etched with snow might have been picturesque, but Stella could not shake off the sense of being stalked. She had been off her guard and had not looked out for Paul when she left the dentist's. Suppose he had followed her from the office and waited while she was having the filling? He would have seen her go upstairs. Dancing flakes darted from the corner of her vision, she increased her pace and hastened over the grass, impacted snow squeaking beneath her feet. A hulking shape stood in the shadow of the church.

The statue was screened from the subway and the street by thick privet. When Stella was small, it had been in plain sight but bushes had already begun to obscure it in the case-file photographs and nowadays no one would see a little boy crouched beneath it. The Leaning Woman had become a secret known only to locals.

That afternoon, when she should have been sourcing a new

window-cleaner, Stella had researched the history of the Leaning Woman. On the Borough of Hammersmith and Fulham's website, she discovered that the sculpture was erected in 1959, seven years before she was born, to commemorate the new Great West Road. She had printed up a grainy black and white image of the unveiling ceremony; elderly men from the council in overcoats and trilbies on chairs by the roadside where she was now.

She checked there was no one behind her and slipped in through the gap in the hedge. Jonathan Rokesmith had sat as still as the statue until a policeman had carried him away.

A gust of wind whipped powdery snow against the brick plinth. In the lagged quiet, Stella's impression that she was not alone was stronger.

He swung Stella off his shoulders and lowered her on to the statue's knee. She was light as a feather, her skinny legs dangling. She wasn't scared of being up high. He worried the concrete would graze her, but she was calm as you like. Afterwards he wiped the river mud off with his hankie and put her boots back on. Her face was blotchy from crying.

'You're my Snow White,' he told her and pulled a funny face. That made her laugh.

Katherine Rokesmith had walked down the subway slope that last day. Stella skidded on the subway ramp and held the rail to steady herself, imagining the young woman walking hand in hand with her son. The chrome on the safety mirror was tarnished and already flecked with snowflakes so she couldn't see into the tunnel. She turned the corner; the passage was deserted. Welcoming the respite from the snow, keeping her breath shallow to ward off the smell of piss, Stella slowed down. With a 'toddler in tow', Kate might have ambled; the day had been scorching, she too had welcomed the shelter of the tunnel. The child might have shouted as kids did in tunnels, but with the traffic above as it was now, it was likely Kate had not heard him.

Stella coasted the slope, her legs trailing. There was chain oil on her dress. He had removed the stabilizers an hour ago and she was proficient in a jiffy. As a boy he had taken longer to get his balance. Hunched over the handlebars, she only braked at the turn, her back wheel lifting. She just missed the wall. Unafraid, she pedalled into the tunnel, getting up speed for the slope at the end. He couldn't keep up with her.

Someone was behind her. Stella spun around, her hands out in self-defence, but the passage stretched away, empty. At the end snowflakes floated, some creeping into the opening. Each time she reached the midway point between the ceiling lamps, her shadow disappeared and reappeared like a person pouncing. She risked injury and ran up the ramp on to Black Lion Lane.

She called Jack Harmon as she neared the Ram; St Peter's Church was striking nine when he answered. He sounded offhand and did not thank her for offering him a job. Stella intended her recruitment process – a lengthy form and an hour-long interview plus the trial in the office – to expose the value of the role and sift out the best. She had allowed Harmon to skip this but did not intend him to be lackadaisical about his success. If she had not seen the quality of his work, if Ivan Challoner had been less enthusiastic and if she did not have a staffing crisis, Stella would have withdrawn her offer.

If she did not want to be Ivan Challoner's cleaner, she needed Jack Harmon.

The Ram, once a modest hostelry for those working in the surrounding streets and on the river, was now the pub of choice of stockbrokers and lawyers. Little was genuine in the nineteenth-century building: sepia-toned photographs adorned oak-panelled walls that might be original, but coated in dark varnish appeared false. Stella was surprised Terry had been comfortable here; he disliked pretension and her mother said he had no time for tradition.

Three men, with the shiny complexions of the cut and thrusting, hair aggressively gelled, trim suits tailored close to the leg, perched on bar stools. They fell silent while Stella ordered an orange juice and a bag of salt and vinegar crisps. Three Pauls in a row: they were mute jackdaws angling for attention. Stella ignored them. When the barman tipped change into her hand she tensed against an impulse to fling the coins into their faces and inflict short sharp pain. They would have been babies when Kate Rokesmith was murdered, if they were alive at all; they had nothing to tell her.

The coin glanced off Stella's forehead. It must have hurt but when he asked her she shook her head. A mark appeared that would be a bruise. Like him she never fussed. He looked for the culprit, but the pool was crowded, kids bombing into the shallow end around them, splashing and shouting. If he spotted who had thrown it he wouldn't trust himself. Stella rubbed her head when she thought he wasn't looking. He plunged underwater and found the coin and, water splashing up, his eyes smarting with chlorine, presented her with a newly minted two-pence piece. She shook her head, this time vigorously. He dropped it into the ceramic gutter under the edge of the pool, meaning to get it to add to her pocket money when they got out. He forgot.

Stella sipped her orange juice and surveyed the room. She did not know where Terry liked to sit. Perhaps he would stay at the bar with the men, insinuating himself into their conversation, getting in a round as he teased out gossip and established facts. Wherever he went Terry sized up the regulars, took note of newspaper vendors, street-sweepers, postal workers; no humdrum daily activity escaped him. On his way to the toilet he would have found an excuse to engage the man doing a crossword in conversation. He would, as he put it, have neutralized him. When Stella was with Terry these ambushes had crippled her with shame and fury. Her mother said he was not naturally friendly; if he spoke to a stranger he was working. Stella wanted nothing to do with the men and women Terry enlisted; she shrank from the strawberry noses, leering eyes and greasy hair. While she sucked on the orangeade for which she was too old – he would not let her have a vodka – as Terry completed his business, Stella fumed at the caked foundation and cheap perfume and resolved never to descend into the unfathomable darkness of Terry's underworld, a place where livings were scrabbled for and the law was there to be wheedled, circumvented or broken. On sunlit pavements, defined by chalked hopscotch numbers, Stella's ambition to run a cleaning company was hatched. Leaping precisely from square to square, the teenager-still-a-girl determined how she would literally get rid of scum.

There were five customers in the bar, including Stella. The crossword-man had a bottle of wine and several glasses on his table; he was expecting company. Perhaps sensing Stella's gaze their eyes met and she made a show of scanning for somewhere to sit but he was looking past her to the door.

She chose a table beyond a chimney breast. Two buttoned wing-backed armchairs positioned either side of a gas-jet fire represented an attempt at intimacy. Stella slid along a pew bench. With her back to the wall she had the room covered.

Post was delivered in the morning. Stella put down her glass. It had not started snowing until the evening so the footprint on Terry's path was recent. She could not kid herself: it must have been Paul; large and clumsy, stomping and angry, he had been to Terry's house. She quelled the sudden knowledge that a good detective would have known this straight away.

She stared at the door; in her corner she was not immediately visible and could slip out the back way, but surely Paul would not come here. He knew she hated pubs.

She took a gulp of the orange juice and told herself that Terry was not a successful detective. He had not been able to prove that Hugh Rokesmith murdered his wife.

The door opened and an elderly man in a tweed car coat, heralded by a gust of snowflakes, stood aside to let his wife pass.

They made for the table with the wine bottle, where the man, presumably their son, was already on his feet pouring the wine without Ivan Challoner's laconic flair. His languor had vanished; he looked twitchy and anxious to please. He was to spend the evening drinking with his parents: an experience Stella would never have.

The envelope icon appeared on her phone, followed by six more. Seven texts.

Call me.

Where are you?

We need to talk.

Call me now.

The other three texts were notifications of voicemails all received while she was at Ivan's, when she had turned off her phone, and all from Paul. He had seen the paint he had advised for her bedroom on offer; they had not agreed he would decorate her bedroom. She had quite liked his choice – another sort of white – but that was all water under the bridge now. In the other calls, each lasting seconds, Paul did not speak, although she could make out his breathing. She set the phone to silent and, as if the handset were Paul himself, shuffled it behind the salt and pepper pots.

In the days since Terry's death her mobile phone had transformed from an imperative requirement to a dreaded enemy. Stella was frustrated at having to resort to avoidance tactics when she had left at four fifteen for the dentist. Jackie, generally discreet about how Stella arranged her life – she arranged the majority of it for her – had reminded her that she was not due at the surgery until five thirty. She fixed tight schedules so that Stella did not waste a minute. Stella's fumbled pretence that she had got the time wrong had not convinced Jackie: she never got the time wrong. After two months – Stella's longest relationship – Paul was wrecking her routine. She was right to finish with him.

This hastily constructed conclusion lessened Stella's lurking guilt at hurting Paul. She supposed she should eat; and consulted the 'specials' chalkboard on the side of the chimney. Yellow sticky-notes spelling 'Sold Out' curled next to 'Fish Soup with Rouille and Gruyère Crouton's' and the 'Rack of Lamb with Apricots'. Both were too fussy, she doubted Terry had gone for them, he would have opted for the gammon, eggs and chips. The sandwich gobbled before her dentist appointment lay like a sodden sponge in her stomach; Stella had no appetite, but as the barman neared her table at that moment, she ordered the gammon.

Ivan Challoner had said that red wine stained ivory if held in the mouth two seconds before swallowing. He allowed himself a couple of glasses of Sancerre a day; one had to have vices. Stella had feared this was a hint so said she rarely drank. He had told her she had marvellous teeth, no crowding, no gum disease. His own teeth were a flawless white.

She made room on the table for the case papers.

One article – from a folder of press cuttings Terry had printed from websites weeks before he died – described Jonathan Rokesmith as 'sitting with his chubby legs crossed, perfectly still like a little Buddha beneath the poignantly maternal statue of a half-naked woman'. A gift for journalists. The boy had shown no emotion and Stella was not surprised: at four he was too young to grasp the meaning of death, but might have cried at his mother's continued absence. If a parent was no longer there day to day it was upsetting but so far, from her reading, he had seemed unconcerned. Jonathan Rokesmith had flown at the constable who tried to carry him off, kicking and punching him, but never making a sound. He fought off his 'rescuers' in silence.

The boy's loss of speech went on for six months, broken briefly when one day with his father he had spied a red Triang steam engine in a shop and demanded to have it. When his father had refused, telling him he had enough toys at home, the boy did not protest and went quiet again. This episode, mentioned in the psychotherapist's report and somehow leaked to the media, earned the child the sobriquet of a spoilt only child. Despite liquid dark eyes and cutesy blond hair, 'Jonny' – as his mother had apparently called him – had, like his father, not won the public's affection.

Although her mother complained she had bought all her toys, Stella admitted to herself that had she wanted a toy in a window Terry would have given it to her; but then buying presents was easy.

According to the psychotherapist's account, Jonathan Rokesmith had not responded to hugs or attempts to kiss him and arched his back when touched, preventing people getting close. In a brown envelope Stella found psychiatric facts lifted from the web in Terry's handwriting. At the end of the page he had scribbled the inadequate reference: 'Google, Sept 2010' followed by: 'Kids are resilient. If they re-enact a traumatic event, firing guns, mimicking witnessed behaviour of criminals, don't discourage. Does not mean without feeling. Not necessarily reliving or repeating damage.'

Terry had no idea about children. Stella's gammon, egg and chips arrived.

Behind her plate she propped up pages Terry had stapled together from a newspaper dated 12 October 2007, inadvertently adding a squirt of ketchup to the stains already there. In the centre of the front page was a photograph of the Pont de l'Alma tunnel in Paris, closed for the 'Diana' inquest jury to visit her crash site. They had arrived in a three-coach convoy flanked by police outriders. Stella had thought the exercise a waste of time and money. What could they find after ten years? The jurors were: 'as ordinary a bunch of people as you might find on any station platform'. A line of suited men descended into the 'Tunnel of Death' like an imported rush hour. Terry would not have been out of place, she thought, searching the text for a clue as to why it was in Katherine Rokesmith's murder file and finding none.

The door opened and this time a man in a black pea jacket like Paul's shouldered into the bar. His hair glistening with snow was darker than Paul's and he was thinner. While the barman poured him a whisky he looked at Stella. She returned to her food.

The jury had visited the bedroom in the Ritz where Diana ate her last meal and had gathered in the tunnel to examine the dents made by the Mercedes on the thirteenth pillar in the central reservation. Stella cut out a square of gammon; loaded her fork with two chips mopped in egg and, as she chewed, appreciated how reproduced images and faded type were a poor substitute for being on the spot. The media attention, quick-fire camera flashes lighting up bystanders, the hum of halted traffic and clatter of helicopters must have whipped up a sense of the frenzy ten years before, helping everyone to step back in time.

She slid aside her half-eaten meal and found her Filofax in her rucksack. Jackie was no longer managing Stella's diary; Stella herself had cancelled two appointments with potential clients, three with suppliers and hopeful reps. In a short time, her business had stopped being Stella's entire concern and she had turned her attention to the cold case. In addition to the columns in her notes about the Rokesmith murder, she had created sub-categories (suspects, victims, neighbours, geography) into which she put key points and timings, alive to any inconsistency, error or vital nugget that Terry had missed or a significance he had not appreciated. Once she had finished the boxes she had brought from Terry's, she would have to return to his house if she wanted to read more. She dismissed this thought.

A chair scraped. The man with a jacket like Paul's had sat at the next table. He had the pick of the pub and could have gone anywhere. Stella returned to her reading: she had guessed what the Diana article was doing in the file. Kate Rokesmith was murdered two days before Diana married Charles. Both women had died violent and premature deaths leaving young sons motherless. Kate died hours before Diana was apparently beginning a happy-ever-after existence and Diana had died on the day that Terry became Detective Superintendent.

Stella had placed her examination of the files at the level of proving a point, an achievement to wave at Terry. *I'm a better detective than you.* But as she studied Kate Rokesmith's smiling face, the even features and perfect teeth unstained by wine of any colour, she was overtaken by a determination to bring Kate's killer to justice as once, years ago, Terry had promised to do. She would avenge the murder of a woman who was not after all a rival for Terry Darnell's affections. Kate had not known or cared about Terry and had not hurt Stella. Blameless and unknowing, one sunny morning in London, Katherine Rokesmith had gone for a walk with her toddler in tow and died at the hands of the husband she trusted to love her.

An obsessive, Terry had duplicated the huge file, determined to prove Hugh Rokesmith guilty even if it killed him.

It had.

She finished the orange juice and stuffed the documents in her bag. On this snowy night, like the fateful day itself, there would be no one about. The beach beside the River Thames where Kate's body was found was two minutes away. Despite the late hour Stella would go to the river to see for herself where Kate's life had ended.

Nineteen

'Now it's my turn,' Justin breathed.

Simon's eyes stared at something behind Justin's head. His shirt was hanging out, his black cat hair slick with sweat and dust; in the watery light his face was a skull.

'No one will find you.' Justin might have been attempting to reassure him.

Simon lay, a collapsed doll on the flagstones.

Justin clasped him, cradling his head on his lap. He tugged on the cord digging it into the skin and pressed the heel of his palm on the cartilage in Simon's throat, making him gurgle like a drainpipe. Justin was impressed so he did it again.

'Don't tease me.' He was elated by the success of his hastily concocted plan. Simon's head was heavy on his thighs. Fact: a human head weighs between eight and twelve pounds. He deliberated telling Simon he reckoned his head was nearer six.

'You will get into trouble.'

Justin thought that was what Simon said.

'I won't. My mummy and daddy are taking me away. No one will suspect me.'

Simon's right shoe had wrenched off and a big toe poked through his sock.

'Your *mummy* is dead.' Simon's voice was thick as if his mouth was full of rice pudding.

Justin's arms were aching from keeping the cord tight; he relaxed.

Simon jabbed his elbow into Justin's ribs and wriggled like a snake out of the loop.

The side of Justin's thumb was bleeding, the cord dangling from his fist.

'I write to her.' This closed the matter.

'They keep the letters in your file, the man told me.'

'What man?'

'The man I spy for.'

Simon had a red line on his skin like a necklace and looked like a girl. Observing this, Justin was unprepared when Simon lunged at him and too late tried to swerve. The Chinese screen folded over him like a dragon's wings.

Simon had the librarian's scalpel.

Jonathan knew the drill: remove all weapons or instruments likely to be employed in combat in advance of the approach of the enemy.

Simon was victorious in battle. Justin scooted back on his bottom until his shoulder jarred against Sir Stephen Lockett. At first he could not trace the source of the water. It pumped in an arc from the gap in Simon's trousers splashing on to his face. Too late he put up a hand to protect himself.

His legs apart and his shoulders back, as he shook off the last drops, Simon looked nothing like a girl.

Justin stumbled, slipping on puddling flagstones; in the passage he bashed against the tiled walls and lost his bearings.

She writes back! he yelled but heard no sound.

The glass in the back door was yellow from the lamp-post in the clearing beyond the wardrobe door; the hiding place where his mummy would find him once he tucked himself within the folds of her soft sable coat. He crunched on crisp snow, his cheeks stroked by the soft ferny branches of a fir tree; he was in Narnia.

I will get you.

Justin repeated the words to make them true.

I will get you.

Fumbling with the bolt, he could not block his ears and Simon's voice echoed along the tunnel.

'Your mummy was murdered and you ran away and let her die.'

Twenty

Thursday, 13 January 2011

Jack comforted himself: despite the rushed departure from his Hosts' house, he had not put a foot wrong. Around him houses were dark – many people went to bed early or drew their curtains against the elements and to keep out those with minds like his own. Only like-minded souls would be out tonight.

He dodged over the A4, between the pillars of the Hogarth flyover where snow blew like polystyrene pellets along the ground. The structure thundered above his head when cars trundled over it. Jack had no fears; he lived with the sense of abandon a tourist has in a foreign landscape that feels insufficiently real to be dangerous.

He stopped by a drain and pulled out his Hosts' door keys and the hammer. He wiped them clean of prints and posted them through the grille; far down he heard a plop when they hit the water. It was nearly ten.

He hurried by St Nicholas' Church where on other nights the sprawling graveyard tempted him in.

Not tonight.

Chiswick Mall had changed little in the last 150 years: from the mansions set back from the road, behind their walls came the smell of wood-smoke; outside, the muffled grind of carriage wheels and the clip-clop of horses' hooves seemed to carry on the wind along the riverside road. At high tide the river lapped on to the camber, strewing it with mud, splinters of wood and other debris. Not tonight.

It was low tide and the eyot at Chiswick, temporarily abandoning island status, was linked to the Chiswick Mall by a ragged causeway of stones. Jack's boots sank in dry snow and with difficulty he walked as fast as he could to the Bell Steps.

A door slammed on Hammersmith Terrace and a man limped up the middle of the road, leaving dragging prints. Stopping by a car, he pushed snow off the windows, front and back, and eased himself into the driver's seat. The engine purred into life and the car accelerated out into Black Lion Lane.

Jack stood in a dark patch of road left by the car. He was at the end of Hammersmith Terrace and on cue came the swell of voices and then quiet as the door of the Ram opened and creaked shut. A woman paused by the snow-topped picnic tables to do up her jacket and pull up the hood on her anorak, which would, Jack noted, hamper her side vision.

He shrank into a porch when she turned towards him, away from the subway. Although she braved solitary paths at night and took gratuitous risks, Stella Darnell was not like him or Michael Hamilton; she did not consider herself beyond harm. Like her detective father, she could not resist a challenge, so it would be with trepidation that, having checked no one was behind her, she made her way down the Bell Steps to the bank of the River Thames on a winter's night.

Jack gave Stella two minutes, then he went after her.

Twenty-One

Thursday, 13 January 2011

Stella had made her decision; she steeled herself to leave the pub. The man and his parents had already gone. The empty bottle and glasses took her by surprise; she had not seen them leave. Terry missed nothing, however trivial. The barman had disappeared and the three men had moved to a table.

In 1981 the doors and windows were open and the place filled with punters, but no one had heard Kate's screams or shouts from the river – if she had called for help.

Stella picked up her rucksack and passing the man in Paul's jacket glanced back to find he was looking at her.

It was still snowing and sharp gusts of wind were bitterly cold. Across the road was the house that she had read once belonged to people called Glyde. The mother was unlikely to be alive, she would be about ninety and the potter-daughter had probably sold up. Stella would check the phone list in the morning and if the Glydes were still there she would get the admin assistant to do a card drop in the street. It would be a way to get in, see what was what. Plus the potter might say something new. Jackie would approve, supposing it was for marketing purposes. If a job came out of it, all the better.

She paused to do up her coat and against her better judgement – for it felt tantamount to sticking a bag over her head – raised her hood.

A footpath along the bank was edged by a wall of arched windows draped with ivy heavy with clumps of snow. The wall was all that remained of a wheatgerm-processing factory demolished around the time Stella was born. Terry had complained about the smell of yeast in the mornings. Or had he? Stella had heard a radio piece about a study that found many childhood memories of events that adults hold dear have never happened. She had wondered how they could know this. She did not know what in her past had or had not taken place; she did not have cherished recollections, real or otherwise.

The pub sign – a ram with curling horns – was buffeted by the wind, the high-pitched squeaking eerie in the snowbound quiet. The clock on St Peter's Church's spire read ten forty. If she left now Stella could be home in twenty minutes; she could process Jack Harmon's details, compile tomorrow's To Do list, answer Jackie's queries – they had not had their morning meeting since Terry's death – and do her emails. Tomorrow she could cold-call the new mailing list and compile a recruitment advert. She could forget about Terry's unsolved case.

The steps to the river were muddy and unlit; it would be more sensible to come in the light, but that would mean a special journey. Since she was here she might as well take a look.

There were three steps up as a flood defence: an odd feature that Stella had seen before as if in a dream. The streetlight did not reach beyond them, so, edging into the inky darkness, she relied on her key-ring torch to make out terrain that although familiar from the photographs was quite different at night.

The tide had ebbed. This was lucky: she had not considered it might be in; she almost wished it had been so that she could legitimately leave. The torch beam did not extend to the shore. Out in the blackness water lapped, in and out, and the odour of river mud filled her nostrils.

She put the same boot down each time, nervous of falling, not moving until sure of her footing. In the daytime Kate would have had more confidence, oblivious of the danger awaiting her.

A hollow whistle, long and steady, carried out across the river. It reminded Stella of the sound she had heard on the motorway the night that Terry died and it chilled her to her bones.

Unsteadily she raked the beam in a lighthouse sweep across the beach. It caught the sundry detritus of snaps and splinters of wood and plastic, frayed and knotted coils of rope bound by a veil of scum. A muffled shape on the surface of the river drifted through the light. She heard the whistle again. Wind was passing over the neck of a bottle sunk in mud; Stella let herself breathe.

Seconds later a rush of wind unwound her scarf and ripped it from her and in a bid to catch it she teetered, sploshing in icy water, mindful that beneath its soupy surface the current was strong and unpredictable. She struggled up the slope and fell on to something that yielded beneath her palm: a car tyre trapped her foot.

'That's it. Lift it so it's under your arms. There. That was easy, wasn't it? Come over to the edge. When I say "Jump", you jump, OK? The ring will keep you floating. I'm here to catch you.' Stella held the ring obediently. It was the only one in the shop, and was for an older child. Her thin arms just reached over the sides. She jumped exactly when he said the word.

Behind her the wall seemed to pitch forward; the driving snowflakes were disorientated her. At her feet her torchlight caught stones, beer-bottle tops and drink-can rings. Here the lack of snow and sodden ground told her that the tide had not long been out. On a plank of rotting timber she distinguished 'KE P TO TH RI HT' in red where the paint had not flaked, the instruction fading as the snow fell faster. Too late she pulled the cord in her hood tight, for water had got in and was trickling down her neck.

She forced herself to focus on her surroundings. Behind her was the garden wall of the house where the two Glyde women had lived in 1981. It was about fifteen feet high and fringed with foliage, a bulbous white in the darkness. Next door a glass panel reinforced with metal replaced the trellis described in the report. There were no footholds on the wall; Kate would have had no means of escape. The Sergeant's report had stated that from the garden it was only possible to see the beach by leaning far over the wall. Stella was determined to see inside for herself; Terry had the right to go into the house but she had no such right. She would have to find a way.

Kate Rokesmith's body had been found close to the wall, hard by the steps. Stella had read how, other than the towpath on the south side, it was only possible – assuming there had been no one with binoculars on a boat – to see the beach from public gardens towards the bridge and from the yacht club pontoon. Except no one had.

The area was secluded and few people would know of its existence. The killer had to be local: with his flimsy alibi everything pointed to Hugh Rokesmith. It must, Stella guessed, have infuriated Terry that a guilty man was living his life unpunished.

She stepped out of the shelter of the retaining wall and was hit by a squall; snow blinded her and stung her cheeks. Her hand could not find purchase on the slimy brick and she dropped her key-ring torch. The wind made a sound that was almost human and smacked at her anorak.

With her hood up, Stella did not hear the scrape of shoe leather on the Bell Steps.

At just after ten o clock, the flood tide began at London Bridge. In a few hours the river would fill and water would wash over the snatch of land near the Ram and engulf the first five of the Bell Steps. The snow would slide off smooth granite and float off in the icy water.

Not all movements were tricks of the eye.

A crunch of stones. A tin was kicked. A dark shape glided over the mud; there was the sound of shoes squelching and releasing with a voluble sucking.

A light swooped down and was extinguished.

Stella fumbled for the torch, her hands slathered with snow and mud. Her fingers grazed the spindle of a key. She snatched for it, missed, tried again and grabbed the bunch. It jingled and gave away her position.

She was out of sight and earshot of the lane where there were few passers-by anyway; by now the pub had closed. The three men, heading for the subway, would not give her a thought. If she shouted, her voice would be lost in the wind.

The steps were not the only way up to the road. She could go along the beach to Chiswick Eyot.

Someone was standing on the spot where Kate was murdered.

Flakes flew at her like flies and, reckless, she plunged into the darkness. All the time the snow fell silently around her, covering the ground. Stella wrenched back her hood. She could see no sign of the eyot: she had underestimated the distance. Twice she splashed into water, veering into the shallows – or was the tide coming in?

If she could get to the eyot she could double back to the Mall and slip up a side street to the van as she had on the day she bent her mudguard. Was it the same man? She wished for her bike now.

Keep to the right.

The snow camouflaged dips and drops in the ground and she nearly turned her ankle, her boots heavy with freezing water swilling around her, slowing each step. The tide was almost to the wall, the water deeper. If she went further she would be cut off. She had no choice but to go back.

She saw nothing but dark feathery shapes pursuing her and struck out for the river. He would expect her to keep to the wall. Again her boots were submerged and she could not avoid splashing. He would hear. Careless of where she stepped, keeping the hazy image of Hammersmith Bridge ahead, she struggled forward.

Above the pounding of blood in her ears she heard him, jumping and hopping from one stone to the next in the furred darkness, heading her off.

She could see the Bell Steps, but in the driving snow they got no nearer. She had lost her scarf, her neck was cold and above the gentle trickle of the approaching tide washing over the stones, her anorak swished with each step, marking her position.

Breath, sour with alcohol, warmed her cheek, hands held her tight and frogmarched her to the wall.

Stella saw Jackie at her sunlit desk – the only person who would care about where Stella was – before absorbing the numb realization: *It's over.*

Twenty-Two

Thursday, 13 January 2011

'Why are you here?'

Stella braced herself. She could not struggle: his grip was like iron. Water lapped around her ankles, a continual running like a tap; she clung to the sound to blot him out.

'Answer me.' He shook her. She bit her tongue as her jaw clenched.

'It's none of your business.' Wrong answer.

'It *is* my business.' He let go, brushing his sleeves as if he had 'dealt' with her. In the half-dark of the intermittent moonlight he rubbed under his chin with the back of his hand.

Paul.

'You frightened me!'

He stroked her face. Then closed in, his coat collar tickling her ear he went to kiss her, his tongue pushing between her teeth. Stella shoved him away but he pressed himself against her.

'I love you, Stella,' he bleated into her neck. 'You haven't answered my calls. I miss you.'

If only he weren't so sensitive. Her fear gone, Stella was furious. Paul had ruined the operation: she had been close to seeing what it had been like for Kate and a few minutes more might have got it, but the image was fragile and Paul had destroyed it.

'You deliberately scared me.'

'You knew it was me, you saw me when you came out of the pub. What are you doing here? Who are you meeting?' His words fizzed though his teeth.

'No one.' Stella heard the guilt in her reply. Even if she had owed

Paul an explanation, she could not explain why she was there: he would not believe she was meeting a dead woman. He had never believed her when she worked late in the office or subbed for her team and he quizzed her about every client. When she had made the mistake of telling him about Mrs Ramsay sending herself flowers, he had sent a bunch to the office every week until she said it would be over if he did it again. Jackie said Paul loved her.

'I saw you talking on the phone. What happened? Did he stand you up? Sitting there with your eye on the door like a lovesick kid. Who did you ring?' Paul was in tears now.

'You've been spying on me.' His crying meant she couldn't be angry with him.

'I won't be made a fool of.'

'You're not a fool, Paul, I don't think that, but please go.'

'So you can see Lover Boy?' He did not move. His efforts to sound threatening were impotent. Jackie would feel sorry for him. Stella told herself that she did not feel sorry for Paul.

She tried to conjure up Ivan's room with its spotless surfaces, tasteful objects and subdued lighting. Ivan would deplore such a scene, so far removed from Beethoven and Mark Whatsit. Mrs Ramsay would have dealt with the Pauls of this world with a tip of the hand while she whirled around her dining room clasping the vase of lilies like a lover. Stella's shame redoubled. 'I'll call the police. This is stalking.'

'Call Daddy?'

She had never seen Paul like this and was thrown. He *was* stalking her. Women were killed by possessive ex-partners who would not take no for an answer. Paul had rung her bell the previous night, he had been outside Terry's house, he texted and called her every hour. He had come to the office, left her heavy breathing messages and now he had attacked her. Stella felt afraid.

'Let's talk tomorrow.' A concession she had no intention of keeping.

'And leave you to betray me?'

'I'm not betraying you.'

'He's stood you up.' He was vicious.

'For the last time, I am not meeting anyone. I need space, time alone.'

'Oh, please! Alone here? Don't give me that shit. We love each other. Let's go home and talk in the warm.' He put out his arms. 'You're grieving; you're in shock about your dad.'

He seemed to have forgotten that a moment ago he had taunted her about Terry. He was losing his mind. Stella edged towards the steps. 'There's nothing to say, Paul, leave it. Go to bed—'

'A woman was once murdered here, did you know that? No, you didn't. I was there! I watched them drive her off in an ambulance.'

Stella stopped. 'What do you mean?'

'I remember it.' Cramming his hands into his jacket pockets, Paul went on: 'I was on the mini-cabs then and working in the area. The cops interviewed everyone at my firm except me because I wasn't on the books, doing a favour for a mate.' He did his braying laugh. 'Your dad was in charge, but he never talked to me.'

Stella clenched her teeth to stop them chattering. She had not known Paul had driven a cab: he was a computer engineer now. He would have been twenty-five in 1981. Jackie would say Paul was not capable of murdering a mouse.

'Why didn't you come forward?' Jackie knew nothing about Paul; nor, Stella realized, did she.

'Interested in me now, are you?' He grabbed her by the shoulders. 'How long has this little affair been going on?'

'I'm calling the police.' Stella wriggled free and patted her pockets for her phone but it was not in any of them. Despite the cold, she was sweating. She must have dropped it on the stones. It would be under water; if not, then buried in the snow. Her only hope of locating it was to ask Paul to ring her number.

His face was lit from below with a greenish glow; his jowls hung heavy; his eyes were cavities.

The light came from her phone.

'What will you use to call them?' He sounded pleasant, even interested. Stella did not recognize him.

'Where did you find it?'

'You left it in the pub.' He tutted. 'Anyone could have nicked it. Imagine losing those confidential numbers, all those contacts. I'll say this, well done for emptying your text boxes.'

'Oh, Paul, don't do this.' Stella was tired. 'Let's meet for coffee after work and talk.'

> *'Today we have naming of parts. Yesterday,*
> *We had daily cleaning. And tomorrow morning,*
> *We shall have what to do after firing. But today,*
> *Today we have naming of parts...'*

Stella cast blindly about, but could not tell from which direction the voice came. Nor could Paul. He wheeled around sharply, stumbling. Stella snatched the phone.

She smelled smoke: roll-ups. She knew the distinctive brand although couldn't place where she had smelled it. The voice intoned:

> *' ... Japonica*
> *Glistens like coral in all of the neighbouring gardens,*
> *And today we have naming of parts.'*

A figure was pacing the stones near the wall with sure-footed ease, the words – intimate in the snow-blanketed air – enunciated like an actor, every syllable stressed, each emphasis precise. Stella could make out only that he was tall and thin.

Her tongue stuck to the roof of her mouth, a swollen dead thing, and she bit down on it to summon saliva. The pain focused her.

'He was at your office.' Paul gestured at the man. 'You're meeting *him*. I was right!'

'I don't know who he is.' But she did.

The way he was moving, his steps economic and sure like a dancer, crazily reassured her.

Soon Stella was picking out stones of the right shape: not too big with flat sides. She grubbed them out, not caring that her hands were getting dirty.

'You're a mud lark,' he told her.

'What's a mud lark?'

'Long ago, kids your age would roam the shores of the Thames on the lookout for bones and lumps of coal to sell for fuel.'

She stared at the place where she had thrown the stone into the water and said it was dead and gone forever.

'Stell! You come out with the funniest ideas.'

One day she would ask a question he couldn't answer.

'So, *Paul*, I gather you're not wanted here.' Jack Harmon had his back to them.

'I'm not leaving her here with you.'

Paul's speech was slurred. Stella could tell that he was frightened and wanted to comfort him. The feeling was fleeting.

'Oooh, I think you will leave.'

Harmon trudged over to them. It might have been a summer's morning, the sun beating down, not a cloud in the sky; he gave no sign of feeling the cold.

Paul lunged at Harmon and in moments, after some swiftly executed moves, Harmon twisted Paul's arm behind his back and held him fast from behind. Stella had seen Terry do it to a man not unlike Harmon in an alleyway off Hammersmith Broadway, when he broke up a fight on their way to her ice-skating lesson in Queensway. The restraint was a police manoeuvre for a person resisting arrest and every time Paul struggled, Harmon hitched his arm up a fraction, which she could see was causing Paul excruciating pain. She was astonished: it seemed Paul's judo classes had done him no favours.

'When I let go, you will go away,' Harmon whispered into his ear.

On the steps Paul turned back to Stella. He dared not ask her to go with him, but obviously hoped she would. Impassive, she watched him mount the steps. Jack was beside her, the tip of his cigarette glowing in his cupped palm. Nonchalantly he drew on it.

'I did that at school,' he remarked.

'Self-defence?' She coughed, her throat felt constricted as if it had been compressed, although Paul had not touched her.

'Naming of Parts.'

Terry said that killers often came back to the scene of their crime.

The clinking had stopped: the bottle had floated off on the incoming tide. The river was nearly at the steps.

Kate Rokesmith had known her killer so did not run. Up to the last moment she trusted him not to hurt her. Had Paul followed her, or had he been here already?

'You OK?' Jack flicked the stub away. It hit the ground with a hiss and the light went out.

'Paul's harmless. He wouldn't hurt me.' She would not discuss her private life with an employee.

'He will be back. Guys like that, they don't give up and he wants you.'

Unlike some people who smoked roll-ups, Jack's clothes and hair did not smell of tobacco. Stella caught shampoo, washing powder and soap on the cold air.

'What are you doing here?'

They were climbing the steps, treading on soft snow.

'I knew you would be here.'

'That wasn't my question.'

'That was my answer.'

He had not sounded surprised when she rang, as if he had been expecting her call. Tonight he had known she would be here. She had given him a job. Had he known she would? She should feel afraid of him, but strangely she did not.

'Have you learnt anything tonight?'

All the lights in the pub except one above the sign were off.

'What do you mean?' Stella knew what he meant.

'You're here because of the Rokesmith murder.' He kicked up snow, making a black scar in the road.

'How do you know?'

'Why else would you be here at this time of night? Oh, and you were looking at the papers when I visited your office and I dare say in the pub just now.'

'This is none of your business. My dad has died, I'm clearing out—'

'You're on a mission to solve the case for your old man. Nice sentiment, although I'm not sure Paul sees it that way.'

'I'm clearing out Terry's house. There's no mission.'

'Not fast enough, according to your PA.'

'Have you been talking to my staff?' Stella was stunned. Jackie had never betrayed her.

'She has told me nothing; she's quiet as the grave.' He walked in long strides, bouncing on his heels.

'I'll pay you what I owe you.' Stella was gruff. They went down the ramp into the subway. Jackie would tell her not to trust this scruffy man; he was too full of himself. His next words underlined this.

'I'm the best cleaner you've ever had.'

'No one is indispensable.'

'We both know that is not true.'

In the tunnel Stella had to take extra steps to keep up with him, their footsteps echoing.

'We match perfectly. Your Paul sees that. I know how people live, when they piss and shit, when they make love; if they never make love. I know when they are having affairs, keeping secrets; living a lie. I know about those who are sick of their partners and those who are sick of themselves. I know what they are thinking and I know what happens next. You need someone like me. When I clean, I see things.'

Jack stopped.

'Are you saying you know who killed Kate Rokesmith?' Stella tried to keep her breathing regular. It could not be him, despite the poetry and the coat; he didn't strike her as the type.

'I have no idea, but together we might find out. We would make a good team.'

'There's no basis to think that and anyway why do you care?'

'I don't care. I like puzzles. Why do you care?'

'I don't care either.' Stella directed her key at her van and the locks shot up.

'I'll come to yours in the morning and see where you're up to in the files.'

'I can manage on my own, thanks.'

'It'll speed things up if there's two of us.'

'No, you're all right. Like I said, I'll manage. Thank you.' Only when she reached the traffic lights where the old Commodore had stood did Stella realize she no longer had her scarf.

Jack watched until Stella had driven away and then returned to the church. Pushing through the bushes, he sat with his back to the Leaning Woman. Sheltered from the snow by sycamore branches overhead, he struck a match into his hand and lit a roll-up.

In the shadow of the statue, he stroked the London street atlas in his pocket. The end was in sight; he only had a few pages to walk. This was not good for so far the journeys had led him nowhere.

He had not known of Stella's existence until he read about her father's death in the paper and saw her name; it explained the dark house and the missing car. He should have realized that the one he needed was the detective's daughter. It must be someone methodical, who did not let emotion interfere with their thinking and would worry at the problem like a terrier with a lamb bone. Stella Darnell was that someone.

While Stella arranged ideas logically and was focused and ordered, he depended on intuitions and dreams to make signs out of numbers and chance events and divined messages out of random words.

Stella would need to be in charge; he liked that about her. He must not act too soon. If she were not in control, he would not get the best out of her. She was not especially perceptive; that would be his job.

He got up and rested his cheek against the sculpture's concrete flank. Under the sycamore and in the shadow of St Peter's Church, she was dusted with only a light coating of snow; he brushed it off.

Jack knew what Stella had been thinking when she drove away. She had sized him up and, although dubious, was interested and would trust him. Until it was necessary, he would not let her glimpse what he was really like. He knew too that she did not think he had killed Katherine Rokesmith. That she would reach that conclusion in the face of so little evidence was what attracted him.

Smiling to himself, Jack ground his cigarette out on the plinth. He blew on the mark and pocketed the stub. He would like to tell Stella that whatever the evidence it did not mean he was incapable of murder.

Twenty-Three

Friday, 14 January 2011

The buzzer went. Stella flicked a dishcloth over the counter and draped it on the dish-rack. She stopped to straighten it unhurriedly; it would be Paul. She would let him in and get it over with. She dried her hands and squirted a bead of hand moisturizer into her palm from a wall-mounted dispenser. On her way through the sitting room, she did an unconscious sweep for anything she did not want him to see. The files. She scooped up the papers, crammed them in the boxes and put them behind the table next to her rucksack. She decided to leave her laptop; it gave nothing away.

Apart from the furniture there was nothing else, although Stella did not consider that the picture-less walls, uninterrupted grey carpet, and bland, blond furnishings would reveal more to any visitor than an empty coffee mug, pieces of opened post or a battalion of ornaments could. She nudged a coaster in line with another.

Paul had his back to the security camera lens almost out of shot. Stella spoke into the receiver: 'Hello.' She released the lock; the figure vanished and through the intercom she heard the thud of the lobby door.

A rat-a-tat-tat inches from her face made her jump and instinctively retreat along the passage. Paul had run up the stairs. Not for the first time she was grateful there was no letterbox. She regretted letting him in. He did not knock again, but he was still there. She pattered back to the door and squinted through the spy hole.

She was staring at Jack Harmon.

She opened the door suddenly and was gratified to see him start with surprise.

He was dressed the same as the day before: black wool trousers, a black polo neck and a baggy black jacket draped from his thin frame as from a hanger. His leather shoes – Crockett & Jones' Oxfords – surprised her for despite scuffed toes and frayed laces they lent substance to the unkempt appearance.

'I said not to come.'

'I've brought your scarf.' He hung it on a hook in the little vestibule by the door and stalked past her down the passage, behaving as if he was at home. Stella hurried after him into the living room.

Landing with a crash, like a small boy, Harmon sprawled on the sofa, one leg dangling over the arm, the plastic covering protesting as he wriggled to get comfortable. Although he had shaved and washed his hair, she was relieved that Ivan Challoner was unlikely to meet him and hoped that any encounter would take place after she had issued Jack with his Clean Slate uniform.

At nine Jackie had rung to relate what she had missed at work the day before. Stella told her she would be sorting out Terry's house which might go on until Monday so would take no calls. She wanted to say this applied particularly to Paul, nor must Jackie take pity on him and make him tea in the office, but could not bear to say his name or think about him. Jackie had been pleased that Stella was getting on with her father's things and had offered to help, which made Stella guilty because she had never lied to Jackie. Now it occurred to her that were Harmon to attack her, no one would know he had been here. No one would hear and the flat, equipped with every cleaning agent, was an ideal space in which to erase all trace of violent crime. She dismissed the thought.

'What's the point of this?' Jack slapped the plastic on the sofa.

'It protects the fabric. Look, thanks for bringing the scarf, but—'

'From what?'

'I'm sorry?'

'If you never take off the cover, it's a plastic sofa.'

'Now you're here, do you want tea or coffee?' Stella had bought the sofa at a good price simply for sitting on. Plastic could be wiped down and she would do so after Jack Harmon had gone.

'I don't drink tea or coffee.'

'Let's get to business then.' Stella pulled out a chair from under the dining table and reached down for the file boxes.

'Please could I have a glass of milk?'

In the kitchen Stella poured half of what little was left in the pint container into a glass and took it back to Jack. He drained it in one go and wiped the milky moustache off his upper lip with the sleeve of his coat.

A film of condensation on the window pane merged the sky, the river, the trees and the snow into a stratified white-grey mass. With a plastic squeak, Jack leapt up, holding the empty glass and rubbed the pane with the milk-stained sleeve. Through the porthole the only movement in an otherwise static scene was a cyclist speeding along the towpath on the far bank. This angle was unfamiliar to Stella; she was never here in the day and, preferring to eat at the kitchen counter, had not until now sat at the table.

'This isn't everything surely?' It was not a question. Harmon settled himself at the head of the table and waved a hand at the two boxes beside Stella's laptop.

'The rest is at the house.'

Harmon sighed. 'Have you been through them?'

'I read the docket which contains the report Terry wrote, and an index to the papers with a front sheet listing reasons officers gave for signing the file out of the General Registry.'

From the depths of his overcoat Jack Harmon produced an envelope of tobacco bound with an elastic band and set about rolling a cigarette with nicotine-stained fingers while he read.

He laid the completed cigarette in a slim silver cigarette case where three others were already in a row and read on. Soon he had made six cigarettes and had nearly finished Terry's report. He was fast. After a bit, without taking his eyes from the page, he shrugged out of his coat, letting it fall over his chair. Stella wanted to hang it up in the hall, but was not keen to touch it.

She took out some papers from the second box and prepared to work, but he had her notes and, besides, she couldn't concentrate. The angular pale man was like a ghost in her flat, the bleak morning light emphasizing his cheekbones and racoon circles around his eyes. He scanned her pages of neat script, sniffing at intervals.

A box of tissues lay beside a flat-screen television and DVD player on the shelf unit. Next to these were various illustrated books on plants and flowers that, despite her having no garden, Terry kept giving her. Stella fetched them and put them beside Jack but he ignored her.

'You have been thorough,' he murmured eventually. It had taken him twenty minutes, and still disgruntled at him being there at all Stella was tempted to test him.

'So you are carrying on where your dad left off?' He rolled another cigarette although the case was full. Suddenly Stella knew where she had smelled the tobacco before.

She dragged her rucksack out from under the table and found the plastic bag in one of the many zipped side pockets. She shook the squashed cigarette end out on to the glass top.

'You've been to Mrs Ramsay's.' She managed a whisper. 'You were in her house. I thought this was hers.'

Jack licked along the strip of paper with a tongue coated yellow, and looked at the filter. 'Yes, that is mine.' He shot her a boyish grin. 'I was using it as a bookmark.'

'I assumed she was going mad when she said someone was there.' Stella gripped the sides of her chair. 'She was telling me about you. I ignored her.' She swallowed hard.

'I wouldn't beat yourself up. Isabel lived in another time and I literally "played" along. She was happier with men and children. You gave her what she wanted too.'

'I was supposed to be there, I was invited.' Mrs Ramsay had not invited her; she paid her on a monthly basis to be in her house.

'So was I. The difference being, no money changed hands.' He was haughty.

'The police think she was murdered.'

'Since when did you believe the police?'

'There'll be proof you were there, a fingerprint, a—'

'A cigarette rich with DNA?' He flicked the butt at her. It spun over the polished wood and landed in Stella's lap. 'The book was a message for you. I was too clever there, it was lucky you turned up when you did.'

'What are you talking about?'

'*Our Mutual Friend*, but you ignored the sign. I realize now that the direct approach works better with you.' He gave a throaty laugh.

'She said she heard doors creaking, and the fifth stair, and she fretted about children playing: in the basement, the garden. She got scared – and all the time it was you.' Stella remembered how Mrs Ramsay had been tormented by losing stuff; she had tried to tell Stella but Stella had humoured her and congratulated herself on doing a few extra hours for nothing. Mrs Ramsay had known she was being mollified; she never waved goodbye.

'We can't work together if you break the law.'

'I was invited. How is that breaking the law? Besides, you're not so squeaky clean. Compromising a crime scene? When did you plan to hand this evidence to Cashman? You shouldn't even have been there, but hey, special treatment for the detective's daughter! As I said last night, we are a match.' He brandished Terry's report: 'Did you see, your dad was the last person to take the file out.'

'Yes.'

'Monday, the twenty-second of June 2009 at three p.m.'

'He retired on the Friday of that week.'

Jack sniffed. 'It must be when he copied it.'

'He would have had to give a reason.'

'Says here that he was going to see the man who found the body: a Charles Jenkins.' Jack was matter of fact.

Stella typed the name into Google, adding 'Rokesmith' to narrow the search.

'Jenkins died in 2010 aged eighty-five, he'd had Alzheimer's for fifteen years.' She pointed at her screen. 'Says he never got over finding her and took early retirement. Odd that Terry bothered talking to him. Kate was dead when he found her.'

'Jenkins might have lied. If you were a murderer, wouldn't a great way to deflect suspicion be to pretend you found the corpse of the victim you'd just killed?'

'Too much of a risk.' Stella wished the theory hadn't come to Jack so easily.

'Anyway, Jenkins was only Terry's excuse to see the files. He could have written anything, he was the boss, no one questioned him.'

'He stuck to the rules,' Stella snapped. Jack was right; she had been granted respect and leeway because of Terry. Cashman had trusted her: a trust that was misplaced; she would not help the police. Terry had been working alone: the rules he stuck to were his own. She did not say this.

Jack returned to the sofa and flopped down, scrutinizing the list. 'It was accessed in December 1992. Someone reported a blue Ford Anglia on the North End Road in Fulham. "The vehicle was registered to a sixty-four-year-old spinster resident in Munster Road. Miss Joan Fellows. She had bought a 1967 model second-hand in 1975 and in 1981 was deputy head at a primary school off the Fulham Road." So what?'

'That's the computer doing it's job: it is matching it with a blue car, possibly a Ford Anglia, seen by a witness.' Stella rifled through her notes. 'Mrs Hammond, aged seventy-four, coming out of Black Lion Lane that day. She was on the Great West Road going to the Broadway, so it was a glimpse. Might have been nothing, but it can't be eliminated until someone comes forward. The fact that no one has, despite the publicity, makes it likely to be suspicious. Hugh Rokesmith drove a blue car.'

'So?'

'It's clear Rokesmith did it.'

'Boring!' Jack jabbed at the plastic on the sofa. 'You've made up your mind. Why go on?'

'I was thinking the same thing.'

'Wasn't that why the police failed? Deciding the guy was guilty and forcing everything to fit their theory.' He sniffed. 'What about having an open mind?'

'There's no mystery. It's obvious he did it, motive, opportunity, means...'

'Motive? What did he gain? The police had nothing: he wasn't even on bail.' He poked at the plastic again. 'This is no fun, you're not doing it properly.'

'He remained a suspect. It says so.' Stella waved her notes. 'They had no evidence. His mother was his alibi; naturally she was protecting him. Hugh Rokesmith had a high-flying career, building bridges all over the world, all that was in jeopardy. She perjured herself to save her son's career.'

'His work dried up, and it's impossible to be in two places at once. The police got that right, yet still you think him guilty.'

'He left at ten thirty, what was he doing for forty-five minutes?' She batted at the box of tissues.

'Like it says here: sitting by Kew Bridge doing calculations in peace. He was a busy man, he rarely got time to himself.'

'We only have his word for that, no one saw him.' Terry knew Rokesmith had got away with it. 'I have a client in Strand on the Green; it takes a minimum of fifteen minutes to get there. Half an hour to plan a bridge? I don't think so!'

It had taken her slightly less time to drive between the two points but she would not give Jack's theory that Rokesmith was innocent ammunition; he was taking over.

'Maybe you'd like to explain why you broke into Mrs Ramsay's house.'

'I didn't.' Jack sucked ruminatively on the arm of his glasses and perused other papers. 'She was my friend. More than that really.' He looked up. 'By the way, why do we think you didn't murder Isabel?'

'What did I have to gain? I've lost a client. I will have to tell the police about you.'

'Can we stop? You have no time for your dad's army and you'd have to explain why you *purloined* valuable evidence. What do they call it… obstructing officers…?'

'… in the execution of their duty.'

'*Exactement!*' He put on a French accent and twirled his spectacles happily. 'Like me – like Terry – you prefer to work alone.' He shuffled the papers and Stella caught a trace of Terry's aftershave. 'You've changed the habit of a lifetime letting me help and we'll only succeed if we approach it like a, well, like a clean slate. Don't be high-horsey!'

Stella covered up a yawn. Over the last days she had slept little more than eight hours and hardly recognized herself. Her previous self would not have given the time of day to Jack, let alone allowed him into her flat. Terry's death had thrown everything up in the air.

'You have the mind of a forensic scientist. Like a detective you will leave no stone unturned.' Jack closed the cigarette case with a snap. 'Don't squander that with blinkered thinking.'

Harmon was right; she had made up her mind. Jackie said Stella jumped to conclusions. Her mother accused Terry of shutting his ears to any other point of view.

'What mind have you got?'

I have the mind of a murderer.

Her mobile rang and without meaning to she answered.

'Hello there, Stella. How are you on this Arctic Friday?'

She could not place the voice.

'It's Ivan Challoner. I do hope I'm not disturbing you.' His tone was intimate, the voice so close he could have been in the next room.

'I'm in a meeting, but it's fine, unless you're ringing to say I need another filling.'

'Your teeth are perfect! I hadn't thought of cleaners having meetings.' Paul would have made this sound patronising.

Stella stepped into the passage. 'You're not with patients?' Ivan was easy to talk to. Trailing towards the front door, she felt a coil of excitement.

'In a moment. The only promise I made to myself as a student that I have kept is not to work on Mondays or at the weekend. I'll be quick to let you get back: would you join me for dinner on Monday?'

Stella agreed to meet him at a French restaurant by Kew station. Unlike Paul's first suggestion of a burger, nothing in Challoner's manner implied it was a date. If he had been flirtatious she might not have accepted his invitation.

She returned to the room, her mood lighter, where she found the sight of Jack Harmon, leafing through her notes, his wire-framed glasses perched on his nose peculiarly reassuring.

'You lie with impunity,' he murmured.

'You should not be eavesdropping. Besides, I am in a meeting.'

He turned a page. 'I'm thinking it would be wise not to tell anyone about this, including your new man.'

'I wasn't planning to and Ivan Challoner is a client, as you know.'

Jack snatched off his glasses, an action that reminded Stella of Terry. 'Perhaps don't let that man – Paul – get wind of it. He was totally in the thrall of the green-eyed monster.'

'I won't see him again.'

'Like I said, he won't give up on you that easily.' Jack flapped the sheet he was reading. 'Isabel Ramsay was the last person to see Katherine Rokesmith alive. It's a coincidence her being your client and your dad's star witness. He never mentioned her to you? Did you seek her out?'

Stella did not admit that, despite reading the notes, until Cashman told her, she had not realized that Mrs Ramsay was so important a witness.

'Of course not. Her daughter contacted us initially; Mrs Ramsay was dead set against a cleaner. I never talked to Terry about work, his or mine. And if you were close, how come she didn't tell you?'

'She did,' he replied simply. 'Read this.' He pushed a slip of newspaper towards her.

It was dated Monday, 21 May 2007. Stella had missed it.

MURDERED KATE HUSBAND DIES

Hugh Rokesmith (65) lost his battle with lung cancer in Scarborough General Hospital yesterday. The civil engineer saw his career designing bridges and viaducts, predominantly in South-East Asia, dwindle after the murder of his wife in July 1981, almost twenty-seven years ago. Kate Rokesmith was found dead by the River Thames on the day that Diana, Princess of Wales, also destined to die young, rehearsed her marriage to Charles. Questioned by detectives, Mr Rokesmith, who in a BBC interview claimed he was 'utterly devastated', stated he was at his mother's birthday lunch two miles from where Kate's body was found. The couple's son, Jonathan (pictured left), who as a four-year-old may have witnessed his mum's death, is said to have visited his dying father in hospital. Believed to live in Sydney, Australia, he has refused to comment on his mother's murder, which a police spokesman has described as 'still an open case'.

'They are guarding against the son doing them for libel or they'd come right out and say Rokesmith did it. I found a website in the States that said a previously normal man is more likely to kill his wife if he finds out she's having an affair, especially if she was younger than him and good-looking. I've written it somewhere.' Stella picked up her notes. 'An affair can be the last straw.'

'What makes you think Katherine Rokesmith was having an affair?'

'I'm guessing. Like you said, keeping an open mind.'

'Let's stick to facts. For example, did you know that a bunch of flowers is always by Katherine's grave?'

The way Jack referred to Kate as 'Katherine' was getting on Stella's nerves, it made Kate distant and unreachable.

'How do you know?'

'It's here. Terry's put it in the margin of his report. It must be recent, he could not have known at the time.

Stella looked closer and, sure enough, there were the words with a date three weeks before Terry's death scrawled beside them. 'Flowers by grave, check.' She had read them before but had made little of it; flowers were often by graves, it was no big deal.

'Who's putting them there?' Jack asked.

'All we need to do is keep a watch on the grave.'

'They appear at odd times with no apparent pattern.'

'Have there been any since the husband died?'

'I'm presuming so, if you go by the date of Terry's marginalia.'

'That doesn't prove anything. It may not be the killer, it's more likely to be a cranky well-wisher. I clean for plenty of those.' Stella stopped. Harmon had not answered her question. How did he know that the flowers were *always* there? Her mobile telephone rang and this time Stella checked the number; although unfamiliar she risked it: 'Hello?'

'Gina Cross. The police in their wisdom say my mother had an aneurism. She was not murdered. My husband says I should sue, but it's paperwork and bother. So back to Plan A. I want your Platinum package as I see it includes outbuildings and attics. I want you to get going right away. Can you do that?'

'I can send a team there now, we'll go into the weekend.' Stella signalled to Jack to put on his coat. Languidly he slid two more newly made cigarettes off the glass table top into his case.

'I don't want to pay double time.'

'You won't,' Stella replied.

The buzzer went as they were leaving. Stella brought up the video and Paul's contorted face filled the screen, his mouth moving – with the intercom off they couldn't hear him – like a bloated fish pressing up to the glass of an aquarium.

'Is there another way out?' Jack was businesslike.

'Only the stairs which come out in the lobby.'

'A basement?'

'It will be locked.'

'Let's not make that an obstacle.' He shouldered his way through to the stairwell.

Less trouble had been taken in constructing the stairs and, racing down the eight short flights, their feet clattered on cheap tiles. At the ground floor they ducked below the window in the lobby door to avoid Paul seeing them and then took the last steps to the basement.

Jack tried the lever handle on a metal-plated door, but as Stella had anticipated it was locked. He groped under the alcove beneath the stairs and extracted a key dangling from a chain; he turned the key in the lock. When he depressed the handle again, it still did not move.

'Lift it?' Stella suggested.

He cranked it up forty-five degrees and the door gave way with a grinding shriek, tracing a rust-coloured curve in the stone. Stella stooped and rubbed it with her forefinger but it made no difference; it would need a stringent agent and could not be done by hand.

Jack removed the key and made the chain a bracelet around his wrist.

'What are you doing?'

'We might need it again.'

They were blasted by a fuggy heat when they went in and the dull hum that was ever present in the lobby grew loud. It came from a generator from which sprouted tentacles of pipes, some bare, others swaddled in silver; they were in the building's engine room. In the centre stood the lift housing with a door giving into the shaft. A grubby notice tucked into a plastic folder listed the date of the last service: five months ago. Judging by fluff and dust coating the pipes, Stella doubted anyone had been down here since. When she moved in she had suggested that the basement be included on the cleaning rota – she knew the value of cleaning what is rarely seen – her request was ignored.

Jack had disappeared. She walked around the lift and found another door. He was already halfway down a breeze-block-lined passage. After twenty yards it turned to the left and stretched ahead to a dead end. Stella fumbled with her anorak and did up the zip; the temperature had dropped considerably.

Recessed into the wall on the right was another door; when she reached him, Jack was unwrapping the key chain from his wrist. He turned the key and cautiously pushed the door. They were confronted by a blast of icy air and dazzled by the glare of snow. An icicle had formed over the doorway, a sharp blade pointing downward; they stepped to the side and found themselves in the garage compound. They crept to the corner of the flats.

They saw Paul attempting to get around the other side of the block, presumably for a view of Stella's kitchen. Any minute he would try their end of the building.

'You have to stop him.' Stella retreated and trod on Jack's foot.

'Me? How?'

In the stark daylight, Jack Harmon was paler still, lost within his black coat, puffing and stamping with cold. She worried that Paul would fold him up like a deckchair.

'Pretend you live here. Take these.' She stuffed her door keys into his hand.

'He'll recognize me.'

'No, he won't. It was dark last night and he was upset. He's crap with faces. Let him inside.'

'Into your flat?'

'Of course not. Go into the lift with him and get out at a lower floor. Come out through the basement or he'll see your footprints. Lock everything after you – and yes, keep the key.'

'You think he'll attempt to break in around the back?'

'Yes I do, he's not stupid. Now go or he'll find us both!'

Jack put his collar up and sweeping a hand through his hair walked around the corner.

'Oh, and Jack?'

'What.' He stamped a foot but did not look round.

'Try to be nice. It's possible Paul murdered Katherine Rokesmith.'

'How do you make that out?' Jack hissed.

'He was in the area at the time and wasn't interviewed.'

'Now you tell me. Anything else I should know?'

'Hurry!'

Stella watched Paul see Jack when he reached the path, sauntering towards him, kicking up scuffs of snow, the keys swinging carelessly, supposedly deep in thought. She noted that Jack Harmon was a consummate actor, giving no sign of having noticed Paul until he was at the door. Paul in the meantime had adopted the role of someone who had just arrived, exaggeratedly patting his pockets as if for keys. Apparently discovering that he did not have them, he hit the buzzer in the resigned manner of a person who hates to trouble others. He made instant way for Jack to indicate he did not expect to be admitted. Jack addressed him, as Paul must have known he would; in his work suit and staid Aquascutum mac he was every inch the man on legitimate business. Stella tried to hear the exchange. Jack laughed: a low modulated sound in the held silence. Then it seemed to her, peering along the side of the building, that the men walked like phantoms into the wall and were gone.

Stella grew cold and chilled further by creeping doubts; she shivered. She had given Jack her keys – what if he didn't return? Paul might recognize him from last night, and if he had been following her he would have seen Jack too.

She started towards the lobby. If she pressed all the bells she could get help. Except so few people lived here it was unlikely anyone would answer. Anyway, what would happen next if she did? Panicked, she raced back to the basement door. It was locked. Suddenly the handle shot up. She pressed herself against the wall behind the door desperately hoping that Paul would not see her.

Jack appeared and saw Stella immediately.

'You're supposed to be getting the van – he'll be here any second!' Jack exclaimed through stained front teeth. Irrelevantly Stella thought he should visit a dentist.

'You have the van key.' She snatched the bunch off him and, skidding on the slippery ground, made for the garages. Responding to the remote control, the door rose with a prolonged screech.

Jack took up position by the flats. There was no sign of Paul.

Stella started up the van and shunted the gearstick into 'drive'. The door shuddered its way down, narrowly missing the roof rack as she accelerated forward.

'He's outside!' Jack mouthed to her and then more urgently: 'He's coming!'

He grabbed the van door, wrenched it open and threw himself in, jolting against Stella. He reached out to shut the door but it slipped from his fingers and swung wide when Stella swung the van to the left. It slammed shut when she veered to the right and sped down the drive, the wheels spinning. Jack pushed through to the rear and fell against a tub of detergent. He crouched out of sight.

'Stella! It's me, Paul!' The shout broke the swaddled silence. 'Sto-op.'

She squeezed on the accelerator, driving as fast as she dared, the tyres slithering on the ungritted surface. Too slowly the drive gates jerked apart. Paul lumbered down the path, clumsy in his smart clothes, yet he was gaining on them. He cut across the lawn and floundered into the ha-ha. Stella braked, her instinct to help him.

'Keep going!' Jack shouted from the back.

She trickled the van through the entrance. In her rear mirror she watched Paul clamber out of the hidden ditch and resume the chase. They had to wait for a break in the traffic. Paul was ten feet away; Jack stretched over the headrest and activated the central-locking system. A lorry flashed its lights and, waving acknowledgement, Stella slung the van out, missing Paul's car by inches. He had parked it facing the other way and he would never catch up with them.

'He didn't recognize you?'

'He was chatty. Rather a nice man, I thought.' Jack struggled into his seat and did up the belt. 'He asked if I knew you. I said only by sight and that you were mostly at work so I hardly saw you. I acted suspicious of him, which shut him up, although he did say "Good to meet you" when I got out. He's a genuine guy.'

Stella drove on in silence.

Isabel Ramsay's hedge resembled a gigantic meringue. One end of the police tape fluttered in the wind. There was no one around and the snow on her path was untrammelled.

Stella turned off the engine. The church bells struck quarter to midday. She glanced at Jack, but he was busy with rolling another cigarette. He lined it up with the rest. Nevertheless, she wondered if he was thinking that it was exactly this time when Kate Rokesmith set off for the river with her son thirty years ago.

Stella kept Mrs Ramsay's keys on her own ring; she never knew when she might call. Chubb in hand she hurried up to the front door.

A bundle lay in the porch. Almost obscured by a drift of snow was a bouquet of white lilies.

Twenty-Four

Friday, 14 January 2011

Stella brought the flowers into the house. The snow on the wrapping paper was melting and soaked her fleece. The hall would have been more of a shock had she not seen it when she met the detective yesterday. The sprinklings of fingerprint powder made the room look dreary. Furniture had been shunted out from the walls; the spindly-legged hall table was in the middle of the room. Stella restored it to its position by the front door; when she lifted it a wave of exhaustion winded her. She listened for Mrs Ramsay's shuffling footsteps, but there was nothing. The clocks had stopped: with Mrs Ramsay dead and Stella absent for a week, no one had wound them.

She snipped off the stamens to avoid staining her fleece, stuffed the lilies in a water jug – Mrs Ramsay having broken both vases – and placed it in the dining-room grate.

Through the window, she saw Jack was on the path finishing his cigarette. On the way, they had detoured off the Hogarth roundabout to the river where at Hammersmith Terrace Jack had pushed a Clean Slate price list through the letterbox of the corner house. Stella had mined the internet and found that Sarah Glyde, the potter in the police interview, still lived there. If she did not respond to the card – which was likely – Jack said he had another idea. Stella put off asking what it was.

They stacked cleaning materials, rolls of plastic sacks, a box of latex rubber gloves and the vacuum cleaner in the hall. Stella sat at the kitchen table where she used to have her morning cup of coffee with Mrs Ramsay. She ignored the empty chair, unzipped her rucksack and produced a fresh spiral-bound pad with the new Clean Slate logo. Her heart lifted momentarily; she was back at work.

She allocated a room per page and by the time Jack had brought in the rest of the equipment she had a list of tasks with respective timings.

He stopped in the doorway. 'Where are the flowers? Her lilies? Did the police nick them?'

'Calm down! I put them in the dining room, where she likes – liked...' Stella ripped off the page with kitchen tasks and slid it across to him. 'You start in here.'

'Shall I make up some flatpack boxes and fill them with crockery and pans?'

'No, do as I've suggested: clean and put everything back.' Stella was stern. 'Restore order, then we'll take stock.'

Jack shrugged in acquiescence and glanced at her pad.

On her way out Stella stopped. Jack was retching. He was going to be sick on the floor. She grabbed his shoulders and shoved him over to the sink. The dead lilies were still there, rotten and foul-smelling; they had smeared the enamel and she scrabbled them out of the way. Jack heaved, gulping in air; he was ashen and blotches of red on his cheeks highlighted a bluish haze of stubble. His fringe swung forward and Stella reached around and tucked the longest strand behind his ear; she supported his forehead.

'Take deep breaths and look out of the window. That's it. In. Out. In. Out. Fix on the horizon.'

Eventually Jack straightened up. She poured him a glass of water.

'Did you eat breakfast?'

'I had milk.'

'Breakfast is the most important meal. If you have nothing else—'

'You're my mother now, are you?' He sipped the water. His face glistened with beads of sweat and he shook, spilling water down his wrist. Stella wiped it dry with her sleeve.

'You should eat.' She went into the hall and returned with her rucksack from which she produced an unopened packet of Rich Tea biscuits. Whipping the tab from around the top, she lifted off the exposed biscuits, four in all, and handed them to Jack.

She pulled out a jar of tea bags and a tin of powdered milk. Soon they were seated at the table, neither of them in Isabel Ramsay's chair, eating biscuits and drinking tea and, for Jack, hot milk.

'If we crack on with this today we'll get a lot done. I'll start at the top and we'll meet halfway by tomorrow evening. You are OK to work, aren't you?' She was brisk, filling further pages on her pad with columns and capitalized headings. Jack still had a horrible pallor and was sitting sideways with his face averted.

'What's the matter?' Stella was not good with illness; she did not tolerate it in herself.

'It's your stationery.' His hands were clasped between clenched thighs. She marvelled that he had scared off Paul, a heavily set man with a black belt in judo.

'What's wrong with it?' No one had criticized her branding, not even Jackie. 'Clients love it.'

'I hate it.' He chewed his bottom lip.

She could not bear it if he vomited; he had eaten a lot of biscuits.

'Don't tell me my logo is making you sick.' Stella had chosen the green and blue with the same level of consideration as stabbing a pin on a map; it might have been mauve or red.

'Pantone 375.' Jack uttered the words as if in a trance.

'Green I call it.' The designer had provided Pantone codes for the printers to be sure the colour was reproduced faithfully in different mediums: the light blue was Pantone 277 and Jack was right, the vivid green was number 375.

'How can a colour make you ill?'

'It always has.'

'You're going to see my logo all the time when you work for me.' Stella waved the pad, making Jack flinch. The masthead consisted of rectangles and squares, the green slipstream of one sweeping brush swishing across blue and green lettering. The logo was on pads for preparing quotes, letterheads, compliment slips and the vehicle livery – one van so far. The others would lose their staid black and white lettering next week.

Jack would have a set of polo shirts in Pantone 375 with *Clean Slate* embroidered in blue on the shoulders where the number is on a police shirt. If he had this reaction to a splash of green in a notebook, he would go into a coma when she made him wear the shirt. Besides reinforcing the brand, the outfit was precisely for people like him whose dishevelled appearance could put off clients.

'It's a phobia. You need to get it seen to because green's hardly rare. There's grass, trees, cars; it's everywhere.' She glanced out of the kitchen window at the snowy scene. 'Except today. This must be a gift!' Stella stifled a wry laugh, knowing better than to make an employee uncomfortable about a physical or mental condition.

'In fact this shade is unusual.' It was a portent but Jack kept this to himself. It was a year since he had seen the colour, when he had fainted in a chemist's and ended up in Accident and Emergency. He had given false details. He had a strategy: he visualized another shade because he could not afford for it to happen while he was driving a train.

Stella left Jack dealing with the lilies in the sink and started in the main bedroom. She opened the wardrobe and Mrs Ramsay's delicate perfume – like the evening scent of garden flowers – drifted out; she inhaled deeply. The wardrobe was in disarray, clothes off hangers and twisted or heaped on the floor. The hangers had tangled with each other and it took Stella twenty-six minutes – putting her behind schedule – to fold the garments and pile the hangers on the stripped mattress, before she could set to cleaning the wardrobe. Mrs Ramsay kept up a commentary urging Stella to direct the vacuum nozzle into the deepest recesses.

For the rest of the afternoon Jack and Stella worked without stopping or speaking to one another.

Stella had turned off the vacuum and was retracting the lead when she heard Jack's phone. She crept on to the landing and halfway down the stairs. The fifth stair strained when she put her weight on it; she lowered herself to the next one. Jack was in the hall speaking quietly. She did not risk going lower or he would see her shadow on the wall.

'I'm not due until the Dead Late... OK, an hour... Earls Court or Acton?'

She heard the click of his shoes on the floorboards and with no time to get back up the stairs darted into the drawing room where she was upset by more chaos. The ceiling-high doors dividing the room were flung wide to create a space the length and breadth of the house and the furniture pushed aside as if for a party. Stella found the cigarette box with the initials 'I' and 'M' on its lid under the coffee table, the contents spewed over the rug. She was on her knees gathering up the cigarettes when Jack walked in; he retrieved two she had missed.

'These are stale.' He sniffed them. 'I doubt the family wants them.'

'I'm tidying.'

'That was my mother on the phone. Family crisis, 'fraid I have to go.'

'What sort of crisis?'

'She's locked herself out. I have a key.'

Nettled, Stella looked pointedly at her watch. The wall clock by the tall boy had stopped at eleven. Her watch read five minutes to five; three minutes fast. They had been working for nearly five hours but she'd intended to go on until at least seven o'clock.

Jack's mother, it seemed, relied on him.

'Do you have to go far?'

'Only South Kensington.' Jack brushed his sleeves and trousers as if dust in the house was why he was shabby. Stella could imagine this mother: absent-minded and needy. She pictured a younger Mrs Ramsay who had Jack at her beck and call. The mother might be a problem.

'Do you need a lift?' Stella liked to know the background of her staff, meet their dependants; this was as good a time as any to see Mrs Harmon.

'Stamford Brook station is up the road.'

'You're OK on the Underground?'

'Why wouldn't I be?'

'What with your green thing, I assumed tunnels might be problematic, claustrophobia or moving fast.' She broke her rule about personal information to offer: 'My mother hates heights and haunts junk shops.'

'Trains are fine. It's only Pantone 375.'

When Jack had gone the house took on a new quiet and Stella decided after all that once she had put the sheets through the machine she would go.

She brought the bedding down and froze.

Jack had transformed the kitchen. The black and white tiled lino gleamed; the bus-like fridge and the grubby Bakelite wall telephone looked new. He had disposed of the lilies and, eradicating their stain, had restored the sink to flawless enamel. Crockery was arranged on shelves, handles pointing in one direction. He had wiped clean the whiteboard and the junk mail was pinned in rows on the cork tiles. Jars of lentils, rice and porridge reflected the warmth of the copper cylindrical lampshade. It could have been 1968 when Mrs Ramsay was in her thirties, beautiful and important, floating about the house: the free spirit she had told Stella that she still was. Stella had not believed her; the way he had cleaned the kitchen told her that Jack had.

As she stared at the battered kitchen table, now a feature with the garish red plastic fruit bowl in its centre, Stella saw jam-smeared children wriggling on the plastic chairs, chubby hands grabbing for bread, and heard their clamour of jokes and demands. Stella's cleaning restored order; Jack had given the room life. She felt remorse that all this time Mrs Ramsay had not had the best.

She crammed the sheets into the drum, tossed in a capful of liquid and chose the 'quick wash' programme before retreating upstairs. In contrast to Jack she had made little impression on the bedroom. She slumped on the mattress and pulled Mrs Ramsay's bedside pile on to her lap. A torn cutting was straining the spine of *Our Mutual Friend*. Stella had not noticed it when she came with Cashman. She took it out and smoothed it out on the mattress. It came from the *Charbury District Advertiser*. Unsettled by Jack's abrupt departure and his work in the kitchen, Stella's energy had entirely gone.

She caught the name Isabel Ramsay in the blurry newsprint and, sliding to the floor, her back to the bed, spread the newspaper over her knees. The entire page was devoted to the opening of Charbury's refurbished village hall. Stella sighed at the idea that readers were prepared to plough their way through trivia such as an apple-bobbing contest and a lucky dip. Villagers had paid two pence to guess the number of marbles in a jar and Iris Rogers, the postmistress, won a *Diana and Charles Wedding mug packed with delicious home-made chocolate truffles*. There must have been a glut of mugs for they featured as a prize in most of the events including the *cake-making competition judged by Mrs Isabel Ramsay (top right) of the White House*. Mrs Ramsay had snipped the ribbon on the strike of noon after a speech by the leader of the Parish Council Geoffrey Markham. Blah blah. Stella was about to get up when she saw the picture accompanying the piece.

A middle-aged but elegant Mrs Ramsay with scissors was in the midst of a mass of faces – smiling, stern, laughing – all gazing at her. A church clock peeping out from behind her shoulder confirmed the time. A string of bunting slanted across the photograph beneath which a caption read: *To the manor born: Mrs Ramsay launches Charbury's new village hall*.

Stella's mind was racing. There was no date, the paper was torn and the opening paragraph splodged with a sticky substance like raspberry jam. Stella turned it over and found two half-page adverts: one for the sale of beds at a shop in Seaford, the other for a car dealership in Brighton: *X-rated! Honeymoon in a brand-new X-reg Ford Escort. Drive off the forecourt now!*

Terry had taught her registration plates. The date of the car sale was Saturday, 8 August, but gave no year. Registrations used to come in on 1 August. She counted on her fingers: her first car, a 1977 Datsun Sunny, was 'S', there was no 'U' so 'X' was 1981. She was being stupid: that explained the wedding mugs, the street party had celebrated the marriage of Lady Diana to Prince Charles on Wednesday, 29 July that year.

Two days after Kate was murdered.

Mrs Ramsay had made a comment on that final Friday morning to which Stella had paid no attention; rushing to her meeting in Chelsea, she had no patience to listen to how Mrs Ramsay was delayed by Geoffrey and his silly shoes: another of Mrs Ramsay's batty remarks. She had been trying to tell Stella about that Monday in 1981.

Stella read the article properly, absorbing information that seconds ago she had dismissed as dull. Mrs Ramsay – *wife of renowned local Professor Mark Ramsay* – had opened Charbury's village hall on Monday lunchtime. The Ramsays had lived at the White House since before Queen Victoria ascended the throne and had been opening buildings and fêtes in the village for generations. The family had funded a stained-glass window, the church roof and Charbury's reading room, now defunct.

Councillor Geoffrey Markham had slipped on the steps and ripped his trousers and grazed his knee. This was linked to the royal couple because Prince Charles had slipped going into St Paul's Cathedral for his wedding rehearsal.

Far below, the washing machine banged and thrummed its way to the climax of the spin cycle and was shaking to a stop when Stella reached the kitchen. She slung the sheets across two clothes horses in the children's playroom; tomorrow she would fold them and stow them in the airing cupboard. Gina Cross would ask her to throw them away.

She was hungry and thought wistfully of Terry's shepherd's pies.

Terry.

The newspaper was where she had left it, on the rush matting beside the bed. She held it up to the light and studied the photograph: Mrs Ramsay wore a light-coloured dress and short jacket. Stella rushed back to the hall and tipped everything out of her rucksack.

The torn scrap she had extracted from the drain cover outside the Seaford Co-op had dried to the texture of brittle parchment. Despite the footprint across the picture she confirmed instantly that it was a photocopy of the article in the *Charbury District Advertiser*.

The house was back to normal: from the landing came the ticking of the grandfather clock and up in the sitting room the Swiss clock on the mantelpiece once again told the correct time. She faced Mrs Ramsay's chair and heard the old lady's voice chatting on, making no sense:

'Delayed by a broken sole, truth be told... one does one's best...'

Stella pulled herself together and punched in Jack's number on her phone; it went to voicemail. She left a message to call her urgently, frustrated that his mother's problems meant he did not even answer.

If Mrs Ramsay was in Sussex at midday on Monday, 27 July 1981, she could not, fifteen minutes earlier, have waved to Kate Rokesmith in St Peter's Square.

There was only one explanation: Isabel Ramsay had lied to the police.

Twenty-Five

He had said he would not be long. She did not like him going but had too much pride to tell him and he put up with the silent treatment because it was better than her not minding at all, which would mean she did not care about him. He thought of inviting her, but they got on better in the house; their private world. She approved of the flowers.

He seldom went after dark. Night was an obvious time – no one would intrude – but she said that night was precisely when those intent on spoiling it would come.

He propped up the fresh bouquet and wedged it with the flint, as she said. He had asked for the flowers to be gift-wrapped this time as a surprise.

'No, just that one, thank you. The other is a present for me!'

The assistant had unfurled ribbon from a roller, using silver without consulting him. He supposed choosing colours kept the job interesting because even selling beautiful, fragrant blooms must pall.

She nipped tape from a dispenser, queuing strips on the counter, using them one by one to swaddle the flowers in cellophane and tissue, curling the ribbons with the scissor blade – one, two, three, four – performing the procedure with expertise born of repetition. With mild ceremony she handed him the finished object.

In the street passing women smiled; a man with flowers attracts feminine approval.

The other flowers had died, but he wouldn't mention it, she couldn't bear death. He had left footprints so kicked up snow to make it look as if children had been playing and then went up the slope, criss-crossing to other graves to further confuse.

He bundled the dead flowers up in the paper and stuffed them in the bin by the lych gate. It was snowing hard which meant that soon his mess of prints around the graves would be undulations, his effort to disguise them unnecessary.

He had promised he would not be long and had been away five minutes. Most people would not think that much, but she could not bear to be without him.

Twenty-Six

Jack stood on the platform at Earls Court and consulted his duty book. The spiral-bound wad of pages, with a picture on the cover of a red and silver District line train, was encased in plastic so scratched with use the train seemed to come out of a fog.

The pages held the details of every shift on the District line for the year: times of trains in tiny print, set to the half-minute. Only when Jack was driving would he submit to the constraints of measured time. The public had no knowledge of this timetable, aware only of what the electronic boards announced: a train was due in three minutes or ten or 'Approaching' with a distant roar and a dusty breeze from the tunnel.

He confirmed the set number of the 11.13 and 30 seconds pick-up. It was '277'. He had no need to ponder what the figures meant, yet he felt afraid. Was he one of those hunters he despised, who live not for capture, but for the hunt itself? When the prey was in sight he wanted to drive his train into a tunnel and ignore the signs. No, he was not one of those, he told himself. He would not shirk his task.

Jack stayed behind the bright yellow gate on the platform's edge, clutching his driver's key. He grew excited, believing that Wednesday night's crack in the pavement had indeed been a sign. When the open cab door slid to a stop precisely next to where he stood, Jack was a god and ready for what would come next.

Jack eased the handle forward and his train slid into the brick tunnel. As the curved roof passed overhead, he allowed himself to think about his day. 'Tired, cold or hungry?' his mother would say when he grizzled in his pushchair, presumably unable to conceive of a child being anything other than these three conditions. He was rarely hungry. Out at night, he was cold, but was used to it. He had never spent so long in the company of someone else. He was tired.

He had not liked leaving Isabel's house so abruptly. What luck it was that Stella had been upstairs when his telephone rang; she had not heard his conversation. These days the Underground was demanding more; he would have liked to walk away except he depended on his times deep below London with only the bricks and the lines for company.

Jack had enjoyed cleaning Isabel's kitchen; it did not nullify her death, but did soothe. He had been aware of Stella two flights above; would she tell him if she found anything? She was not the sharing type.

He pulled into the station and in the monitor saw a man and a woman boarding different cars; the night-time rush was over. Once more up to Upminster then to Earls Court and home, except that since leaving Michael and Ellen Hamilton's he had no home.

Jack Harmon had told Stella the truth; he did not know why the colour green – Pantone 375 – provoked such violent symptoms.

He mulled on the other colour in Stella's branding: Pantone 277. He had hidden his shock well when she told him: twenty-seven and seven didn't take working out; the signs were thick and fast. Today the set number for the relief train was 652 and as was often the case it had not immediately communicated anything.

He took the train along the open track after Ravenscourt Park towards Stamford Brook. This was his favourite part of the journey. Jack loved the tunnels, but he also appreciated the long vista at this point. The stations with the highest death rate are those near mental institutions. This was a good place: a Piccadilly train passes the unprotected platform at Stamford Brook at speed; no driver can stop in time.

None of the drivers referred to their shifts as journeys; they were shifts for which they were remunerated, but for Jack every minute counted, every mile travelled was progress.

It was one o'clock in the morning when Jack came out on to Earls Court Road. He avoided the crack in the paving that had got him the other night. Half an hour later he cut under the Hammersmith flyover, dodging between the supports where with no snow it was easier to walk.

There was no green to bother him at night. Jack remembered the light blue: Pantone 277 and got it: the two colours, 277 plus 375, added up to 652: tonight's set number.

He was getting hotter.

He entered Furnival Gardens and skated along the icy path to Hammersmith Terrace, singing softly:

> 'This is the dog that worried the cat
> That killed the rat that ate the malt
> That lay in the house that Jack built.'

Outside Sarah Glyde's house, by the Bell Steps, he turned on his phone; Stella had left a message asking him to call. He turned to page 141 of his *A–Z*. The next page in his quest took him to Biggin Hill. Too late tonight, but with so many signs he must persevere; he texted that he had to take his mother to Biggin Hill and switched his phone to voicemail.

With insistent stealth, snow fell over the sleeping city, rendering it timeless. No one saw a tall, loping figure, hands in the pockets of a long black coat, enter the subway tunnel that came out beside the statue of the Leaning Woman.

Twenty-Seven

Monday, 17 January 2011

Stella went by train after work to meet Ivan Challoner. It was seven thirty and, waiting on the platform at Hammersmith, she regretted accepting his dinner invitation. Then she recalled the piano music, the peace and lack of complication and was pleased she had agreed. Ivan was, she guessed, about the same age as Paul, who would be fifty this year, but being wiser he seemed older.

The indicator board flashed up: 'Train Approaching'.

Boarding, Jack Harmon came into her mind. He had not been available to help her at 48 St Peter's Square on Saturday and had not returned her calls for two days. Had she interviewed him she would have been explicit that she expected flexibility and availability and established his other commitments, making it clear where Clean Slate was on the priority list. He had not signed a contract and behaved as if she was lucky to have him. She had no idea when she might next see him. She dialled him again and left a snappish message insisting he be at the Ramsay house by eight the next morning – Tuesday just in case he was unclear – and resisted adding 'Or else' because she was not sure what the 'else' would be. She had called Gina Cross and told her they would be finished in a week. She hoped that was true.

On Friday morning Jack had spoken as if they were detectives capable of solving a murder together. Then he had vanished.

She wanted to tell him about the photograph and that Isabel Ramsay had not seen Kate Rokesmith when she said she had which meant there was no firm sighting of the murdered woman and alibis needed to be revisited. Despite her striving for an open mind, it meant that more than ever it was likely Hugh Rokesmith was the killer. Hugh Rokesmith had been at his office that morning but said he had popped back at ten to change and left at ten thirty. Because Mrs Ramsay was supposed to have seen Kate alive at eleven forty-five, the interval after Rokesmith left his house and arrived at his mother's did not in the end count. The truly grey area had been when he popped out for wine around midday. Now, everything was up for grabs: the article had effectively torpedoed his alibi. The window of opportunity was flung wide.

The only person with a solid alibi was Mrs Ramsay: she had been in Sussex that Monday and there again for the royal wedding party on the Wednesday; it was unlikely she returned to London in between. Yet she had lied, so had to be a suspect of sorts.

The train slowed outside Gunnersbury, and peering into the darkness Stella made out the clamps holding the cables to the walls, one clamp halted in the centre of the glass. They had stopped. She disliked being late and did not want Ivan to consider her unpunctual. The engine ceased throbbing and went silent.

'We apologise for this delay. A train has broken down at Gloucester Road and we are waiting for it to be towed to the depot which should not take long.'

The driver sounded genuinely sorry and reminded her of Jackie who was excellent at customer service. While Stella could send a text jilting her partner, she never kept a client uninformed of progress. It was ten to eight; if the train moved now she could make it. Seated in the front car behind the driver's cab she heard tapping, a rustling and a staccato voice over the transmitter.

The cable clamp passed off to her right, then another and another and soon were out of focus as the train gathered speed again. In minutes they were at Kew Gardens station.

Stella crossed the concourse in front of the station and following Ivan's meticulous instructions she found the restaurant. When she entered she saw immediately that Ivan had dressed up. Stella had changed into dark green trousers and wore a loose linen jacket over a T-shirt; Ivan was decked out in an immaculate suit. As if to emphasise his sharp attire, Ivan shot his cuffs before lifting a bottle of white wine from an ice bucket beside him to fill their glasses. Stella had the sense that until she arrived Ivan had been lingering in the wings and that now she was here, his performance could begin.

A packet lay on her plate, tied with a silver ribbon.

'What's this?' she demanded, refusing the waiter's offer to take her coat and sitting down.

'First things first.' Ivan held up his glass. 'Here's how!'

She raised the wine glass, putting it down again without drinking.

'Open it.' Ivan's gold tie pin glinted in the candle flame. He contemplated her over the rim of his glass.

Stella began to rip off the paper. He snatched it away.

'Not like that!'

Ivan cradled the package, tipping it between his fingertips. He undid the paper and handed her a cardboard box within a sleeve. Inside was a hardback book with no writing on the cover, dusky red and reeking of mould. Stella was reluctant to handle it before giving it a proper wipe. Ivan, like Terry long ago, was watching her expectantly so she could not say she did not have time for reading.

'It's a first edition by Duckworth with engravings by Claire Leighton. Her brother, Roland Leighton, was killed in the First World War. He's the one who features in *Testament of Youth*. As you know, she was well known in her day.'

Stella did not know. She found gold lettering on the spine: *Wuthering Heights*.

'I remembered you spotted this on your first visit. I'll be honest, as I am guessing it will make you feel better, I didn't pay for it. Grateful clients give me presents. I'm sure you know that one!' He quaffed some wine. 'You must be constantly receiving gifts. Anyhow, thing is, I don't need two. I have kept my original, it's in fairer condition. I could flog this, but it would be tricky, the client would be bound to find out. She's a rare book dealer; they are a tight web so please do me a favour and accept it?'

'Even so, it is generous...' Stella faltered. Her own clients stuck to the baskets of soap, candles and the odd bottle of single malt which she passed to Terry for Christmas and birthdays.

'It's not generous. I am offloading an unwanted copy on you and keeping the one with less foxing.' He bent beneath the table. 'Now, I am really going to be for it!' He brandished a bunch of flowers.

Almost euphoric that Ivan Challoner had read her correctly, Stella accepted the slender bouquet, noticing with further relief that he had not got them gift wrapped. She settled in for a pleasant evening.

Anxious about eating in company, Stella ordered soup that could easily be consumed and a risotto which she could cordon off into bite-sized amounts and efficiently demolish. She waived dessert, but agreed to coffee.

She listened to Ivan describing his love of the countryside, days by the sea with his son and his passion for reconstructive and cosmetic dentistry. Some patients came to him after accidents, others with inhibiting defects or damage due to poor oral hygiene. Everyone came dissatisfied with their appearance and left feeling happier. His calling – and it was a calling, he insisted as with dextrous fingers he pulled the tail off a king prawn – was to make patients feel good about themselves. He restored their smiles. He dabbled his fingers in the water dish, drying them one by one, observing that, for some people, his work amounted to a rebirth.

'It must make you feel powerful.' Stella surprised herself with this comment; she did not dwell on motivations or feelings.

'On the contrary, I am humbled,' Ivan replied, patting his mouth with his napkin. 'We are in the same business, of course.' He sat back supping his wine.

'I don't see that.' Stella isolated another portion from the mound of food and embarked upon it, chewing the glutinous mass. The idea of seeing business in terms of improving clients' opinion of themselves was an anathema to her.

'You too restore order. As the giver of purity you, or specifically your staff, scour, mop and dust away the accumulated filth in our lives. You and I, with our commitment to perfection, add to the sum of happiness.'

'I hadn't thought of it that way.' Stella regretted the risotto; no matter how much she ate the amount was not diminishing.

'I can hear how pretentious it sounds, yet you get the point.' He refilled Stella's glass before she could stop him. One glass was her limit even when she wasn't driving.

Ivan, too, was scrupulous in not broaching anything personal. He stuck to discussing business, seeming genuinely curious about how she managed her staff because, he admitted, his management skills were minimal.

Nevertheless Stella was troubled. She cleaned her client's premises to the highest standards because she despised mess. She could not bear smudged glass, scuffed walls or carpets spattered with tea or coffee or worse, tables stained with food or streaks of grime. She hated creases in fabrics, papers and useless objects on every surface. She went to war on her clients' homes with an assortment of cleaning weaponry. At no point while she was disinfecting and deodorizing did she consider the owners themselves – other than as an irritating distraction when she was vacuuming around them or an income stream enabling her to continue cleaning. That Ivan strove to improve his patients' lives was extraordinary. There was no one whose existence Stella wanted to improve – with the possible exception of Mrs Ramsay, and she was dead.

Watching Ivan mop his plate clean with a pinch of sesame roll, Stella reflected how she had cleaned the darkest and most obscure places for Mrs Ramsay. She had never done this to make the old lady happier, she had done it because she loved to deep-clean.

Ivan insisted on escorting Stella to the station, which was, he assured her, on his way. The pavements had not been salted so they walked on the road, retreating to the kerb to avoid cars. The snow had immobilized the population and, picking their way along Sandycombe Road, they were alone.

At the station entrance Ivan was diverted by a tramp listing on a bench outside. Stella was repulsed by his filthy clothes, his wrinkled skin darkened by dirt, and was anxious that his drunken swaying meant he was going to throw up. She wanted to be far away if that happened.

'Do excuse me, Stella.' Ivan approached the man. Sure Ivan was going to move the tramp on, Stella felt stirrings of triumph. The seat was for members of the public, not for drunks to pass out on.

Ivan squatted down and, fishing under the seat between the man's boots, he picked up a coin. He stood over the man and clasped his shoulder, touching the dandruff-speckled wool as he might guide a patient into the operating chair. He had not touched Stella.

'I think you dropped this, sir.'

The man struggled to focus, squinting blearily at Ivan. Unsteadily he picked the coin out of Ivan's palm and stared at it. Then he smiled. His front teeth were missing. 'Verr...very shen-er-russss.' He worked his lips hard to form the words that Stella herself had used about Ivan earlier.

'No, not at all, it was yours.' Ivan let go of his shoulder. He returned to Stella. An expression of sadness passed over his face but, pulling himself together, he breathed: 'I have enjoyed myself tonight, thank you, Stella.'

On the end of the platform, as she watched a dot far down the line expand into an eastbound District line train, Stella confessed to herself that she quite liked Ivan Challoner. Jackie said she was a bad judge of character and she imagined telling her that her first impression of Ivan had been right; he was someone she could trust.

Stella did not see the driver of the train when his cab slid past her to stop just beyond where she stood, nor did she know that he was observing her in the platform monitor as she boarded his train.

Twenty-Eight

Tuesday, 18 January 2011

A magpie was busy above their heads on the snow-insulated roof, raising flurries of snow in front of the glass doors. There was a beating of wings.

Silence.

Through the glass, the lawn was marked with animal and bird tracks, virginal patches of snow sparkled with a bluish haze in the morning sunshine.

Jack and Stella were in Isabel Ramsay's summerhouse. Wrapped up, Jack in his greatcoat, Stella in her padded anorak, they lounged awkwardly in motheaten deckchairs beaten free of spider webs and the husks of insects, nursing mugs of tea in Stella's case, milk with honey for Jack. The semi-circular structure with a glass frontage had sun all day long and, even in freezing temperatures, was warmer than the house where the central heating had died along with its owner. Jack had arrived, punctually at eight as Stella had requested, and she had assigned him the basement. At eleven, by way of a truce, she had brewed tea in Mrs Ramsay's chipped Woolworths' teapot, boiled a pan of milk and then bade him follow her down the garden.

Mrs Ramsay refused to sit in her summerhouse, saying, 'Mark always got there first. He did it to get to me, he hated the sun.' Lately Mrs Ramsay, apparently having decided that Stella had passed her tests, had initiated beverages mid-shift and made Stella drink the glass of fruit juice – to keep up vitamins – as soon as she arrived. Stella never thought about vitamins and doubted that Jack did. She had rather liked Mrs Ramsay's caring what she ate or drank.

'Do you know what it means?' Stella took too large a mouthful of tea and burned her tongue. Swallowing she panted in cold air.

'She lied.' Jack had a milk moustache.

'Yes, obviously, but how did she get away with it? How could so glaring a discrepancy not have been spotted? How many villagers were at that opening?'

'Easy peasy. Although the murder got national attention, it was brief. The Royal Wedding saturated the coverage. I'm guessing that in deepest Sussex, the drama was a councillor ripping his best suit when he slipped.'

'He tore his trousers.' Stella mimed wiping her lip. Jack ignored her.

'Don't get bogged down with detail.'

'Just as well I do.' Stella warmed her hands on the china. 'The police missed it.' Terry had missed it.

Jack looked more frayed than ever and Stella suspected that unless he had a stock of black shirts and trousers, he wore the same clothes every day. She was nerving herself up to insist that he put on her uniform. In the meantime she had to reserve him for where the client was out or dead. It was not ideal: Jack was too good to be on the subs' bench. They were discussing the new timings; Jack did not agree that it locked down Rokesmith as suspect.

'He left his house at ten thirty and arrived at his mother's at eleven fifteen, then went out again just before midday for wine and returned about twenty minutes later. He didn't have time.'

'I tell you he is our best suspect. He could have killed her any time between, say, eleven and two when she was found.'

'It would have been mad to have agreed to a walk to the river when he was pressed for time. Is that likely?'

'If he planned to kill her the walk would have been his idea, and he would have intended time to be tight to give him this very alibi.'

'There were others at the lunch,' Jack reminded her.

'Only from twelve thirty after he returned with the wine.'

'Kate told him she had a headache: why would she agree to a walk when she didn't feel up to the lunch?'

'We only have Rokesmith's word that she had a headache; actually at one point there's mention it was the son who was ill.' Stella blew on the tea to cool it.

'Why are you fixating on the father?'

'Why aren't you?' she retorted.

The glass was steaming up, gradually fading the view to blotches of whites and greens.

'I'd ask why Mrs Ramsay put herself into the picture when she was miles away and had a cast-iron alibi.' Jack wiped his mouth on his coat sleeve. 'What about your Paul?'

'He's not *my* Paul.' Stella swallowed some tea. Speaking the words out loud made her question the truth of them.

'By giving that false statement Mrs Ramsay became the key witness. Why did she put herself in the frame?'

'She made up things all the time, she said her children visited, but a neighbour told me they never do.' Stella took a gulp of tea; already it was cooling.

'Maybe the neighbour was wrong.' Jack murmured. 'I saw the youngest daughter once and besides when did you last see your mother?'

Stella's mobile trilled with a private number – Ivan? – and she answered it.

'It's Jeanette's the florist here. You left a message cancelling Mrs Ramsay's flowers.'

'Yes, I'm afraid so. ' Stella shuffled her feet on the wood floor, hot despite the cold temperature. 'She has died.'

'I *am* sorry. Normally we would not take a cancellation except from the sender but in the circumstances… I take it the sender knows of Mrs Ramsay's death?'

'She can't cancel them herself.' Stella could not resist it.

'Mr Jack Harmon pays for the flowers. Are you in touch with him?'

The summerhouse swooped. Stella gripped her mug, spilling tea on her lap. 'Yes I am.'

'Perhaps you wouldn't mind informing Mr Harmon that we

will stop his order and please pass on our condolences for his sad loss.'

Stella put the phone back in her pocket. Jack was draping a skein of milk skin on the rim of his mug, not looking at her.

'Reasons she would have lied. One: she didn't want anyone to know where she really was. Two: she was covering for someone.' Stella struggled out of the deckchair and rubbed the glass in one of the windows. 'Rokesmith, maybe. Maybe she was having an affair with him. Or with you,' she added, turning round.

Jack's fingers were like raw chipolatas. She would have to get him gloves; she could not risk him damaging his hands. Terry's gloves would fit, but were brown and Jack might insist on black. She should make him wear green: his best way of solving the problem was to tackle it head on.

'She was forty-eight and he was in his thirties,' Jack protested. He fell silent.

Stella did not want to think of Mrs Ramsay having an affair. 'It happens.' She imagined Mrs Ramsay bored by a precise civil engineer. 'We should crack on. This evening we'll get a takeaway and head over to mine and get up to speed with the notes. No use speculating, let's comb through what the police thought they knew. Already we've uncovered a crucial error.'

'I can't tonight, I'm busy.'

'I'll pay you.' She had not meant to say that.

'I'm still busy.' Jack stalked off up the path.

Stella returned to the sitting room.

Five hours later, Stella hauled down some of the cartons and plastic sacks that she had stacked on the landing the day before. She emptied the contents of Mrs Ramsay's linen cupboard, her stacks of unused sheets and stuffed them in rubbish bags. Jack had been right. Gina Cross wanted it all got rid of.

The smell of a horsehair blanket put Stella in mind of her nana.

It was never explained to her why Terry had stopped taking her to stay with his mother. The reason, she learnt later, was simple: her nana had died. Stella did not remember this but did remember her nana allowing her milky tea like a grown-up and counting up the buttons in her button box. Terry must have bagged up his mother's bedding as Stella was doing. Maybe he had cleared her flat and chucked out the objects that lose value once their owner is gone: indifferent, outdated crockery that will never come round again, keepsakes from seaside towns and horsehair blankets smelling of camphor. The blankets were rough and heavy; their weight strained the plastic, splitting it. Stella could only manage one bag at a time. In the hall she could not see or hear Jack and after the third trip stopped at the top of the basement stairs and called: 'Jack?'

No answer.

'Jack?' Louder. He must still be in a huff. Like Paul, he was too sensitive, perhaps due to the business of the green.

The back door was unlocked. She peered out. Beside her was the fire escape – black, ugly and, Mrs Ramsay believed, an invitation to thieves – it ended on a flagged area outside the children's playroom that, never getting sun, was coated in moss but was now hidden beneath inches of snow. Jack was not on the metal stairway.

To her right, marks on the door frame tracked the heights of the three Ramsay children. When Stella had pointed them out, Mrs Ramsay had wrung her hands in her odd way and lamented that Lucian was not like his father. Stella had presumed she was talking about height.

Stella was as tall as Terry.

She was about to lock the door when she saw Jack huddled by the side of the summerhouse where brambles and weeds had been left to grow because Mrs Ramsay had wanted a place for the bees. He was rubbing something against his trousers. Stella could not make out what it was. He held it up to the light and then put it in his pocket. She would have to explain that 'Finders' was not 'Keepers', a phrase she had not used since she was little. She supposed it had occurred to her now because Mrs Ramsay had said that the wooded spot in which Jack was standing statue-still was perfect for children to hide.

Jack did what he liked when he liked; he smoked, questioned her decisions and was not available at short notice. She was about to call out to remind him of the deadline, but then reminded herself that Jack Harmon was the best cleaner she had ever had and instead of berating him, she strayed back to the hall, fractious and forlorn. Gone was the grey powder: Jack had washed the walls, the skirting and cornices using bleach and polish, but he had done what she said and kept the doors open so the smells were faint and the air fresh. He had vacuumed the rug and laid it exactly in the centre of the boards as it had been. She did not have to lift it to know that the stains she had laboured over, which for a time the police had thought were Mrs Ramsay's blood, would be gone. He had buffed up the hat stand till the antlers shone.

Jack's coat was hanging in the hall.

The last day she saw Mrs Ramsay, the old woman had been fumbling with a coat when Stella was leaving. She had given the impression of sulking, but now Stella realized her mood was agitated. Mrs Ramsay had been pulling at the pockets, trying to get her hand inside. The cloth was rough, like the blankets. Stella sniffed it: an outside smell that somehow lessened her anger. What had Mrs Ramsay been looking for?

She swung the coat around and found a pocket containing Jack's packet of tobacco. The coat was weighted by a lump in the other pocket. Stella ran to the back door and confirmed that Jack had not moved.

Stitches were broken in the seam and she pulled two more, manoeuvring out a compact booklet encased in brittle plastic which, like his tobacco, was held with an elastic band. She pulled off the band and flicked through the spiral-bound book. Each page was filled with columns of printed numbers: 20.02.15, 21.04. It might have been a timetable, but for three digit numbers under a heading: 'Set No.' On the cover was a London Underground train, like in a child's story book, retaining only the main features: headlights, wheels, windows. One of the pages was marked with a gold paper clip. Stella manipulated the scruffy volume to that page and, holding it at some distance to accommodate her growing long sight, tried to make sense of the numbers.

The fire escape shook; Jack was coming back from the garden. She shut the book. It would not close properly and when she tried to bind it with the elastic band, running it off her grouped fingers, the band snapped and flew towards the garden door where any minute Jack would appear. She rammed the book into the pocket, tearing another stitch, and hurried to the stairs where she did an about-turn as if descending when Jack came in. He paused and wiped his feet on the mat, which he had made look new. He was trembling with cold and did not see Stella.

'Hi there. All right?' she enquired brightly, jumping off the last step, one hand on the newel post.

He eyed her with surprise. 'I went for a smoke.'

He did not smell of smoke.

'It's lunchtime, I thought we might wander along to the Ram.' Only on special occasions did Stella offer staff lunch; she preferred to eat alone.

'Thanks, I'll work through.' Jack indicated the plastic bags. 'Do you want help bringing down the rest?'

'I'm fine.' Stella had completed the upper floors. She stood in the back bedroom on the top floor. Gina Cross had instructed her to be ruthless in the bedrooms; if her siblings wanted anything they would be in touch. If she didn't hear, she should 'dump the whole caboodle'. Good, clear instructions: Gina Cross was Stella's kind of client.

Why did Jack have a driver's timetable in his pocket? Why had he bought Mrs Ramsay flowers?

Once the vacuum had started up in the basement, Stella checked her mobile to find no messages. Jackie had taken her at her word and was not disturbing her. She would be grateful that Stella was back on the job, but had made several hints about progress on Terry's house such as grieving could not be swept under the carpet. This was precisely where Stella thought it could be swept, but had instead agreed that time was a great healer.

Jackie picked up on the second ring.

'You tell me not to answer the phone, where's thingy?'

'Beverly. She's at the dentist – I sent her to your man. She broke a tooth on a pear drop, would you believe!'

'He's not my man.'

'No, I meant… Why are we whispering?'

'I'm not.' Stella cleared her throat and raised her voice as much as she dared. She could still hear the vacuum. 'Could you give me the numbers for Jack Harmon's referees?'

'Oh-kay, tell me what's happened.' Jackie's tone implied she had expected a problem and here it was.

'Nothing, I want to confirm them. Normal procedure.'

'I have already, I told you. One was lukewarm but basically good and the other man, if I remember rightly, was impatient, though he said he'd have Mr Harmon back.'

If a person wanted to fake a reference they would be clever enough to avoid fulsome praise; Stella kept this to herself. If she were asked, she would have difficulty not raving about Jack. She took the numbers down on an old laundry list of Mrs Ramsay's, airily enquiring if Jackie had heard from Paul.

'Not a dicky bird. I'm taking it that he's not your man either?'

'You are.'

'So you're out if he calls?'

'I am.'

The vacuum motor went up to a pitch; Jack was using the nozzle on the stairs and would finish soon. Feverishly she stabbed at the buttons, squinting at the digits on the tiny screen. She got one wrong and had to start again, mouthing the numbers as she dialled and pressing the green button with only moments before Jack would appear because the vacuum had stopped.

No one was answering. Downstairs she caught the sound of a standard Nokia ringtone. It was Jack's phone. That would delay him, and if he was talking he would not hear her.

'Nick Jarvis.' The deep voice was clipped and irritable: the sort in too much of a hurry to give a decent brief for a job, but with plenty of time to complain if objectives omitted were not met. She leant on the sill ruminating at the overgrown lawn. The man was breathing as if he was running. Downstairs she heard the back door open.

'It's Stella Darnell from Clean Slate Cleaning Services. You offered to give a testimony on a former employee, Jack Harmon. Is now a good time?' His breathing was irregular and she could hear what could be the shuffling of shoes. Jarvis must be outside somewhere.

Jack was in the garden, tracking his own footprints back to the wall, this time looking back at the house. Stella ducked out of sight.

'If you're quick, but I did speak to someone from your company.' Stella checked her watch: it was nearly five. If Jack turned out to have been sacked from his previous job, it was unwise to confront him alone in a client's house.

'I need his dates of employment and the reason why he left.'

'Has he embezzled the petty cash?'

'Would you expect that?'

'Best cleaner we had in the whole wide world. Aren't you pleased with his work?' Jarvis sound rather belligerent. Why should he care?

'Yes, very.'

St Peter's Church bells struck the hour. The sound came through the phone. How was that when Nick Jarvis was in Muswell Hill?

'No good on timings, I'm afraid. My advice is that you trust the guy.'

Stella hung up. At the same moment Jack lowered his arm and was off the phone.

It was not coincidence.

Nick Jarvis did not exist. She felt desolate. Confident he could fool anyone, Jack had faked his references. He had fooled Jackie and if Stella had not heard the bells he would have fooled her.

Now he would know she did not trust him.

Stella crept out on to the landing.

'Be here same time tomorrow, yeah?' Jack called up.

He was leaving.

'I'll ring you.'

The door slammed. She remained where she was, contemplating the drop down the stairwell. The plastic bags behind her rustled, easing and settling. More sounds. This was how it felt to be Isabel Ramsay when Stella was not there to keep the ghosts at bay. Out they came from their hidey-holes while Mrs Ramsay tried to manage what was left of her life.

She brought another bag down to the hall. The broken elastic band was on the newel post. Jack must have found it. She stood on the spotless rug and breathed in the lavender fragrance. She knew what to do next.

Twenty-Nine

Wednesday, 19 January 2011

Jack was breaking London Underground rules: he had left his phone switched on in the cab. He would not answer it, but he had to know if she called. It was fifteen minutes past midnight and his phone had remained silent. Stella was making him suffer.

He did not know if Stella had guessed it was him being Nick Jarvis. But calling the referees when her PA had already done so was proof enough that she did not yet trust him.

She might believe she did not need him. Yet again he combed through their conversation in the summerhouse for something that had caused her to verify his references just when he thought they were getting on. Perhaps she had always doubted him? No, something specific had prompted her. He suspected it was Isabel's lilies.

Mike Thorpe and Nick Jarvis had been adequate Hosts: he had modelled their ruthless and dispassionate approach; even down to how they boiled water for tea or tied their shoe laces. Jarvis's brutal disregard for space, pushing through crowds, taking up more room than necessary; Thorpe, unaware of anyone, never getting up for anyone on a bus or a train. Their utter lack of empathy had been gratifying and staying with each of them he had been sure he had found men with minds like his own. Until the facts belied this.

A good liar believes his own lies. By making the men his referees Jack had given them new life.

'*Naked came I out of my mother's womb, and naked shall I return thither: the Lord gave, and the Lord hath taken away; blessed be the name…*' he muttered, the words comforting although Jack did not think of himself as religious.

Jack had stayed with Nick Jarvis in his Barbican flat for two months and could not pretend it had been pleasant. He did not have a cleaner because he did not want snoopers prying into his business. Jack had known Nick Jarvis as soon as he saw him on the platform at Sloane Square; there were too many Nick Jarvises, standing where the doors would open, pushing their way in, taking the last seat, they projected respectability and belonged to the Rotary Club and Neighbourhood Watch while behind the scenes they were getting away with murder.

This afternoon Nick had stepped out of character to give Jack a good reference, but Stella had seen through him; she had not called Mike Thorpe. Jack had been ready, knowing he would have to work to get Thorpe's voice right. On the other hand, maybe it was a positive sign: Nick had convinced her.

Stella was taking her time.

Tonight's set number – he had done a short shift so there had only been one – was 242. Jack tried to divine the answer from the rails and the cable bundles strapped to the walls and gantries but on this journey they too were impervious. All he could see was all there was: no signs, no messages; he had been abandoned.

Above ground, triangles of snow, bisected by silver lines hatching off across Chiswick to Ealing and over to Ruislip, were translucent in the London-dark. On a segment of land between the District and Piccadilly route track-side workers had built a snowman and dressed him in a 'hi-viz' jacket with a woolly bobble cap and sticks for arms, but no face.

Jack had not noticed Ealing Common. He must have stopped there, would have operated the doors and seen who boarded and who alighted; he was not concentrating.

Stella should not have let him leave without going through the rooms he had cleaned. To assert authority she should highlight any blemish: a forgotten corner, a wisp of cobweb. Not liking to praise, she needed to catch him out. She had not done so; she was avoiding him.

Stamford Brook was the next stop. He imagined himself as

static while the world outside his cab passed by in rolling scene changes: a line of lights, a canopy, the London Underground roundels; the passengers.

The platforms were deserted; few travellers went up to town at this time. He was steering his train through a deserted city; cheered he began to sing:

'*Incy-wincy spider climbing up the spout. Down came the rain and washed the spider out…*'

There was someone on his platform; involuntarily Jack jerked the handle, jolting the train like a novice. His fingers clammy with sweat, he gripped the lever. The man was close to the platform edge and Jack imagined him getting ready to execute a perfect dive – *on your marks, get set* – right in front of Jack's cab. Instead the man turned away and went down the steps; Jack let himself breathe. He loved trains, the engine, the cab, the carriages for their stolid intent: so oblivious to the frailty of a single life. Flowers were laid beside roads where 'loved ones' had died, but none were put on tracks. Death was better glimpsed from cars than contemplated by waiting commuters who might get ideas of their own.

Waiting passengers took no notice of the driver, although they stared at the cab; it was the train they eyed impassively as it entered a station. He saw the same expression on hundreds of faces. When he was a boy Jack had not grasped what, if people had eyes, noses, mouths and chins, made them different from one another. It was not true that under the skin we are all the same because, as he had learnt, only some had minds like his own.

Pick a face, any face. He could enter a tunnel and wipe them out.

A person was looking straight into his cab.

Stella Darnell had no need to call his mobile. She knew where to find him.

Thirty

Wednesday, 19 January 2011

Snowflakes were swirling; the church tower was a pencil sketch, its lines indistinct. Stella had lost sight of Jack and thrust aside rhododendron branches, tipping snow on to her head. Ahead, lit intermittently by traffic and what lamplight penetrated the dense foliage, was the statue.

They had not spoken on the drive to Terry's house and Jack had got out of the van as soon as Stella turned off the engine. He had not seemed surprised to see her at Stamford Brook station, nor had he avoided her on the platform at Earls Court where she waited while he took the train to the depot. Implicitly they had both known where they were going and why: Stella could not return by herself to Terry's house for only the second time since his death. She had to take Jack with her.

Wind had blown snow into the clearing; bushes and the spreading sycamore offered scant protection. It covered the Leaning Woman's head and shoulders like a shawl. Stella tramped around the sculpture and found Jack, his knees up to his chest, curled in a ball. He clasped his hands as if in prayer, perhaps in an attempt to keep them warm. Stella resolved to find Terry's gloves. She would heat up a shepherd's pie because in the half-light, despite all the milk he drank, Jack looked more malnourished than ever.

'You didn't mention a "day job".' Her voice was level.

'Night job, to be accurate. I do the Dead Lates four times a week. Tonight I finished early because I was a relief driver.'

'This is early?' Hampered by manic flurries of snow, Stella

could not see the time on her watch. In the van, it had been about midnight.

'The night is young.'

Stella lowered herself beside Jack. 'Where do you live?' She raised a gloved hand. 'Don't bother making it up. I contacted the address on your form. A Michael Hamilton and his wife Ellen – who actually live there – had never heard of you.'

Jack lit a cigarette; he had taken a risk putting a real address on the form; the best lies were mostly truth. The Hamiltons had been his family for longer than was wise since they were not part of the main task. They had not given him what he was looking for, but he at least had found what he had lost: a home. He cleared his throat.

'Have you any idea what paltry issues can form the basis for a catastrophic rift in a relationship? Which way a lavatory roll is fitted in the holder, pulling from the top or from underneath, can be a reason for murder.'

'Don't change the subject.'

'This is the subject. In the afternoons, I'd hear the gabble of kids' voices from the gardens, that way they talk, excitable and dramatic, then it goes wrong and they're quarrelling. "It's not fair", "It's *my* turn" and so on. I'd want to join in.' It was upsetting to hear that the Hamiltons claimed he was a stranger.

'One more time and then I am going. Where do you live?' Stella's back was numb and she zipped up her anorak to cover her chin.

Jack blew on his hands. 'There are so many secrets.'

'Here, take these.' Stella gave him her gloves.

She balanced on her haunches trying to avoid the cold and wet, which was already seeping though her trousers. 'How can you expect me to trust you when you come out with this stuff?'

'I don't expect anything. However, you do trust me, or you wouldn't have me cleaning for you.'

Stella considered the truth of this and kept it to herself. 'Did you steal anything from these Hamiltons?'

'No. I gave them back their lives.'

'How exactly?'

'So much is hidden in homes: affairs, private hurt, injustice. I shone light on some of it and moved events along. I am a catalyst.'

'So where *do* you live?' She pulled her hood over her head.

'Why do you care? I do the work and you have my number.'

'I care if you break into people's homes, I know you were in Mrs Ramsay's. You claim she invited you, but why would she do that? And why were you sending her flowers?'

'I told you, Isabel was my friend.' Jack struggled to his feet. The statue had vanished beneath snow and he brushed it off, his actions frantic, as if her smothered state was distressing to him.

'Since you were such good friends, why didn't Mrs Ramsay tell you that she lied to the police about Kate Rokesmith?'

'As I keep saying, we have private lives. Perhaps she might have, had she not died.' Jack swept snow from the statue's head. 'Although I doubt it. Isabel was made of steel and rigorous in committing nothing to paper.' As he worked, more snow fell, undermining his efforts.

'What makes you sure she didn't write stuff down?'

'I didn't find anything. No letters, cards, journal nor notebook: Isabel Ramsay was the sort of woman to write about her every move; she fascinated herself and would imagine her children fascinated after she was gone, but there wasn't even an appointments diary.'

'I didn't say you could sort her papers. That was not part of the brief.'

'Terry solved his cases with a squirt of polish and a buff of a duster, did he?' Jack swished snow from the outstretched arms with one of Stella's gloves. 'If we want to learn stuff, we have to be nosy.'

'Terry didn't solve this case.'

'Rather than protecting Hugh Rokesmith, my guess is she was protecting her own husband. She was always grumbling about Mark Ramsay. You knew that. She wouldn't believe he was dead.'

'Protecting him from what?' Stella retorted. 'Her husband was a professor, a doctor.'

'Doctors kill people. Take Harold Shipman.'

'I know they do.' Stella was on her feet. 'He wasn't interviewed because he was at work at midday.' She stamped about, churning up snow, to get feeling back in her toes. 'My money's still on Rokesmith. Will you leave that bloody concrete monstrosity, you're not making any difference.'

'We already decided Rokesmith had no motive.' Jack ignored Stella's outburst. 'What about Mark Ramsay, since midday has been discounted?'

'I read he was at work at the National Hospital for Neurology and Neurosurgery. You're setting up dummies.'

'And Paul, did you check him out?'

'How am I supposed to do that?' Stella huffed. 'I think Rokesmith was having an affair and wanted Kate out the way, the oldest reason in the book.'

'We have no evidence.' Jack put Stella's glove back on. 'He never remarried.'

'What does that prove? Nor would I if I'd murdered my wife.'

Jack scuffed at the ground with his boot. 'This is where the boy was found.'

'This is where *we'll* be found if we stay any longer.' Stella moved to the edge of the clearing. They were in the middle of London beside a major road, but it might have been in a remote wood insulated from the world by thick snow and dense bushes.

'Hugh Rokesmith lived under a cloud of suspicion all his life. Commissions for work ran out except the occasional job at a derisory price and so-called friends stopped phoning. Women were still interested, the kind that correspond with murderers in prison. By the time he died he was, like Isabel Ramsay, a recluse. His cancer would have been treatable had he gone to the doctor sooner.'

'How do you know this?'

'It's all there on the internet.'

'It's not.'

'The Leaning Woman took care of the boy.' Jack walked around the plinth. 'See these lines?'

Faint marks had been painted on the concrete.

'They represent the jointing of a carcase.' Jack trailed his gloved finger over the woman's stomach, making marks of his own in the new snow. 'We are looking for a man with a mind that could do this because such a mind killed Katherine Rokesmith.'

'What makes you so definite that man wasn't her husband?' In the poor light Jack looked older. Stella realized she had never actually established his age. It was not on his form. He was still talking:

'... Rokesmith gained nothing. She wasn't insured and had no money. Her death shattered him and he was lumbered with the son. On top of that he had to live with the world's certainty that he was the culprit.'

'He didn't do much to prove otherwise.'

'If you are not guilty you don't have tracks to cover.'

'Not like you.' Against her better judgement Stella blurted out: 'How innocent are you? Why are you so interested?' She retreated to the gap in the privet.

'I was Jonathan Rokesmith's friend.' Jack spoke to the Lady.

'What sort of friend? Where is he now?'

'We were at school together.' He rubbed his face. 'Jonny's dead.'

'You're too old!'

'Thanks.' He smiled grimly. 'We are the same age. He would be thirty-three now. Same age as Jesus when he was crucified.'

'Why wasn't Jonathan Rokesmith's death in the news?'

'The Rokesmiths aren't news. There have been other murders, other murderers.'

'So you snoop into people's lives and steal their identities for the sake of a dead friend?'

'The best detective thinks like a murderer, didn't your dad tell you that?' He smiled briefly. 'Call it unfinished business.'

'Terry was not the best detective.'

Jack had played games with her. Stella turned on her heel. He could follow her or stay talking nonsense in the icy cold: it was up to him.

They heard a sound; it could have been a gust of wind blowing snow off a branch, but the second time it was further away. Footsteps. Jack pushed past her and sprinted out to the road.

There was no one going towards the square or the other way along the north side of Black Lion Lane. Then came the drone of an engine and a brake light sparkled on the camber at the far end.

'This ground was virgin.' Jack pointed. Apart from their tracks there was another set of indistinct prints along the pavement by the bushes, leading to where they had seen the car.

'These are forefoot-struck,' Stella announced.

'What?'

'Whoever made them landed on the ball of their foot rather than their heel, which is more common.' She straightened up: 'I use my heel and so do you. The heels on your shoes are worn while the front part of the soles are only scratched.'

'Are you suggesting that, like Hugh Rokesmith, I can be in two places at once?'

'I said that this person uses the front of their foot, didn't I? Besides, I'm your alibi. If we can't trust each other...' Stella began to walk back to Rose Gardens North, speaking over her shoulder: 'Someone was on the other side of those bushes, they must have heard everything.'

'We might be closer than we think.' Jack's voice was almost inaudible.

'Here, take Terry's keys and let yourself in, I'll be back.'

'You trust me now?'

'I must be mad.'

'Where are you going?' Jack's hair tufted at the back like a child's after napping in a cot. 'You're not bottling out, are you?'

'No, I am not.' Stella snapped. 'I have to sort something.'

Thirty-One

He might have slipped on the ice, she admonished him. He was
too old to take risks.

The snow had given him away, crunching underfoot. If there
had been no snow he would have been able to hear what they were
saying. She admitted that snow made the place deathly quiet when
he was away; a blanket of white suffocating her. Desperate to keep
her smiling he continued, divulging too much.

They were talking about the Rokesmiths, he told her. The man
was Jonathan Rokesmith's friend. They both knew that Jonathan
only had one friend and he was called Simon.

He could see the subject upset her and he tried to come up with
another: she loved to hear the tales of his day. On summer evenings,
sitting out on the terrace, they mixed gin and tonics and watched
the rooks; fewer nests this year. He associated her with sunshine
and told her so.

He would have to go. He called a goodbye up the stairs. She
would probably demand that he come up to the bedroom and kiss
her but she did not reply. This had not happened before so he went
up anyway and popped his head around the door.

She was smiling. He kissed her long and tenderly and then left
the room without looking back.

He let himself out by the back door. It would not be long before
he returned.

And with her new television, she would hardly notice he was
gone.

Thirty-Two

Stella found the car immediately. She got out of the van and inspected it: the bonnet was cold, the windscreen hidden beneath a thick layer of snow that sparkled blue in the moonlight. It was still snowing, meaning Paul could have returned as little as twenty minutes ago and the car would look like this.

Paul Bramwell lived in a 1980s block off the Goldhawk Road that consisted of two buildings forming an 'L' shape surrounded by bushes and shrubs. One element of whatever Paul and Stella had shared had been the communal gardening days. Stella had surprised herself by rather enjoying taking part in planting, clipping and pruning along with Paul's elderly neighbours; more than he had done himself. Terry's gardening books, unopened on her living room shelf until then, had finally come in handy.

There were no footprints to the front entrance but again this would be because it was snowing.

She had not wanted Paul's key and had only agreed to keep it in case he locked himself out.

Paul would not credit her with reading clues and reaching a conclusion; he would not expect her. Stella was both relieved and surprised that he had not confronted them by the statue.

His flat was on the second floor. Music was thumping from the flat opposite. Paul could sleep through anything, although Stella doubted that he would be asleep. He would be planning his next move. He might not be there; he might be at her flat. Briefly she let herself appreciate the irony of each of them spying on the other before remembering that she had seen his car.

She turned the key and slipped inside.

There were three bedrooms. Paul used the box room for playing online games and mending computers. She could hear fans whirring in servers and laptops ranged on a rack.

The kitchen had a serving hatch through which Stella would catch Paul watching her while he prepared supper as she sat in the living room. Over steak and oven chips he would confess how special it was to have her there and she must treat it as her home. Stella had not known how to.

The table was a mess of plates and dishes of half-eaten food. Paul never cleared up after a meal; not wanting to spoil the mood he left the crockery to soak beneath a film of greasy water overnight. At first, drawn in by his skill in networking her office computers, his boyish charm and their agreement that there were 'no strings', Stella had gone along with it, but soon her anxiety at the task burgeoning in the sink overwhelmed her attraction to Paul and she would rush out to clear the kitchen.

Motorcycle boots stood on the parquet floor in the hall, one balanced on the toe of the other where he had taken them off. Stella switched on the light and picked up a boot: the leather was dry. The tread on the heel was worn thin. This did not make sense.

Bags of shredded paper awaited recycling: Paul was neurotic about identity theft – another concern they had shared.

He would only just have gone to bed; he was usually up later than this, trawling the internet. He was using bed as an alibi.

The bedroom blazed with light: on every surface was a candle, lines of tea lights covered the chest of drawers and the window sill. There was a funny smell. Paul had complained of being allergic to room deodorizers. Incense sticks burned in a pot. Stella tripped on a heap of bedding at her feet.

It took a moment for Stella to comprehend the scene. Paul was naked and face down on the bed. Then she saw two more legs either side of him, the knees raised. She backed out.

She had accidently deadlocked the Yale; Paul caught up with her fumbling with the front door.

'What are you playing at?' He was struggling into a dressing gown.

Stella could smell him. She could smell both of them.

'How come you are here?'

'You were spying on me!' Even as she spoke, Stella knew she had made a mistake. Paul had got drunk, picked up a woman and brought her back. He had used for her the romantic candle display meant for Stella. In the morning he would regret it, but he would let it slip to Stella, hoping to make her as jealous as she made him. Hoping she would change her mind and they would live happily ever after.

Stella was jealous, an all-purpose jealousy that did not belong in this bachelor flat but somewhere else out of reach.

Paul had been here all night, setting up candles, ordering a takeaway and the rest.

'The only one spying on anyone is you, on me.' Paul was reasonable.

'I'm sorry,' Stella whispered.

'Why don't you hurry on home to your toy boy and find him something to clean.'

Paul could not help himself and Stella allowed herself to feel vindicated.

They heard shuffling from the bedroom. Paul would have portrayed himself as a rolling stone, unattached and without baggage: Mr Cool.

'You *have* been stalking me,' Stella insisted.

'I love you, that's all. I'll ask her to leave, then we can talk.'

'You never have time, you put work first, you care more about your computers and your silly kids' games.' Stella did not know where the words came from. She would rather he was interested in computers than in her.

The hallway swam, the walls wafting like card; her head throbbed.

'This is bollocks, Stella. It's you who is always too busy.' Paul did up his dressing gown, looking at her strangely.

She put the key on the telephone table and rushed out of the flat.

On King Street a thought filled her with dread.

If Paul was telling the truth, then someone else had been listening by the statue. Instinctively she pressed the central-locking button and checked her mirror.

Still she did not see a car behind her.

Thirty-Three

Wednesday, 19 January 2011

Jack was in Terry's study. He had obeyed Stella's instructions not to turn on lights in the rest of the house and parking up she had been gratified to note that it looked from the outside as if no one was there.

Jack was lounging on Terry's desk chair, his feet propped on an open drawer. He was examining papers from the filing wallet: car insurance schedules, MOT certificates, utility bills that Stella had set aside for probate. She dismissed the ripple of annoyance at this. As she had suggested, he had eaten a shepherd's pie. The smell caught in her throat.

'Did you sort Paul out?' he said without looking up.

'How did you know...? Yes, I spoke to him.'

'Don't tell me, he'd been in all night having a romantic dinner for two.'

'Something like that.' She leant on the sill and looked over at Mrs Ramsay's summerhouse. In the light of the moon it looked like a house in a fairy tale. 'It was probably a passer-by who got scared and ran away.'

'Never believe in the obvious.' Jack slipped the document he had been reading back in the file. He swung his feet down and trundled the chair up to the desk.

'Have you found anything?'

'Not so far. He was meticulous, your dad.' Jack tapped a file box. 'He kept his life in date order. There are art exhibition programmes with the date of his visit, bills with cheque number and date of payment. I see where you get it from.' He clawed his hair back from his face. 'Birth, marriage and death certificates. He's even kept his divorce papers from 1974. Poor guy, eight years was not much of a marriage.'

The angled light heightened his pallor. Stella wished he would stop calling Terry 'her dad' or worse, 'poor guy'.

'Art exhibitions?' she echoed.

'Like I said, never believe the obvious.' Jack angled the monitor to face him. 'Have you been in his computer?

'No.' Stella had not come to the house since she had rushed out and she was sure Jack knew this. 'I suppose he got it to occupy himself in his retirement.'

'He had an occupation.' Jack switched on the machine. The fan was loud in the quiet house and blew out the smell of scorched dust as it came to life.

'That's a bugger.' A white background striped with horizontal grey and letters and digits in Courier font spread over the screen.

'Any ideas what his password was?'

'None.'

'He must have had some technical know-how – this needs a BIOS password. Burglars often test a machine before nicking it and if it asks for one they tend to leave it. Only a professional can crack it. I disturbed a break-in at the Hamiltons and they dumped Michael's laptop because it had a BIOS request.'

'Pity you couldn't have caught them.'

'I did. While they were doing the bedroom I called the police from the study extension and they arrested them on their way out. I had to escape through the study, which was awkward.'

Stella knew a fantasist when she met one. Jack clearly believed what he was saying was true, so it wasn't lying in the strictest sense. Terry put up with all sorts to get answers. She asked: 'Why don't people find you? I would.'

'Yes, you would, but you're not like other people.' Jack tilted back the chair. 'What was Terry's warrant number?'

'How should I know?'

'I know my dad's national insurance number and his car registration.'

'If this is a competition, I'm happy for you to win,' Stella retorted. 'Why would I need to know?'

'It would be a help now if you did.' He tapped the keyboard. A message flashed up saying the password was wrong, try again. 'I thought you were close to your dad.'

'You thought wrong.'

Jack flipped through the document wallet and eased out Terry's payslips. He ran his finger over the paper. 'Here we are.' He punched in a six-digit number:*130253.*

Password incorrect, press return for a retry.

'It will lock us out after ten goes.' Jack leant down and scratched his ankle. 'What's that?' He pointed at the wedge of paper tucked half under the leg of the desk.

'It's keeping the desk steady.' Some detective he was.

Lifting the desk, Jack pulled out the paper and unfolded it.

'It's blank.' Stella wished he would leave things alone.

'No it's not.' He smoothed out the deep creases. 'Why does Colin Peterson ring a bell?'

It had meant nothing to Stella when she used the paper as a stabilizer. It did now.

'He was a suspect in the Rokesmith murder.'

The church clock chimed one.

'Let's call him.'

'He'll be asleep. Besides his alibi was proven.'

'When the time frame was fifteen minutes to midday, but now?'

'He was at Doncaster Racecourse. I think we can rule him out.

'He may know something.'

'Such as what?'

'Wasn't he decorating the spare room? He might have overheard something but not appreciated its significance.'

'Don't you think the police would have got that by now?'

'They were treating him as a suspect, not a witness. Come on, Stella, it's at least worth meeting him.'

They agreed to go the next afternoon. Jack helped Stella load the computer and remaining files into her van.

'I'll give you a lift home.' She was weary and aware she had done no clearing up.

'Nice try. I'll walk.' Jack smiled.

'It was a simple offer,' Stella barked, thinking as she spoke that this was not true.

The snow had stopped and there were no new tracks outside the house or on the road. Jack skittered off in the direction of the Leaning Woman.

When he was out of sight Stella climbed out of the van. Jack was pretending he had the power to conceal himself in people's houses. He was like some little kid being a spy or Batman. She would find out where he lived and make him cut the crap.

Stella floundered through the snow to the church and tiptoed into the dark clearing with the statue. Jack was not there. She did not linger and shuffled through powdery snow past the subway. What with the graveyard and bushes, there were many places to hide. Jack would keep still until she had gone.

The ground was uneven where snow had been trampled and overlaid by another fall. She returned to Terry's street where she spotted fresh tracks on the pavement leading to St Peter's Square. Jack had doubled back from the Leaning Woman. He had got the better of her. She stopped and listened, but heard only traffic on the Great West Road, still busy despite the late hour.

The footprints went diagonally over to the park where, with a flick of the heel, they were lighter. Jack had run, perhaps to make little impression, and then halted by the gate, its horizontal bars picked out in white. The top was clear of snow where he had climbed over or he had wiped it clean to fool her.

Stella nearly gave up. Except giving up was what Jack expected her to do.

She put a foot on the bar above the lock and pulled herself up and over. She had done this before. In the hours before dawn, clothes on over her pyjamas, she had filled a basket with conkers. The cane on the basket was hard and lumpy like a Christmas stocking, or was that from the conkers?

Long shadows fell across the blue-white lawn. For a moment Stella forgot why she was there. Her eyes became accustomed to the dark and gradually she distinguished shapes on the path where Jack had not bothered walk on the edge. He probably thought she would not get this far.

Abruptly prints tracked back the way they had come, along the pavement parallel to the path. He had exited opposite Mrs Ramsay's house.

She clambered over the gate and ran over to 48 St Peter's Square. There were no lights in the windows but Jack was not stupid. Nor were there footprints to the door, and the snow on the yew hedge was pristine. She hovered in the porch. She had a key, she could go inside, but it was late and she was tired; her mind was playing tricks; Jack was not here.

Stella stopped by the hedge. So faint she might have missed them were footprints from the park gate – heel first – that went up the steps of the house next door to Mrs Ramsay's. The house which until 1981 had been Kate Rokesmith's home.

Thirty-Four

Stella made her way from the garages to the lobby in the dark; the lights were still on the wrong timing. She had copied the boiler-room key in case Paul ambushed her but could see from the lack of footprints that there was no one about. For this, if in no other way, the snow was proving useful.

It was numbingly cold. The crunch of her boots carried across the silent compound. It took six journeys to transfer the Rokesmith boxes and Terry's boxes to the lobby. Stella was relieved to get inside. For once she would have derived comfort from meeting another resident.

She loaded the boxes into the lift and pressed the button for her floor. She padded back and forth along the corridor until she had got everything into her flat.

The novel Ivan had given her lay on the hall table where she had left it and aimlessly she carried it through to the lounge where the DVD clock read two minutes past three. On the dining table the case papers she and Jack had been reading were scattered across the glass. This reminded her that Jack had confessed to knowing the boy.

Perhaps he was lying about that too, but somehow she believed him.

She left *Wuthering Heights* on top of the microwave while she brewed a cup of tea, and then, the scuffed volume in one hand, the mug in the other, she went to her bedroom.

Stella had lied to Jack. She did not want to solve the case to vindicate her father as Jack imagined, but to show Terry Darnell that she was a better detective, and to get Kate justice. Now a new impetus was creeping in, which Stella could not put into words. She shivered: the sense that Terry was present had followed her from his house.

She sat in bed drinking the tea, *Wuthering Heights* propped up on her knees, and turned the tissue-thin pages. Other than Jackie, Ivan Challoner was the only person she had met who was genuinely interested in Clean Slate, she mused.

He was wrong about *Wuthering Heights* – she had no time for fiction, real life was full enough – but she rather liked that he thought it was her favourite book. Something fell out of the pages, skimmed off the bed on to the floor. She bent to retrieve it and nearly toppled over. It was a postcard. She flipped it over. It was not stamped and in turquoise ink were the words: 'T, Five. "Cathy" x'.

The writing was scrawled, as if written in a hurry. Described on the back as a 'Winter Scene in Woodland', the picture showed Queen Charlotte's cottage in Kew Gardens, the roof laden with snow, surrounded by trees, not unlike the scene outside Stella's bedroom window.

This presented Stella with a dilemma. The card must have been given to Ivan and if she returned it, he might feel bound to explain who it was from and risk their conversation straying to intimate subjects. Beyond discovering that each was an only child and Ivan referring to a son, neither had given anything away.

If she did not return the card it would be stealing. The scribbled words might be one of the few mementoes he had of his dead wife, whose name was Cathy – or perhaps not, given the inverted commas. It might seem insignificant, but he had kept it so Stella could not throw it out, nor did she want to hold on to it.

No, it was not Ivan's; the novel was second-hand, it had been sent to a previous owner. There was no signature on the flyleaf to offer a clue; no name starting with 'T'. The edition was eighty years old and the card had no date. Ivan had probably never even opened the book. She laid the postcard on the bed. The Rokesmith papers had made her question everything.

More questions: when had Ivan's wife died? How long were they married?

Wide awake now, Stella turned to chapter one and began to read.

Thirty-Five

Sarah Glyde did not hear her brother come in. It had always been like that; Antony entered and left rooms without anyone noticing. He had a key because it had been his home, but since their mother died this was *her* house and she wished he would ring the bell. It was worse than that: Antony never announced himself but lingered in the doorway of her studio until she sensed his presence. She would look round and there he was. She never felt alone.

'You gave me a start.' She was by the sink scraping clay from her fingernails. The cold water splashing down from the loose wall-mounted tap made her hands ache.

He was dressed for work so she did not kiss him and risk dirtying his suit. He was flourishing a bunch of flowers like an Olympic torch.

'You always say that. What are you doing?' He sounded incurious.

'Nothing.' Sarah flung a wet cloth over the beginnings of her sculpture; not that he would see more than a lump of clay. It would not work for her this morning, it was thick and sluggish, refusing to comply or submit to manipulation.

She had seen the man several times, but it had taken only one sighting, when he crossed the road outside her house, for her to retain the intricacies of his face: the straight nose, high forehead and full lips. Her hands could feel his skull beneath the sallow skin and in her mind she stroked the defined planes, the rise of the high cheekbones and the jutting of the jaw. He was not one of those she collected and catalogued, to be accessible whenever she needed an ear, a pose, or a dimpled chin. He had more substance than the faces that populated her dreams. He was beautiful. Sarah had learnt that when a person burned so indelibly into her consciousness she must work on him or her immediately. She would give the clay shape and life and make it her own.

She had been in the studio since dawn, her strong hands with their nimble fingers shaping, slapping and pressing the sullen material to little avail; after several hours it remained unchanged and she quelled a rising panic that she no longer had the skill; her inspiration was used up. Her temples pounded and her eyes ached; she would get nothing done today.

As he so often did, Antony had caught her in one of her bleak moods. In vain, she reminded herself it was like this at the start of every new piece. All the things she had ever feared had happened, but she had survived. This was life. She incorporated the fear into her work, striving to make permanent what was temporary, and to find the enduring in the ephemeral.

Sarah Glyde turned people into sculptures who gazed out from alcoves and corners. The heads, busts and masks she placed everywhere did nothing to break the silence in the many-floored house that, ever since she was a child, had unnerved her. It was a silence that Antony did not break now, as stock still – a statue himself – he communed with himself until she registered he was there.

'Do you want tea?' Sarah had resolved to be nicer to him and, weaving her way between pedestals supporting commissions in various stages of completion, kissed his cold cheek.

He was flapping a leaflet. It was the flier advertising cleaning services that had come through the door. She had meant to hide it from him.

'This was in the hall.' He spoke as if she had deliberately set out to cross him by leaving it there.

'I thought of giving them a call. This place is more than I can manage.' She affected nonchalance.

'You should go by recommendation. Don't choose whatever drops on to the mat.'

'Can you suggest a cleaner?' A Stella Darnell owned the company and Sarah did not say that she would have gone by the name because she liked it. Such minor considerations often precipitated her into making major decisions and infuriated her brother.

'I don't have a cleaner.' Antony screwed up the paper and hurled it accurately into the dustbin by the kiln. He made no attempt to sound convincing and Sarah did not believe him. He was being obstructive. In that moment she hated him.

'It was a whim. I doubt I'll get around to ringing.' After her father's death their mother had made no decision without consulting Antony. Sarah gave him the mug without the chip and, in an effort to be pleasant, patted him as he took it from her. His shoulder was thin and hard. She reminded herself that Antony bought her pieces and gave them away as presents. He was her self-appointed patron and she should think him a good brother.

'What are brothers for?' He had read her mind.

'Do they have to be "for" anything?' Antony put her on the back foot; he did not think or speak like other people. Not for the first time she marvelled he was so successful; he must be different at work.

'What can I do for you? Is this a social call?'

'I came round to see that you were all right.' He seemed mildly aggrieved.

'I am, but why wouldn't I be?' For over thirty years, since Antony had bought his own house, the siblings had exchanged no intimate information or confidences; their relationship was set in clay.

'The weather's making it hard to get out. I've had a plethora of cancellations.'

'The snow brings everything to a halt. It's fabulous, it encourages reflection.' She did not expect him to understand.

Antony took a sip of tea with a smile that did not reach his eyes.

He was sitting on their mother's chaise longue. Antony disapproved of his sister bringing it into her studio to be caked with splashes of slip and stained with paint; he had accepted tight-lipped the clean cloth she laid on the fabric to protect his trousers. Wintry sun warmed their faces. The river was filling, the beach beneath Sarah's back garden was submerged, water rising up the Bell Steps. Sarah knew this: the times and turns of the tide were in her bones.

'I don't like to think of you stranded, unable to get out. Have you enough food?'

'I'm fine. Stop worrying.'

Sarah went around the screen and washed up the cups. When she came back Antony had gone. The bunch of flowers was on the table next to the sculpture. She checked the cloth and was sure it had not moved. As usual there was no message on the flowers but she presumed they were for her. She would have to ring him and ask, and then be suitably grateful; he would be upset if she did not thank him.

Later that afternoon, Sarah called her brother before she could change her mind. The crabby Mrs Willard knew her voice but as usual asked for her name and was only marginally more polite when Sarah told her. She was possessive of Antony and resented any attentions he paid his younger sister. Today was his day off, she reminded Sarah, and Antony had gone to the country. She suggested Sarah keep the flowers, doubtless they were for her.

Sarah chucked the flowers into the dustbin. As she did, so she saw the screwed-up cleaning flier on top of snips of wire and floor sweepings. Still in what she called 'doing mode', she rang and asked for Stella Darnell. The nice person who answered – she called herself Jackie – said Stella was out all day but booked an appointment for Ms Darnell to come that evening to scope the job. It sounded rather too official, but Sarah agreed. She was also told to expect a polite young man called Mr Harmon who, should she sign a contract, would be doing the work. Sarah was reassured: it sounded like Clean Slate took trouble.

She was about to start work when she remembered the flowers. It was no use; she took them out of the bin – chrysanthemums, her least favourite – and deposited them in a jug she had made for her mother. Putting it on the window sill, Sarah wished again that Antony would find a more willing recipient of such gifts and stifled the fear that she was the only woman he cared about.

This notion, although uncomfortable, was more palatable to Sarah Glyde than admitting that her brother did not care for her any more than she did for him.

She lifted the cloth off the clay. The feeling of dread, which had abated when she booked Stella Darnell, returned. Sarah contemplated the ill-formed features, dabbing at them with a moistened cloth, and tried again to recall where she had seen the face who was its inspiration before.

Thirty-Six

Stella arranged to meet Jack outside her office on Shepherd's Bush Green at three o'clock to avoid him finding out that she had told Jackie she had an afternoon appointment with a man in Paddington. Jackie had raised her eyebrows at the name: Nick Jarvis. Not practised with untruths, Stella had inadvertently used one of Jack's fake referees.

She concluded that it would worry Jackie less to think she was struggling with bereavement than that she was investigating a murder with a man she knew little about beyond his cleaning skills, who had been at school with the son of a murdered woman.

She had not told Jack she suspected he had broken into the old Rokesmith house in St Peter's Square for two reasons. One: while he imagined he could hoodwink her, he might let his guard down and she would learn more about him. Two: she did not really believe that he had broken in.

Jack was lounging against the bonnet of the only van not kitted out with the new green livery. Stella had delayed the respray; she did not want Jack to collapse. He had washed his hair and lost some of the pencil-grey pallor. He had on a clean shirt and his trousers were pressed, his shoes polished. He had made an effort; Stella inadvertently waved.

There was no sign of Paul. After her visit he must have got the message.

As they sped along the Westway they concocted the story for Colin the plasterer. Stella would have to say she was Terry's daughter; they would not reveal the new timings and Stella promised to keep an open mind. Jack would just be Jack.

The satnav guided them into a network of streets behind Wormwood Scrubs Common in the shadow of the prison. Terry had grown up nearby; Stella could not remember where.

Colin Peterson lived halfway down Mellitus Street in the only house in the two-up-two-down thirties' terrace painted white and adorned with hanging baskets. The regulation council house door had been replaced with ornate oak and leaded stained glass of red and yellow diamonds. They passed between a trimmed privet and up a concrete path, the snow shovelled aside; Jack pressed the doorbell and precipitated a clamour of Big Ben chimes within.

A sandy-haired man in jeans and a polo shirt, with a toneless complexion as if coated with foundation for a television appearance, opened the door.

'Not interested, I told the other lot: I don't give handouts to street callers. On your way.'

'Mr Peterson, my name is Stella Darnell. You met my father.' Stella spoke rapidly to get his attention before the door shut. She took a chance he had met Terry.

Peterson appeared doubtful, but stayed where he was.

'He has your notepaper.' She reached into her pocket.

Peterson took the sheet, creased from the weight of the desk.

'It's mine but I don't recall your dad. Tell him I've got no space until the back end of March if he's still interested. What did he want doing?'

'It's about a job you did.'

'You tell him from me: if plastering ain't working, you see it right away. No use complaining after the fact. If he has a problem it'll be the paint, the age of the wall—'

'We're not complaining. I wanted to ... to follow up on your conversation.'

'To be honest, Miss er ... I don't know your dad and need to be in Acton for four fifteen.'

'Terry Darnell. He was here about a month ago?' Stella stepped away; they were wasting their time.

'Bloke a bit taller than me? Grey hair, black jacket, paunchy, late sixties?' Jack intervened, his new-found Shepherd's Bush voice catching Stella by surprise. She had forgotten Terry's accent; the imitation was faithful. Only then did it occur to her to wonder how Jack could describe Terry.

She glared at him, trying to catch his eye.

Peterson smacked his thigh. 'Why didn't you say? The private detective with ex-copper written all over him – but I told him, "My memory's like an elephant, I know who you are, you put me through the mill and nearly ruined my life."' He spoke as if it were Terry on his doorstep. 'He wanted to rake up that murder. I was doing up the spare room where the poor lady lived. I should have sent him packing and the same goes for you.'

He had worked himself into a rage and tried to shut the door.

Jack put his shoe into the gap and his hand on to the door jamb. Stella admired his courage, his shoe would be ruined and his fingers broken.

'This is Detective Superintendent Darnell's daughter. We're after answers for him and with your ring-side seat hoped you could help. We're doing it for the little boy who lost his mum and still doesn't know why.'

Were they? That was a new take on it. Stella waited: it could go either way. Their hastily devised strategy had collapsed; they had not reckoned on Peterson being intractable.

'I got enough grief off of the police at the time, I don't need it dug up.' He addressed Stella: 'I told your dad, I'm set up, remarried, free of those clowns at the Inland Revenue and making OK money.' He nodded at her ruefully. 'He said you and him was checking up on loose ends? I had a lot of time for that lady. The newspapers and the police chewed me up and spat me out without an apology, although I grant you, when he was here, your dad said sorry.'

Stella guessed this last bit was wishful thinking. Terry never apologized.

'Would it be all right if we came in?' Jack spoke softly.

Sighing, Peterson let them into a hallway with smooth walls.

He led them into a front room so tidy it might have been prepared for putting on the market. A patterned carpet gave off the deodorant some clients used to hide the smell of dogs or cigarettes. Stella caught a whiff of protection cream off the stark white leather three-piece suite into which she and Jack sank. Someone looked after this house; she debated asking Peterson if his wife wanted work, but he was speaking to her.

'It was before Christmas; we had the tree so he had to sit over there. He said how his little girl liked lights on a tree. I told him mine did. Not that little, though, are you!' He gave a wheezy laugh. 'He said he would bring you. What happened? He bale out and make you do his dirty work!'

Stella shrugged out of her anorak and folded it across the back of the sofa behind her.

'Could you go over what you told Terry?' Jack asked.

Peterson raised his eyes, then with a shrug went on: 'I was there for a fortnight in June 1981. I checked my old diary for him. I'd been gone a month when the tragedy occurred.' He adopted the manner of a witness in court.

'We aren't after facts – they must be hazy after so long – but we'd love to hear your impressions, your feelings about your time there,' Jack encouraged him. Stella tried to catch his eye. Facts were precisely what they were after.

'Why were you there so long? Surely it's a day's work to plaster a room?' she demanded. Jack frowned at her.

'Your dad asked that the first time around and like I told him, I was doing chippy work too and painting. My trade's plastering and nowadays I stick to it. If I never see another paintbrush it'll be too soon, all that sanding and coat after coat and the customer is never happy. Like I said, what made up for it was that Mrs Rokesmith was nice. Have you been in the house?' Stella glanced at Jack but now he was gazing out of the window, making no effort to appear to be listening. If only he could behave consistently.

'She tried to keep her little lad away. He was desperate to help; he had his own brush and bucket. My kids were the same. Not that they've either of them stuck at it. The youngest might—'

'You saw her son?' Jack interrupted. Stella fixed on him but he avoided her eyes; he had no idea about being a team.

'In the end she asked if it was OK for him to watch. He sat in his little chair, chattering like a bloody canary. I couldn't shut him up. It beat Radio One. I got to look forward to him scampering in to show me his toys. He had names for everything. Odd kid. He didn't have brothers and sisters so he made up friends. I'd never come across one like him.'

'What do you mean?' Jack asked.

'I'd catch him staring like he could see right into my head. Then he was off again: what I was doing, why was I doing it and what would happen next. He held the hawk like a pro, ready to slap on the plaster. He goes and informs his mum he's going to be a plasterer. She was well into it – not sure Mr Man would have approved. At eleven on the dot, we'd have coffee and a natter. Not often a customer is so friendly.'

'Was she interested in you?' Stella saw Jack stiffen. He was going to be no use to his dead friend if he could not be objective.

'Lovely looking girl. I was married and so was she. It wasn't like that. I told the police. I would never have hurt her. People's minds are filthy. More so than ever.' He made a steeple of his hands; the skin was dried and cracked. 'I finished the job and moved on. She was lonely, that's all.'

'What makes you say that?' Jack seemed to have shrunk into the white leather. Stella decided he lacked stamina, probably vitamins too.

'I never saw no one there. I would of expected a lady like that to be having coffee mornings, other mums round – the usual. She had her lad, and that was it. Not unless you count Uncle Tony.' He laughed.

'Who was Uncle Tony?' Jack sat forward.

'I remembered that when your dad was here at Christmas. I told the lad I had an Uncle Tony, which tickled him. He wanted to be like me – the kid I mean – he'd go on about my Uncle Tony and his Uncle Tony. Long dead now, bless him.' Colin Peterson rested one ankle on his knee. 'I didn't have my kids then. I've got three now.' He gave a guffaw that ended in a starter-motor cough.

Jack took out his pouch of tobacco and set about rolling a cigarette. He placed it in his case, which Stella noticed was full.

'What was this Uncle Tony like?' Jack began another cigarette, licking along a paper.

'He wasn't real. The kid made him up. Copying me, I suppose. I forgot about him until your dad was here. It brought back the fuss about the engine.'

'The what?' Jack snapped shut the case and returned it to his pocket. The room was fuggy with heat, but he had not taken off his coat.

'He said his Uncle Tony gave him the toy engine. I had to see it, he insisted, made me have a go, you know push it along. He let me be the driver.' He shook his head.

'What sort of steam engine?' Stella was puzzled: Jonathan Rokesmith had wanted his dad to buy him an engine he saw in a shop window after his mother's death yet he already had one. The article had said Rokesmith refused to buy him the engine in order not to spoil him; no wonder, if Rokesmith had agreed, the boy would have had two engines.

'It must have cost an arm and a leg. It was old even then, more my time, but in good nick until sonny boy got his hands on it. One day it all went pear-shaped, he comes to play and there's me up a ladder doing the ceiling. No way I could play but he was going on and on.' He raised his arm in demonstration: 'You got to do it in one hit with the same mix or the line shows so I didn't dare stop and my, was he put out? I saw another side of him, he went ape!

'I did warn her she should be more strict. I wouldn't put up with that.' Peterson scratched his forearm and added: 'Get away with murder otherwise.'

'Did you see anyone else?' Jack broke in.

'No, I said, apart from the husband, and him only once, which was fine by me.' He pulled a face.

'Why was that?' Stella did not look at Jack. Later she would talk to him: he was behaving as if she was not there.

'You minded your p's and q's when Mr Rokesmith was about. He had to find fault. He spots the ceiling right off. I felt like saying, blame your boy, but it wasn't fair on the lad. These days I know not to be distracted even if the house is on fire. Ceilings are a bitch!'

'What was Hugh Rokesmith like?' Stella pressed on.

'He was fussy – not that I was as good then, mind. She said he blew hot and cold. I couldn't be doing with that. Drive you mad.' He flicked an invisible speck off the arm of his chair. Stella wondered how sensible it was to have white leather in the house of a plasterer. Her experience of plaster was that it did not respect dust sheets or closed doors; it got everywhere.

'Why didn't you say about Uncle Tony to the police at the time?' she enquired carefully.

'He was fibbing about Uncle Tony, like I said. Her bloke was an engineer; they're the worst sort of customer. These days, I'd turn the job down. They're so finicky. Small step to kill his wife, I'd say.'

'What's wrong with engineers?' Jack was taking it personally. Stella tried to nudge his foot, but he was out of reach in the corner of the sofa. She would remind him, they would only spot clues if they paid proper attention.

'They work to much finer tolerances. They're dealing with machines; it's all certain, no room for slippage, no approximations. I'm doing it by hand so it's bound to be rougher. Like I said to Kate, any problems, there are British Standards. My dad could quote them for breakfast, so I was up on them. He wants an argument, I'm out of here, I told her. That's when she said it was just his way and she could handle him.'

'Do you think he killed her?' Stella was struggling to sit straight amidst the squashy cushions.

'He said he was with his mum. Like my first wife was fond of saying, my mum argued cats were dogs for me.' Peterson assumed a wise expression. 'He might have done it. Then again he might not.'

A wall clock struck four. The design was one of those that make a feature of the mechanism at the expense of telling the time. Stella thought it more of an engineer's clock than a plasterer's. She stood up.

'I told your dad, I hope he gets the man this time. I'd be in the queue to have a pop at him. For the aggro he caused me and for that poor girl. People don't trust you. I thought about changing my name, but what to and why should I? He should change his.'

'Perhaps he has,' Jack murmured.

On the doorstep they shook Colin Peterson's hand and, perhaps because it was over and in a minute they would be gone, he confided: 'He's all right, your dad – some of them flash their badges soon as look at you. They get off on it.' He seemed to appraise Stella for the first time. 'Got you doing his leg work, has he!'

'Something like that.' She wanted to be gone, but forced herself to pay attention.

'He hadn't forgotten his roots.' He leant on the gate, his appointment in Acton apparently forgotten. 'We did have a laugh about the old days. Funny bloke isn't he, cracked me up! He went to Old Oak Primary like me but was a couple of years above. My sister Joan remembers him – a "dish", she said! She used to hang about outside his house – you can tell him that. He's still a QPR man, ain't he? Said he dragged you to the Cop once. My boys defected to Spurs.'

'His house?' Stella was casual.

'Primula Street. Forgotten what number. Joan will know. He said he was taking you there.'

'If you think of anything else.' Stella saw Terry flipping open his wallet, removing his card. She would lie in bed and worry about the criminals who had his number and would come to find him. She offered her Clean Slate business card.

'Your dad's never let this go, got to admire him. Give him my best, yeah?'

On the street Jack skidded and grabbed her arm, causing Stella to lose her balance. They teetered like starfish.

'Why didn't you tell him Terry was dead?' He let go.

'It wasn't important.'

For the first time since Terry's death, Stella Darnell began to suspect that perhaps it was.

Thirty-Seven

Thursday, 20 January 2011

Jackie rang to confirm the appointment with Sarah Glyde as they were passing Wormwood Scrubs Prison on Du Cane Road. She had liked Stella's idea that her cleaners come to initial meetings to impress clients. Stella would have to come up with a reason why this only applied to Jack.

He suggested they leave the van outside Terry's house and walk under the foot tunnel to Sarah Glyde's. Stella soon saw why. At the Leaning Woman he cleared off a new layer of snow and scraped icy patches from around her face and along her thigh with a coin.

In the growing dark, the statue diminished in size and the ravages of the years was apparent. It was a lump of concrete which, over half a century, had fallen victim to decay and vandalism. Jack worked frenetically exposing the pock-marked surface demarcated into butcher's joints, a tinge of colour in his cheeks. It struck Stella that, like a vampire, Jack drew life from the sculpture. His hands flitting over the Woman's thigh, her face, brushing and sweeping, he was not the zombie of an hour earlier. As the statue had shrunk, so Jack had gained in stature.

Sunlight flashed on the hearse. Stella was beside him, a tiny thing on the wide seat. Already her tights were wrinkling. Her feet fidgeted in new patent-leather shoes. She had expected to visit her nana and although he'd explained what a funeral was, she had not taken it in. Her mother had dressed her up. Wearing a dress had, he could see, put a dampener on the day for her. Until Du Cane Road Stella chattered away; it was exciting, they had a whole huge car to themselves. Did prisoners go in it? He didn't get this until she announced that the man driving them was a policeman like him. She became subdued when the traffic slowed and the hearse in front filled the windscreen.

Suzanne had said four was too young for a funeral and besides Stella hardly knew his mum. He said she had loved her nana. He had to be right so she came, no arguments. Stella was upset and he was sorry; he didn't care if he was right, just that he didn't make her cry.

Du Cane Road was solid; nothing could stop the world, not even his cranky old mum. He had gone mad with flowers despite her warning no fuss. She would have given Stella juice and biscuits afterwards. His family: his mum and his little girl. When he told his mum about his matrimonial problems she said at least you have 'fin-fan'; her name for his Stella. The sun was hot and it was only morning. They passed the prison. He shouldn't have brought her.

'When I get there I'll sort your father out.' His mum's dying words had got a laugh at the station but wouldn't work on Stella.

'Is Nana getting boiling hot?' She jerked a wet thumb at the coffin.

'She can't feel anything, not pain or sun.'

Satisfied, she put her thumb back in her mouth; he wouldn't stop her, not today.

His mum could not feel sunshine.

Stella might have been mulling it over the way she crinkled her forehead. She worked problems out step by step, taking after her nana. One day perhaps he would have his practical businesslike mother back by way of his daughter.

Stella slipped a damp hand into his and they squeezed fingers when the hearse entered the crematorium gates. She would not forget her nana, he told himself. He was right to bring her.

Look after the living, his mum would say.

'I wanted to scream when he was waffling on,' Stella said. 'All that about Terry and primary school.'

'I didn't see anything about an Uncle Tony in the files, did you?'

'Of course not. He made up him up,' Stella snapped. Jack also knew about 'made-up'. She rounded on him: 'What was the matter with you back there? He obviously reckoned Hugh Rokesmith did it and you kept contradicting him. Peterson was there, he should know, that was why you suggested we went.'

Jack's ear was against the plinth as if he were cracking open a safe and listening to the tumblers. Stella hoped he was not going to have another 'Pantone 375' attack.

'He was biased, he hadn't liked Hugh Rokesmith because he was a perfectionist. In an engineer's world errors are not permissible. If a bridge is wrong it shows – at worst it falls down – so your mistakes are public.'

'Did you meet him?'

'What do you mean?' Jack brushed off the last of the snow.

'You were Jonathan Rokesmith's friend. Did you meet his father?'

'He brought the son into the class on the first day.'

They walked in silence through the subway.

In Black Lion Lane Stella trod gingerly; she could not afford to break an ankle. Even when Sarah Glyde's house was in sight, Stella did not let herself increase her pace. Jack, his coat unbuttoned, flapped ahead of her, silhouetted against the lamplight like a great bat.

Stella gave the knocker two sharp raps. She craned up, certain that she would not like to live in such a large house on her own. Mrs Ramsay had managed it by filling her draughty home with dead people and making up others for company – except she had not made up everyone: Jack was real.

'You made it! Come out of this perishing cold!' Sarah Glyde ushered them in.

Jack stepped into the light and Sarah Glyde stopped smiling.

The moment was brief and, shaking her hand, Stella decided her impression that the woman had for a moment been terrified was mistaken.

Thirty-Eight

Thursday, 20 January 2011

They parted outside Sarah Glyde's house and again Jack refused a lift. This time she did not argue; she knew where to find him. Neither of them suggested a debrief about the meeting; since the afternoon, despite a slight improvement in his mood at the statue, Jack had been heavy and sullen and Stella was as keen to part with him as he seemed to be with her. Jonathan Rokesmith might have been his friend, but if they stood a chance of solving the case he had to put his own feelings to one side and be professional.

They arranged that Jack would be at Stella's flat the next afternoon; he was busy in the morning. Stella stopped herself pointing out that he had said he only did late shifts on the Underground. Jack was one of those people who liked to weave a mystery around themselves to appear interesting, so she would not indulge him by quizzing him.

Jack set off down the path to Hammersmith Bridge; he would have to double back, perhaps via the Great West Road. Grasping gateposts, walls, even hedge branches, Stella snailed her way along Black Lion Lane.

Every few paces she checked behind, as she had done on the way to Sarah Glyde's, looking out for Paul. Jack would not be suspicious were he watching. Paul's silence since her visit to his flat was making her nervous. Just before the ramp, she clambered over a mound of snow in the gutter and hid behind a four-wheel drive.

Jack would pass by on her right; she was ready to move around the large vehicle to avoid him. She arched her back to alleviate the stiffness. She had concentrated on the Rokesmith case over the past week so had not picked up cleaning shifts which she relied on for exercise; she was out of condition. She gave up and stepped into the road.

Jack was by the Bell Steps. He was staring at her. She had been stupid: he had reeled out his line, let her swim towards the bait, now he was winding her in.

He moved and she realized he was facing the other way and had not seen her. She took her chance and, careless of injury, scooted into the subway.

It took Stella ten minutes to stumble through the snow and ice to St Peter's Square, by which time she had decided what to do about Jack.

Thirty-Nine

Thursday, 20 January 2011

After the Clean Slate people had gone, Sarah Glyde went outside without sufficient warm clothes. She did not think Antony would visit now, yet she hesitated on the brick coping step, her lungs hit by cold air. A thick mist lowered the sky and shrouded the river. The country was complaining about productive hours lost, injuries, traffic jams, car accidents and cancelled trains. As she had told Antony, the white-out afforded an opportunity for meditation. She had cleared a path to the garden wall by smashing up one of the blocks of salt she kept for children's sculpture classes and sprinkling it on the bricked surface but had left snow on the path to her studio so she would know if Antony had been there. With enough work she could sit tight and share in the joyful spirit of those adults who had taken to the hills on tea trays and – willing huskies – dragged their offspring on toboggans through streets to stock up on provisions. These people had souls; Sarah was not alone.

She had willed him to come to her and tonight he had; the strength of her powers scared her. He was called Jack Harmon and would come to her house every week. She would not tell Antony; he would spoil it.

She had planned to go out to the studio and continue with Jack Harmon's head. She felt naughty; her mother would have disapproved and if he appeared Antony would tell her it was too cold, too late, she should take more care. The idea that she was flouting their authority should not have mattered to a woman in her fifties, but old habits die hard and the fact that her behaviour lacked parental sanction added spice to her decision.

She leant on the garden wall and damp crept through her father's Aran jumper, making her bones ache; she pulled the cuffs over her hands, hugging herself, comforted by the ghost of his smell.

Her mother had been dead ten years, her father longer, but still Sarah's sense of freedom was tenuous. She jealously guarded her slivers of independence: people came to the studio as models; when the piece was fired, their relationship, such as it was, ended. They paid for their time with her.

Jack was different. Sarah was prepared to pay a high price for him.

With no buildings there were few lights on this stretch of the Thames. The surface of the river was black as oil; slick and treacherous. On the horizon it reflected the kindling lights of Hammersmith Bridge like stars leaping, vanishing and reappearing when chill gusts whipped the water. The whoosh of traffic on the Great West Road was in counterpoint to an irregular tink-tink at the river's edge of a bottle washing back and forth on the encroaching tide, tipped against a brick jutting out of the mud. The insidious sound was a warning to those who ate, drank and were merry in the cafés, pubs and clubs of London amidst the rigour and tumult of the city, that mortality awaited them as it had their forebears. The metronomic sound pointed up the hubris of human endeavour as mere flotsam and jetsam. The river had flowed when hansom cabs, broughams and horses dragging carts log-jammed the thoroughfares of London. The tide came in. The tide went out.

The man was there again. Sarah's euphoria ebbed with the tide. He was by the shoreline, negotiating the slippery stones, squelching through mud with the poise of a dancer, behaving as if the terrain was his own. Sarah ripped at the fronds of ivy, their leaves stiff with ice, and the man looked around. She kept still. He continued to the yacht club pontoon.

It was never truly dark in London and she could make out that he was by the shallows, letting water wash around his ankles, unafraid of the river. Sarah imagined the freezing water parting for him as for Canute.

She went into her studio and, leaving the light off, made her way to her work table. She switched on her mother's standard lamp. The colours of the shade were dulled with clay dust and sunlight. The cloth was draped like a veil over Jack Harmon's unformed head.

Antony's visit had cast a pall over her studio, his presence a contamination. She needed to air the place. Jack Harmon would make the house finally hers.

She whipped off the material with a waiter's flourish and perched on her stool. The light illuminated only her corner of the room; the rest was in shadow. She did not need to see to create his features; she could have worked blindfolded.

The river filled. The relentless pull and draw of the tide hitting slime-hung walls gave a base rhythm as, methodically, mechanically, Sarah Glyde worked on.

The face that gazed back at her in the blue light of dawn was a face she had not seen for thirty years.

Forty

Thursday, 20 January 2011

Someone was leaning on the bonnet. Stella, cursing under her breath that she had parked outside Terry's house, crept forward. Her steps squeaked on the crisp ground. At any moment the man – she was sure it was a man – would come over and search the bushes. She lowered a branch.

It was Paul.

Stella struggled to her feet. If Terry were here he would send him away. She was grateful he was alright.

If Paul had been following her, he would have been outside Sarah Glyde's house. Perhaps he had not liked to confront Stella with Jack there – he wouldn't want a fight – but as soon as they separated he might have tackled her and he had not. He could not have been following her. Paul had expected to find her clearing Terry's belongings; he knew her well enough to be certain that, anxious not to lose time in the office, she would come in the evenings. Seeing her van, he must have congratulated himself on being right. Jackie was right, if Stella bothered to get to know people she would feel the benefit. Stella appreciated this pearl of wisdom, although not in the way intended. Had she taken the trouble to know Paul she would have anticipated that he would become too involved and avoided him.

He looked frozen. Stella guessed he had been there for some time.

She thought back to how Paul had been by the river. She had been relieved that Jack – and there was little about him that reassured – had seen him off. For a split second she had been

283

convinced that Paul would kill her. It was an extraordinary idea: he was mild-mannered, cowardly and indecisive. Or so she had assumed. Such an underestimation of the capabilities of a lover or an ex-lover could cost a person their life. Paul had been in the area on the day of the murder. She should grill him, but to do so alone in the dark was plain stupid. Why had he not gone to the police? Terry had said murderers returned to the scene of their crime; supposing Paul had not followed her to the river, but was going there anyway? She pulled a face; having an open mind was doing her no favours.

Paul was keeping vigil; it was not Stella herself he wanted, he wanted to stop her discovering the truth. The van told him she was there, or that if she was not, that she would return.

She could go up Black Lion Lane, take a left into the square by the Cross Keys and get to the Rokesmiths' house from the north side. It would take her fifteen minutes with the snow. That was too long; Jack would come any minute.

Paul would see him.

She should warn Jack. Or should she warn Paul?

Jack had lied. He had not told her he was a train driver or that he had known Jonathan Rokesmith; he had promised that they would be a team, but did not answer her calls or do what they had agreed.

Paul was fiddling with an object; Stella saw too late that it was his phone as her own handset buzzed. She had five seconds before it would ring, faintly first, then louder. Frantic, she scrunched up her anorak, feeling for it; she had too many pockets.

She found it, but dared not take it out, or Paul would hear. She fumbled at the keys, sliding the flat of her thumb over them. All the time the harp melody she had assigned to Paul's number was increasing in volume. She found the mute button. She was sweating in the padded jacket and, wiping her face, dared to shuffle on her haunches to ease her muscles.

Tinny chatter came through her gloved fingers and she held the handset close to prevent light penetrating the bushes. Paul's name was on the screen. Digits counted up: *30 secs, 31 secs…* She had not cut off the call, she had answered it.

Stella closed the line but too late; Paul was walking towards her. She was unable to move. She had to maintain a sense of proportion; it was Paul, he could not kill anyone; and surely not her. She shut her eyes. The phone buzzed again; she let it go to voicemail.

When she opened them Paul was by her van, cupping his hands around his face to peer inside. He tried the doors and then to her horror resumed his position by Terry's gate. He was going nowhere.

She scrambled along the undergrowth until she reached the edge of the flower beds. Ahead was the subway. She cleared her throat quietly before she dialled Paul's number.

He answered: 'I've been trying to get you. Why were you ignoring me? I knew you were there all the time.'

'I didn't hear it ring.' Stella knew she did not sound convincing.

'I know you're in there. Your van's outside.'

Paul spoke coldly. If Stella had not been able to hear his voice carrying across the snowbound street she would have doubted it was him. There was a nasty edge to his voice.

'I'm at the pub, the one by the river,' she replied without thinking.

'I can't hear anyone.'

'I'm on my own.'

'It's open just for you, is it?'

'No, I mean, I'm outside. That's why I didn't hear you ring. I came to check my messages and saw you had called.'

'Nice of you to call back. Is *he* with you?'

'No.' This bit was true. 'Why don't you go home?' He would know she was lying if she agreed to meet him. Paul understood her better than she did him.

'I'm coming. We need to talk; I need to explain.'

'I won't be there.' Without intending to, Stella rang off.

She flitted into the shadow of the trees. They would not hide her if he looked her way, but Paul was running to the subway looking at the ground. Near the statue he skidded but recovered himself. He might have spotted Jack and Stella's footprints leading from the van towards the river, but he was no detective.

As soon as he entered the subway, Stella broke cover and crunched over the frozen turf to St Peter's Square. The steps up to number 49 were covered in snow: Jack had not been back. Her own footprints would give her away. There was no other way to the front door, except the surprise element was essential. She looked wistfully over at Mrs Ramsay's house, dark and empty, next door.

She still had her keys. In a snap decision, Stella walked as if on a tightrope at the edge of the path, leaning into the hedge dividing Mrs Ramsay's garden from what had been the Rokesmiths' thirty years before. Inside the porch she took a stride to the doormat and, peeping around the column, checked behind her. A halo of light had formed around the lamp-post beside the park and within this shapes appeared and disappeared. It was snowing again.

Her prints would be covered.

Inside the tang of cleaning agents sharpened the still air. In the light from the landing windows the balustrade coiled into the darkness. Her heart crashing against her chest, Stella began to ascend, gripping the beeswaxed wood. After her experience at Terry's house she was relieved to find the doors on the first landing still shut as she had left them. In the sitting room the partition doors were open wide; the French windows lit the sweep of polished space on which Mrs Ramsay had danced the night away.

There would be no more parties, she had informed Stella on her last visit, implying it was punishment. Stella had become a stand-in for one of Isabel Ramsay's children just as the vacuum hose had been her substitute dancing partner, so the punishment was intended for the children. Perhaps, after all, her mind had been going; Stella had heard it said that presuming your family were stealing from you was an indication of dementia. Mrs Ramsay's agitated search for the dolls' house fitted this picture.

The glass in the French doors was so clean it was invisible. She had done this room. She was still good.

Outside she could not see Jack or Paul.

All the doors on the top floor were ajar. Stella had purposely closed them to cut down the risk of fire spreading. She felt panic rising; Jack had no reason to come here; she had taken the top floors. Had he broken in after all?

He kept insisting that Mrs Ramsay invited him. For some reason Stella believed this. She tried to stop the jumble of questions and doubts: perhaps she was going mad herself. Jackie said grieving could make you mad; Stella had wanted to say she was not grieving.

A scattering of grit lay on the carpet at the top of the stairs. She had cleaned the landing so the only way it could have got there was through an open window. The landing window across the stairwell was nailed shut and even if it had been possible to open it, the grit was only in one area. If it had come through the window it would be on the stairs too.

She had forgotten the attic. Her least favourite job, it had slipped her mind, as it had at Terry's, even though she had longed to have a go at it when she cleaned at Mrs Ramsay's. For some reason Mrs Ramsay never included it in her lists.

Stella gave the hatch a push and caught it as it swung down; peeping over the hole was a wooden ladder. She tried not to think of the last time she had climbed into an attic but already a cold fear was uncoiling. The wooden rungs strained when she put weight on them, but held. She was surprised to find no dust; the ladder was tacky as if it had been wiped down.

Stella poked her head through the hole, cautiously, blood hammering in her head. There was something attached to a vertical support. She went all the way up and gingerly stepped on the joists. It was a Bakelite switch; she flicked it and filled the loft with light.

Piles of boxes, books, riding hats, a child's scooter and roller skates were amongst heaps of clothes, the material greyed with dust. The attic was a dumping ground for broken or discarded objects: the clobber of living. Here were the toys Mrs Ramsay had insisted her children had lost: a deflated Space Hopper, a child's painting of an aeroplane flying over fields, a naked Sindy doll and, behind a rickety wheelchair, a gigantic house. She had found the dolls' house, but it was too late.

Someone had laid down boards and moved boxes and bags to create a walkway; Stella followed this makeshift path and got an answer to her question.

Jack had not needed a key or an invitation to Mrs Ramsay's house. Once he had broken into the Rokesmiths' house next door, he could come and go from Mrs Ramsay's as he pleased.

There was no fire wall.

Forty-One

Thursday, 20 January 2011

Paul Bramwell had spent the evening drinking Famous Grouse, a Christmas present from his brother, and – adept at adopting motives to disguise real ones – convinced himself he needed to clear his head. As soon as he'd left his flat he knew he really wanted to see Stella. He knew also that he had drunk too much to drive, although for a moment the smack of night air fooled him that he was sober. Still he hesitated: the side roads were not gritted, he could not afford to lose his 'no claims'.

No claims. Paul mumbled this as he fell against a signpost. He was free, single and not so young. He waited for the pavement to stop tipping like the deck of a boat, then set off for Stella's.

At Young's Corner he stopped. Even if Stella was in her flat he had no way of getting in because she turned off her buzzer and she would not hear him shouting through her double glazing. Like Stella, the flat was hermetically sealed from the world; perversely this idea prompted a wash of affection for her. They had got this far, that must mean something. She had dumped him because her dad had died; it was a reaction and he should cut her some slack. It was his birthday in two weeks. He wanted to spend it with Stella, not with a stranger. Or worse, alone.

Stella would have gone to her father's house. She would not neglect her business to deal with his stuff so she would go at night. Although Paul Bramwell had provided himself with an excuse not to walk all the way to Brentford, he was right about where Stella was.

At the sight of her van, Paul was joyful. By now he had assured himself that Stella loved him as much as he loved her. He slouched against her van and planned his speech. The whisky had enabled him to forgive her for the poet with the spider legs and even for the tosser with the flash car he'd seen waiting for her by the river. As he had assured the policewoman, he was a family friend and he was there for her.

An hour went by. Initially the alcohol and the walk from the top of Goldhawk Road had made him hot; soon he cooled down and his feet went numb. He would not ring her. He imagined her checking her mobile and there being no call. Her secretary had dropped a hint that girls needed the chance to miss their partners. She had been right; he had laid low and Stella had come to his flat.

Maybe, he thought, Stella did not know where he was. He could pretend he was at home, which would mean she might think it safe to come out. But he ought to check she was all right – he had been drunk for a week when his father died. Yes, Paul Bramwell told himself, he should definitely call her.

He would tell her what he knew about the Rokesmith murder. He regretted now that he had not come forward; he might have met Stella's dad – that would have impressed her.

He called Stella. It rang and rang and just as he was giving up he got through.

'Hello?' he whispered. She wouldn't be happy if he woke the neighbours. He clamped the phone to his ear and picked up rustling and shoving. *She was in bed with that man.*

'Stella. It's me, Paul. I'm… I'm at home. I've been here all evening. Where are you? I know where you are.' The line went dead. He dialled again.

'*Leave your name and number and a short message.*'

Stella did not promise to return calls, nor did she ever call back. Paul tightened his fist as a red mist of fury descended.

He was brought back to the present by his phone ringing.

'I've been trying to get you. Why were you ignoring me? I knew you were there all the time.' He forgot to talk quietly.

'I'm at the pub, the one by the river.'

'I can't hear anyone.'

'I'm on my own.'

'It's open just for you, is it?'

'No, I mean, I'm outside. That's why I didn't hear you ring. I came to check my messages and saw you had called.'

'Nice of you to call back. Is *he* with you?'

'No. Why don't you go home?'

'I'm coming. We need to talk; I need to explain.'

'I won't be there.'

She rang off. Paul could wait for her to return to the van or go and meet her. He was too cold to stay still, he told himself, so, fortified by her voice, he slithered and skidded to the subway. The tunnel was a break, without snow he could walk faster. The tiled walls and stone floor seemed to be merging: he was still drunk and must not let Stella see.

Halfway along, he checked each way and then peed into one of the gutters at the sides. His pee steamed as it hit the tiles and he swayed slightly. Stella hated him pissing outside. But these were special circumstances: he could not risk her leaving while he went to the lavatory.

Tucking himself in, Paul forgot to do up his zip because now he was concerned she might have left the pub. He careered up the ramp.

Demons chased him, leaping and grasping at him: another man's hands had been on her; another man had been inside her. Whenever Paul thought of Stella when she was not with him, he supposed her the life and soul of the party, lively and spontaneous, surrounded by men wanting her. His jealousy was a kind of insanity.

The pub was shut.

He put a hand on the wall of a house to steady himself, and then stumbled up the three flood defence steps. He teetered at the top before dropping unsteadily down to the river.

He should have thought to bring a torch. He had his mobile. He nearly fell over as his feet sloshed through water. There was water everywhere.

'...nor any drop to drink,' he murmured, faintly pleased with himself. That bastard was not the only one who knew poetry. Paul inched along the shore.

Stella was not there. But it was all right: she loved him, she would be looking for him; she'd probably crossed the Great West Road, wouldn't like the tunnel at night. Before his eyes danced black shapes of cut-out paper and when he tried to brush them away they got reinforcements and stung his cheeks. He thrust out his fists.

'Oh, it's you!'

The black shapes joined up to equal nothing.

Forty-Two

Thursday, 20 January 2011

After leaving Stella, as she had anticipated, Jack did double back. He trod in other people's footprints along Hammersmith Terrace. In Eyot Gardens the snow was thick, which made walking easier.

He noticed he was not the only one to have come this way since the last snowfall. A tall man, he guessed, looking at the distance between the prints; someone who stepped with the ball of his foot first.

He retraced his steps. Not literally, for he made no attempt to be precise, even kicking snow up to blur previous prints with the present ones; that would confuse. He stooped and made a snowball; compacting it to ice, he hurled it across Hammersmith Terrace. It splattered against the wall of the old laundry, making no sound. He ran to where it had landed, chips of snow on the flawless surface. Snow on snow. He scooped up more and, moulding it between his gloved palms, lobbed it at the spot where he had been standing. *Bull's eye.* He went through this caper twice, shuffling back and forth across the road each time. If anyone noticed him they would think him drunk, or eccentric, but not suspicious. He hopped and jumped over his tracks until there was a muddle of footprints.

Once more he went down Eyot Gardens, further obscuring his tracks. The Great West Road had been salted. With offices on the south side and bushes and trees on the north, he would not be seen by a sleepless resident. A camera might catch him so he wore his woolly hat and affected a limp for the benefit of the lens. His disability was not pronounced; they would congratulate themselves on their observation skills if they spotted it. He pretended to struggle climbing the central barrier of the Great West Road and crossed the eastbound carriageway in a lop-sided stroll, hands in his pockets, head down, partly for the CCTV, partly because he felt like it.

It was two in the morning and with the city to himself Jack was in excellent spirits. He squatted down to make another snowball and hoped nothing would happen to spoil it.

Forty-Three

Jack was not alone. He had to move but his legs would not work. He sank to the floor.

It took temerity to slip in through a front door when the Host was only by the bins and he had nearly been discovered many times. He always stayed calm, remembering that his Hosts did exactly what he had planned. They were puppets in his private theatre. People saw only what they expected to see. They did not expect him to be there so they did not see him.

Now he had lost his nerve and was sure the man with the mind like his own had found him instead.

The change was imperceptible; most would have missed it. He could not say what had altered. The air may have been fresher; the temperature may have been colder. He believed in ghosts and there were plenty to choose from in these rooms.

It was not a ghost.

When he returned from the river he had confirmed that there were no marks on the steps, so they must have got in through the back. Yet the rear of the house was impregnable: a high wall by the Great West Road with holly bushes hard against it and a gravelled patio to warn off intruders. There were strong locks on the doors but this person knew those tricks.

The hands on the brass dial of the grandfather clock had stopped. He had not wound it.

He *had* wound it.

It was ticking.

He was making elementary mistakes. This simple error was one of the kind his benign Hosts made.

A shadow fell across the peeling William Morris paper on the landing wall.

He hid amongst the folds of the fur coat waiting for her.

She was coming down the stairs.

'You took your time.'

'How did you get in?' he croaked.

'Same route you used to scare Mrs Ramsay, through the attic.' Stella Darnell was as cold as ice. 'Now you know what it feels like. What I want to know is how *you* got in here? No, no.' She reached the last step. 'Don't bother, I can't bear to know. Get up. We're going next door to Mrs Ramsay's before we both end up at Hammersmith Police Station. At least we have a vaguely legitimate reason to be there – and a key.'

Jack hugged his knees, waiting for his heartbeat to return to normal. He wiped his clammy hands on his trousers and did not move.

'So who lives here now?' Stella persisted. 'Don't give me rubbish about a Host.'

The clock's pendulum oscillated: back and forth, back and forth.

'Jack!'

'I do.'

'Enough!' She was brisk. 'I mean who *really* lives here?'

'This is *my* house. I live here.'

Stella stopped, her hand on the front-door handle and looked down at Jack, crouched in a ball at her feet.

A woman sprawled on a beach, her skin bleached by light and lack of life.

'You are the little boy.' She breathed at last. 'You are Kate Rokesmith's son.'

The steady tick-tock was louder in the silence.

'I made a mistake.'

'You could say that.' Stella stood over him.

'I have the mind of a murderer.'

'Sure you do.'

'I can imagine how a killer thinks and behaves. I recognize them: in streets, in cafés, libraries, on station platforms. They are not as rare as you'd think. They have little connection with the world; their attitude to those around them is clinical and derisive. They keep a tight rein on their lives and on other people's.' He got his cigarette case out of his pocket and shakily placed a cigarette between his lips.

'But each of my Hosts had an alibi: their own crime was elsewhere, either geographically, or in the future, or kept at bay by some means. I haven't found him but I won't give up until I do.'

'Found who?'

'I got distracted by those not like me who gave me somewhere warm and brightly lit, with a piano sonata to send me to sleep or a radio playing that was like a bedtime story. On her way to bed, my mummy made sure the duvet was straight and tucked right up to my chin and shooed away ghosts and aliens.'

Jack slapped wetness from his cheek. The cigarette, stuck to his bottom lip, bobbed when he spoke.

'I don't understand.' She did understand. Jonathan Rokesmith had gone mad.

'The clue is in my name, but you didn't guess.'

'Jack Harmon?'

'Jon Rokesmith.'

'You've lost me.' To distract herself, Stella pulled out her phone and confirmed that Paul had not called. This reminded her. 'Did you see anyone on your way here?'

Jack ignored her. 'You've not read *Our Mutual Friend*?'

'I might have seen the film. I've only read W*uthering Heights*. I don't see the point in stuff that's not true.' She replied absently. How could Jack have missed Paul?

'That's not by Dickens.' Jack put his head in his hands. He had misread the signs and was back at the beginning. He only had the street atlas filled with journeys that so far had taken him nowhere. He had wanted the killer to recognize him and had been sure they were moving around each other; closing in. All he could do was huddle on the floor in the last room his mother had been in before she was murdered and shiver like the coward he was. Everything: the visits with Hosts, the journeys – by Tube, through the streets, and virtually on Street View – were for nothing. The murderer was out there and he had no idea where.

'You are the little boy,' Stella repeated.

'Yes.' In a little boy's voice.

'Have you lived here ever since the… ever since?' Stella could not say the word.

'I told you that Katherine Rokesmith's son went to boarding school and then abroad.'

'Yes, you did tell me that.' Jack had told her a lot of things. 'What about Hugh Rokesmith? He was your father!' No wonder Jack wouldn't consider Rokesmith a suspect. She was in the doorway of the room that in Mrs Ramsay's house was the dining room. Beside a table – the Rokesmiths had evidently not entertained on the scale of the Ramsays – was a piano. A book of music was propped open. She went over. It was a collection of Beethoven Sonatas, the page turned to the 'Pathétique'. Mrs Ramsay had told her to listen to the piano music coming through the wall. Stella had heard nothing when she was cleaning. Jack had cared for Isabel; he had pretended to be her admirer and sent her lilies every week. He made her happy.

'Do you play?'

'It was my mother's.'

'That wasn't my question.'

'No.'

The tall windows were shuttered. Stella had noticed the windows of the house next door were always closed when she came to Mrs Ramsay's and, scrupulous about not delving into what was not her business, had never asked who lived next door.

She was not a real detective. Until Terry's death it had not been her business.

'My father stayed here when he was in London but when he got less work he stopped coming. His aunt left him a cottage in Yorkshire, outside Whitby. He lived there until he died.'

'Did you see him?'

Jack examined his hands. 'I nursed him.'

'It's clean, considering,' Stella remarked brightly.

'I clean it.'

Stella nodded. People thought they knew what 'clean' looked like. This place would show them that they had no idea.

Sitting on the floor, Jack was the same height as his four-year-old self.

'She banged her head.' He crawled on all fours over to the table.

'Who did?' Stella came back into the hall.

'My mother.' He jumped up and ran up the stairs. Stopping where the staircase curved, he peeped down through the spindles. 'I can see the table from here,' he exclaimed excitedly.

'Your point being?' Stella asked in a level tone. His mother had been murdered; it perhaps made sense of the sneaking about, the thing about green and making up the life he had missed, the friends he had not made. Death did funny things; she knew that from her clients; from herself.

'She had a cut on her forehead. The police came here looking for the blunt instrument that might have caused it and they found traces of blood on that table. If you remember, they concluded that she had argued with Hugh and he pushed her. A man who could do that might kill his wife, was their thinking.'

'You do think he did it after all?' The table had a marble top and the corners were sharp. It made sense: Jack had argued that Hugh Rokesmith was innocent because he could not bear his father to be a murderer. Terry had told her that life does not mean life. A man who murdered his partner could be released from prison and, as next of kin, get custody of the children who were the only witnesses of his crime. It was a crazy world. Jack had polished the table beautifully; the marble was like a life-force.

'I can still see you.' Jack was prattling like a toddler. Stella tried to remain patient.

'Pretend you're looking in the mirror,' he commanded from the stairs.

'What mirror?'

'It's oval and dotted with silver blotches. Above the table.' He pointed.

There was an oval shape on the peeling wallpaper, lighter than the surrounding area; in the dim light from the streetlight outside, the pattern swam. There was no mirror.

She peered in the oval mirror. It was spotted with silver, but she could examine the cut on her forehead, delicately dabbing at beads of blood, wincing when it stung.

'She bent to straighten the rug – that rug – and banged her head. I was here, watching. I had been hiding in her wardrobe.' Jack stomped down. 'She didn't come to find me.'

'Was your father there?'

'He left in the morning. I didn't see him again until the police brought me to him.'

'You remember now?'

'It's a fog.'

'Do you have such a thing as a kettle?' Stella rubbed her hands. 'And any chance of putting on the heating?'

'We'll get tea and light a fire in my study.'

The kitchen was in the basement. A cave-like room lined with teak cupboards darkened with age, it was a time capsule for 1981. Shelves were piled with crockery, orange and steel pans hung from butcher's hooks and dishes were stacked in an overhead draining rack. Stella had not imagined it was possible to make so many objects look ordered. When Jack filled the kettle the pipes clanked and whined. She knew the sound; she had heard it many times while she cleaned next door.

Mrs Ramsay had talked of letting a boy play quietly. Stella had assumed she meant Lucian. She had meant Jack.

'Did you tell Mrs Ramsay who you were?'

'Isabel knew who I was. She said I was a train driver because like my father I was looking for something.' Jack splashed tea into two mugs out of a brown teapot with a chipped spout. There were no tannin stains in the mugs. Nothing had changed for decades; everything was clean, although Stella would not have kept a damaged teapot. Jack wiped the tea drops off the table and replaced the cloth on the draining rack. 'I drive trains looking for her killer; that's my reason for everything.' He spoke more to himself. Isabel had actually said he was looking for his mummy, but he did not say this.

'What happened to your hand?' The blood on his knuckles had not been there at Sarah Glyde's.

'I slipped.'

'You were lucky not to break your wrist.'

Jonathan Rokesmith had known Mrs Ramsay all his life. He had not been an intruder; she had invited him; they were on first-name terms. He did not work for her. Stella dismissed these thoughts. She had liked working for Mrs Ramsay.

'Do the neighbours know who you are?'

'Only Isabel; it was our secret. The rest know me as Jack Harmon. I keep myself to myself. Of course your dad suspected.'

Stella swallowed tea. The liquid travelled like a fireball to her stomach.

'You spoke to Terry?'

'I got rid of him.'

'What does that mean?'

'He knocked on the door about two months ago, asking for Jonathan Rokesmith. I told him I had moved in recently so couldn't help. Being a detective, he asked about Isabel and kept me talking. Isabel wouldn't speak to him. Like you she avoided the police.'

'Terry didn't guess who you were?'

'He worked it out.'

'I doubt that.'

'Out of the blue he asked me if I had seen *Our Mutual Friend* on the telly. I said no. He asked if my parents had named me after the character, John Harmon. He knew who I was.' Jack drank the rest of his tea. 'I rather admired him for that.'

'Why didn't you tell me?'

'You would not have known what to say. You would have been awkward, like everyone else. We would have got nowhere.' He took their empty mugs over to the sink.'

'I'm not everyone else.'

'Yes, I know that now.' He had his back to Stella. 'I don't want sympathy.'

'I'm not sympathetic.'

Jack washed the mugs and dried them. He replaced them on the shelf next to the others. 'I don't trust anyone.'

'Fair enough. Not sure I would if I were you,' Stella replied peaceably. 'Nor do I,' she added.

In the strained features of the thirty-three-year-old man, she saw the ghost of little Jonathan Rokesmith with his unfathomable brown eyes and home-made haircut.

'Terry must have discovered that the house had not changed hands since Kate's death. The press gave the impression it had been sold and the family moved away. He worked out I was Jonathan Rokesmith. He knew my name was John Harmon, probably from the electoral roll. What's more he had met me before – albeit thirty years ago. Terry did not forget faces.'

Jack emptied the tea leaves into the bin. Stella looked up from her phone, absently registering that like Mrs Ramsay Jack did not use tea bags. Paul had still not called; it was not like him.

'The house came to me when my mother was murdered. My dad had put it in her name when he started his business to exclude it as an asset if anything went wrong. Wise move because of course everything went wrong.'

'That would be a reason for him to kill her. He would get it back.'

'You will not find a motive any more than your dad could. Stop trying.'

Jack was surely mistaken. Terry would not have made the connection between the two names. Plodding up the stairs behind him, she asked: 'Did Terry tackle you about your name?'

'He pretended to take me at my word.' Jack stood aside to let Stella into his study.

The small room was filled by a large desk, with a chair and an armchair. Stella relaxed.

'When he did not come back, I was surprised. I'm rarely wrong.' He turned on his laptop, and added gently: 'I read about his death on the BBC website.'

'That must have been a relief.' Stella did not want Jack's sympathy any more than he wanted hers.

'Far from it. I regretted I wasn't honest the first time. Between us all maybe we could have got somewhere.'

'Where exactly would that have been?'

'He wanted you to help – Peterson as good as said that.'

'What makes you think that?'

'You heard Peterson. He wasn't surprised to see you. Terry had talked about you. He wanted to show you where he grew up.'

'I should go. Are you still going to work for Clean Slate, or was that just a ruse to get to me?' Stella could not move.

'It was.' Jack pushed back his hair. 'There's no doubt where your priorities lie!' He liked that about her. 'I'll go on with Sarah Glyde; we might learn something.' He had a feeling about the middle-aged potter, but would say nothing until he had evidence. Stella liked facts.

'What about Ivan Challoner?'

'How does he fit into this?'

'He is expecting it to be you that comes.' Ivan would not care who came to clean but Stella did not say this. Ivan would, however, demand the best.

'We'd better not let him down then.' Jack tapped in his password and the laptop sprang to life. 'Can't have you doing his cleaning.'

'He's just a client.' Stella knew no more about Ivan than she had about Paul but liked herself better when she was with him. Ivan made people relax; he wanted them to be happy. Suddenly she understood. 'She knew him.'

'Who?' Jack looked up.

'Your mother. She knew her killer. She didn't put up a fight because she did not expect him to attack her. She didn't take him seriously until it was too late.'

'You said, but it wasn't my dad.'

'OK, for argument's sake, suppose it wasn't Hugh Rokesmith, but I *am* sure she knew her attacker.'

'How can you be so certain?' Jack got up and, making up twists of newspaper, began arranging them around logs in a small grate.

'That other night at the river, I was so relieved when it was Paul, I knew he would not hurt me, but I was way off. If you hadn't turned up I don't know how far he would have gone. He is an obsessive.' Why had she gone out with Paul?

'What were you doing with him if he was obsessive?' Jack asked.

He could read her thoughts. Was that the mind of a murderer? She thought not.

'I assumed he was a normal everyday computer engineer. He took my computer apart without fuss, diagnosed the problem and screwed everything back into place. After he had gone, it was as good as new.'

'From such minute considerations is love kindled. You think my father was like Paul?' Jack lit a match and hovered the flame beneath a chunk of firelighter.

'We said we'd leave your dad out for a minute. Your mother recognized her killer so did not put up a fight. I'm sure she had gone there to meet someone she knew. Don't you remember any more than her banging her head? Think!'

'How much do you remember from when you were four?' Jack fixed a sheet of newspaper over the fireplace. 'He had on his best blue gum boots. There was a problem with the Leaning Woman and his mummy had promised to look after her but she didn't.' Jack watched the newsprint glow orange as oxygen fed the flames.

The newspaper caught alight and flaming scraps floated out into the room. Stella rushed forward and, flailing, sent them towards the fire. Leaping flames licked up and snatched them.

Jack had not moved.

'So he didn't save his mummy,' he finished.

From the hall below came the steady ticking of the grandfather clock.

'You saved me from Paul,' Stella offered eventually. 'You were a kid, what were you supposed to do?'

Jack went to his desk. 'OK, who have we got? Paul, Mark Ramsay and I'll add my father for your sake.'

'There's also the wild card.'

'Like the Joker?' He frowned.

'The person no one has thought of: a woman, for instance.'

'We have to stick to the facts, you know that. Add whoever Terry suspected.'

'That was your dad.' Stella was apologetic.

'No, I don't think it was.' Jack stared at his screensaver: the statue beside St Peter's Church, taken from the ground up through the crook in her arm. It was a child's perspective. 'I think Terry had a new lead. When Peterson mentioned the steam engine I remembered it. Bright red metal, made by Triang and in its original box. He was right, it was special: not the sort of toy for a kid. I drove it into the river.'

'What about your Uncle Tony? Maybe you didn't make him up.' Stella was being sympathetic, but hid this from Jack.

'What are you talking about?' he snapped. She was rubbish at pretending.

Stella blundered on: 'Maybe there *was* an Uncle Tony. Peterson thought the boy was trying to be like him, but that doesn't explain making up pretend relatives.'

'Both my parents were only children. I don't have any uncles.'

'Concentrate! Was there a Tony?'

'There was no Tony.' He went to the fire and rearranged a stick; placing it in the centre of the flames then he returned to the desk.

'Was there another person that morning apart from you and your mum?'

'The Lady.' Jack tapped the keyboard and up came Google Street View displaying a street in Stanwell. 'The Leaning Woman told them to stay with her but his mummy ignored her and kept on going down the ramp.'

'Jack, now you are being weird.' It was best to tackle his behaviour head on. 'We're talking about you, stop saying "he".'

'You sound like your dad.'

'I sound dead on my feet. I'm going to bed. Don't forget you're at Sarah Glyde's tomorrow – today. I'll complete Mrs Ramsay's. We'll go to my flat when you finish and take stock. Come for me next door. Or are you "busy"?'

'I'm on annual leave for two weeks. I'm all yours.'

When Stella opened the front door, wind blasted into the hall and snowflakes fluttered on to the wrinkled kilim.

It was a blizzard. She struggled through the swirling mass and only when she climbed into her van at Rose Gardens North did she think of Paul. She scanned the area, but he was nowhere to be seen.

At Chiswick High Road, it occurred to Stella that she had not asked Jack if he had liked Terry, either when Terry had come to the Rokesmith house or when Jack was little. She had not asked if Jack had noticed if her dad had seemed unwell. Presumably he had not noticed anything wrong with him because he had expected him to return. She did no more than twenty miles an hour on the deserted road to avoid skidding.

Jack, like Stella, had not expected Terry to die.

Forty-Four

Friday, 21 January 2011

Sarah tidied up before Jack arrived. Antony would laugh at her for cleaning for the cleaner. She explained to her absent brother as she scrubbed at a pan, excavating years of burnt food, that a cleaner was not there to do her washing up or tidy up after her. Yet as she scoured her blackened cooking utensils, rinsing a film of grease off glassware with scalding water, cleaning for Jack Harmon was precisely what she was doing. Sarah would hide from Jack how careless of hygiene she was.

Antony had a dishwasher; if it broke he got in an engineer.

You solve your problems with a phone call and a cheque.

She ground the wire pad into the sides of the stewing pot. Calling Clean Slate had been a passing idea that she might have abandoned, but for her brother's dismissive response.

Shovelling papers and unopened post into the cutlery drawer, she declared to Antony that it had paid off. She had found who she was looking for. She did not care what he thought, she uttered firmly, keeping to herself that she had booked Jack Harmon for the days when Antony was in the country.

This is my house and you are welcome to visit, but only when I invite you.

She chucked out a two-year-old packet of dried apricots and a tin of rock-hard cocoa powder.

I can do what I like.

She flurried about her bedroom, throwing shoes into the wardrobe, hanging her kimono behind the door. She was in the bathroom dusting incense ash off the sill into her palm when there were three knocks on the front door.

Jack Harmon was not talkative. When she invited him to have coffee before he started, he shook his head and got straight to washing down the kitchen cupboards.

Sarah retreated to the sitting room to consider her next move. She could not go to her studio with Harmon in the house. She wanted his photograph and had an hour to obtain it.

She would wait until he was vacuuming the top floor and take him unawares. A photograph was a poor substitute for him modelling for her, but would allow her to study his face and make a sketch which would define him in lines and shade. Asking his permission was out of the question.

Jack was not real to Sarah Glyde. Not until the head under the damp cloth on her work table was complete would he gain life.

She unclipped the lens cap and rubbed the glass and viewfinder with the corner of her blouse, aimed the camera at the marble fireplace that, preferring the intimacy of her studio, she seldom lit. The battery was charged; it was ready.

Jack was in the doorway, his hand poised to knock. His soundless presence reminded her of Antony and she suspected he had been there some time.

'Miss Glyde, sorry to bother you, but the back room is locked and there's no key.'

'Sarah, please.' She attempted to be airy and tried to hide the camera under a sofa cushion, but it tumbled to the floor. Jack pulled it up by its strap and kept hold of it.

'I'm sorry if I gave you a start.'

Sarah felt heat rising in her cheeks.

'It looks OK.' He turned it over and switched it on. 'So, the top room?'

She wanted it cleared out and filled with sunshine.

'It's not mine.' Sarah patted her hair, fitting a strand behind her ear that immediately fell forward. ' The room. I should have said.'

'You did say to give everywhere an "overhaul".' He repeated her term without mockery, apparently to mollify her.

'My brother has the key – it's his old bedroom. He's older than me. It's ridiculous but that still counts so there's nothing I can do about it.'

'Not a problem.' The lens zoomed out; Jack retracted it.

'Tony has his own house. Two actually.' Sarah could not stop herself and offloaded oft-rehearsed phrases of injustice like ballast. 'One in London where he works and a country cottage, yet he still has his room in *my* house. It shouldn't matter because there's loads of space. My mother took his side, you see. She believed he was fragile and needed extra support. He could eat what he liked, while she rationed my food because it was family lore that I was fat. He never put on weight. The silliest things upset one, don't they?'

'It's working.' Jack handed her the camera.

'I'll have a word and see what he wants doing.' As she said the throwaway line, Sarah imagined that this was possible. She had only to say: *I want it as a guest room.*

You don't have guests.

That's because I don't have a room for them.

It's my room.

Dad said it could be mine when you left.

He's dead. I'm in charge now.

'Let me know when you want me to do in there.'

Sarah sank on to the sofa. Jack had switched the camera to display mode and his clay head, its shape defined, his jaw kneaded and moulded, was on the screen. She had smoothed the clay, working and reworking it, wiping it down, shaping it; caressing it. This would be her best creation. Jack Harmon must have seen it.

Jack Harmon. The name was familiar. She gazed at the face, the unformed features ghostly in the poorly lit image, seeking to reassure herself that Jack could not have recognized himself. Few recognized their own beauty.

She heard squirts of an aerosol, bumps and scrapes: above her

Jack was shifting furniture in her mother's room. Her bed – single once Sarah's father had died – squeaked and rumbled as he manoeuvred it. Stella Darnell was right, he was thorough. The vacuum motor droned, overlaid with taps of the nozzle probing along the skirting boards.

By the time Sarah had nerved herself to creep on to the landing and up the stairs, Jack was in the bathroom. The window was painted shut and, like Antony's bedroom, it overlooked the river. He had the best view in the house.

Keeping out of the way of the door, she confronted the vacuum: one of those red spherical machines with eyes and a mouth on its body. It was coy, grinning at her from the sink pedestal, its tube snaking out of sight. The lavatory lid banged.

He was using the lavatory. Sarah wanted to see him pissing. She wanted to hear him. She wanted that knowledge of him. Switching on the camera, she raised it to her face and inched closer.

Jack was standing on the lavatory seat with his back to her, his face pressed to the bathroom window set high in the little room, which unlike the lower panes was not frosted.

In the mirror above the sink Sarah had a perfect shot of his profile. She snapped, once, twice and then a third time. The shutter made no sound. She ran down the stairs, out of the house and into the studio where she collapsed on her work desk, panting and heaving to get her breath, exhilarated by her temerity.

Only when she had printed the pictures and placed them in a folder marked 'Suppliers' – that Antony would never pry into – did it occur to her to wonder what Jack Harmon had been doing. What was he so interested in looking at?

After he had gone she went up to the bathroom. The ceramic sparkled; the limescale that had stained the bath since her mother died had gone, as had the grime around the pipework. The taps shone. The room looked as it had when her father was alive.

The lid was still closed. Gripping the downpipe on the overhead cistern, Sarah climbed on to the lavatory. Below her, the river flickered with black and silver when wind rippled its surface. It was low tide, the muddy shore was exposed; she craned down, but could not see what had attracted Jack Harmon's attention.

Sarah Glyde was still standing on the lavatory when her brother walked in.

Forty-Five

'She keeps the top room facing the river locked and went peculiar when I asked her to open it.' Jack cupped a hand under his chin to stop crumbs as he bit on the biscuit. They were in Stella's flat. Jack was sprawled on her sofa, the plastic covering squeaking as he fidgeted.

'Peculiar how? She wanted us to do everywhere.' Stella was annoyed. 'I quoted her for that room. Did you say?'

'So, you come out ahead.' Jack wiped his hands on his trouser legs. 'I could hardly insist she break the door down. Apparently it's her brother's bedroom and she went on about him, harking back to old resentments. Sibling shit.' He sniffed.

'It's a waste of time you being there if you can't see out of that window.'

'It can't be much different to the bathroom so we can assume that anyone in that room would not have seen where Katherine Rokesmith died. No one was there that day so it wouldn't help us.'

Jack crunched up the last digestive biscuit. He had eaten half the packet; Stella wondered again if he ate properly. His kitchen was well equipped, yet she could not envisage him cooking.

'I'll get someone else on the contract; you've found out what we needed to know.' If they were at Terry's she could have heated up a shepherd's pie for him. Next time they were there, she would get one out of the freezer.

'We promised her the same cleaner each week.'

'Listen to you, Mr Customer Care.'

'I'd like to go again.' Jack poured himself more coffee from the stainless steel cafetière. 'I've got a feeling.'

'What kind of feeling?'

'I had left the vacuum on to check the window. I can't swear to it, but I had the sense that someone was in the room, yet when I looked round there was no one.'

'Maybe she fancies you.' Stella was losing patience. She had spent the morning at Mrs Ramsay's. She would not confess to Jack that all the time she had been convinced Mrs Ramsay was present. It would encourage his fanciful thinking. Nor did she tell him that Paul's continued silence was troubling her. There had been no contact from him since yesterday. When she was driving, she kept tabs on her mirrors; at her flat she kept checking the communal landing to see if he was outside. He had never been silent this long; if Paul was playing games, he was getting better at them.

The door buzzer went.

Jack put his finger to his lips and tiptoed out. He had the video picture up by the time Stella got there. A motorcycle courier was gesticulating at the lens, a parcel under his arm.

'Are you expecting a delivery?'

'Yes. Can you see anyone behind him?'

'No. If your man has sense, he'll keep out of view until the last minute.'

'I'm not risking it.' Stella activated the intercom and spoke into the microphone: 'The entry button doesn't work, have your helmet off by the time I get down there.' She turned to Jack. 'After I've got the package, watch to see if Paul appears.'

The ping of the lift and Stella's heels clicking on the marble broke the cladded silence.

It was the same courier who delivered lilies to Mrs Ramsay but he gave no sign of recognizing Stella. She took the padded bag off him, executed an illegible squiggle on his handheld device with the stylus and slammed the door. As the lift door slid shut, a silver SUV was passing on the main road, but otherwise nothing moved. If Paul had been out there, he would have appeared, she assured herself. She rather wished that he were; then at least she would know he was all right. His silence was oppressive. Nothing in these flats made any sound: the rapid ascent of blue-lit numbers on the control panel was the only evidence that the lift worked.

The Friday morning arrival of Mrs Ramsay's flowers belonged to a remote time. The packed-up house was soon to be empty of all the furniture she had kept clean, making Stella doubt that the two years she had cleaned for Mrs Ramsay had ever happened.

Jack was still in the hall. He had stayed as she requested, which gave her hope for what she planned next. She sat on the sofa, the plastic squeaking, ripped off parcel tape and broke open the padded bag.

That morning the new uniforms had arrived in the office and she had asked Jackie to courier over one large polo shirt for Jack.

She held it aloft. The Clean Slate logo was embossed on the shoulder, the silk thread – Pantone 277 – contrasted with the Pantone 375 material; it was smarter than she expected.

'This'll impress Sarah Glyde.' She went for the light approach.

Jack glanced up from the papers he had returned to and blanched.

'Take it.' Stella laid it on the table in front of him.

Jack rushed out of the room. Stella couldn't hear him being sick – her soundproofed walls did their job – but went cold and clammy at the thought of him kneeling in front of her spotless toilet bowl.

She was kneading the top-quality material busily, berating herself for being rash when Jack reappeared. She did not think it possible he could look any paler, but he was chalk-white.

'Don't look like that. I never throw up.' He skirted the room, avoiding the shirt, which she had draped over the arm of the sofa. 'Green makes me ill, while you practically pass out at the prospect of vomit. What a team!' He retreated behind the case files on the glass table. 'We need Terry.'

'How would he help?'

'You really didn't rate him, did you?' Jack mopped his forehead with a wodge of lavatory paper.

'He was a crap detective and a worse parent.'

'What sort of daughter were you?'

'It wasn't my fault he was never there.'

'He had to work. You don't mention your mother. What's her excuse?'

'She lives in Barons Court with her budgerigar.' Her mother loved the tiny yellow bird that talked as much as she did.

'You are second best to a bird?'

'I'm forty-four; I don't need a mother.'

'We all need a mother.'

Neither of them spoke.

'I stopped existing for my father the day my mum died. As soon as I was old enough, he enrolled me in a remote Dotheboys Hall boarding school.' Jack fished into the packet for another biscuit until he saw there were no more left.

'I thought you nursed him when he was ill.'

'It didn't make us close. He was bitter. The world believed that he had killed his wife and, in the absence of the police, the press and the public, his resentment was aimed at me.'

'You believed he was innocent.'

'He knew that I wasn't sure. Children know their parents the least of everyone. He never mentioned her and we never visited her grave. I wondered if he could kill someone. He knew that.'

'What is it about green?' Stella had depended on her shock tactic curing Jack. She was eager to see him in the new uniform; she wanted him on the next Clean Slate brochure.

'It should have sun on it.'

'Talk normally.' Stella shook the shirt. Jack flinched.

'It is absolutely terrible.' His eyes were mournful. 'I can't say more.'

The telephone rang.

'Yes?' Stella rapped.

'Stell? It's me, love, listen I've had the strangest call.' It was Jackie.

Stella prepared herself: it would be a client wanting to mix and match services and Jackie had found the idea of straying outside the pricing structure strange. To Stella such requests were opportunities.

'A man has called saying he's Paul's brother. Your Paul.'

'He's not— Oh, never mind.'

'He was supposed to have a fish supper with him last night and he never showed up and isn't answering his mobile. The brother told me you were going to marry him. Paul, I mean.'

Jackie was trying not to be peeved that she hadn't been informed, Stella thought.

'Jackie, if I ever marry, you will be the first to know. Why is he panicking? Paul's a grown man. He can drop out of a fish supper if he wants.'

'He wasn't panicking, he presumed Paul was with you. He was expecting to meet you too. I said as far as I knew you were not in touch with Paul and had not been for a while. I said he had misunderstood.'

'I haven't seen him.' Stella chose not to mention her visit to Paul's flat, or last night; it would involve confessing that she had tricked Paul. She was not proud of it.

'I do hope he hasn't done anything stupid. He cared too much for you.'

'He's probably mending a computer in a place with no signal.'

'His work hasn't heard from him since Wednesday.'

She hung up and looked at Jack. He appeared to have resumed reading, his glasses on the end of his nose, the cut on his hand livid against his skin and his face pointedly averted from the polo shirt.

The only person Paul could have met on the way to the pub was Jack.

He raised his eyes.

'I slipped on the ice, Stella,' he said. 'Have you checked he hasn't cottoned on to Ivan Challoner? He may have seen you with him. Why don't you give your friendly dentist a call?'

'Let's not talk about Paul or my dentist.'

Stella went to the toilet. As she dried her hands, she thought it was likely that Paul had seen her with Ivan. She could not ask him if Paul had been to see him. She hit upon an idea.

She pulled her mobile out of her trouser pocket and rang his surgery.

The starchy receptionist answered.

'I wanted to check the dates of my appointments with Ivan' – she deliberately used his first name – 'as I'm filling in a claim form. They might have sent an insurance rep round, they're pretty diligent.'

'It's not usual. I give patients their receipts and they post them.'

'No one has been in asking about me? Would they have got in touch with Ivan directly?'

'I am sure they would not. However, *Mr* Challoner is not here, he's speaking at a conference in Rome and will not return until next week.'

'Thanks for your help.'

There was no reason why Ivan should have told Stella he was going away, but still she was disappointed that he had not mentioned it on Monday when he had talked of their meeting soon. Presumably it would not be soon.

Jack was absolutely still on the sofa, the Clean Slate polo shirt balled up in his hands.

'Katherine Rokesmith was wearing a scarf the colour of Pantone 375.' His voice was level.

Stella took the polo shirt off him and folded it.

'It was not on her when they found her body.'

'Her killer took it to remind him of her. He has a box of trophies.' Jack's face was almost the white of the sofa.

Stella fitted the shirt back into the bag and placed it on the table out of his sightline.

'We have the murder weapon,' she said softly, and drew up a dining chair close to the sofa, their knees touching: 'Jack, he strangled your mum with her own scarf.'

Forty-Six

I saved you.

He had planned saying this to her all the way home. The curtains were drawn, lights on and the fire lit. He was her hero and she expected nothing less.

You're mine, she would say and he would feel the truth of it.

He tucked her in, promising to come upstairs after a quick drink.

'You have a wonderful reputation.' She stroked his hair. 'You must do everything you can to preserve it. You have saved us both!'

She drifted into sleep. It was his reputation he had saved, he thought, contemplating the bruise on his face in the hall mirror. It would show and he would have to explain it. She was the only person he could tell. Once he had discussed it with her, he felt better and everything shrank to normal.

His mother used to say that most things looked better after a night's sleep and something about a trouble shared.

The man should have minded his own business, she agreed. The man had been itching to start a fight, he told her.

He poured himself a finger of whisky. His hand shook and he caught the neck of the bottle against the glass, splashing liquid on the table. She was good to him. Not a day went by when he did not tell himself this.

It was too dark to see the rooks. He raised the glass to his reflection in the kitchen window.

'*You saved me*,' he whispered.

Forty-Seven

Saturday, 22 January 2011

Mrs Ramsay's house was finished. Her daughter had sent a consignment of bright yellow plastic crates from her company: Gina-Ware. They had packed them with crockery, vases, figurines, books; the paraphernalia of fifty years would go into storage. Stella had sprayed the rooms with a sandalwood and ginger spray from the Body Shop she had not used before. She wished Mrs Ramsay could offer an opinion, although feared she might consider the scent dreary. It was not usual for the family of the deceased to ask Clean Slate to sort the contents and Stella had disliked taking responsibility for deciding what to keep and what to take to charity or the rubbish tip. Lucian and Eleanor had not been in touch; Mrs Ramsay would have called them naughty. Stella had been wary of throwing out something valuable and knew Gina Cross would not welcome the number of crates.

She had not thrown out the spiral notebooks indented with Mrs Ramsay's heavy script and stained with multiple mug rings: the weekly task lists. These were still on the shelf in her bedroom. Stella had read them, but found nothing to shed light on why Mrs Ramsay had not told the police the truth.

Each list – addressed to Lizzie, the Ramsay's live-in help in the sixties – was dated with the completed item scrawled through. Many were carried over: 'Clear Mark's Study' appeared frequently and was never crossed off. There was no study; Stella guessed it must be at their country house. A lot of the items – cleaning, general tidying – were delegated to children. Mrs Ramsay would cook special meals: *Boeuf en Daube popped up the most*. Later notebooks covered a greater span of time but the names assigned for the tasks stayed the same, with Mrs Ramsay seemingly unaware that they no longer figured in her daily life.

In the last notebook it had been Stella not 'Lizzie' who actioned: 'Sort Broom Cupboard, Do basement and Tidy coal cellar.' She had shovelled damp coal in the hole beneath the pavement, the cramped chamber enmeshed in spider webs as thick as rags. For no apparent purpose, she moved coal from one part of the cellar to the other. Mrs Ramsay did not light fires. Stella would tell Gina Cross about the coal, but did not think she would want it.

Stella did not feature in Mrs Ramsay's notebooks.

She should arrange handing over the keys but was delaying the moment. She locked the front door and walked around the corner to Terry's house.

Jack arrived at 11 a.m. on the dot as she was booting up the computer.

'How did you get in?'

'You left the back door open.'

'Yes, but … OK. We need to crack this password.'

'It's possible to bypass the BIOS with a desktop computer, but newer laptops have a security chip on the motherboard. We need an engineer; Paul would know, you needn't explain why we want it. Just a thought.' Jack knelt down beside her chair, and picked up Terry's silver ballpoint. Once more Stella breathed in a mixture of washing powder and fabric rather than stale tobacco smoke.

'Can you really not guess it? Your dad wasn't that complicated, was he?'

'We've been through this. You carry your parents' vital numbers and now I understand why. Plus you're obsessed with numbers. All the same, did you know your father's password?'

'My mother's birthday,' Jack replied promptly, sucking on the ballpoint.

'Terry wouldn't be using *my* mum's birthday. She still complains he never remembered it. She holds a grudge that Terry was on a job the day I was born.'

'What was that?'

'Twelfth of August 1966.'

'No, the job.'

'The Braybrook Street shooting.'

'Do I know about that?'

'You're too young.' Stella was dismissive. 'So was I, come to that.'

'When was it? What was it?' He pulled forward a blank police notebook from the pile Stella had yet to clear.

'Three policeman were shot dead in Braybrook Street, West London, when they approached a suspicious group of men in a car. It's right by Wormwood Scrubs Prison, so at first it was assumed they had escaped. I had just been born and Terry was on his way to Hammersmith Hospital, and was diverted to join the search. They didn't find the ringleader, Harry Roberts, for three months. He camped out in Epping Forest. Terry didn't see me for two days.'

'I vaguely remember reading about it.'

Jack was bluffing. He did not like it when she knew something that he did not.

Stella carried on: 'The room, used as the incident room at Hammersmith Police Station in the eighties, is named in honour of the fallen officers: the Braybrook Suite. They ran Kate's investigation from there.' She trundled the mouse around the mat; the pointer did not show up on the screen. 'It's a meeting room now with pictures and a plaque to the officers. It was the worst loss of police life since 1911 and wasn't matched until the IRA Harrods' bomb in 1983 when another three officers died.'

'Considering your view of the police, you're well informed.' Jack got up and went over to the window.

'Terry showed me the room.'

'So, when *was* your birthday?'

'I said, twelfth of August 1966.'

'That makes you...'

'It makes me older than you. Can we get back to breaking into this thing?'

'Try your birthday.'

'That's one date Terry will not have used.'

Jack came over and, leaning over her shoulder, pecked in: '12-08-1966'.

The screen returned an incorrect password.

'Told you.' Stella flung back in the chair, pushing it away from the desk, just missing Jack's feet.

'Three of his colleagues were killed on that day and his daughter was born. Terry cared all right.' Jack frowned. 'One, two, zero, eight, six, six.'

Password incorrect, press return for a retry.

He shook his head. 'What time were you born?'

'How would I know? You know that too, I suppose.'

'Do you know what time you were born?' Jack repeated.

'No.'

Stella swivelled the chair back and forth. She could get crates like Gina's to store Terry's stuff until she had time to deal with it. Gina-Ware offered good rates.

'Where's your birth certificate?'

'Certificates only have dates.'

'Do you still have Terry's files here?'

'The case files? You know I don't, they're at the flat.'

'His personal files, the stuff you're meant to be giving to the lawyer.'

Stella tipped a languid hand at the buff concertina file on the floor where she had left it the night she had fled Terry's house. That seemed a lifetime ago.

'You've already been through that. This is a waste of time, Jack.'

'We'll see.' He clapped his hands. 'Eight six six!'

'What?'

'My set number on Tuesday was your birthday. See? It's a sign!'

To humour him, Stella typed in the numbers.

'No luck.'

Jack wasn't listening. He spilled the papers on to the carpet tiles and, cross-legged, scrutinized each paper, giving a running commentary: 'His dad's death certificate, his leaving certificate – exemplary service – meant to show you this, not that bad a detective then. You should display this. His mum died four years after you were born, do you remember her?'

'Four is too young to remember anything.' Nana.

'Quite possibly.' Jack bit the side of his thumb.

Hunched over the papers, Jack Harmon – or Jonathan Rokesmith – could have been playing cards or arranging his toy cars. With a shock Stella saw why she had taken the risk of allowing this shabby man who looked in need of a meal and older than thirty-three into her flat and on to her cleaning schedule. She understood why she was prepared to be alone with him in a succession of empty houses late at night. She had a new reason for finding who killed Jonathan Rokesmith's mother. Against her better judgement, she liked Jack.

Her mobile rang.

It was Ivan. She answered, pretending she did not know the caller so that he would not guess she had programmed his number into her handset.

'I am so sorry but I will have to postpone dinner for a bit. I'm at a conference in Paris. Paediatric dentistry is not really my thing, but one has to show one's face. I'll be away until next week. May I call you when I'm back and see how you're fixed? I feel rotten, I should have rung earlier.'

Stella assured Ivan that she did not mind. Privately she was rather relieved: eating in a restaurant twice in one week was a challenge she did not relish. She enjoyed the fact that the dentist's receptionist had got it wrong; she had said he was in Rome.

'Here we are!' Jack waved a faded pink card. 'Stella Victoria Darnell – Victoria was his mother's name by the way. Born in Hammersmith Hospital, weighs ten pounds, one ounce – that's *heavy* – on Friday the twelfth of August 1966 at two minutes past midday. Your adoring parents sent this to their friends and relations announcing you were here!'

He crawled over to the desk and kneeling up, tapped in the keys like a pianist picking out a melody.

'One, two and a zero, then another two. A one, a two and zero-eight. I'll bet he dropped the nineteen so lastly six and six. *Voilà!*'

Nothing happened. Then the hard drive light on the left of the keyboard flickered, the screen went blue and up came the Windows password request. Jack repeated the sequence of numbers. They were in.

'Most important day of his life,' Jack said under his breath.

[I. Ramsay Statement, T Darnell 11092010.docx]

Isabel Ramsay, 77. Flirts like a girl. Complimenting her jacket got me indoors despite my being police and her not liking Hall. (Looked up: D. I. Hall – Howland case 1968.). Mrs Ramsay appears demented, talks as if kids still young and husband still alive. Could be shamming.

Showed her local paper piece on village hall opening in Sussex (Charbury). She admitted lying. Didn't think it serious, 'silly mistake'. Possibly acting. Was in Sussex until mid afternoon. Thinks husband (Prof. Mark Ramsay, fifty-six at time of 29/7/81, died 1999, likely suicide but coroner ruled Acc. Death) saw Kate R. Doesn't know and never asked. Could be covering for him. 'He is a doctor. He has signed the Oath.' Became animated and insisted the husband did not know she had 'made stupid mistake'. I told her she was compellable to give evidence against her spouse: she tried to end conversation. When I pushed the point that Ramsay had not come forward to contradict her evidence she said: 'He loved me.' Said this phrase several times, her lie possibly because she can't remember and not hiding evidence.

NB: Saw Clean Slate card on IR's fridge. Ring S.

Tried to contact D. I. Richard Hall, passed in 2001.

Talk to SD then MC.

'Terry was good with people,' Stella remarked after they had both read the document on the desktop. 'So she did speak to the police.'

'I didn't know,' Jack admitted.

Mrs Ramsay had not shared all her secrets with Jack, Stella noted.

'Terry seems to have assessed her correctly: he wasn't taken in by her charms,' Jack said. 'He didn't speak to you.' He jabbed a finger at the 'SD'.

'He had the wrong number,' she admitted. She cleared her throat. 'We need to look into Mark Ramsay. Something's not right there.'

'I don't feel that was where Terry was going.' Jack was gnawing at his thumb.

Nevertheless Stella underlined Mark Ramsay on their list of suspects, which numbered four: Hugh Rokesmith, Mark Ramsay, Paul (who surely did not count but she left him there anyway) and the wild card: the 'nominal' in police-speak.

They spent the next fifteen minutes exploring Terry's computer but found nothing else. According to a receipt in his files, Terry had not had the machine long before he died. He had not created any other documents.

Jack clicked on the browser to find out the five-day weather forecast.

'What do you care? You're underground most of the time.'

'Not when I'm walking.'

'Walking! Where?'

'It depends which page I'm on.'

'What do you mean?' Stella looked at her watch. It was only thirty-five minutes past eleven. She was sorry not to be meeting Ivan; she could do with a glass of wine at the end of the day.

'I found a London street atlas on a Richmond train. It has pen marks on every page. I thought at first they were a child's scribbles, but when I looked properly I found that the lines trace a journey. They are a sign.'

'A sign of what?' She had thought it was going too well.

'Only if I complete all the journeys will I find out. I trace each one on Street View before I go in real life. It's not cheating, it's another way of seeing.'

'Why would it be cheating? It's not just a sign that someone forgot their *A to Z*?'

Jack groped in his coat and produced a filthy battered copy of the *A–Z*. Stella thought again about a therapist. She would not like Jack to go off the rails. Literally.

'I'll show you.' He clicked on Google maps.

Stella grabbed his wrist: 'Stop! It's showing what was looked at last. Why didn't I think of that? We can see the history of Terry's searches.'

'I'm walking this last page tomorrow.' Jack was gazing at the book. He paused, then: 'Isabel loved my tales.'

Stella found that hard to believe. Mrs Ramsay was not a good listener. She pulled the monitor towards her.

'Pay attention, Jack. Where is Bishopstone?'

'East Sussex. It's where my mother grew up. She's buried in the churchyard there. You know this; it's in the notes. It's near a town called... um what's it called?' Jack looked up and ran his finger down the screen. 'There, Seaford. Anyway, when I'm not working I go on these expeditions following—'

'Seaford. Are you sure?'

'It says so there.'

'Seaford is where Terry died.'

Jack jerked his head. He crammed the book back in his pocket and clutched at the desk to steady himself. He grabbed the mouse from Stella and enlarged the window.

'You're a star, Stell.' He batted the arm of Stella's chair.

No one but Terry or Jackie called her 'Stell'.

Jack switched to Google Street View. 'Your dad must have gone to see her grave or the house where she lived. Why did he do that?'

'Like the jury going to see where Diana died?' Stella ventured.

'No, it was something else.'

'His car is still in Seaford – I meant to go and get it!' Stella exclaimed.

'Let's go.' Jack leant on the desk to get to his feet, making it tip forward. He did up the few remaining buttons on his overcoat.

Stella typed 'Broad Street' into the Street View search. A picture of the high street where Terry had died came into focus out of a cluster of pixels. She manoeuvred the cursor along the road to the Co-op store on the left. Most pictures for Street View were taken in brilliant sunshine, giving the scenes an upbeat unreality, but the weather the day these images were taken had been overcast, cold and spitting with rain. Somehow she expected to see Terry going into the supermarket to buy his breakfast. The cursor swooped out of control and she was in the next street: a figure was heading towards the camera. Stella thought it familiar, but in the course of her job she met many people; they merged into types. Most people looked like other people.

'Terry's car might hold a valuable clue!' Jack was on a treasure hunt. Ever since she had learnt his real identity Stella could not shake off the impression he was a small boy treating everything as a game. Despite bags under his eyes and lines around his mouth that made him look nearer forty than thirty-three, Jack could seem four years old.

Jack looked over at the screen and divined Stella's motivations for looking at the Co-op better than she did herself. He spent as much time in Street View's static landscape as he did walking the actual streets, searching the pixellated faces on sunlit pavements for the parent he had lost. Since 27 July 1981 his life had had only one purpose. He brushed Stella's shoulder: 'Terry had a massive coronary and wouldn't have known about it. It's the memory of pain or trauma that makes it bad. It's worse for those left behind.'

Stella turned off the machine. 'We'll take the train so we can come back in Terry's car together and debrief.'

Stella did not add that she wanted Jack's company.

Forty-Eight

Saturday, 22 January 2011

Bishopstone was less than half a mile from the A259 – the route from Brighton to Eastbourne – but with no through road and any road markings or signs lost beneath the snow it was remote and timeless. All the way from Seaford Stella had kept the fan on, but Terry's car had not warmed up by the time they found the church.

In Seaford they had searched the car, squatting down by the door sills to peer beneath the seats, but Terry had been a tidy man and there were no used tissues or chewing-gum wrappers; they found nothing.

It was late afternoon; they had been travelling for two and a half hours. Their journey had begun with an Upminster District line train to Victoria station. To avoid fuss Stella had waived expense and proposed they hail a taxi, but Jack was reluctant. He had a staff pass for the Underground and Stella, thinking it would do him good to feel in charge, agreed. He insisted they face forwards in the front carriage and had sat with his left hand clenching and unclenching, his eyes on the door to the driver's cab at the end of the gangway like a child steering. Stella understood; her left foot would depress a phantom brake at junctions and bends whenever she was a passenger in Jackie's car.

They had changed trains at Lewes for Seaford. There, they struggled along icy pavements, past a church, a police station and a post office, to a wide street called the Causeway, to the sea where Stella had left Terry's car. The cars were covered with snow and Jack stomped ahead clearing registration plates until he found the Toyota.

Neither of them had considered the risk involved in moving the car. Snow had banked up around the wheels but they found a small shovel in the boot – there was also a hazard triangle and a first-aid kit – and dug around the tyres. The street was as slippery as an ice-rink and when Stella finally started the engine and manoeuvred out, the wheels spun and they slid gracefully over the camber stopping just short of the smaller shape of a motorbike. Stella coaxed the vehicle forward; the brakes were spongy and the wheels' response to the steering approximate. They missed a parked car by inches, knocking the wing mirror, making it spring inwards, which Jack insisted on getting out to correct. At last they reached the Bishopstone junction.

The village was at the end of a long winding lane. Stella was relieved to turn off the engine and dared not contemplate the drive back. She got out of the car and leant on the front wing. The air was fresher and colder than in London and she took a long breath.

Despite their speculations on the train, they were no closer to finding out what had brought Terry to Bishopstone.

'Why would he come here?' she mused out loud.

'Perhaps he had wanted to visit her grave; remind himself why he was doing it.'

'How often do you come?'

'Hardly ever.'

Jack had told Stella about the set numbers and knew she had found it hard to contain herself at the idea that he made life decisions on the basis of a train's identification number. He would not admit he had come to the grave two years ago, on 6 December, because on that day his first train's number had been 612.

'How far are we from Charbury?' Stella was speaking.

'About ten miles, maybe a bit less. Why?'

'It's where the Ramsays have a house. Maybe we should move Mark Ramsay up the list.'

A gust of cold wind blew in from the open car door and something fluttered out from the sun visor on to Jack's lap. He held it up to the interior light.

Newspaper had been torn roughly with no care for the text; it was probably rubbish and he was about to stuff it into his pocket, when he caught the words 'vacuum cleaner' in the fragment of headline: *riticize lazy security guards for failing to check vacuum cleaner.*

Until he worked for Stella, Jack had not realized how much there was to know about cleaning: the equipment, cleaning agents, solutions for specific stains, hazard signs, buckets with wringers and wheels, brushes for every kind of dirt. He had stumbled upon an art form. He knew he was a good train driver but received any praise and promotion with stolid indifference. He did not care. Stella had not told him she admired his work, but let it slip to his mythical referee on the phone. He was pleased.

The article was dated 30 September 2008. The story was about the fire on the *Cutty Sark* the previous year. The incident was the major news story on the day his father had died. Jack had sat in the hospital watching the BBC lunchtime news on the monitor opposite the bed. Once, such a report would have gripped Hugh Rokesmith, who considered every eventuality when designing a bridge or a tunnel, but the world had diminished to an irrelevance and he did not respond when Jack reiterated the events of that early morning in May 2007.

Now it seemed that a Planet 200 industrial vacuum cleaner had been left on and overheated, causing a fire on the nineteenth-century clipper. Jack knew the vacuum, set on a platform with braked castor wheels at the front and a guiding bar at the back. Stella used them for commercial jobs. There had been one in the back of the van when they visited the plasterer and he had sneaked a look. Made in Italy, its stainless-steel cylinder with a little gauge was like a steam engine, although it operated on different principles. He longed to touch it, polish it and hear its motor; it was a feat of engineering. Unfortunately it wasn't necessary for Ivan Challoner's flat or Sarah Glyde's house, despite its years of neglect.

Jack had been shocked to see tears running down his father's cheeks. He wasn't looking at the television but out of the window at the sky. Jack had never seen him cry and had walked out of the ward. He kept walking, out of the hospital, on and on until he reached the sea. He ended up in Scarborough's Grand Hotel where he bought a coffee. While he was drinking it, a call came from the hospital. His father had died.

It was a sign.

He flipped the paper over. In jagged blue biro was a string of letters and digits in the margin: 'CPL 628B. Does this mean anything to you?'

Stella floundered through ankle-deep snow and leant in through the open door. 'Nope.'

'A serial number.' Jack handed her the paper. 'Or a password?'

'It's a registration plate.'

'Foreign maybe.'

'No, in the UK the suffix series started in 1963, the last letter is the age of the vehicle. This is 1964. What with your number thing, I'm surprised you didn't know that.'

Jack got out of the car and slammed the door. The sound startled rooks in the graveyard, their clattering wings and a burst of cawing broke the quiet.

'Me too! Good work, PC Darnell, your time on traffic paid off.'

'Terry told me.'

Jack could have said he treated numbers as a coded instruction; he dwelt on the message that they carried. His set numbers might tell him which train to pick up, but their meaning was deeper. He rarely considered numbers in the context of their own system; that was mundane.

'Terry had a string of stolen cars in his head, he'll have spotted this and written it on the nearest thing, no doubt while driving.' She crumpled the paper and stuffed it in her anorak pocket.

'I'll show you where Katherine Rokesmith grew up.'

Jack led them up the lane and on to a track narrowed by blackthorn bushes so high they were effectively in a tunnel. Here there was less snow, but the frozen mud pitted with ice made walking treacherous, so Stella was grateful when he stopped by a gap hidden amidst foliage which she would have missed.

A gate with the name 'Rose Cottage' carved along the top bar was held by one hinge; beyond it a path of terracotta tiles wound through tall grasses and bushes to a glimpse of a roughly stuccoed house with missing roof tiles. It looked deserted, but for a light in a downstairs window.

'Who lives here?' Stella breathed.

'No idea. When my mum's parents died she had to move.'

Stella stepped back and tripped on a plastic milk bottle holder with an indicator dial for the milk required. Two empty bottles had toppled out. Righting the carrier, she caught the manufacturer's name on the dial: 'Gina-Ware' – the company owned by Mrs Ramsay's son-in-law; now she too was seeing signs. She dropped the bottles back in.

'Let's get on, the light is going.'

'Different to St Peter's Square, isn't it?' Jack was conversational on the way back to the church.

'How did Kate meet Hugh Rokesmith?' She could not call them Jack's parents.

'It's a fairy tale. She was walking her dog in a place on the south side of the A25 – we'll pass it when we go. Tide Mills is the ruins of a nineteenth-century village by a railway halt. My father was returning from a meeting and fancied some air and pulled off the road. He petted her dog and they got talking. He might have driven on by.'

They reached the car.

'It might have been better if he had,' he added.

'How do you know this? Didn't you say he never mentioned Kate?'

'Isabel told me.' Jack opened his silver case and, taking out a cigarette, put it in his mouth. 'To be precise, she didn't tell me, she assumed I knew. She said what a charming way to fall in love and it must have rubbed off on me.'

'You wouldn't be here if they hadn't.'

Stella led the way through a gate beneath a gabled roof and strode ahead up a salted path to the church. In the gloom she thought the row of mausoleums looked like buildings in a miniature city.

Jack read out an inscription: "'William Catt, 1770 to 1853.' I used to wonder why cat was spelled with two Ts. It was a word I could spell because of Brunel, our cat.' Jack was animated. 'I had forgotten Brunel.'

The church tower was forbidding against the darkening sky. Stella knew they ought to return to London; in the country it seemed lighter than it was and already the driving conditions would be dangerous.

In the porch Jack tried the door; it was locked. He veered off the path. Thick snow made it hard to distinguish the graves and more than once they stumbled into troughs and over hidden mounds.

They went between two rectangles of snow: topiaried bushes and down a slope. A gravestone was on its own near a low flint wall beyond which fields had already merged in the twilight.

'Are you the ones who bring the flowers?' The strident voice carried over the hushed ground. A middle-aged woman lost in a wool coat and angora scarf scurried down the slope, pulled along by a small shaggy poodle straining on a lead.

Jack and Stella drew closer together.

'I'm sorry?' Stella said.

'The flowers. They are there again! Even in this atrocious weather they're here. I walk Mansfield here most days and I've never caught anyone by the grave or putting them there. The old ones are taken away. So thoughtful. I assume it's her son. The husband is dead and there was a little boy who would be grown up now.' The woman glared at her dog, which caused him to sit down, sinking into the snow, a paw tentatively lifted up and down.

'We're not locals, so no flowers, I'm afraid. We read about St Andrew's in a thingy in the tourist place so thought we'd pop in to take a look. I gather this is the oldest church in Sussex. What a thing!'

Stella watched as Jack rattled on, his accent pure public school. 'Unfortunately it's locked. Such a pity they lock churches these days. We are admiring the view, then heading off home.' He waved a hand into the gloom.

The woman rummaged in her pocket and produced a handful of little bone-shaped dog biscuits. 'Paw.' The dog did as it was told and snapped up the proffered treat.

'You must have heard about the young woman callously murdered in London. This is her. She came from here. Tragic. She was with her son. I went to the funeral. The whole village turned out. It was terribly sad. I supposed you might be relations and I wanted to give you my condolences. You don't see many at the grave, thankfully really. I do hate these shrines that are springing up everywhere, willy-nilly. On the other hand, apart from the flowers, our Katherine is rather neglected.'

'Did you know her?'

Terry would have talked to the woman, too, while Stella was fighting the urge to run away.

'We were in the same class at school. I can't say we were friends. When Katherine met that husband, she left and never came back. Or not while she was alive.' She grimaced and popped another biscuit between the poodle's lips. 'The poor thing. Such are the twists of fate. We've had more than our share of tragedy here, what with the plane crash at Shoreham that killed thingummy. I want to call him Flyte because he was a mad-cap pilot type and besides that's the Waugh novel, anyway the man with the frosty big-wig of a son. Years ago all this was, his grave is here too somewhere. I should set up a tour, the way I'm going on. Mansfield! Ssssh! No begging.' She dropped the lead, squeezed the biscuits back into her pocket and did up the button.

'You're not meant to speak ill of the dead, and especially when the death was in such appalling circumstances. But Katherine Venus – that was how we knew her – wasn't warm. She didn't have friends, apart from the son, Lord Snooty. Such a shame.'

'What son?' Stella was paying attention.

The dog set up a furious barking, shrill and intent and scattered away over the snow.

'Mansfield! He sees ghosts and won't let up.' She set off in pursuit up the slope, her legs kicking out behind her. The area under the trees had become dense and impenetrable. The woman's distant tones of admonishment faded to quiet.

'Let's hear it for nosy bloody parkers,' Stella muttered. 'Does the young man she mentioned mean anything to you?'

Jack shrugged. 'Probably a boyfriend. I expect she had many. Mrs Poodle-Person no doubt disapproved.'

The headstone, iced with snow, gave the date of Kate Rokesmith's death – 27th July 1981 – and stated only that she was 'Wife of Hugh Rokesmith'. Lichen had blotched the inscription and it was sprinkled with snowflakes. Stella brushed these away.

'It doesn't say when she was born.' Nor did it mention Jack, but she did not say this.

'I hadn't noticed.' He was looking in the direction the dog had gone.

'No label, no message, nothing.' Stella examined the flowers. 'They don't smell. I didn't know you could get orange roses.'

'They mean something.'

'Do they?' Stella was tiring of Jack's signs.

'The colour of roses signifies different emotions. Black roses mean death. I can't remember orange.'

'I wonder why your father didn't put both dates. Birthdays are nicer to think about than death.'

'Perhaps the only date that mattered to him was the one on which she ceased to exist.' Jack went towards the path. Stella wandered over to the wall despite her concern that they should leave. There was a drop of about six feet on the other side of the wall – more maybe, the snow made it hard to tell. She sat astride it.

Everything swooped and she had to clasp sharp flint to balance. Terry had been here. He had climbed this wall and sat where she was sitting. He had jumped down; Stella felt for toe-holds, clinging to stones to prevent herself pitching off. She lowered herself by degrees until her boot, kicking about in the snow, encountered solid ground. She was out of sight of the graveyard. She trod on something – a plastic disc. She held it up to the failing light: it was a lens cap.

Terry had been here and taken a picture.

They had not found a camera in the car, nor was there one among his belongings. Terry was here; she felt his presence. Panicked, Stella lunged at the wall. It was harder to climb and twice she fell before struggling over and tumbling into the graveyard. She brushed slabs of snow off her anorak and knees and made her way past Kate's grave up the slope to the path. There was no sign of Jack.

A gate clanged. The sound came from past the church. She skirted the building where there were more graves and a beech hedge which stretched to the lych gate. She found footprints and tracked them to an iron gate in the hedge. Through this she could see nothing because another hedge blocked the view. The gate was fastened with a padlock glinting silver in the last light. Stella could make out the twin gables of a house above the second hedge; she presumed it was the vicarage.

At the crunch of footsteps she saw Jack emerging from trees where the dog had gone.

'There's another way out.' He was grim-faced and pale. 'Someone was there recently.'

'It was the dog-woman.'

'There's more than one set of footprints. That dog heard someone.'

'I should think this path must be a cut-through.'

'It's not the best way, but good if you don't want to be seen. Those roses are fresh.'

'Did you follow the tracks?'

'They disappear. It's like the person took off into the air.'

'That's impossible.'

'Nothing's impossible.'

Stella looked at him, but he was staring through the gate at the house. To bring him back, she said loudly: 'The flowers had snow on them and there are no footprints by the grave. They were not put there today.' Then she headed for the car.

Terry's boxy Toyota was ten years old. He would have looked after it, but earlier, having not been used for nearly two weeks, it had only started after several attempts. This time it fired first time. She rolled the seat back and stretched out her legs and rested her head back. There was a compartment above the mirror, flush to the fascia. They had missed it. Stella was sweeping her hand over the plastic, feeling for the mechanism, when Jack climbed into the car.

Their fingers brushed as he reached up and depressed the plastic cover; it sprang upwards. The space inside dipped down to defy gravity, so Stella had to poke far inside. Behind a roll of toilet paper, her fingers encountered a hard object. She knew it was Terry's camera before she pulled it out. She knew too that the lens cap would fit.

'He carried this everywhere. Mum would go on about how much time he spent in his darkroom.' She groaned. 'I forgot about his darkroom. It's in the basement.' She cradled the camera in her hands. 'She'd be talking and Terry would take a photograph, of a passer-by, a number plate, a street, cars with a broken tail light or a dent. He was discreet. He snapped pictures because a person looked suspicious or familiar; they never knew. He built a bank of images he hoped one day would provide evidence or a clue. My mum said that after they were married he stopped photographing her.'

'You're lucky; he took pictures. The only ones I have of me are passport pictures and driving licence, a nursery school snap they used for the media when my mum was murdered.' He rubbed his ear and added: 'That one of me as a baby with Kate has gone missing; the press nicked it.'

Stella was about to contradict him – she had no pictures of herself – when truth dawned: 'Terry was taking pictures of Kate's grave.' She cradled the camera.

'Turn it on.' Jack fiddled with his case, drew out a roll-up and stuck it between his lips.

Stella turned a dial to the right as she had seen Terry do. It had no effect. She tried it the other way and the lens motor buzzed, the lens shot out, firing off the lens cap and then retracting.

'Battery's dead.' Jack took the unlit cigarette out of his mouth and held it with his fingers and thumb. 'He must have a charger, perhaps in the darkroom.'

Stella could not go into Terry's darkroom. There, more than anywhere in his house, he would be present; she kept this to herself.

'Where did you find the lens cap?'

'Behind the graveyard wall.'

'Why would he take a picture of the grave from there?'

'Terry was particular about perspective and framing.'

'So why take the headstone from behind? I didn't know where you were; you were out of sight.' Jack put the cigarette back in his case. 'Terry hid there.'

Stella pulled down the seat belt and clicked it into place.

'He was taking a photograph of the person leaving the flowers.' She spoke in a whisper. She released the handbrake and the car slid off the verge on to the lane. 'It will be on the camera. We must find his battery charger.'

'I desire you.' Jack banged the dashboard with his cigarette case.

Stella hit the brake. The car continued moving.

'Orange roses, that's what they mean. Or "I desire to get to know you better."'

Stella played the wheel, giving it enough slack to avoid skidding.

'Jack, do you suppose that the person who puts the flowers on Kate's grave is the person who murdered her?'

'I do,' Jack replied. 'It's what I would do.'

Forty-Nine

Saturday, 22 January 2011

They were waiting for a break in traffic on the A259, Stella drumming on the steering wheel. They would not get to London until the late evening. She groaned as the headlights travelling down the hill from Seaford dazzled her.

'All right my side,' Jack said helpfully, leaning back against the headrest to give Stella a clear view. A vehicle slowed, its left indicator flashing.

Stella let the other car swing on to the lane and then accelerated out. Jack glimpsed the car – a bulky four-by-four – as it swept away up to Bishopstone.

Stella's phone rang in her rucksack.

'Would you answer that?' she rapped. 'Unzip the side compartment,' she added as Jack's hand fluttered over the many pockets. Eventually he pressed the phone to Stella's ear, which was not what she had intended.

'Are you driving?'

Jackie's voice was too upbeat. Something was wrong. Stella's hands tightened on the wheel. She had never taken time off from work before and was about to pay for it.

'Yes.' Stella did not want to say where she was or who with. Nor did she want to lie to Jackie. 'It's Saturday. Why are you working?'

'Can you stop? Are you sitting down?'

'No and ye-es.' The headlights lit a barn at a bend in the road; it was a fairy-tale house coated in marzipan. 'Put it on hands free,' Stella mouthed to Jack. He had another unlit cigarette in his mouth.

'It's Paul. I know you don't want him mentioned.' Jackie's voice boomed over the speakers. 'The police have rung. They've pulled him out of the river.'

A footbridge curving over the road ahead was a silver rainbow.

'Stella, I am sorry to have to tell you this, but the nice policeman said that Paul has drowned.'

Fifty

Sunday, 23 January 2011

Traffic was queuing behind a white police lorry outside Hammersmith Police Station on Shepherd's Bush Road. One back door was open; red letters on the other spelled 'Police Ho'. A policewoman in riding gear slammed the door.

Police Horses.

Stella watched the officer climb into the passenger seat and the lorry roar off in the direction of Shepherd's Bush Green and her office.

Police. Ice. Lice. Pile. Pole. Lope. Clip. Clop. Lip. Lop. Nice.

'Ten words is a lot to get out of one word. Clever girl!' At six years old he could barely read. His daughter could break words up to make new ones. The idea would not have occurred to him. 'You spelled "Like" wrong.'

'Da-ad! It's "Lice". A girl in my class had them on her head. She had a comb with disinfectant put in her hair, like the wicked stepmother in Snow White, *you remember!'*

Reading Stella her bedtime story was the best bit of his day.

'OK, but there's no "N" in police, Stell. You can't have "Nice".'

'You're nice, so I can.' She got down from his lap, off on some new mission.

Police. After Kate Rokesmith's death Stella had willed the word and all that went with it to disappear. Jack had once counted up words visible while they sat at traffic lights and reached twenty-three: street signs, vehicles, retail signage, a T-shirt, a notice on a lamp-post about a lost wedding ring and an advertising hoarding.

The modest frontage of brown brickwork and beige cladding of the police station was three storeys high. A Lion and Unicorn supporting the police crest above the portico and the two lanterns on wrought-iron arms were the only ornaments. On each of these lanterns, Stella read 'Police' engraved in the blue glass.

Metal bollards at the entrance were not there when she was little and a barrier boxed in the ledge where she waited for Terry to come off shift. She had pattered back and forth, braving the drop to the pavement, singing to her mother:

'I'm the King of the Castle.'

'Stella, get down or you'll be arrested.'

Hammersmith Police Station.

Terry's castle.

Aside from a spell there in the eighties, Terry Darnell had seen out the last nine years of his service, until he retired in 2009, at the station where his career had begun in 1966.

His daughter climbed the steps he had used, the surface stained orange-brown with grit, slush puddling in a dip on the third one. Hammersmith Police Station had seen its best days. The police would move to new premises and the life that Terry had known would be history; his forty-three years of service amounting to a framed certificate, a beer tankard and the boxes of an unsolved case in his attic.

Glass doors slid aside and in the foyer it dawned on Stella that Terry would not come out to greet her. The woman behind the grille raised enquiring eyebrows; she did not know Stella.

'I've come to see Detective Inspector Cashman.'

'Is he expecting you?'

'Yes.'

The person on the end of the phone must have said Stella was the late Borough Commander's daughter because the woman came to life, asking if she would like tea or coffee and urging her to sit down. It might have been better to see Cashman at her flat after all, as he had offered, but to avoid him coming there she had volunteered to drop in on her way to a client. It being a Sunday, there was no client.

Afterwards she would check Terry's camera, left charging in her kitchen. His charger was in a drawer in his desk. Jack had gone on his last *A–Z* walk, refusing to cancel despite the pointlessness of following routes traced by a stranger; he wanted time to himself, then tomorrow afternoon she had put him down to clean for Ivan and then he was coming to her flat. The thought of Ivan made her feel better and she wondered if he was enjoying Rome or Paris. He had not rung; after Paul's full-on communication this should have been a relief, but it left her uncertain: had she only imagined that they had got on?

She sat where she used to sit, bolt upright, furthest from the desk, her rucksack on her lap. The seat, too, had changed; no longer wood, it was blue metal like a piece of Meccano. Soon, despite herself, she was keeping a weather eye on the door; alert for Terry. What would he be like? How would he be? Each time she saw him she had to get to know him all over again. Sometimes a beard, neatly trimmed, at others a moustache, or clean-shaven with a crew cut. Always a stranger.

The last time: a day's growth of beard, milky eyes staring at nothing.

A friendly man at the counter had given her a paper and a pen saying 'Metropolitan Police' on its side and told her that her daddy would be late, so why didn't she do him a picture in the meantime? Stella was not the kind of child that knew what to do with an expanse of paper and a world of possibilities. She had a colouring book in her bag, but did not say so. She wrote her name in the corner and drew a handgun with lines coming out of the barrel to show the velocity of the bullet. A voice had told her that little girls did not do guns. It must have been Terry's.

Over the reception hatch were the names of officers who had died in the war and now Stella supposed that the idea of a gun had come from seeing these. Her thoughts were interrupted by D. I.

Cashman. Wringing her hand, he had an air of hurry, as if he had left a situation that could go wrong in his absence. He held open the heavy oak door.

On the bright central staircase, Cashman issued a sober 'Morning' to everyone who passed them. A young man called him 'sir' and nodded to Stella, who nodded back. As a teenager, she had found the status conferred on her by being Terry's daughter mortifying. By then no longer holding Terry's hand, she would slink behind him to his palatial office with a private toilet and its door always open.

Martin Cashman's heels were official on the parquet floor. Windows filled the passage with sunlight. Stella paused by a wooden batten on the wall in which was fixed a bronze rule reaching to eight feet.

'This tells us the height of villains. Stand up, that's it, good and straight. Put your back right up against it. Four foot six! You've grown since... since...'

He could not remember the last time he had seen Stella. She would be tall like his mum. As tall as him.

'I'm not a villain.'

'Course you're not. You're completely innocent, you!'

The rule started at four feet five inches; Stella had supposed the police did not imagine that anyone under that height could be bad. Through the window she counted nine cars in the car park below, ranged in rows of three, the number '10' in blue on white roofs. The cars had changed too. Cashman was waiting. Behind him was an outdated enamelled street sign:

Borough of Hammersmith
BRAYBROOK STREET. W12

Stella had assumed the meeting would be in his office but they were going to the Braybrook Suite, the murder room for the investigation into Kate Rokesmith's case. Cashman gave a peremptory knock on the door before opening it.

'This was your dad's favourite place in the station. He'd only been in the force five minutes when it happened, but I guess you know this.'

Stella said nothing. Cashman left his pad and pen on the table and went to a shelf near one of the windows. There was a large book open there; he flipped through it. He was a curator preparing to guide her through the venerated contents of his museum.

The room was used for meetings: six grouped tables around which were high-backed chairs. Commemorative silver cups were displayed in a glass-shelved vitrine. Terry taught her that word.

'Here we are.' Cashman beckoned to Stella.

Reluctantly she stepped past a television on a trolley and joined him.

'That's Terry, second from the left.'

A black and white photograph showed policemen crouched down, their hands white against the dark of their uniforms and the grey of the grass. Behind them, other men crept forward like kids playing Grandmother's Footsteps. Terry's face was half in view; he was kneeling, one hand supporting himself, the other hovering over the grass; he was staring down. His hair was a John Lennon-style mop and although dressed like the other officers, he looked different. Stella felt that at any minute Terry might glance up out of the image and see her.

In the background was Braybrook Street; a taxi and a police van were parked beside trimmed hedges. This was what Terry was doing instead of meeting his newly born daughter.

'When I found the room was free, I nabbed it for old times' sake.' Cashman was pleased with himself. Stella managed a tight smile.

A slate plaque read:

THIS ROOM IS DEDICATED TO
CHRISTOPHER HEAD
GEOFFREY FOX
DAVID WOMBWELL
WHO WERE SHOT AND
FATALLY WOUNDED IN THE COURSE
OF THEIR DUTY AT
BRAYBROOK STREET, SHEPHERD'S BUSH, W12
12th AUGUST, 1966

Cashman sat at the table and busied himself with his pad. Stella sat opposite.

The shaving cut on his chin, fresh when Stella had seen him a week ago, had healed to a line drawn with a dark red pen.

She could have drawn a detective. That would have pleased Terry.

'I am sorry about Paul Bramwell.' He jotted '23/1/11' on a clean page. 'What with the old lady and more specifically your dad, this is a tough time.' He pursed his lips.

Had Cashman brought her to the Braybrook Suite and shown her the picture of Terry to soften her up?

'You were his girlfriend, weren't you?'

'It wasn't serious.' Stella felt herself grow hot. It would be ridiculous to cry when she didn't feel like crying.

'You probably knew Mr Bramwell as well as anyone. His brother hadn't seen him for months. I want to get a sense of his last days. Did he have fallings out? Any reason to feel bad?'

Stella shook her head. Paul had a school friend he had found on Facebook and the brother; she had not wanted to meet them.

'When did you see him last?'

'At my office eleven days ago when we agreed to end it.'

'Was he upset?'

'It was a mutual decision.'

'So he was OK with it?'

'It was never serious.'

'I have here that he was forty-nine, an IT engineer for Robbins and Robbins, a PC maintenance firm in Uxbridge. He had a flat near the Goldhawk Road and apart from a spell in the army had lived in Hammersmith all his life. One brother, parents deceased, single.' He looked at Stella. 'No kids. Is all this correct?'

'Yes.' Stella had not been interested in Paul's past. She did know about the army because of a tattoo of his number on his upper arm; an arm now lifeless in a mortuary drawer. She blinked.

'Was he depressed, suicidal? Did he bring it up, even as a joke?'

'No.' Stella was careful not to elaborate. She had made that mistake about Mrs Ramsay.

'How he fetched up by a pontoon at Hammersmith Bridge is a mystery.'

'He couldn't swim,' Stella volunteered.

'Not much help to him if he could, I'm afraid. I'm sorry to put you through this, Stella, but you know the score: how did you meet?'

'He mended an office PC and then came back to set up a local area network, an LAN.' She was pleased to recall the acronym, although the sheer weight of acronyms in Paul's conversation had soon palled. Now it triggered a flash of fondness. 'How did he die?' She steeled herself.

'The post-mortem is in this morning. I do know he was in the water a while so I'm not sure how conclusive the results will be.' He sat back. 'His brother says you and Mr Bramwell were planning to marry.'

'That was never on the cards; the brother's got it wrong.'

A knock and a woman police constable entered with an A4 envelope. She spoke in Cashman's ear, but Stella could hear. 'The PM results, sir.'

'Thanks, Mandy.' Cashman was like Terry, he knew everyone's names, and gave full attention if only for a second.

He withdrew sheets of paper stapled together and, tipping his chair back on two legs, consulted them. Behind him was a photograph of Sergeant Christopher Head and another of his coffin being carried from the church. Terry had gone to the joint funeral for the three fallen officers. He showed her a newspaper picture of him saluting the coffins.

'Seems Paul had drunk a distillery's worth of whisky. We found an empty bottle at his flat, with only one glass. There was a hundred and ninety milligrams of alcohol in his blood. By rights he shouldn't have been able to stand. Was he a drinker?'

'Not with me.' One picture showed the cortège of black limousines along a rain-soaked Uxbridge Road lined with crowds huddled beneath umbrellas. On 1 September 1966, Stella was twenty days old. Terry was a recently married man with a brand-new baby daughter. Had he felt lucky that day?

'We do have one problem. He appears to have called you the night he died. The line was open for eleven seconds.'

Stella made a show of looking puzzled. *Phone records.* She took the handset out of her pocket and keyed her way to 'Received calls'.

'It says here he called me at 11.03. Missed call.' She kept her voice level.

'You called him back moments later.' Cashman grimaced as if the whole thing were a nuisance.

'It must have jolted in my pocket. I forget to lock it.' She made a show of locking the handset and placed it on the table between them as if it were a revolver she had emptied of bullets. 'We spoke briefly – but I thought that was earlier in the week.'

'Did he – I hate to have to ask – did he sound drunk?'

'He did. We didn't talk for long. He was going to the pub.' Breathe in. Breathe out. They would not have transcripts of the conversation.

'Did he say which one?' She watched Cashman write 'pub' on his pad.

The three dead men's expressions bore the same neutrality: prepared for duty, like Terry, officers with a job to do.

'The Ram. He wanted me to meet him. I said no.' If they checked where the handsets were when the conversation happened, they would see they were only feet from each other.

'This is looking like accidental death. Paul has a gash on the back of his skull he likely got from falling. No idea what he was doing by the river. I have to say my guess is that he was urinating: his zip was undone.' Cashman laid down the report. 'He was unconscious, but alive when he fell into the water. I am sorry, Stella.'

'Me too.' Stella meant it.

Cashman slipped the report back into the envelope. 'A hell of a way to go.' He got up. 'Stella, thank you for doing this. I think we can say that Paul Bramwell was careless. Happens to the best of us, but he's paid a high price. I hope you can put it behind you. You've given us all the help we need. There'll be an inquest, but I doubt you'll be called.'

Stella got up.

'One more thing.' D. I. Cashman's hand was on the door handle.

Stella kept calm. His tactic belonged on television.

'We wondered if it is family only.'

'What is?'

'Terry's funeral. There's many here want to come.' Cashman had the expression of the officers in the photograph. 'You know, Terry could have a Force Funeral. We do the arranging.'

Stella had opted for the crematorium's early-morning fifteen-minute slot and was not going herself. Her mother would not attend and Terry's only relative – an older sister – had emigrated to New Zealand before Stella was born. She had sent a condolence letter but would not be coming. Terry's colleagues had more right to be at his funeral than his daughter; they knew him better.

'We had this running joke with Terry about a bench: for the man who never sat down. Not so funny now, but the girls were saying it would be a special gesture for a super cop, Top Cat we called him because—'

'I know.' Stella folded her arms.

'Course you do. I said I'd pass it by you.'

Stella looked into a display case by the window. A Police Notices book for 1966 was opened at a black-bordered page announcing the three deaths. On the facing page were the lighting-up times for

13, 14 and 15 August of that year. For the families of the men it must have felt dark whatever the time.

The men would never know what their children did next.

'It is a nice thought,' Stella agreed. 'Tell them, yes.'

'I'll be honest, they've gone ahead and got up a collection and Janet's chosen a three-seater. We want to know where you'd like it to go.'

'I'll leave it to you.' The sun had gone in, making the room seem smaller.

'The bench?'

'Both.' Stella made a decision. 'The funeral and the bench. Terry would be … Thanks.' Terry was dead and would have no idea what she did next.

Cashman led Stella out of the station the back way. They crossed the yard in front of the stables. A whiff of urine-soaked hay caught Stella in the throat. Cashman was unlatching the doors.

'Terry said he brought you here when you were little. Come on, I'll show you.'

Stella hesitated; she was afraid of horses. There were no bits of straw in the aisle between the stalls and white brick-bonded tiles were washed clean.

The floor was chocolate, she declared. He didn't get it at first and then he saw what she mean: the raised non-slip squares did look like a bar of chocolate. He said she could have some later. She said nothing. That was not what she meant; he should have known. She's never been one of those kids demanding stuff. He lifted her to see the horses. Omega stuck his head out. 'He won't bite.' She touched his nose, softly stroking. They were bringing out Hadrian in full livery for a parade. He sat her on top of him. Sitting sideways. 'You are the Queen.' She looked even more of a tot on the enormous beast.

'I'll get you riding lessons if Mum is OK with it.'

Stella said later she didn't want them, but 'thank you for showing me, Daddy'. He got a feeling when she called him that.

Outside on Shepherd's Bush Road, Stella sneezed and pulled a tissue from her pocket. A ball of newspaper fell to the ground.

'You dropped this.' Cashman stopped it with his foot and picked it up.

It was the paper they had found in Terry's car.

'It's a plate number. I don't suppose you could tell me the name it's registered to?' Stella grew hot. She should not have asked.

Cashman rocked on his heels. In the harsh winter sun his face was sharp, almost ugly. 'Nineteen sixty-four. Going back some. Stella, I'm sorry, I hate it when this happens, it'll have to be a no. They are tight on rules these days.'

He made to hand the paper back. Stella shook her head. He could chuck it – who was she to have hunches? Cashman would have done it for Terry but she was only his daughter, with her the favours ran out.

'I'll be in touch.' Cashman was placating her. A police officer approached him and already his mind was elsewhere.

Furious with herself, Stella walked briskly away. By the steps to the Hammersmith and City line on Hammersmith Broadway someone stepped into her path.

'Don't get yourself locked up, I'd have to bail you out.'

Ivan Challoner belonged to a world that was shiny and certain. He would not fall drunk into the Thames or fail to return her calls. Despite being keen to examine Terry's camera, Stella accepted his suggestion that they grab a coffee. It was Sunday; he was having a weekend, he said. She caught his mood: she would take Martin Cashman's advice and put it all behind her.

Watching him dextrously tip a teaspoon of milk into his double espresso, she considered telling him about the Rokesmith case. She and Jack were too close to it and were getting on each other's nerves and therefore nowhere. She was not a detective and Jack bordered on bonkers. Ivan was methodical and intelligent and, Jack would agree, had the right kind of mind.

Fifty-One

Sunday, 23 January 2011

'I'm investigating a murder.'

Stella felt a tingle down her spine. They were out of earshot of other customers. The nearest to them, two men and a woman, were huddled around a laptop as if keeping warm.

'How intriguing.' Ivan looked quizzical.

'It's a long story.' Stella gulped down the tepid latte. 'My father was a detective, in the Met. He's just died.'

'I am so sorry, you never said.' He leant forward. Stella noticed with surprise that he looked as if he wore foundation. One cheek was caked with it and then powdered as if covering a spot or a cut. It had worked; she could not see a blemish of any kind.

'It was nearly a fortnight ago. I'm going through his stuff. It's taking a while.'

'If only we could step off this world with no fuss and paperwork.' Ivan spoke with feeling. 'I prefer to think of death as a transition, not so much an "after-life" as "another-life". Our loved ones never leave us. Or so I feel. We find our own way.'

'He had copied the files for a murder. It's not allowed but it happens. It must have got to him. Detectives – most police officers probably – are on the lookout for people they didn't catch or who got off. They can't let it go. Terry – that's my dad – was obsessed with the Rokesmith case.'

'I can relate to that,' Ivan agreed. 'I dwell on treatment I might have done differently, or better, particularly if a patient goes against my advice. I'm with your father, I like to see a job to completion. I lie awake at night roaming people's mouths, picturing the perfect operation that has eluded me. With a crime it must be worse.' He ate the last of his croissant and wiped his hands on his paper napkin.

Stella was relieved he did not appear to judge Terry for committing an illegal act. She had taken a risk telling him. The problem of clearing out Terry belongings became less onerous as it receded into the business of normal life. It had happened to Ivan. She went on: 'It was famous at the time, you may have heard of it.'

'Doesn't ring bells.'

Stella had decided Ivan Challoner was in his fifties, but his tall figure was trim and muscular, he moved with the suppleness of a younger man. A skilled dentist, he was detached from the basic and disagreeable; the Rokesmith murder had received national attention, yet Ivan had missed it.

'A young woman called Katherine Rokesmith was out with her son. It's likely he was there when she died. In those days a detective superintendent from Scotland Yard appointed a local team of detectives including sergeants and detective constables. My father was the senior investigating officer and handled the operational side. Although he wasn't formally in charge, he was on the ground and so responsible. Career-wise it was a break, except he did not find the killer.'

'I see.' Ivan put down the napkin, folding it. 'He receives credit if he gets his man and plenty of recrimination if he does not. Damned if you do etc. So you have taken over the mantle and are bent on solving it for him. What a good daughter.'

Stella felt awkward. Ivan presumed she was a much nicer person than she was. He thought only the best of people.

'I got drawn in.' She cast about. 'The police are doing nothing, the file is "put away", as they call it, and no one, apart from Terry, has opened it for decades. There's no DNA, no murder weapon and no clues of worth. The police can't tie up valuable resources looking for a needle in a haystack. Now my dad has gone too.'

'I see.' Ivan was gazing at Stella. 'Do you think you can succeed? Don't mistake my question: I have more faith in you than in the average Met detective. In a short time I have gained an impression of you as resourceful and intelligent; nevertheless Kate was strangled many moons ago. I'd hate you to set yourself up for failure. We can't answer for the sins of our fathers. We must lead our own lives. The one perk of being "orphaned" is that one is free to be oneself.'

Ivan had never spoken so personally and Stella did not after all dislike it. Nor had she noticed how blue his eyes were.

'I'm not sure I can solve it, although I have found fresh evidence. I think that Terry had a new lead, which I may be close to discovering.'

Ivan offered Stella a lift. Her first instinct was to refuse, but in the last hour she had begun to see the Rokesmith case as no longer a stifling dream from which she could not escape. Ivan was interested. Besides, the visit to the station had lowered her spirits and she wanted his company a while longer. She also wanted to get back quickly; the weather had caused delays on public transport. In Ivan's big swish car she could be at her flat in twenty minutes.

As they joined the Great West Road and edged out into the third lane, Stella described the visit to Bishopstone the day before and told Ivan about finding Terry's camera.

She did not tell him about Jonathan Rokesmith.

Fifty-Two

Sunday, 23 January 2011

At midday Jack was in Stanwell.

He walked each page of the *A–Z* in order and, apart from one slip, did not skip numbers to get to the areas he preferred. He did not impose significance on numbers where there was none. It would not help to return to what he had missed, the secret would be apparent only if he faithfully traversed the path of each journey. A true reader understands that the only way to appreciate a story is to read each word, from the start to the end.

Over the months Jack had been soaked by rain and stung by sleet; he had greeted streaks of dawn light as he took a left or a right to stay on the path drawn. He'd slithered on footpaths, avoided sick, dog shit and litter. Wind tore at his clothes as he battled across grass, tarmac and the wasteland depicted on his map as blank space. Walking, Jack was never somewhere.

He was nowhere.

One by one he had walked the pages – and today he was on the last one.

He had passed the Hammersmith and City exit minutes before Stella was about to go down the steps after her visit to Martin Cashman. Neither saw the other, although they were so close. When a man stepped in front of Jack, forcing him to give way and without apology ran down the stairs, Jack considered going after him. The man's indifference was what he looked for in the perfect Host. But Jack had spent months working towards this final journey in the atlas; he would not change plans.

He wished he had not told Stella about the street atlas. She was a police officer's daughter; she relied on evidence, not fanciful thinking; he worried it had put her off.

Before he found the book, Jack had not had much use for an A–Z. In his driver's cab the tracks were his guide. But over time the atlas had offered him another way to achieve his quest.

The marked-out routes were a set of instructions: the area of Inner and Greater London was divided into a grid of 144 squares. The numbered grids followed the western reading pattern: from left to right, then down to the next line. A convention broken at square 142, which along with 143 and 144, was tagged on to the left of the grid covering Uxbridge, West Drayton and Stanwell respectively. Of these districts, only Uxbridge was familiar to Jack because it had an Underground station.

Jack had been walking for two and a half hours but did not know this because when he was tracing a route he wore no watch. He did not need to measure time. He had passed the new Terminal Five building at Heathrow, which in his 1995 deluxe edition was described as the 'Proposed Terminal Five Development Area'. He was on Clockhouse Lane.

This was long and for the most part straight, a line of tarmac demarcated by snow heaped in the gutters. He stayed on the left where he could make out a pavement beneath the snow. He kept hard by the link fence to avoid spray from speeding cars. He had not met another pedestrian but was accompanied by a set of footprints going in the same direction. Whoever had passed this way was not in sight.

The top of the fence was strung with three lengths of barbed wire. On both sides of the lane was scrubland; today a landscape of white mounds. The map depicted a lake, and squares representing warehouses. At the junction with the A30 there were playing fields and an industrial estate. He had seen them; he did not stray outside the pen-line.

He reached the white of grass surrounding a lake glittering in the thin light, with trees punctuating the shoreline: vestiges of countryside that would disappear as the city encroached.

He was on the last grid square, the pen-line, firm and competent, went along Clockhouse Lane and trailed off a square with no coordinate. When he stepped off it, he would be invisible.

One step, two step and he was gone.

Jack found himself by metal railings, through which were tennis courts, their nets slackened within a wire enclosure. He unfastened a gate and crunched over to a bench. Clearing off snow, he sat down.

Around page twenty Jack had begun to prepare properly for his expeditions. He carried a flask of hot milk and honey and, since he had met Stella, a packet of digestive biscuits. He was strict about where he stopped; there must be no one nearby and if there were, he moved to avoid conversation. He must not be remembered.

He had once loved snow, but now it was his enemy. Stealthy and insistent, it blotted out clues and signs while giving away his own actions. Lost in his coat, the collar up, his damp hair slicked to his head, Jack sipped his milk, savouring the sweetness, but today it did not work its magic. He was not resting in the middle of a journey full of promise, he was at the end of the line and did not know where to go next.

Stella was right, his conviction that the atlas would give him a clue to his mother's killer was absurd; he was wasting time. He chucked the rest of the milk on to the ground and it hissed a hole, like a wound, in the snow.

He leafed to page 144. In the top right-hand corner – so small he had initially mistaken it for scribble to check if a pen was working – he saw: '242'.

Jack rummaged in his pocket for his timetable. He found this week's shift pattern. The second set number for his last train on Wednesday had been '242'. The train Stella boarded on the day he told her he was at school with Kate Rokesmith's little boy. Was that a sign?

He fitted the little book back into his pocket and felt something cold and hard. His amulet. Even in the flat light the glass glowed green. Suddenly he remembered: that Mummy had tried to swap it for his engine, telling him it would bring him luck. He had insisted on taking the steam engine. As he tried to gather the loose strands, tenuous images dissolved back into the mists of the past.

He stared at page 144, willing it to give up its secret, but perhaps the secret was not his to know. It belonged to a stranger. Perhaps some mysteries were destined to remain unsolved. Jack was overwhelmed with futility; nothing could alter the main event. It had happened and that was that.

Nothing will bring her back.

He would have to look for real signs to get him to a station. He was off the map and could not go back the way he had come.

Still clutching the green glass, he put it to his lips. His mother had been right: about good luck; the talisman had saved his life.

He willed the *A–Z* to give up its message and as if his wish was granted he saw a wardrobe in his mind, but, trying to hold it, the image evaporated.

Jack had not told Stella that when he found the man who had murdered his mother, he would kill him.

Fifty-Three

The car splashed through thawing ice into one of the visitors' bays outside Stella's flat. There were no other cars. Ivan turned off the engine and the Schumann violin concerto was cut off; Stella half expected it to continue. Cushioned in the heated leather seat, the music and purring engine had the soporific effect of Ivan's dentist's chair and the sofa in his sitting room. She relished playing truant with Ivan; not a soul in the world would find her.

'Would you like to come in for a cup of tea?'

'That would be lovely, but then I'll get going, I don't want to disrupt your Sunday.'

Ivan came to Stella's side of the car to open her door. When Paul had done this she had been irritated, but Ivan did not do it to impress. She tried not to think about Paul.

The lift pinged. Paul was not dead; a drowned body was easy to misidentify. Stella felt a surge of hope.

A woman yelped when she saw them, and then recovered herself. 'It's rare to meet anyone in this ghost of a building!'

Ivan stood aside to allow her out before ducking into the lift.

Stella did not know what led her to introduce herself: 'I'm Stella Darnell, I live on the fourth floor.'

'Oh, it's good to meet a friendly face. I simply never see anyone. Emma Chaplin, second floor, number twenty-five.' She peeped into the lift where Ivan was scrutinizing the buttons. 'Lovely to know you're here!' As the doors closed, she called out and put out a hand. 'Isn't it...?'

Ivan hit the button again, the doors shut and soundlessly the lift ascended.

'Did you know her?'

'She might be a patient. They can't place me, the white coat confuses them.'

Stella suspected Ivan was unhappy she had encouraged conversation. If he did not want people to think they were together he should not be seen with her in public. In the car he had renewed the cancelled dinner invitation and they were meeting at the French restaurant in Kew where the staff no doubt assumed they were a couple.

Once they were in the flat, Ivan brightened.

'What a splendid place. I long for such peace but only get it in the country. And you are right beside the river. Perfect.' He was gazing out of the window. 'I would have thought these properties would be snapped up.'

'There's no tube station. Tea or coffee?'

'Coffee, if you don't mind. Where's that camera? I'll take a look. I'm good with equipment. One has to know about much that's not directly to do with teeth in my job.'

Stella had forgotten that Ivan's offer to bring her home had been prompted by her telling him about Terry's camera.

'It's by the kettle.' She went into the kitchen and unplugged the charger. Ivan was behind her and took the camera. While liking his enthusiasm – she'd taken a risk in confiding in him; he might have judged her absurd for trying to solve a murder – Stella wanted to check the camera herself.

While the coffee brewed she had a twinge of doubt: the Rokesmith case was a project she shared with Jack. He had advised they keep it to themselves and although she had not officially agreed, she had not even told Jackie, whom she could trust. Jack trusted her, but without asking him, she had told Ivan.

The sun was out, the snow was melting; everything seemed possible. Stella was certain that Jack would understand.

She plunged the coffee and placed it on a tray with milk and two mugs. She had no biscuits but doubted she should offer sweet things to a dentist.

Her mobile was ringing. Stella found it on the dining-room table in the living room; she had no memory of putting it there. Ivan sat at Jack's end of the sofa, fiddling with the camera. Stella saw what Jack had meant about the plastic. Ivan would never cover his furniture with plastic.

It was Jackie. She did not want to speak to Jackie with Ivan listening. Besides, Jackie should not be working at the weekend.

Ivan sighed. 'No luck, I'm afraid.'

'You can't fix it?'

'The problem lies with the memory card. There ain't one, m'lud.'

'Are you sure?'

'See for yourself.' He pulled open a flap in the casing to reveal two slots. Stella recognized the one to connect with a computer. The other was long and thin and empty.

'Your father must have removed it.' The plastic shrieked as Ivan got to his feet and laid the camera on the table.

'Or someone else did.' She would not see the last pictures that Terry had taken. She would not see what he had seen. Stella's mouth went dry.

'Extraordinary – why would anyone steal the card but leave the camera?' Ivan breathed in the steam from his coffee.

'It is unlikely,' she agreed.

'You'll come across it amongst his belongings. He must have been infuriated to forget it. What about his computer – did you find pictures there?'

'No. There was only an interview with the witness, a Mrs Ramsay. It doesn't matter. The whole thing's a wild-goose chase. I'll give it up. How can I find a man the police never found?'

'Why assume it was a man?' Ivan sipped his coffee and gave an approving smile. 'When those we love die, we snatch at gossamer: a voice on an answer machine; a bus ticket in a pocket; shopping lists. The missing card *does* matter. It might have given you a pointer to the solution to this frightful murder.'

Stella nodded. Maybe she had been trying to hold on to Terry. To bring him back, if only to tell him he had failed as a father. Had he failed? Jack had asked her what sort of daughter she had been. She could not say. Not that great, though. It was not possible to mourn the loss of a father that you never had, she told herself with lessening conviction.

After Ivan had gone, Stella remained in the hallway watching the entry screen until he appeared. She caught her breath when he glanced up into the lens and smiled as if he could see her. When he had disappeared from shot, Stella thought of Jack. He would mind that she had told Ivan. She would tell him what Ivan had said about the murderer: maybe their wild card was a woman.

She went into the living room. She had been positive that they were on the verge of a breakthrough: Terry had taken photographs; the lens cap proved he had been by the wall.

Before she set off for a job, Stella would draw up a list of all that she needed: brushes, chemicals, spare vacuum bags, client's key, alarm code. She was prepared. Terry was meticulous; he would not have forgotten to slot in a photo card.

She switched on the camera.

'Insert card'.

Terry would have seen there was no card as soon as he looked through the viewfinder. He would not have discovered its absence in the graveyard; he would have tested it before he left the house and again by the car. He tested his camera on Stella before using it to take a car or a person. Then there was the lens cap: he had taken it off to use the camera and something had made him forget to replace it.

He had followed the person putting the flowers by the grave.

She sat on the sofa. The plastic squeaked. She leapt up, put the camera on the floor and dug her fingers into the sofa. At first she made only an indentation, stretching the plastic. She dragged her thumbnail along the mark and the plastic rent; the rip travelled a foot. She pulled at the opening. The plastic made the sound of a zip undoing as it tore and soon she was knee-deep in plastic as if she had opened an enormous present. She hefted it into the kitchen and crammed it into a rubbish sack.

Stella came back and lowered herself gingerly on to the pristine white sofa. The fabric was soft and smelled of ultra-clean cotton. There was no noise when she shifted or patted the material, appreciating the fine weave. She swivelled around and sprawled, as Jack did, her feet propped on the armrest. She was comfortable. There was a piece of paper under the table. The sofa made no sound when she reached for it. The type was single-spaced:

[J. J. Rokesmith, 25 August 1981]

On Jonathan's next visit, I prepared a place for Walker the Bear at his table. As before I laid out crayons and paper and invited him to make a picture. This time I proposed that he might like to give it to Walker. This idea engendered mild interest. Jonathan neither agreed nor disagreed. He did address the crayons, removing the turquoise-green crayon from the box and snapping it in two. A specific action, free of malice, that I observed as preparation for the activity. He got up from his chair and went into the kitchen and threw the bits into the bin. D. I. Darnell made to object, but I stayed him with a finger on my lips. When Jonathan returned, I waited a moment then asked if he disliked the colour. As before, he gave no impression of having heard. His actions were brisk: he chose the black crayon and pressed hard on the paper, doing stabbing motions, daubing the white space.

He drew a crude house with gables and a hedge depicted with lines coiled like barbed wire and dashes for branches. The house had five windows, one each side of the front door, three on the second floor. He went over these until they were black, his movement of the crayon implied he was making vertical lines over the glass. I asked if he was putting in bars, invisible because he had coloured in the window black. He did not reply or appear to hear but he abandoned the windows.

Darnell asked if Jonathan had seen the man who had attacked his mummy and if the bars were to keep this man out. Would he know him again? The only indication that Jonathan gave of being aware of the detective was by thrusting motions of his crayon whenever Darnell spoke.

I had given him several sheets of A4 paper. In each session he used only one. When he finished he flipped the paper over and stalked into the garden. The garden is where Jonathan goes when he has had enough of the questions.

On this day, when Jonathan came back in he returned to his picture. He has never done this before. Once an activity is abandoned he does not resume it in the same session. He found the black crayon on the floor and with furious strokes stuck what looked like a garage on to the side of the house. He put down the crayon and at last acknowledging the detective, made his fingers into a gun and pretended to shoot him.

This was Jonathan's fifth session and he has yet to communicate verbally. If Walker the Bear, his transitional object, is moved or addressed by adults in the room, he glares protectively. He shows no interest in anyone else nor in the chocolate biscuit but drinks the milk I give him on each visit. He shows no pleasure in activities and performs them as if out of duty, then goes to the garden or if it is raining sits on the doormat.

Stella looked at the end of the sofa where Jack always sat. She had bought a pint of milk, but he hadn't been back so it was still in the fridge. She wanted to tell him about the plastic.

She lifted the camera from the floor and balanced it on her stomach. After a bit she closed her eyes, and pictured Terry's car by the church gate. In the light of the interior lamp above the dashboard she had examined his camera.

The memory card had been there then.

Stella rang Jack. She got his voicemail and asked him to call. She waited a moment and then dialled Ivan Challoner's number. When she got his voicemail too, she did not leave a message.

Fifty-Four

Monday, 24 January 2011

Jack was in his study, the fire unlit. He huddled in his coat, although it was damp from the night-time walk. He pulled out the *A–Z* and tossed it on the desk; it fell open at page 144, his last journey. He had spent three-quarters of an hour on Google's Street View nursing the cursor – Jack imagined the clicks as 'paces' – along the route ending on Clockhouse Lane that 'in real life' yesterday had taken him a long time to walk. Street View's photographs were stitched together to create a seamless virtual landscape of streets, houses, open space, roads and sky.

His mobile buzzed. He ignored it; he never spoke to anyone on his journeys, real or virtual. He had yet to respond to the message Stella had left; she would break his concentration, he needed mental space to understand the signs.

On Clockhouse Lane, being straight, it was easy to manoeuvre the mouse. In this parallel world there was no snow; on this Clockhouse Lane the fence and scrubland were drenched in sunlight. Jack enlarged a line of white print at the bottom of the picture and read: 'August 2008'; two and half years before his visit to the Lane.

He was halfway along the Lane before he noticed the motorcyclist. A figure in black, face obscured by a helmet, visor down. Jack zoomed in and the image fuzzed to coloured squares like an Impressionist painting, but he could distinguish a jacket zip, a buckle on the boot and the bike's headlight.

Each time he clicked forward along the road, sometimes in leaps, sometimes in minute steps, the bike was coming towards

366

him. He magnified the photo: there was the zip, the buckle, the anonymous rider approaching but never passing him, while Jack made good progress along the lane.

He reached the recreation ground where yesterday he had stepped off the map and sat drinking his milk. The biker disappeared as if he, like Jack, was invisible. Jack used the screen's quadrant button to navigate and swung back the way he had come. He expected see the motorbike driving off, having overtaken him, but the road was clear.

He swivelled to face his original direction and there was the bike coming towards him. He inched along, keeping it in his sights. The view swooped when he accidently hit the down section of the quadrant button, filling the screen with the mottled grey of tarmac. Jack spotted a puddle – a bluish-coloured wrapper was half submerged in its centre – pooling in the gutter. At edge of the screen he read the words: 'Image date: November 2008.' He jumped a couple of feet forward and again the biker had gone. He paused and angled the picture to show the kerb with the puddle: it was dry and there was no litter. He had returned to August 2008. Despite his coat, cold crept into his bones, but Jack did not think to light a fire.

With one click he had entered a different time: three months after the biker had ridden down the road. The photographs of Clockhouse Lane – after Rosa Avenue when the bike vanished – had been taken in the winter of 2008 on a day when it had rained, when there was a motorcyclist and a blue wrapper floated in a puddle.

The car capturing Street View images would have been in front of the bike, both travelling in the same direction. A passenger watching out of its back window would see the bike following. When Jack mouse-clicked counter to the direction of the camera-car, he saw what had been behind it as if it was approaching him. Street View captured this perspective for its vast tapestry. The tapestry was static but Jack could 'walk' in it, going in any direction he liked within a different month and year to his own.

Jack wound the clock back with every mouse-click: he was going where the motorbike had been, while moving forward in his own time. When he turned back and headed in the same direction as the biker, he of course vanished: he had not yet reached that point in the road. Jack had entered the biker's future.

Jack rubbed his eye sockets. Walking the street atlas had not been a waste of time. It proved that what he had told Stella was true: time measurement was the invention of humans; it could be manipulated. When Jack mouse-clicked along a street – in the past, the present or in the future – he eliminated time. This was the feeling he had when he walked the actual streets at night.

Simon had been wrong. Jonathan Rokesmith was not a coward. He had not run away; he had been trying to save his mummy by running back into her past. He had belted down Black Lion Lane, looking for her on the route they had walked together: along the subway tunnel hooting like a train, up the ramps on the other side to where he had snatched his steam engine off her. At the Leaning Woman he shouted 'Boo!' to his mummy in the time before *it* happened. If he could find her in the 'before', he could stop it happening.

Ever since that day, Jonathan who became Justin who became Jack had tried to go back in time – through tunnels beneath the city, along roads using a defaced map – to undo what could not be undone.

Jack shrugged out of his coat and, letting it drop to the floor, rolled up his sleeves. He lit the wood in the grate and sat down again. His mouth twitched and he sniffed, hands poised over the keyboard, readying himself. He would start where the detective had ended. He keyed 'Broad Street Seaford' into Street View's search bar; he spelt the Seaford wrong: time wasted.

He was at the intersection of Broad Street and Sutton Road, the light was dull, signposts made no shadow and there was no one on the pavements. A broken window in the Pound Shop was crudely mended with cardboard and gaffer tape. A man, perhaps smoking a cigarette – his hand was blurred by movement – perched on a bench beneath a lamp-post decorated with baskets of trailing flowers. Along the kerbs were parked vehicles; a bright yellow van stood near the Co-op where Terry Darnell had died. Despite the flat light, the date the images had been taken was July 2009.

At Woolworths Jack focused in: the store had shut down and through the glass he panned over empty shelves, some on their side. Leaflets, free newspapers, takeaway menus lay amidst a confetti of leaves curling on the mat; evidence of another past.

By the building society called the Abbey – in Jack's present renamed Santander – the sun came out and the vehicles, including the yellow van, were replaced by others. He had travelled back eight months to November 2008. Jack moved forward one step and the yellow van was there; it was July of the following year again. He had entered two different years in the past while in his own present.

Jack knew enough about cars to identify the make and model of the car parked by the kerb of Broad Street in July 2009. Despite the efforts of Google to fuzz out plates and manufacturer badges, this was a BMW X3. If the registration details were visible Stella would have given him the year, but his own knowledge of the series put it as brand new for that year. He zoomed in on the silver four-by-four.

A four-by-four had been exiting the A259 onto the lane at Bishopstone the day they came to see Kate's grave. Jack had seen it only for a second as they waited at the junction.

He clicked rapidly away from the Co-op, back the way he had come, to the junction with Sutton Road, which lay on the A259. He charged through the time when it had been sunny to when the light was bleak; storm clouds were brewing beyond the supermarket. He clicked left on to Sutton Park Road and past the station. The BMW – like the bike in Clockhouse Lane – was coming towards him. Jack was in its past; he was going where it had been.

It was falling into place; he did not need to travel back in time to know that the silver car that had stopped at the zebra crossing on Earls Court Road the night he stepped on the crack in the paving was a BMW. Jack had sensed the driver had a mind like his own, but was diverted by his mistake. It was a sign and he had ignored it: a much bigger mistake. The car had waited at the zebra, although there had been no one waiting to cross.

He swooped the cursor over the Buckle Bypass to the junction with Bishopstone. The snow and the darkness of his and Stella's time in the graveyard, while in his own past, still lay in the photographed world's future. The BMW disappeared. He clicked back and forth around the junction, making it reappear and then vanish again. He frowned. The light remained the same. Despite the fizzle and crackle of flames from the grate, he could not get warm. The time frame had not changed, so where was the BMW?

He forced himself to concentrate. Grey and white clouds spread above the Downs, their pattern illustrating perspective, the vanishing point at the port of Newhaven in the distance. The BMW had disappeared, not because the months in which the pictures were taken were different, as was the case with the biker on Clockhouse Lane and some of the vehicles on Broad Street in Seaford, but because the silver four-by-four had turned off at Bishopstone. Jack clicked back to the junction and took the same turn-off as the BMW had done the afternoon when he came with Stella. There was the silver four-by-four.

Jack clicked along after the car towards the village. The church spire protruded through the trees; he stopped where Stella had parked Terry Darnell's Toyota, or where she would park in Street View's future. Out of range of the camera a bunch of fresh roses would be propped against his mummy's headstone. In the screen-world – the scene, bright with green trees, dappled sunlight and azure sky – Terry Darnell and Isabel Ramsay were alive, but his mother was still dead.

There was no BMW.

Jack had entered a new time frame – November 2008 when

there had been no silver car: it belonged to the dull July day in 2009. The trail had gone cold.

He was out of time – off the map – alone in the village where Katherine Rokesmith née Venus had briefly lived and where now she was buried forever. Jack was nowhere.

He grabbed his phone and dialled Stella. He got the engaged signal and closing the line saw that she had called him again, but left no message. It was nearly four in the afternoon: he was due at Sarah Glyde's in five minutes. He snatched up his coat and ran out of the house.

Jonathan Rokesmith took the same route to the corner house by the Bell Steps as he had walked with his mummy before it all happened.

Fifty-Five

Monday, 24 January 2011

Martin Cashman put back one rasher of bacon, a concession towards a diet, and shoved his tray, heaped with a full English breakfast, along the rails to the drinks machine. He poured himself a coffee. No milk, no sugar.

He had awarded himself this late afternoon's breakfast because he had completed the General Register Docket on an aggravated burglary. This, along with the Paul Bramwell Docket, could be put away. Such days were rare. In the past month he had handled two sudden deaths that had been suspected murders but were not. Coincidental, he considered as he crammed his mouth with egg, sliced sausage and a square of bacon, that Stella Darnell had been tied to both 'nominals'. In his job Cashman had learnt not to read much into coincidence. Stella was like Terry, she didn't suffer fools: she had defused the first murder to natural causes by explaining away evidence and she had neither wasted his time nor got too emotional about the second.

She wanted little to do with the force; Cashman was used to that. He had attended two funerals where the widows, fuelled by fortifying drink, had lost it at the wake, letting rip how a husband in the police was worse than him being with another woman. One said his death would be more of the same, he was never there anyway and now at least she knew where to find him. Cashman had assumed Stella Darnell would agree; Terry's wife had bailed out early. He had been taken aback when she asked for a favour and said no.

Terry Darnell would not have refused one of Cashman's girls a favour. He had looked after his own.

THE DETECTIVE'S DAUGHTER

Martin Cashman left half his food uneaten and ran upstairs. In his jacket pocket he still had Stella's reg plate. He punched in his access code to the police database and typed the number into the search box.

The owner had no previous convictions, not even a traffic offence, and meant nothing to him. He flicked through his card index for Terry's contact details. He could not bring himself to throw them away. Stella was Terry's next of kin; there were three numbers: her work, her home and her mobile phone.

The receptionist told him Stella was out for the rest of the day. Cashman tried her mobile but a recorded voice said the number was no longer in use. He called the home number and it went to answer machine. He toyed with trying later to tell Stella in person and hear her pleasure that he had changed his mind, but in the end left a message with the registrant's name and address. He insisted that if there was anything he could do, Stella must always ask.

When Cashman returned to the canteen, his plate had been cleared away.

Fifty-Six

'She's not here. Can I take a message?' The mobile phone line was breaking up. Jackie was patient, knowing better than to offend a potential client. So far she had made out that the man was Colin something and wanted Stella about plaster. She circled 'plaster' on her pad: that must be wrong.

'It's ter-rib-ly hard to hear YOU!' she bellowed into the mouthpiece.

'... she said core ... *crrr* if I thore ... of ... anythi ... *crrrrrrrrrr*membered ... *crrrrrrrrrr* about *crrrrrrrrrr* ... okesmith's ... *crrrrrrrrrr*ncle ... childhood *crrrrr* ... freh ... I told *crrrrrrrrrr* ... poli ... *crrrrrrrrrr* ... Miss Darnell wanted ... *crrrrrrrr r*...'

The line went dead. Jackie replaced the receiver. If it was urgent he would call back.

'Where was that from, Australia?' Beverly the admin assistant was kneeling on the carpet surrounded by filing.

Stella had said she would be in mid-morning after meeting a new client. Jackie had found no record of this client on Stella's calendar – the flouting of a Clean Slate rule Stella was hot on – and it was now afternoon. Stella had not come to the office for days. She was, Jackie believed, losing interest in her business. Grief did funny things. In the meantime Clean Slate had to carry on.

The man was probably a time-waster. Many people badgered either herself or Stella with questions over several calls and then went with another company. The message provided her with an excuse to find out what Stella was doing.

'Earth to Jackie?'

'It was for Stella.' Jackie pulled up Stella's mobile on the quick-dial menu.

'Stella rang.' Beverly was banging metal cabinet drawers like sporadic gunfire as she filed.

'When?'

'Ages ago, she said to say she's working from home and not to disturb. I was going to tell you.'

'In your own time, I'm guessing?'

'She's not here, so it's obvious she's not coming. Time for tea?' Beverly slammed another drawer.

Jackie watched the young woman leave the room to fill the kettle in the toilets. She did at least make a good cup of tea.

The phone rang. A pub on King Street liked Stella's quote and wanted a cleaner tomorrow. Jackie spent the next hour arranging a contract and reorganizing the rota because Stella never said no to new business.

She was in bed when she remembered she had not recorded the plasterer's call in the day book or rung Stella. It was five to ten but Stella worked late. Or once upon a time she had; nowadays Jackie had no idea what Stella did.

There was no reply on the landline so she rang Stella's mobile and, apologizing, left a voicemail consisting of: *Colin, plaster, uncle and childhood*. It was the epitome of the incomplete message she was training out of Beverly, but Stella might understand.

Jackie Makepeace could have no idea of the importance of these words or that by the time Stella heard the message, it would be too late.

Fifty-Seven

Sarah Glyde appeared in the kitchen doorway and collided with Jack as he carried out a half-filled bin liner.

'I have to go out.' She barged past. 'You know where to find everything. Concentrate on the kitchen and bathroom, I want them done thoroughly.'

Jack tied up the bag and placed it on the steps to take to the basement area when he left. He considered the instructions issued with such brittle authority. When he had met Sarah Glyde last week she had seemed every inch the artist, floating about her sitting room, only vaguely listening to the earthly matters of limescale removal and grout-bleaching. However, like his Hosts, such as Nat, Nick Jarvis and Michael, it seemed Sarah could switch to peremptory and ruthless. In a short space of time she had reverted to type.

From the sitting-room window he watched her walk towards the subway and out of sight, and counted to ten in case she returned. When it was safe he put on his coat and went into the garden.

Like her brother's locked bedroom, Sarah Glyde's studio was not on Jack's cleaning itinerary. On his first visit, she had called it 'out of bounds', instantly putting it in Jack's mind very much 'in bounds'. He resented anything marked 'Private'. He had seen Sarah fishing about in a ceramic pot by the back door so knew where she kept the key.

The studio was a detached brick and wood structure that, Jack estimated, had been built in the 1940s; its guttering was loose, the felt on the flat roof buckling and the brickwork crumbling. The house was in a similar state: Sarah Glyde did not look after her property.

Climbing plants smothered with snow grew in a flower bed beside the path. Existing footprints were Sarah's; there were no others so she would notice his tracks. He knocked into a board, lumpy with dried clay and paint, propped by the back door. Jack supposed it was a discarded surface for works in progress. He laid it over the snow and stepped on to it. From there he leapt into the flower bed; the plants shivered as he landed, a shower of snow falling on to his shoes. He balanced precariously and reached for the board, managing to lift it, leaving only a mild indentation. He repeated the procedure up to the door. The path around the side of studio was clear, which struck him as strange. Why would Sarah Glyde neglect the bit she walked on the most?

She had laid a trap to tell her if her brother had been there. On the other hand, Jack thought, finding signs of an intruder, she would assume it was the brother.

The area between the studio and the garden wall was laid to paving on which was the statue of an angel, her wings outstretched, between box bushes trimmed square.

A honking disturbed the quiet: a flock of geese in 'V' formation flew over the house, across the river towards Hammersmith Bridge.

Jack peeped over the wall. Wind stung his face. He slipped on compacted snow and grasped cold brick to steady himself; someone made a habit of standing here. So what? Deflated, he flopped to the ground, his back to the wall. He had a child's-eye view of the French doors into the studio.

He had been here before.

He got up and peered through the glass and skipped backwards. Someone was looking at him.

He blundered up the path, leaving footprints, scratched the key in the lock, strode past the sink and a potter's wheel to a table on which unglazed pots awaited their turn in the kiln.

The head was stuck on a metal tube that crudely resembling the cervical section of a vertebral column. The lower lip was chapped and cracked in the middle as Jack's had been until Stella gave him a salve stick.

Jack was face to face with himself.

It was not a faithful rendition; the forehead was lumpy like Frankenstein's monster and lacked his own deeply etched lines. Yet the skin was tight over the cheekbones and hair slicked close to the head and down the back of the neck like his own. Jack stroked the bridge of the clay nose. So exact was the copy he could have been stroking the rise of bone on his own nose, except he could not feel the touch of his finger.

A spiral of wire with a wooden handle at each end lay coiled beside the model. He yanked the wire taut and poised it behind the head. As it bit into the clay he caught sight of a photograph pinned to a cork board. He rolled up the cutter and slipped it in his coat pocket; it would be a nice touch, one up from a ligature.

He had climbed on to the lavatory to see out of the bathroom window, and left the vacuum going so that she would think he was cleaning. He had not fooled her; she had spied on him. Sarah Glyde had a mind like his own.

Jack had never once thought his Host might be a woman.

It was no coincidence that Sarah Glyde had rung Clean Slate asking for a quote. She wanted him. If he had not turned up with Stella last Thursday evening, she would have come for him.

Her desk was grainy with clay dust and lost under papers: orders, invoices; whatever else she might be, like him, when it came to her own papers Glyde was not organized. The invoices were for hundreds of pounds: dinner services, vases, busts; she was busy.

He stirred the papers around and found more photographs. All were identical and of the place where his mother had been found dead, taken from where he had just been, by the garden wall. The light was poor, dusk flattened the contrast and made reflections on the river as substantial as the bricks and rubbish on the shore.

A ghostly figure stood at the water's edge. He held it up to the window. Printed on gloss paper, light made the image merge into the sky. Jack gathered up the pictures and put them in his pocket with the cutter.

On a table by the French doors was a glazed panel of clay the size of a tea tray. The horizontal layers of green and turquoise interspersed with maroon and mauve put Jack in mind of Exmoor. A motif – Glyde's signature – had been scored into the corner: a child's depiction of an aeroplane with wings crossing the body and upright tail.

It was not an aeroplane; it was a glider.

Jack rushed out of the studio.

Minutes later he was in his parents' bedroom at St Peter's Square. He pulled open his mother's wardrobe door; Kate Rokesmith's clothes – dresses, coats, skirts eaten by moths, stiff with dust mites – hung where she had left them. Jack would crawl beneath them to the back, not realizing it was her hiding place too until the day he discovered a surprise.

The cardboard box was there; a side tore when he pulled off the lid. Jack sneezed as he dusted the box off with his coat sleeve. He pushed aside the flaps, fitted his hands in and lifted out a clay head identical to the one in Sarah Glyde's studio. He got to his feet and set it on his mother's dressing table.

Glyde's fingers must have been on familiar ground as they manipulated and shaped his eyes to life; the eyes on this head were like his own. He passed a hand before them, half expecting them to blink. Her mouth was perfect, her lips slightly parted, her hair snaked around her neck and over her shoulders. Unlike his sculpture, this piece did not stop at the head, but continued to the swell of her bosom.

It was Kate Rokesmith only days before she died.

'I hid it in there as a surprise. Ssssh! It's our secret.'

He had only been interested in the aeroplane on the back of her shoulder and insisted on inspecting his mummy's real shoulder to see if one was there too. No one had drawn on her skin or marked her out for jointing.

'I don't like it when you kiss like that.'

'Kiss who, darling? Daddy?'

'No.'

'Don't be silly, Jonny.'

The temperature was bitter in the bedroom and Jack hugged into his coat. He picked up her blue plastic hairbrush from the dressing table and played it along the terracotta tendrils on the clay head. There was no hair in the bristles; he had clawed off what there was and kept it in his trophy tin. For the first time in thirty years, Jack risked turning to stone, and met his mother's gaze.

Sarah Glyde had lied when she had claimed not to know Kate Rokesmith. She had known Kate and Jonathan. Kate had commissioned a bust of herself as a present and they had visited her regularly. She had been their Host.

He had been right to keep faith with the *London A–Z*: it had led him to the Host. She had visited his mother's grave in a silver BMW; she had lured his mummy and him to the river to see the lovely colours and shapes.

Sarah Glyde would not be Jack's Host because this time he would not be staying.

Fifty-Eight

Monday, 24 January 2011

Jack let himself in through Stella's basement. The scrap of thread he had wedged in the jamb drifted down; no one had been here since he'd used the exit to avoid Paul Bramwell.

He was unlikely to meet anyone in the lift, but just in case he used the stairs, the box clasped to his chest.

He put his ear to Stella's door. It was a ridiculously thick security door and he did not expect to hear anything, but a particular stillness confirmed she was out. Stella was becoming as unavailable to him as she had been for the drowned Paul. He rang the bell, pressing the button and holding it. Stella did not come.

Jack had taken Stella's key off her ring when he handed back her car key the day they escaped from Paul. He had had a copy cut and it was back before she could notice it had gone.

'Stella?'

No answer.

Jack's footsteps and the click of the front door were deadened by the carpet, the fire doors and the triple glazing. It gave him the irrational sense that he was a ghost, and entering the living room he coughed to dispel this impression. He half expected to find Stella among the files, trying to solve the case by herself, but the room was empty.

He tried Stella's mobile number and left another message: 'I'm in your flat.'

The sun had almost set and streaks of orange across grey sky tinged the river a dusty pink. Jack Harmon watched the yellow disc sink below a bank of smog on the horizon. The light faded incrementally until his own reflection – holding the bust of his mother in his arms – stared back at him.

He was startled when the answer machine snapped into action; Stella had turned off the telephone bell.

'I'm not able to take your call. Leave a message. Thanks.'

Jack shifted his mother's head and sat in his corner on the sofa.

'Hi, Stella. Martin here. Martin Cashman from Hammersmith? I ran a check on that item we discussed? Like I said, it's an early plate, the second year into that scheme which started in 1963. It's 1964. The present owner bought it new, so now it's a classic, although must be on private property as no tax paid since, oh wait a sec.' Jack heard a shuffling and breathing. 'Here it is: 1981 and the owner is S. A. I. Glyde, address at the time was Fullwood House, Church Lane, Bishopstone, Sussex. If I can do anything else any time at all, please just ask, I insist … It's Martin speaking, by the way.'

The machine went quiet. Stella had not told him she was going to trace the number plate; in fact she had behaved as if it was not important. He had believed her.

In the dimming light his mother's head was more lifelike than ever: her features fluid, her mouth on the brink of a smile. Katherine Rokesmith's clay facsimile was moulded by the woman who murdered her. Some murderers collected trophies as mementoes of their crimes. Sarah Glyde had crafted a clay bust of her victim.

He had given Stella a chance to stop him. He had come to the flat, trusting they were a team, to tell her about Sarah Glyde. But like Terry Darnell, Stella worked alone – or no: it seemed, despite her avowed dislike of them, she worked with the police.

Jack was on his own.

He sprang up and roamed the flat, still holding Kate's head, convincing himself Stella had forfeited her right to privacy. In the spare room was a desk, as basically furnished as Terry Darnell's, lit by a lamp shaped like a spider's leg, the bulb the size of a bullet.

Jack was surprised to find a novel by Stella's bed: *Wuthering*

Heights. A postcard three chapters in marked her place. He held open the place with his thumb and took out the card. It was of Queen Charlotte's cottage in Kew Gardens; he had been there during page seventy-one of his street atlas expeditions. He turned it over: 'T, Five. "Cathy" x'.

It was his mummy's writing but her name was spelt wrong. He had other cards like this in his biscuit tin of trophies.

Twenty minutes later the Clean Slate van was outside Sarah Glyde's house where a solitary light shone in an upstairs window. At last Jonathan Rokesmith was doing what for most of his life he had planned he would do.

This time he did not ring the bell first. He opened the door with his key.

Fifty-Nine

Monday, 24 January 2011

Stella paid the bill when Ivan was in the toilet; he had insisted on covering it the last time. She was enjoying herself: Ivan had unwittingly offered her a refuge from Terry, from the office and from the Rokesmith murder. Jack had called her, but typically not left a message. Paul used to do that; she had no time for games. Her mobile was in her rucksack; if it rang she would not hear it. She sipped her frosted glass of Sancerre and silently toasted her respite. She might have been mistaken about the memory card in Terry's camera; she was tired.

'Will you do something for me?'

'Of course.' She had not heard Ivan return.

'Come to Fullwood House.'

'I've been, haven't I?' He surely had not forgotten.

'Not my flat, that's a billet for when I'm working. I feel nothing for it, as you probably gather. It's sterile.'

Stella liked sterile but did not say so.

'I want you to see the house where I was born. It's a beautiful place. I seldom take guests there. Most would not understand, but you would. Come!'

'If you're sure … that would be nice.' Stella felt her reply was inadequate to his enthusiasm. She had never seen Ivan so animated. He must have lived with his wife and son in the house. He was coming out of the shell of grief. She should not knock him back by refusing his invitation.

'I could go next Saturday,' Stella said, getting out her diary to show she was serious.

'I mean now.' Ivan put down his glass. Stella saw that he had hardly touched his wine.

'Now?' she echoed.

'It's only ten past eight. We can be there in no time. It will be dark, but it is a place that benefits from mystery.'

'I need to be at work in the morning. I wasn't there today. I have my father's stuff to sort and there is that murder.' Stella picked up her empty glass and put it down.

Ivan looked crestfallen. 'I find that plans kill the spirit of an adventure because the experience has to measure up to the plan and is not of itself.'

'I could do either day at the weekend. Actually Sunday would be better.' Stella tried to mollify him. 'Or shall we leave it open?' She liked to plan and was disappointed he saw it differently. Paul had been big on spontaneity, but even he knew better than to give her no notice at all. To shore up her argument, she added: 'The weather might have improved by then. Already it's thawing.'

'A smattering of snow is nothing. My car is designed for bad conditions. Once there I light a fire, I have towels and night things and a spare room. I'll get the bill.' He folded his napkin and rubbed his palm at the waiter. 'Never mind. It can't be.'

'I've sorted it.' Stella tucked the bill into her purse.

Unsmiling, Ivan bowed his head. Stella remembered when she had thrown up at Earls Court Underground station: one mistake with Terry had led to another, as was horribly confirmed by Paul's death. Ivan would not offer her another chance to see his home. Already she could see he was regretting it; he would be thinking he had been wrong about her. Perhaps that was true.

Kew Station village looked like a Christmas card; branches of kerbside trees white with snow twinkled in the lamplight. Stella climbed up into Ivan's big four-wheel drive. When he shut the door, it locked automatically. He walked around the back of the car to the other side.

Terry would have accepted the invitation. He was not a spur-of-the-moment man but he knew an opportunity when it presented itself. Ivan could have helped her with the case and she had let the possibility pass by. Stella did up her seat belt.

Terry's dull brown case boxes were awaiting her, smelling of damp paper and failure. Her flat was no more of a home than Ivan's clean and uncluttered living quarters; it was no more than a pit stop. She had turned off the heating. It would be cold.

Stella had a speech prepared to explain her refusal, but when they stopped outside the lobby Ivan was out of the car as soon as the ignition was off and opening her door.

'Will you come up for a cup of tea?' She used the same words as she had the day before, hoping they would elicit the same response and that Ivan would accept.

'I want to get down to the country before it is too late.'

The evening was over.

Sixty

Monday, 24 January 2011

The Ram Inn on Black Lion Lane had closed early, so few customers had ventured out. Although a thaw was setting in, by nightfall the pavements had frozen and an insidious grey fog hung over the Thames and crept up the Bell Steps. The clock in the St Peter's Church tower struck ten.

Jack had not entertained the possibility that his mother's killer was a woman. It had not felt right, nor did it still, but it did make sense. When people had said they had not seen anyone suspicious, or noticed a stranger in the area, they meant men. Sarah Glyde was not a stranger, nor would she inspire suspicion.

The police report said it had taken strength to apply the ligature to his mother's neck. Sarah moulded clay, she lifted heavy pieces of sculpture and wielded tools that could kill. She was strong.

Despite his cleaning, the air in the hallway stank of decay, its contents absorbing moisture, gathering dust, the wallpaper yellowing and peeling and brittle. Framed photographs of eminent Victorian ancestors were obscured by silver in the prints rising to the surface. Sarah Glyde's home was her studio. The house was impervious to life.

Jack's ghost-self moved on soundless feet, the clay-cutter wire spiralling in his hands. He unlatched the basement door, the box containing his mother's clay head digging into his armpit. The basement stairs strained and flexed as he descended. At the bottom step he let his eyes grow accustomed to the hovering shapes in the half-dark. The fridge trilled and then shuddered into silence. Ethereal light from the garden called forth ogres and spectres of his childhood and evoked the spirits of animals and trees turned to stone by the White Witch. He was in a gallery of statues that wanted only his touch to bring them back to life. He turned on the light and chose the longest kitchen knife from a row on a magnetic strip. The blade was sharp.

Jack may not have been a guest in this house, but he had cleaned every inch of it. The telephone wire was clipped beneath the barred window facing on to the back garden. Jack had wiped it free of cobwebs. His hand jerked as he fitted the blade between the wire and the wall and levered out a clip. He steadied it and then prised out another clip, loosening the wire, which he severed.

There was a light in her studio.

Snow had receded from the path; he left no tracks and his footsteps were silent. The studio door creaked when he stepped inside and he was enveloped in the fuggy warmth of a calor gas stove.

'Who's that?' The voice came from behind the partition. She was scared. Jack was gratified to discover she could feel fear. He brandished the knife, flashing the long silver blade to disguise the tremor in his hand. The cutter dangled from his fist; he had a choice of weaponry.

Sarah Glyde, in a stained man's shirt and torn jeans, was seated on the stool by her work-table.

'Oh, it's you.' She gave a wan smile. 'Did you want your money? I pay the agency, they should have explained.'

She saw the knife.

Jack was intrigued at how quickly colour can drain from a face.

'No amount of cash will cover your debt to me.'

She shrank back, crashing against the heater, the jolt opening the stove door. Jack kicked it shut. His clay head was on the table. She was working on it.

'A good likeness.' The clay eyes followed him as he strolled to the patio doors and confirmed they were locked.

'I'll pay you for being a model. This is only a rough start.'

He wanted to say: *What's the next stage – you strangle me and leave my body down there?* It would be crass, the pleasure momentary.

She was allowing herself relief, Jack could see. He wanted money; that was it, she could pay him off. She was used to disposing of problems with a cheque and was making rapid calculations: would a cleaner know the going rate for an artist's model? Could she undercut it?

She was edging closer to the telephone beside his clay head. He smiled as, the knife slicing the air, he got there first. He pressed the green button and handed it to her, in a trance she put it to her ear.

Now she was *truly* frightened. That was more like it.

'I don't keep money here. We can go to a cashpoint. I can take out five hundred at a time. I don't have a car, we'll have to walk, unless you … The nearest one is in King Street.'

It was extraordinary how people fixed on the more prosaic facts of life at times like these. She still had the temerity to lie: oh yes, she had a car.

The blade rat-tat-tatted against the worktop as Jack's grip on the handle lessened. Intent on finding the murderer, he had not considered the logistics of his revenge. Like Stella, he hated mess.

Glyde's hands fluttered over the head as if by destroying it she might destroy him. Suddenly Jack understood that this was true. If she smashed the clay piece on the tiled floor he would be nothing.

'I don't want your money.' He spoke in a weary voice.

He took the box from under his arm and placed it on the table. Gently taking out Kate's head, he positioned it next to his and stood before the two faces. They were indistinguishable.

Sarah Glyde backed as far as she could go, stopping by the wall that abutted the Bell Steps.

The heads had identical bone structures: a straight nose with a lump below the bridge and square chins and wide mouths and full lips over which played the ghost of a smile. The gender difference was not apparent beyond a thickness of neck and an Adam's apple on the newer sculpture.

The real difference was in the mastery of the clay: over the decades the artist had developed a deeper relationship with her material. The first head had the strained perfection of a younger and less confident sculptor: she had cut and smeared, pushed and pummelled to achieve verisimilitude and technically it was exceptional, but it lacked a soul. The clay for Jack's head had been moulded at its maker's behest: coaxed and massaged to her will. While Jack's jawline was sharper than his mother's, it was fashioned with a lighter feel.

Sarah dropped the handset. It hit the table, bounced to the floor and chips of plastic flew across the tiles. The casing lay at Jack's feet, the light still glowing.

'She was beautiful,' she whispered. 'She had seen my advert for pottery classes in the newspaper but didn't want to join a group. She insisted she was musical, not artistic. She commissioned me to make her likeness as a surprise. We had several sessions: I sketched her first. Her son had to come with her so I gave him clay to keep him busy. He didn't make soldiers or sausages like most kids; he created a half-naked woman with folded arms. I recognized the statue by Karel Vogel beside the Great West Road. He had paid attention to what he saw; it was an incredible likeness. We fired it.' She was talking to Kate's head. 'I don't think she realized how talented he was. She was astonished.'

Sarah bent over his mother, her palms tenderly cupping the face, not making contact, echoing its shape with butterfly movements. She went on: 'I saw you in the street. I wanted you to model for me, but before I could get your attention, you had gone. When you appeared on my doorstep with your boss I thought you were a ghost. I worked from photographs and memory, but I was certain I had been here before. I knew the planes of your face, the way the light plays on your cheekbones. I *knew* you.'

'Why did you kill her?'

Jack had asked his mother's murderer this question as he watched Miss Thoroughgood chalk up sums on the blackboard, as he walked London according to the street atlas, as he drove his train beneath London. When he was with the Leaning Woman.

Sarah Glyde was as tall as Jack. He remembered his mother as tall, but in the case notes he read she was five foot six inches. He was six foot. If his mummy were here, he would tower over her. Sarah Glyde had easily overpowered her.

For years he had scoured the streets for the monster he would capture and slay. This wiry woman in her fifties with a grip of steel was that monster. Sarah Glyde's head was cadaverous in the angled light; a bluish vein pulsated on her forehead, her hair escaped in coiling springs from a careless bun. Her bones would snap with a mild blow. The knife would slice into her with little resistance and she would feel a cold pain and look, uncomprehending, at the quiet pumping stream.

Jack swallowed hard.

For a moment he longed for her to hold him, to grip his throat, squeeze down on his neck and, as she had made a head identical to Katherine Rokesmith's, by killing him she would reunite him with her.

You killed my mummy.

He had dreamed of uttering these words. He had spoken them into the night, whispered them in spare rooms, from rooftops, in tool cupboards in the homes of his Hosts. Yet faced with the mind like his own, Jack's lips were as immobile as clay.

She came towards him and he lifted the knife.

'You have made a mistake.' She flinched from the blade. If he used the cutter he would not have to touch her, just draw the wire through her flesh, like butter.

'You told the police you didn't know Kate.'

'It was her secret.' With an unsteady hand she supported his clay cheek, refining the bone beneath the left eye. 'They would have asked questions I could not answer. She had taken the piece away and wasn't coming back. She never paid me and I did not want her husband to cover it, he was going through enough. Then when it was he who murdered her, there was no point.'

She began on his other cheek. Jack had not thought the head

could look more like himself than it already did. His own strength seemed to ebb as, retreating from her fear, Sarah Glyde smoothed and stroked the clay.

'I talk to her. I talk to all my pieces. I liked her. Why would I kill her?'

'The police asked about your car?'

'What are you talking about?'

'Don't lie.' He would pierce her heart. Tuck the blade under the left side of her rib cage and give a firm push.

'I couldn't drive.'

'A 1964 blue Ford Anglia?'

'I don't even know what one looks like.'

It was a while since Jack had seen someone so frightened, but any gratification he felt was dull, for she had not expressed remorse. He could not kill her until she said she was sorry.

'What has that to do with me?'

'It was registered in your name. After 1981 no more road tax payments made. I know a lot of facts about that year.'

'How could that be?' She clasped her hands under her armpits as if to warm them; the stove had gone out. Beads of perspiration glistened on her bone-pale forehead and her lower jaw quivered. She was lying.

'S. A. I. Glyde? Sarah Annabel, Isabel, Anne, Ingrid ... am I close?'

'My initials are S. M. Glyde, Sarah Matilda and my mother's were C. E. for Clarissa Emma. She couldn't drive.' She got up. 'I did not kill Kate Rokesmith and nor did my mother. Can we stop this?'

She was hiding something, busying herself paring strips from a block, dragging the wire through the clay. He pulled up a stool and sat down at the table. The lines converged, the shapes coalesced; the air shifted. Day by day she had turned his mother into a statue.

Jack raised the blade, the fingers of his other hand curling around the clay cutter.

The clay had rolled beneath his palms, thinning as he pressed down with all the weight a four-year-old could muster. Too thin.

He had bunched it up and started again until it was long and quite thin, then worked at the legs, the folded arms, the head. When he visited again she had put it out ready for him; moistened by a damp rag it was soft. When the Lady was finished she had got a box for him to take her home in.

His mummy had said he could not keep it. Their visits were a secret.

'I had no reason to want her dead,' Sarah repeated, addressing the heads. 'If I had been here, in my studio, I might have saved her. If she had cried out, I might have heard. In the summer I hear people down there. But I was at my brother's and when I got back, it was pandemonium. The streets and the river were teeming with police. There was even a helicopter. I had to argue to get into my house.'

'You told the police you were at the dentist.'

'My brother is a dentist. Antony has always done my teeth.'

Jack was floating somewhere on the other side of the space. Only the heads had substance.

'For God's sake, not like that!' Tony cradled the ripped box as if it were a hamster that he loved and Jonathan saw that although Tony made a fuss of him, he did not like him. He had supposed until then that all grown-ups liked children.

Uncle Tony.

His mobile phone rang. He checked the screen. Sarah Glyde lunged at a bodkin on the table and he thrust the blade at her; catching the bodkin, he sent it skittering over the wood. She crashed against the French doors and slumped to the floor.

He put his fingers to his lips and answered the phone, the blade poised. If it were him he would still shout for help.

'Is that Jack Harmon?'

'Yes.'

'It's Jackie here at Clean Slate. I'm sorry to bother you so late. Stella's not picking up on her mobile or at home. She said she was going to see you – is she there?' The words filled his ear. Jack tapped the table with the point of the blade, making nicks in the wood.

'She's not,' he replied pleasantly.

'I left her a message. It's not like Stella not to return calls. If you know where she is …'

'What's the message?'

Sarah Glyde was quaking, hugging her knees. She looked defeated; he knew the signs. Now that she was penitent, he imagined soothing her. It was his Achilles heel that he wanted to take care of his Hosts.

'A man called Colin rang. He may be a plasterer. I'm relying on guesswork because the line was terrible. I think now he said "teeth" and I've been going over it and I think it must be a dentist. It might be a referral. We have one dentist on our books, as you know, but he's called Ivan, so it's not him. Never mind, I suppose it can wait until the morning.'

Afterwards Jack slipped the telephone into his pocket. Signs were all around him, like a game of Patience falling into place.

'What was your brother's name?'

'Antony.'

'Do you ever call him Tony?' The answer was nudging him before she spoke. He too was shaking.

'No.' She was staring past Jack and he looked quickly around but there was no one there. 'Some people do, it depends when they knew him.'

'Tony Glyde?'

'Antony was my mother's son from her first husband who died in a plane he was piloting back from France. It went down in the sea off Shoreham. His name was Challoner. He was a dentist too. Really Antony's my half-brother.'

The words were lost in a rush of white sound. A woman with a dog vanishing amongst the trees.

'…I want to call him Flyte but that's the Waugh novel, and anyway that was the second husband…'

The room reeled, the clay heads tipped crazily in urgent conference, skulls crashing. Someone was shouting. His throat hurt because it was his own voice.

'No. No. No.'

The wall was cold on his forehead. He felt a hand on his shoulder.

'Are you all right?'

'Is he buried in a village called Bishopstone?' Jack walked towards the heads. Sarah Glyde encircled them with her arms. She was not fearful for herself.

'How did you know?'

'Does he ... do you, have a brother called Ivan?'

'That's Antony's third name. Simon Antony Ivan Challoner. Bit of a mouthful – in the family we've always called him Antony. At work he prefers Ivan. What about him?'

'I clean for him,' Jack muttered. For once he could not marshal facts.

'He told me he didn't have a cleaner.'

'You saw him on the day of the murder.' Jack was trying to keep to the point. 'What's the address of Challoner's surgery?' He knew the answer.

'Two hundred and forty-two Kew Gardens Terrace.'

Two hundred and forty-two. His set number the day Stella boarded his train and the number on the last page of the *A–Z*. Nothing is a waste of time; everything leads somewhere.

'I had an eleven o' clock appointment with Antony. I did tell the police. He wasn't working; he never does on Mondays. He gave me a filling. I remember because he caught my gum and made it bleed. Peculiar slip for he never makes mistakes.'

'The time was wrong.'

'What time?'

'What happened when you got there?'

Sarah Glyde addressed his mother's sculpture. 'He didn't answer the door, but I had his key so I let myself in and sat in the waiting room. It's silly, but I didn't feel I could go upstairs to his flat. He's a private man. He used to hate it if I went into his room when we were young – as you know I still can't. I read a magazine.'

'How long for?'

'It felt like an age. I was about to go when he arrived. So maybe about forty-five minutes? It wasn't like him to be late either.'

'Why was he late? Did he say?'

'Neither of us mentioned it. I supposed it was my fault. I'm absent-minded. Antony never gets appointments wrong. As I said, he never makes mistakes.' The last words were spoken with less conviction.

'We now know that the murder could have happened at least three-quarters of an hour earlier.'

Jack gripped the table to stop himself from falling. Neither of them had noticed that he had put down the knife.

'How was your brother?'

The light in the bulb burned out with a ping. Moonlight gave the studio the appearance of a negative image.

'He was flustered and irritable and forgot to give me an injection.'

They did not move; statues both.

'Where is Ivan Challoner now?'

Imperceptibly she shook her head. 'I don't know.'

The calor gas heater ticked as it cooled. The clay heads were silhouetted in the glass of the French doors. Mother and son faced each other in wordless communion as they never could in life. The knife was on the table between them. The quiet in the deserted studio was broken by the call of geese flying over the water, wings beating the night air. Their honking died to nothing as the birds headed towards the wetlands out at Barnes.

Beyond the garden wall the ebbing tide of the River Thames and traffic on the Great West Road marked the passing of time.

Sixty-One

Ivan lit the candle and placed it on the dressing table where she could see it. The flame flared and steadied, triplicated in the three-way mirror and the room came to life. She was watching. He loved how she observed him, her expression unchanging, taking him in. In her presence his simplest action was witnessed. The flame nearly went out; shadows jumped and danced on the walls. The room was busy, but she had eyes only for him.

There was a draught; he had promised to locate it and block it up. She felt the cold. The house was old; there were cracks in the skirtings and gaps in the floorboards; seams ran through the plastered ceilings and sashes were swollen so that windows did not shut properly. She minded less than him about the state of the house; she agreed it would be disruptive to have workmen crawling all about the place. However, this was the room in which she spent her time and he had promised to keep it perfect. Tonight he would tell her about Stella Darnell and she would have good advice to give him.

No one had ever said no to Ivan before and he did not like it.

He risked another look and found he was right: her eyes were boring into his back, undressing him, caressing him. These days he rarely felt desire; he felt it now.

As this was her room, so the house was his special place. He had shown her his boyhood carvings in the tree, helping her so that she could climb up to the next branch and sit in the hollow. She had been more agile than him; he had not dared climb, telling her he was frightened of heights. She had laughed. She was not laughing *at* him, he told himself. Unlike Stella she had jumped at the chance to come.

She would not betray him.

When she had asked for his news, he had been reticent. Oh, where to begin, he had prevaricated, instead going to make her a cup of tea. Now he was putting off talking about Stella Darnell, repositioning the make-up on her dressing table, which in a minute would annoy her. Not yet; her smile was genuine. He had wanted her from the first moment he had seen her, he told her again.

It was the smile. People's mouths were his first impression and how he judged them. He had wanted to disappear into hers.

Ivan turned from the mirror, his arms outstretched. It was his job to do what he could to keep her safe; he could say nothing of what he was thinking.

Her smile was warm, her teeth whiter than white and not once did she blink. Her hair was flaxen in the mellow candlelight as if bathed in summer sunlight.

The church bells struck eleven times. The night was young. After so long, neither of them needed to speak to communicate with each other.

Ivan knew what she wanted him to do.

Sixty-Two

Monday, 24 January 2011

Jack followed the instructions on the van's satellite-navigation system until, coming out of Newhaven, he recognized where he was and switched off the relentless voice. He travelled the remaining miles in silence. At the sign for Bishopstone he checked his rear mirror but there were no headlights. Indicating left, he flicked down to sidelights and bumped slowly up the lane.

He was looking for the silver BMW four-wheel drive. On the seat beside him was a printout map of the area. After he had left Sarah Glyde's studio, his instinct had been to come straight to Sussex but he had forced himself to prepare. He had returned to his parents' house in St Peter's Square and brought up Broad Street in Seaford on his screen. There it was, a silver four-wheel drive, fixed in time, making its way towards the Co-op supermarket in the sunshine, its driver a shadow behind the wheel. He had clicked the magnifying glass icon and enlarged the image; cropping the surrounding street from the frame, he pressed *Print screen*. He confirmed that the vehicle was the X3 model on a dealer website.

There was always a silver X3 outside the surgery when he came to clean and on his last visit it had been missing.

As he remembered from when he had come with Stella and from his journey in Street View, the lane wound for a long way, with no dwellings, hedgerows overgrown; the van's sidelights accentuated the density of leaves and groping branches. Fullwood House was remote; Ivan Challoner did not want neighbours.

Outside the churchyard his phone rang, and he fumbled for it, sending a blue light over the dashboard when he hauled it out of his coat slung over the passenger seat. Stella had left another voicemail: 'Jack? Stella. Where are you? Ring when you get this. You've taken one of the vans. Why were you in my flat?'

They were no longer a team. Jack told himself Stella had abandoned him. He had her van; she wasn't telling him anything he didn't know. She had not answered his calls. He mounted the verge where they had parked last time and cut the engine. He would not tell her where he was; she would find out soon enough. Jackie would have told Stella she had spoken to him.

It was over.

He turned off his telephone and dropped it in the handbrake well between the seats. Stella would not call the police to report her van stolen. He felt a twinge: he was sorry that he would not see her again.

He found a torch in the glove box. He had not brought the clay cutter or the knife. Neither were suitable. Challoner would have plenty of tools that would do the job.

Shrouded by thickening fog, in his black coat and treading quietly, he was invisible but avoided the light of a single lamp-post as he surveyed a Gothic Victorian villa with a deep arched porchway beyond a twisted hedge. On the gravel outside, parked at an angle, was a silver BMW X3. He shone his light quickly on the number plate; it was registered in 2009.

Jonathan Rokesmith was as near to happy as he had ever been in his life.

Sixty-Three

Monday, 24 January 2011

The blinds in the surgery were shut and Ivan's sitting-room window was unlit. He must have already left for the country. Stella was sorry for refusing the invitation to his family home and, jumping into Terry's car, had driven down to Kew.

She deliberated whether to phone Ivan, but could not bear the idea of him not answering or not returning her call or, worse, putting down the phone. She had no idea where Fullwood House was so could not go there and surprise him, and besides Ivan was like her: surprising him was out of the question.

She was disappointed not to find Jack at the surgery, although he would have finished cleaning hours ago. She had left him a peevish message which now she regretted. More than not going to Sussex, she regretted not answering Jack's earlier calls; there was so much to discuss.

She had perceived too late what it had cost Ivan to invite her, so intent was she on keeping her routine and not repeating her mistakes with Paul. Stella had not noticed that since Terry's death she had no routine and, as for having space, well, she had plenty of that. She wished Paul were alive to get on her nerves. She tramped over melting snow to the front steps, the clinging fog chilling her to the core.

She had listened to Ivan's account of the new kinds of treatments he was researching and in return described her new compact and easily manoeuvrable walk-behind scrubber-drier with attached cleaning system. Unlike Paul, Ivan did not hanker after owning her; she enjoyed his company.

Tonight she had found out what was precious to Ivan and rejected him; there would be no second chance. She stared at the sign: Ivan's name and qualifications were solid in the lamplight suspended above the two brass-studded doors: 'Dr S. A. I. Challoner. Dentist'.

Strange that he wasn't called by his first name, she thought. She tried Jack's number again. No answer. She pictured him sulking because of her message about the van. Where was he?

Car headlights raked the steps, momentarily dazzling her. Ivan was back; it was all right – although ideally she did not want him to find her. She cast about with the crazy thought of hiding, but that would make it worse. She prepared a bright smile.

The headlights on full beam captured her in their glare and suddenly Stella panicked. Her first instinct had been right. She did not want to spend a night with Ivan in a house in the middle of the country, miles from anywhere. Terry would not have liked her to accept.

Sarah Glyde got out of the car.

'It said in the case papers that you couldn't drive.' Something was very wrong.

'I can now.' Glyde slammed her car door and sloshed through the melting ice up the stairs. 'Is Antony here? Are they inside?'

She shoved past and to Stella's astonishment prodded a key into the front-door lock.

'There's no one there.' Stella remained on the top step. 'Who did you say?'

Sarah Glyde appeared not to have heard.

'Jack's a very disturbed young man. He was coming here when he left me. He had a knife.' She rushed inside and, after jabbing in an alarm code, switched on a lamp in the hall.

Stella splashed after her. 'How come you have a key?' It was inconceivable that Ivan would be friends with a hayseed in ripped jeans and a filthy shirt too big for her. Sarah was circling the receptionist's office, tapping and stroking the filing cabinet, the desk, the computer and its monitor; muttering incessantly as if casting a spell.

'I rang to warn Antony but...'

'Who the hell is Antony? What was wrong with Jack's cleaning?'

'You call him Ivan.'

'Do I?'

Dr S. A. I. Challoner. Dentist. Rule: never call clients by their first name.

'I didn't know you knew each other,' Stella whispered.

'Why should you?'

Terry would have established every connection, however trivial; he found out who knew whom, what they did. He covered every angle. Sipping her lemonade and munching crisps while she sat with him outside pubs, Stella had seen him in action.

'What did you say about Jack?' She felt dread.

'He cleans for Antony. I had no idea. You know of course. We must find him before it's too late.'

Nothing was making sense. Stella's phone was ringing. She glanced at it before she answered it. The number was not programmed into her phone.

'Stella, it's Martin Cashman, sorry to call so late. I got this number off your P.A. – she works late too! You got a moment?'

'A moment yes, I'm with someone.'

'Your question was niggling, so I did a bit of homework.'

Stella did not know what Cashman was talking about. She had a mounting unease.

'I checked up on S. A. I. Glyde? You know, the owner of the Anglia? It was registered to a man who changed his surname in 1982. You still there?'

'Yes.'

'He became Challoner. Simon Ivan Antony Challoner. Odd maybe, but nothing wrong with it – all above board. Like I said, his residence is listed as Fullwood House, Bishopstone.'

Stella wrote the information on a copy of *Hello* magazine, although she would not forget it.

'While I've got you, about the funeral, one of our sergeants – a nice lady called Janet – will call you. She worked with Terry for donkey's years, and is handling it. Say if we're stepping on any toes.'

'It's fine.' Stella rang off.

Sarah Glyde was roaming the waiting room, touching every object like a child engrossed in an elaborate private game.

'Who is Antony Glyde?' Stella shouted.

Sarah tilted her head as if hearing the sound from outside.

'My brother,' she said eventually.

Antony. Tony. Uncle Tony.

'What about Jack?'

'What do you mean?'

Stella was impatient. 'You said he was disturbed.'

'We need to stop him—'

'Why did you say Jack was disturbed?'

'He told me it was his mother who was murdered outside my house.'

'Why did he tell you?'

'He found my sculpture of her. Kate commissioned me as a surprise for … well, I thought it was her husband, but I think now … I'd have done it for nothing, a face like that is what one dreams … Instantly I saw Jack I got such a sense, and as soon as I worked on the face my fingers told me they had been there before. Today I found out why.' Her voice had a faraway quality. 'I brought him to me.'

'Stop talking garbage. You told the police you didn't know Kate. You said you were out when the murder happened.'

She was at the dentist.

'Jack knows. I'm worried Antony might …'

'You didn't think to mention to the police that your alibi was your brother?'

'At the time Kate was killed I was having a filling. Look, there's no time for—'

'And did Jack also tell you that the time of the murder was wrong?'

Sarah sank into one of the red chairs, the colour increasing her pallor. 'Yes.'

'What time was your appointment?'

'I've been through this. You're not listening to me, I think—'

'Was Ivan or whoever here when you arrived?'

'No.' Her mouth was dry, her speech tacky. 'I let myself in. It was Mrs Willard's day off.'

'How long did you have to wait?'

Sarah Glyde was motionless.

'Don't tell me, you have wondered about it ever since.' The other woman's ashen features told Stella that she was right.

Sarah hugged herself. The room was cold; the central heating had gone off. Stella detected lavender: like Mrs Ramsay Ivan had taken her advice. Jack did not clean the surgery; Ivan preferred to do that himself. Of course he did.

'I don't know my brother well. He was older so we didn't grow up together. His father was killed in a plane crash and our mother remarried and had me. He holds me to blame for everything, which is patently unfair. My mother loved him better.' Sarah jangled the office keys, her sense of urgency gone. 'I might have known – he has always frightened me – but for the time of death. Antony was with me when Kate was supposed to have been murdered. I clung to that fact.' She gave a strained laugh, which ended abruptly. 'I've been so grateful that Antony does my teeth for nothing, he charges a fortune.'

'I know.' Stella thrust the torn page from the magazine in front of her. 'Do you recognize this address?'

'Yes.' Sarah stared dumbly at it. 'It's where my mother lived with her first husband. Antony was born there. We moved to London when I was a baby. Antony went every weekend as soon he could be trusted on his own. My dad hated it, so my mother went less often until he died. When she died, she left it to Antony. I got the London house because it had belonged to my father. My family are terribly strict around money.'

'Would Jack know this?' Stella was brutal.

'He was going to kill me.' Sarah Glyde clasped herself tighter.

'Why did Ivan – Antony – Tony – change his surname?'

'Did he tell you to call him Ivan?' Sarah frowned. She implied Stella had taken the law into her own hands and renamed her brother. 'He changed it out of the blue, in homage to his father. My mother was upset. She saw it as a slight to my dad who put him through school. Not that she told Antony; ultimately he could do no wrong.'

'When did his wife die?' Stella's hands were tingling, her thoughts racing. She had shown Ivan the case files. After she had given Ivan the camera, the memory card was missing. How had he known she was at the police station? When they bumped into each other on Hammersmith Broadway he had been walking towards her so could not have known where she had come from.

If Jack had been in her flat he would have heard Martin Cashman's message. He would think that she had betrayed him.

'Antony never married. Like me, he prefers his own company.' Sarah had a faraway look.

'What about his son?' The little boy whom Ivan tucked in bed before reading him a story. The little boy who had loved to hear his mother playing Beethoven's 'Pathétique' on the piano and who Ivan said was frightened of the dark.

'You all nice and comfortable? OK, excuse me while I have a sip.' She made him say this phrase or they couldn't get going. Stella squirmed under the covers and then settled down.

'Then I'll begin…'

He bookmarked their place. Tonight it was The Lion, the Witch and the Wardrobe. *She always knew where they had left off and read out the first line. The teachers told him her reading age was older than seven. He sometimes thought it was older than his own.*

Sarah Glyde was talking: 'Antony doesn't have children, he hates them, he couldn't bear me when I was small. I'm sure he disliked other children even when he was one himself.' She looked up as if suddenly aware of Stella. 'Did he say was married? Have you and he been having a…?'

'No.' Stella was emphatic.

Jack had found out that Ivan Challoner had murdered his mother. He had gone to Fullwood House.

Sarah was talking more to herself than to Stella: 'Antony never invites me to Fullwood, not that I would want to go. The place gives me the creeps.'

Jack wanted to help Stella solve the case, not simply to get justice for his mother, but to find the murderer and get his revenge. He was going to kill Ivan Challoner.

Stella pushed past Sarah Glyde and rushed out.

The wheels spun on the ice, but when they gained traction, the Toyota jumped forward, spinning out on to the road, the rear wheels skidding. Stella glanced in her wing mirror and saw Sarah Glyde silhouetted in the porch.

Jack had several hours' start; he would be there. It would be too late to save him from crossing the line, yet she had to try.

Only when, hunched over the steering wheel and driving as fast as she dare down the M23, did Stella think of calling the police. By police she meant Terry.

Sixty-Four

His hand hovered an inch from her face, tracing her flawless smile. Her teeth gave him joy; he kept this to himself because she would tease him. He did not like to be teased.

He had once told her this.

His voice broke their reverie: 'Darling, do you remember me going down to the garage to fetch a gas canister for the heater?'

Her smile, as ever, was encouraging.

'I was about to leave when the strangest thing happened. I heard a telephone. It could not be mine as I had left it with you, so I was stumped.'

'This has a happy ending.' She was anxious; he hastened to allay her worries. If he were to stroke her skin, it would be soft and smell of sunshine.

'I found a mobile phone by the garage doors. Now this is where I don't want you fretting, but I found the canvas cover thrown back. It could not be you as you never go in there. I'm right about that, aren't I, darling?'

Her teeth were even, no gaps, no shrinkage in the gums; good and strong. They looked capped, but he knew they were not.

'It was still ringing when I got to it. The caller was one 'Stella mob'. I waited for it to stop then went through the previous calls. I know this is weird to you, but there is a list of Received calls and Dialled calls, then there are messages, some sent, some received. A whole history – yes, it's terribly clever. I began with the sent messages.'

It did not vex him that he was losing her attention. As long as he had told her, she couldn't accuse him of keeping it from her. It helped him to go over everything and get it clear.

'I found two messages on the detective's phone. They were both to this Stella. One read: *Meet me at the Ram 8pm.* The next contradicted this with *Can't make it. Will call. Dad xx.*'

She was gazing at him, still smiling. Naturally she expected him to have a solution and was not interested in detail. He did not have a solution.

'I couldn't find the details of the owner. What I want to know is why they were in our house and if whoever it was came up here.'

The intruder could not get into the house without breaking the front door. He told her to keep it bolted. They must have got into the garage because although he found the garage door open, it was unbolted from the inside. This meant the back door had been unlocked. She was maintaining her smile.

'So you see, I think they had guessed about us, which means they will be back. Nothing has been moved or stolen, I am sure you would have told me.' Still she did not respond.

Her shoes had moved; they were at the foot of the bed and not where he had put them, under the chair. She had promised never to betray him.

'The intruder left in a hurry. Perhaps you remember teasing me for forgetting to bring the gas canister? You said I would forget you next!'

She had laughed. Her laughter shrill and mocking, her head thrown back, her teeth white and flawless in the sunshine.

She had known he had found the phone, but said nothing. From that day the house was no longer a refuge. They were under siege.

There had been nothing in the phone's Inbox. 'Stella mob' had not replied, or if she had the owner had deleted the message. He found her in the contacts list along with lots of numbers referenced only with initials. The owner of the mobile had a lot of secrets, he told her.

We just have one.

'I did toy with telling Mrs Willard I was ill, but didn't want her telling Sarah. You know how they hate each other. Mrs Willard can't resist showing off about me and, whatever you say, it is useful that she is like that; she protects me from patients. I am never sick; they would both be concerned so I had to ride it out.'

The candlelight made the liquid in her wine glass a rich crimson. He couldn't remember what they had been drinking; she had liked Merlot. It must be Merlot.

'The next afternoon it was on the local news that a Met detective had died of a heart attack in Seaford. I knew immediately it was that detective, Darnell his name was. "Smart arse", you would have said. I went on the internet and my suspicion was correct: the man had a daughter named Stella. It's all there: she owns a cleaning company. She arrived at the Royal Sussex County Hospital in Brighton too late. Don't look like that; it was always too late. The man died in the street. I went up there and found her van in the car park and since then I've kept an eye on her for you. I gave her little gifts, the flowers, a book to flatter her, not that she reads. She's not like you, my darling.'

He could not decipher her expression. Did she already know about the detective? Had she talked to him or, worse, had she been expecting he would return? In case she had, he repeated: 'The detective is dead.'

'For half an hour – and it was literally that time – I was on top of the world. At last we were free. But then a woman from Clean Slate rang to book an emergency appointment for her boss: Stella Darnell. With two "L"s, she said. I know, I nearly said. I took the call because it was too early for Mrs Willard. I acted cool, of course. You would have been proud.'

She lay on the bed, the glass in her hand, poised for a sip, listening now.

'The detective had told his daughter and she came straight to me.' He had reached the tricky part and heard himself picking up speed, trying to sound normal. He had nothing to be guilty about.

'She needed a filling, so I got her back in again and invited her for a drink to trap her. Her teeth were in terrible shape – not like yours. She was boring. I'm sorry, but there is no other word. I talked about the boy and she was suitably interested. She would have seen nothing in the flat, although she checked it for cleanliness. I saw her through the hinge gap.'

'After I invited her upstairs and she said nothing, I thought, incredible as it seems, that it was coincidence she had come to me. She has not the imagination to pretend. She is like her father, no care for people, just intent on getting the job done. She did rather seem to enjoy my company, but believe me, darling, it was purgatory.'

He had her attention so he kept going. He would tell her everything.

'It's been stressful. Stella Darnell had this lovesick man in tow. He is gone. An unfortunate accident – I know you understand. He went down like a ninepin. He recognized me; bloody patients get everywhere. The problem is, I think Sarah suspects, my lovely little sister is not as much with the fairies as we think.'

He never got sick of looking at her teeth, their perfection made his job worthwhile even though it left him redundant.

'Stella Darnell has a new man – one of her cleaners. He cleans for me. Fickle madam: if I were truly a widower, she would be leading me a merry dance. Yesterday she went to the police station about her dead boyfriend. She didn't mention the cleaner to me. I am disappointed; people let you down.' He smiled at her. 'Except you, my love.'

She smiled.

She continued smiling. Ivan was encouraged: 'She sent her boyfriend on a wild-goose chase; she has not told the police she spoke to Bramwell; she thinks he did it. We will remind her about her lapses in honesty, starting with the twenty-pound note at the automatic teller in Seaford; failed that one, Ms Darnell!' Ivan raised his glass to her and drank some wine. He had let it breathe and it was at the right temperature: it was delicious.

'Darling, we needn't concern ourselves with Mr Bramwell or the detective any more. There's just the daughter now.'

She toasted him, toasted them both.

'Luckily Stella is keen to confide in me because my hard work listening to stories about commercial floor care have paid off. What she has told me is good and bad so I want you to pay attention.' She was still smiling. He did not trust the smile. Did she already know what he was about to say?

'I invited Stella Darnell here tonight. No, don't look like that; I know what I'm doing. We would have dealt with her but she refused to come. However, it's a matter of time. Her new man cleans for me. I haven't met him but I heard her talking to him by that statue; the night you told me off for taking a risk. Aren't you glad I did go out on a limb? Who else loves you like I do? They are weaving a web, my darling; one that you and I will not be caught in. I will have to get another cleaner – a shame – this Mr Harmon is terribly good.'

An owl hooted from the direction of the church. The lattice windows were opaque with fog. Ivan was lighter for unburdening himself; she had put the problem in proportion. He could deal with Stella Darnell and Jack Harmon. He would not allow them to ruin a life that had taken thirty years to build: Fullwood House was sacrosanct. Bramwell had been easy; the detective's daughter would be too. They would soon be safe.

He ran nimbly down to the basement, which he called the surgery, for that was what it had been in his father's day. He had the only key so he knew it was unsullied by the detective's intrusion.

The surgery was soundproofed and for this reason once he closed the door he did not hear a floorboard creak in the utility room, nor did he hear someone going up the stairs to the bedroom.

Sixty-Five

Monday, 24 January 2011

After he opened the back door, Jack pressed against the wall and let the minute hand go around his watch-face five times. Ivan Challoner had a mind like his own and would do everything he could to outwit him. He gave him time.

Jack glided along a flagged passage. Outside the fog was thinning and a moon appeared. Fact: a waning gibbous moon. It gave enough light to plot the room: a large kitchen. A carving knife lay on a long table but his experience with Sarah Glyde had told Jack he could not stomach blood and mess.

So far it had been too easy. He gauged the silence; it was too quiet.

He did not need to orientate himself. As in a dream, he knew the way. The doorway ahead led to the main part of the house and upstairs, as he expected, Jack found a corridor with five doors.

Five doors in a row,
Ready steady go.

His boyish sing-song verse reverberated off the walls. He had been before.

Far off, a rook cawed three times. Rooks. He had heard them before too. A bar of light shone beneath the fourth door.

The last time he had turned the handle it had been higher up and difficult to grasp; he'd had to use two hands. Tonight the china knob turned with no effort.

A candle burned and, after the comparative darkness, the

bright light hurt his eyes. His entrance caused a draught; the flame flickered and then flared up so the room seem to tip. The candle was in a silver holder with a snuffer attached. The wick was half submerged in molten wax. Jack estimated that the flame had another quarter of an hour.

A campaign of items advanced across the top of the dressing table: lipsticks, foundation, face powder, mascara, eye-liner, combs, hairbrushes, moisturizers, cleansers: the tools of magic. A used cleansing pad, pinched by fingers, stained by lips, lay next to lumps of cotton wool stained with red nail varnish. The black snood that she used to pull her hair back from her face when she did her make-up dangled from the mirror.

Minute fibres clung to an exposed lipstick, the surface of the open pot of face cream had crusted to a custard yellow. Balls of cotton wool were grey and dirty and a scent hung in the air, laced with the heavier tang of damp; it made his stomach clench. He could not touch the bottle of Eau Savage Extreme.

'Boys don't wear perfume. I bought it for your mother.'

'It says it's aftershave.'

'And I said, put it down.'

The artistry created authenticity: the make-up, the potions and creams, nail scissors, nail varnish and nail-varnish remover had not been used for decades. This was the stage-set of an abandoned life; he was looking into the past to a time that had petrified; he could not obliterate the evidence with the click of a mouse or the turn of a street atlas page.

Downstairs, a clock struck the hour, followed by church bells, their volume varying as they were carried on the wind. He stopped counting after five and took the candle; cupping the dying flame, he walked egg-and-spoon-race style over to the bed.

He had made Stella count up the number of words she could see out of the car window while they sat in a traffic jam.

He lost count as words swam before his eyes: headlines which provided more context as time went by and the case became history. There had been other murders, other Kates.

Thames murder: Kate killer left no trace
Clueless detectives – Kate hunt stepped up
Kate: tragic boy speaks
Ten years: Kate TV appeal
Was Rokesmith Hammersmith Murder no. 7?
Murdered Kate's boy is school bully
Rokesmith loses battle with cancer
Mystery flowers on murdered woman's grave
Kate Rokesmith detective dies

Beneath each headline Jack read and reread the story of his mother's murder. He could not change the ending: at the end of each article his mother was dead.

Mixed in amongst grainy images – newspaper orange-peeled with damp – were colour prints of Kate. Jack recognized the back of this house. Kate was in the kitchen filling a kettle, smiling brightly: the perfect housewife.

The kettle whistled like a train.

'Give me that. It's not for blowing through. You'll fill it with germs.'

Kate lying fully clothed on the bed in this room, upon the same counterpane as the one on the bed now. She held a glass of red wine to the camera, smiling over the rim; her teeth were white and even. Three Kates reflected in the bedroom mirrors; Kate picking flowers in the garden; Kate outside the front door.

Jack lifted the candle close to the flaking plaster wall. Many photographs had been snipped; he examined one of Kate on the bed: the hand not raising the wineglass was holding a hand smaller than hers. Although he had been there, Jonathan Rokesmith had been excised from the picture.

Jack had lain on the bed beside his mother so that Uncle Tony could take their picture. He had picked flowers in the garden, carefully choosing her favourite ones. He had stood outside the front door and, while they waited to have their picture taken, asked when they were going home.

'Sssh, darling, smile for Uncle Tony.'

'After this, you're to go and play in the sitting room, there's a good boy. Your mother and I have much to talk about.'

A length of material was draped across the back of the bedstead. Jack directed the candle towards it and a heady scent filled his nostrils.

It was a silk scarf. Even in the guttering light Jack could see that it was a livid green.

Pantone 375.

He set the candle by the bed and with tremulous hands wound the scarf into a pool of slippery fabric around his hand. He put it to his face and breathed in; he shook with sobs.

The flame died.

Jack wrapped the scarf around his neck and blundered out of the room. Jack knew about the second staircase. All his life he had wondered if the house with two sets of stairs was his invention. There had been no one to ask. He stopped: suddenly he pictured seeing the man called Uncle Tony talking to the boy called Simon by the gate in his secret garden at school. He had kept very quiet so they did not see him; but then perhaps that was a dream.

He glided along the passage, the scarf – the last sign – caressing his skin. He did not feel sick.

The door beneath the main staircase opened and a man came out into the hall, his shadow enormous and then diminishing when he reached the front door. He paused at the foot of the stairs.

Ivan Challoner left his father's surgery, satisfied that everything was in order for his patient. He trusted Stella would come and that his treatment would be effective. He put a kettle on for tea. Kate liked chamomile at this time of night. He unhooked two cups, deciding he would join her. There were drops of water on the floor and he presumed some had splashed when he filled the kettle. He stopped. They were not by the sink and were not splashes; they were footprints. They led to the cloakroom where the bulb was low wattage but enough for him to make out that the trail started by the back door.

Someone was here.

Kate. He must make sure she was unharmed. It was then that a nasty idea came to him: Kate had not expected him tonight and she had let someone into their house. He went swiftly along the passage to the hall – and froze.

Kate Rokesmith was standing on the landing, her hair framing her face. The scarf he had given her for her birthday was arranged around her neck in elegant folds, pale moonlight highlighting the fine green threads. Slowly, gracefully, she descended the staircase.

The kettle came to the boil, the whistle rose to an urgent hoot like a child hurtling through a subway tunnel, pretending to be a train.

The piercing sound hurt Ivan's ears.

Sixty-Six

Monday, 24 January 2011

Stella found the van by the church, the driver's door hanging open. The new Clean Slate logo showed up in bad visibility; she hoped Jack had been able to bear the green. Where was he?

She slewed Terry's car beside the van and jumped out. She stumbled down the lane past the church; she nearly missed a track to the right because a hedge jutted out, obscuring the entrance. There were no houses. After ten yards she saw the dark hulk of a barn and directed the torch at it: the light barely reached but she could see great cylindrical hay bales piled to the roof. Jack was not here.

Thawing snow had mixed with mud and by the time she had retraced her steps to the lane Stella's shoes were soaked through. Twice she veered into a wall and once she slithered into a ditch. Soggy earth clung to her trousers and anorak. The darkness was thick and she longed for London's many sources of light: lamp-posts, headlights, signs, shop windows. Mad shapes were dancing and ducking on the edge of her vision: she saw what Jack meant about seeing signs and spirits in every inanimate object.

Her torch made the darkness more intense. She stopped, her insides shrivelling: entrails of fog were twisting up from the tarmac like cobras charmed out of a basket. She had seen the phenomenon before on a day trip to the country with Terry. Travelling home at night, she had been secure in his warm car, with him there to protect her. Stella could not feel his presence any more.

Somewhere a twig snapped and with a whirring of wings a bird flew out of the hedgerow and away. It might be a rook, or a crow;

she didn't know the difference but had thought all birds slept at night.

She was not afraid, she told herself.

The plaque for Fullwood House was almost hidden by fronds of ivy spreading over brick piers either side of imposing gates. When she lifted the catch, it gave a squeak and the gate shunted down and sank into the gravel.

There was still snow on the drive, which revealed one set of footprints, the tread with the ball of the foot first. Ivan. Where was Jack?

A lethal mix of holly and pyracantha barred the way to the back of the house. Already wet and shivering, Stella launched herself at the tough branches. She found a gap and on her hands and knees crawled along the ground, her knees scratched with dried leaves. She rolled out on to a lawn behind the house; still covered in snow, it was ethereal in the insipid light. Through the thinning fog she recognized the hedge that separated the garden from the church. Ivan lived a stone's throw from Kate Rokesmith's grave.

The back door was locked. Stella had jumped in her car and hared down here like some invincible hero, without thinking that when she got here she would not be able to get inside.

She checked each window: all were dark and locked. At the other side of the house a flight of steps led down to what must be a cellar, although no windows were visible. The lower steps were obscured by brambles that trailed over a barred window next to the door. Stella gingerly put a foot amongst the prickly branches. She ripped away ivy to clear a gap and shone her torch at the glass, risking being seen from within. The window had been walled up on the inside with planks of wood. No one could see out and she could not see in.

A hand grabbed her arm. The game was up.

Tugged by strong hands, she had the presence of mind to shake off the grip and aim the torch in the face of her assailant.

It was Sarah Glyde.

'What are you doing here?' Stella hissed.

'I came after you.'

'To warn your brother?'

'If I wanted to do that, I'd have rung him on his mobile phone.'

Stella digested the truth of this and wrung her hands. 'They're in there, but the windows and doors are locked.'

'We ought to call the police. I should have before I left, but I had to catch up with you.' Sarah was matter of fact.

'We need to find Jack.' The police would arrest Jack. Revenge was not an excuse for murder. He would not survive a jail sentence.

Stella had found Kate's murderer. She had solved the case. Damp, cold and in the middle of nowhere, this realization gave her no satisfaction; Jack and Ivan might be dead. Terry would not have let it get to this.

She flashed the beam at the wall. 'There's an alarm box, but it looks dead. If we smash a window round the side, the chances are he won't hear and what do we have to lose? Jack's in there.' Stella was channelling Terry; she had to keep her nerve.

'Or we could use this?' Sarah Glyde held up a key on a chain.

'I thought he never invited you here.'

'This is my mother's. Antony doesn't know I have it.'

'What are we waiting for?'

Stella snatched the key off Sarah Glyde and stalked around the house to the back door.

Sixty-Seven

Monday, 24 January 2011

'She sends me cards with the time of meeting. It's a game; she loves the secrecy and fooling others. She fears being ordinary; the drudgery of daily life. I would have to cancel what I was doing, often at short notice. This was before mobile phones. The postcards come to my flat, unsigned, in envelopes marked "Private and Personal". Her handwriting would be identifiable but it's never come to that. She trusts me to destroy them. I could not reply in case he intercepted them. Mr Rokesmith may have suspected we are in love, but he couldn't prove it.'

'I don't believe you.'

'Yes you do.'

He thought of the cards written in his mother's hand that he kept in his trophy box. Isabel Ramsay had given them to him. Until now he had supposed they were sent to Isabel by his mother. In fact she had known of his mother's affair and kept her secret all these years. It was why she had lied to the police about seeing Kate. Mark Ramsay must have known too; it was why he did not contradict his wife's evidence.

The basement was lined with ceramic tiles. Two lights with gun-metal shades shed white light on a dais in the centre. On this was set a luxurious red-leather dentist's chair with chrome fittings. Challoner had seated himself in it and at his request Jack had poured him a glass of water.

Above a counter in which there was a sink, a lit panel displayed a series of X-rays showing what Jack judged to be the same set of teeth from different angles: front, down, side. The lips drawn back were a grey mass at the periphery of the image. The teeth were that of a child and flawless, although one on the lower jaw was missing. Jack read the label on each negative: the years progressed from 1968 to 1969, but the name was the same.

Katherine Venus.

As a small boy, passionate about the Romans, he had taken it for granted that his dead mother had been the goddess of love and beauty, with a planet named after her that in 2012 and 2117 would transit across the sun. Buried in the churchyard, her teeth would be perfect; her smile long gone, her own transit was over.

'That is my father's work; such tremendous skill, he nurtured your mother. He had this surgery soundproofed because my dear mama couldn't bear the drill or any dental treatment. Consequently she had dreadful teeth, which mortified my father. She only let him set up his practice in here on the condition that she didn't have to meet his patients or hear the equipment. Apart from the income, I doubt if she noticed when he died. He might have still been down here, working away. We can shout as loud as we like, not a creature will hear – the nearest houses are weekend retreats and will be empty. At this time of night we are only twenty-five minutes from Brighton and a mere hour and a half from London, yet we could be on the moon. We are alone. Welcome to your mother's sanctuary, my dear Jonny.'

Ensconced on his throne, Challoner was the True Host; his manner expansive, he sought to make Jack feel at home.

'No one calls me that.'

'Your mother does. By the way, you are the spitting image of her, a credit to us both.'

'I'm not your son.'

Challoner sipped the water with ruminative pleasure. He placed the glass on a ledge beside the little rinsing sink and rested back on the cushioned leather. He was quite unlike his sister; about to die, he was not afraid or concerned.

'Ah, Jonathan, you were always so intractable.' Challoner shut his eyes. 'You'll have to forgive me my confusion earlier. I thought you were Kate chasing her cup of tea.'

'I don't forgive you anything.' Jack examined the polished steel instruments on the counter. With previous Hosts he had allowed time to understand their movements, their preferences and habits. He had spent weeks observing them, becoming familiar with even minor behavioural patterns. Had he seen Challoner during a cleaning session, he would have recognized him. He had known him on the zebra crossing in Earls Court the night he stepped on the crack in the paving.

'If you tell me what you think I have done, I can perhaps exculpate myself.'

'You know what you have done.'

'Kate is dying to see you. It's been too long, although she understands you have your life to lead. We must let our children fly free; they do not belong to us, she says.'

'Stop talking about her as if she is alive.'

Challoner returned to the water and sipped at it with quiet complacency, seeming not to have heard Jack.

Apart from a jumble of debris on the counter, the room was ordered and clean. Despite the outdated equipment, it had a contemporary feel, but as in the rest of the house Jack detected decomposition beneath the cocktail of stringent polishes and detergents. He could imagine why Challoner's mother had hated going to the dentist, even if it only involved going down to the basement and the dentist was her husband. People had not been happy in this room.

Ivan Challoner had treated Jonathan's mummy here.

The chair reminded Jack of a 1950s American automobile, the shiny chrome reflected his face warped in the curving silver. He was told to wait upstairs and draw pictures – adults were always asking children to draw pictures – but the profound quiet had distressed him. After a while he had pattered along to the door and, pressing his lips to the wood, had called: '*Mum-my!*'

She had ignored him. Fact: in the soundproofed basement,

with the door sealed shut, Kate Rokesmith had not been able to hear him.

The rubbish on the counter was tangles of frayed twine, snaps of wood dried grey and smooth, rounded shards of glass scattered amongst stones and pebbles. These last were arranged according to size, the smallest at the front, then graduating to polished cricket-ball size. Some were flints, others pockmarked wedges of chalk: every item was arranged to depict a beach.

A beach seen only at low tide.

In the twine Jack sniffed river mud; in the chalk he caught the salty tang of the sea. Sunshine warmed his face and a gentle hand brushed his fringe from his eyes. He had discovered the pebbles in the garden by the church and used the twine for mooring rope to tie up his boat and lash together lolly sticks for his bridge. The lumps of chalk he'd dug up from amongst seaweed in the abandoned village. He had lived through the shape and colour of every object; his memories, hopes, fears and dreams were locked within these found and lost treasures. His mummy had said their days out or walks to the river or to the big house in the country were a secret and like the treasures found on his walks at home, she'd taken them away from him.

Meticulously, Ivan Challoner had placed each object where it belonged as if it were a giant three-dimensional jigsaw. All that was missing was the Bell Steps.

'Grown-ups never appreciate the value to children of what they find. Those treasures are the bones of our lives. I kept them safe for you.' Challoner smiled fondly at him. 'We've been preparing the house for you, Jonathan. You are our very special guest.'

Deep within the silence of the phantom surgery, Jack heard the wash of the incoming tide and he distinguished voices.

'What do you mean you've prepared the house? You're not expecting me to move in with you, are you? It needs redecorating, modernizing! And having got away from that dull as ditchwater village, you can't imagine I want to go back? I have a home here, as do you. Tony darling, don't spoil it. Hold me and enjoy this, now. I've

had Hugh doing the silent bit about me not coming to his mother's frightful birthday lunch, and Jonny is crotchety about your engine… he's not speaking to me. I've had a bloody morning. Please be a sweety and be nice. Be my Heathcliff!'

'He's brought my engine with him? Christ, he'll ruin it.'

'He won't be parted from it. I even tried bribery with some lump of glass that dear sweet Isabel gave me for luck. Come on, Tony, don't waste this time on a silly toy.'

'It's not silly, my father gave it to me.'

'You shouldn't have given it to a baby then.'

'I've talked to a lawyer. If you give up your rights to the house, it can go through pretty smartish.'

'What can?'

'Your divorce, obviously. We will marry.'

'Oh, Tony, what a funny idea. One husband is enough. Do talk normally. We haven't got long, Jonny needs his lunch.'

'Don't tease me.'

'I shall tease you if it makes you see sense. I shan't leave Hugh. He would be devastated and I would hate that. He's so kind, when he's not working. I couldn't do it to our little boy. He loves Hugh and besides all his toys are there.'

'Not all his toys. Look me in the eyes and tell me you don't love me.'

'I don't love you. There. Tony sweetheart, I would drive you potty if you saw me all the time, you'd soon be bored of me. You are a wonderful dentist and my special friend. Won't that do? I wish Hugh would come to you. He's got a nagging tooth that makes him so grumpy. He and Jonny are a bit much at the moment.'

'You have to leave.'

'I might as well tell you now, I'm having a baby. At this moment I'm not going anywhere except home. Hugh doesn't know yet, so it's our secret. I've told you first. Jonathan, come on! It's time to go.'

'You cannot go anywhere until you say you love me. Especially with our baby.'

'She lied to me.' Challoner broke the spell. 'They did a post-mortem. She was not pregnant.'

'She owed you nothing, least of all the truth.'

Jack looped his mother's green scarf under Challoner's chin and pulled it tight.

'You gave this to her for her birthday and lucky for you she was wearing it that day. My father had never seen it so did not miss it when he identified her body. There was nothing to link Kate Rokesmith with you except these X-rays of your father's and her dental records. Police didn't ask you for those. You were calculating: you left her body knowing the river was filling and the tide would wash it downstream and then you went after me. If you had found me, I would be dead. I am your only witness and ever since you have lived in fear of me finding you. Isabel Ramsay, for reasons of her own, unwittingly did you an enormous favour; she made your alibi watertight.' Jack did not add that he could not remember what had happened on the beach; he only remembered the colour of the scarf.

He held the fabric taut and pulled the lever on the chair, making it tip up until Challoner's feet were as high as his head; he was helpless. His voice was thick as the scarf cut into his neck.

'Did you stay to fight the dragon-slayer, like a brave little soldier? Did you rush to the aid of your beloved mummy?'

The fine green silk was a second skin that he could not shed.

'No, you ran away. I'm no psychotherapist, but don't they call it "projection"? You need to put your guilt on me. Go ahead. I am here for you, I always have been.'

He made no effort to loosen the makeshift ligature.

'Kate was a trophy to your father; he didn't want her but he didn't want anyone else to have her. She was merely existing in his tomb. I saved her. Had you stayed, I might have saved you too.'

The sun was bright and made golden arrows on the water. Jonathan had wanted to drive his engine into the river and see if it could be a boat.

Jack let the scarf loosen.

His voice stronger, Challoner continued: 'You and he leeched her life. If you didn't get your way, you punched her and threw things at her. Is there a name for mothers abused by their children?

I love her for who she is and I won't let anyone spoil our life, not even you, who, despite everything, she longs to see.'

Challoner's skin was white against the green silk. Jack moved his hands further up the scarf.

'As I clasped her to me, a bird – a phoenix, I now believe – beat its way through my rib cage and I fought for breath. She entered my heart. I carried her home.' Challoner reached behind and stroked Jack's sleeve. 'She is upstairs now, Jonny.'

Jack snatched his arm away and pulled on the scarf, making Challoner choke.

'Cathy – that was my pet name for her – teased me and my sister will tell you that I do *not* like to be teased. Cathy promised to leave Rokesmith: we would have our life, the mornings waking up together, the rambles by the sea. I gave you my engine to make her think I would love you too. I brought her here to show her the house. You had to come. She adored our bedroom and was ecstatic when I said I was giving you the attic all to yourself. She said I was so generous. You rampaged along the passages, up and down the staircases, crashing through my house like a tornado. She said how happy you were. We toasted our little family with the last of my father's Château Latour, laid down the year I was born. We did so because she had promised to leave him.'

It had been cold although the sun was out. Jonathan had made a bridge over the rivulet in the sand running into the sea. First he laid a stick along the mud and propped it up with stones, creating supports to make it solid. Then he dug into the mud to narrow the course so that the water flowed faster. When it was finished he called for Mummy to come and see. They were close to each other, walking amongst the ruins of the mill owner's house. He had meant for his mummy to see it, but Uncle Tony came instead. He said it was very clever. Jonathan wanted him to go away.

He said so.

'I have to preserve our peace. You are welcome here, but Stella Darnell doesn't have your sensitivity and blunders in regardless of feelings. She's like her father. You take after me.'

'You are not my father. You are no one.'

'We cannot host Ms Darnell. I have a mind like yours, but you know that, don't you? We are one, you and I. I took better notice of you at that school than Hugh Rokesmith. I was a better father to you. For him, you were out of sight so out of his mind. I rang up every week to find out how you were.'

'You're lying; it would have been to check whether I had given your description to the police.'

'You would never have done that. I was certain that your guilt had silenced you and I was right. Jonny, you misjudge me, my calls were proof of how I care for you.' Challoner grimaced and put a hand to his neck, then let it drop. 'I couldn't get your house-mother off the phone. She said Simon was your special friend until the bullying. I was disappointed in you then, Jonathan. However, I understood: we all have our "Simons", mine was Detective Darnell.'

'Did you kill him?'

'Jonathan, darling, please! I thought we understood each other. He killed himself: too many beefburgers and beers. Would you pass me my water?'

Jack loosened his grip and gave Challoner his glass.

'I was with one of my late-night patients when Stella Darnell called her father's phone. I shouldn't have answered, a stupid mistake, but after the first call, when I found the phone, I couldn't resist it. I forgot about background sounds of water rinsing into the sink; still no matter, she wouldn't have noticed; she is a cleaner, not a detective, after all.' He tilted the cup; this time he just moistened his lips. 'She had to be better than her father. She had to poke about in our business.'

'Stella loves her dad.'

'She doesn't understand love. The Stella Darnells of this world do great damage with their lack of insight. They hurt the likes of you and me.'

As the scarf closed on his larynx, Challoner spluttered: 'If you kill me, you kill her.'

The little boy had collapsed, hot and panting, against the plinth.

Unable to reach, Jonathan promised the Leaning Woman he would bring a knife and cut off the plastic box tied to her arm. He promised to set her free.

'I will save you,' he told his mummy.

The scent of Eau Savage was overwhelming, the silk of the scarf cool in Jonathan's hands.

Sixty-Eight

Tuesday, 25 January 2011

The light switch did not work. Stella switched on her key-torch: they were in a cloakroom. Signalling to Sarah, she trod lightly on the tiles but tripped over a wellington boot. Beside this was an industrial-sized top-loading washing machine and on a shelf above were packets of soap powder. Sarah gasped and jolted Stella's elbow, making the torch dip wildly. Sarah Glyde was a liability; Stella should have sent her back to her car.

'Those were my mother's.' Sarah indicated the soap powders.

'Sssssh. How can you tell?' Stella lifted down a box. It was empty.

'These boots are mine, that coat was my father's. Antony has kept everything.'

They crept into a passage which went in either direction. When Sarah stumbled against her for the second time Stella clenched her teeth: for an artist the woman had little spatial awareness.

'Left or right?' Stella hissed.

'Your choice.'

'No, I mean what is the best way?'

'Left takes us to the garage and back stairs and that way leads to the kitchen and through to the main stairs and the sitting room.'

'Right then.'

Stella kept the torchlight down as they felt their way to the kitchen. She played the light along the wall until she found a light switch. When she flicked it on, nothing happened. She sighed: she had done this stuff too recently in Terry's house. She was used to empty houses, but this was straining her nerves.

She manoeuvred around a long deal table and opened the fridge. It was an old Lec model, over forty years old. The lamp inside remained unlit, even with the door ajar. In such an old model the motor would have been noisy: 'He's turned the power off,' Stella breathed.

'Why would he do that?' Sarah spoke in a normal voice.

'Why do you think?'

'Can you just tell me rather than talk in riddles. Antony doesn't suffer from power cuts, his father had a generator installed.'

'He's expecting visitors. Your brother is prepared for us.'

'You don't seriously think he will harm us?'

Stella gave her a look. Not having siblings she could not be certain she would believe it if someone she hardly knew told her that her brother was a murderer. She might demand evidence. She suspected Sarah Glyde of long closing her eyes to clues.

Sarah gripped her arm, her terror palpable. Stella straightened. Only the fact that she would not admit to feeling afraid kept her from tearing out of the house. That and knowing that Terry would not have done so.

They tiptoed past a breakfast table laid for two; Sarah knocked a packet of Cornflakes off and in her effort to catch it batted it across the floor. The noise echoed in the cold silence.

There was no sound from above. Stella retrieved the box: it was light even for a packet of cereal. She looked inside. It, too, was empty. She caught sight of the sell-by date and squinted at the tiny figures. *December 1981.*

That could not be right. She trained the light directly on to the flap of the packet. Even if the one was a seven, and she was sure it was not, the eight was definitely correct. The cardboard was worn and had been reinforced with clear tape. The cereal box was nearly thirty years old. She directed the beam on the table. The marmalade jar was empty; nor was there any ketchup in the old-style glass bottle. The breakfast table was a museum exhibit.

Stella pulled the kitchen door open quickly and thrust the quavering torch forward as if its beam might save them and turned left into a passage. At the end was the hall and the front door, its stained-glass lights casting watery triangles over the mosaics.

Out of the corner of her eye Stella caught a glint. Sarah Glyde had a carving knife, its sharpened blade tapering to a point. She was unblinking, her mouth grim. Stella was stunned: she would be prepared to kill her brother. This did not make Stella feel better.

The door led into a garage. Stella got a vague sense of comfort from the smell of petrol, paint, chemicals, garden implements, bags of compost. It reminded her of Terry's shed. She got another feeling too: Terry had been here.

A dark shape draped with canvas filled the space; everything else – the lawn mower, flower pots, spades, a strimmer, canisters of calor gas – was ranged around the walls.

Challoner had another car.

Stella held the torch at shoulder height and scooted along to what, judging by the shape, must be the bonnet. She had little room to bend down and had to crane sideways. Sarah Glyde stayed by the door with the knife.

The strings holding the tarpaulin had been cut. Stella flung it back and a cloud of dust stung her eyes; she had to pinch her nose to stop a sneeze. The car's windscreen was greyed with dust; cobwebs obscured the wing mirrors as if a massive spider had been at work wrapping the vehicle as it would a fly. The front tyres were flat, the rubber perished. Stella tried to see the registration number. She expected to find it obscured by grime.

It had been cleaned.

Terry had been here. She felt a rush of heat. In the quivering torchlight, she read a registration plate – black against white – she could have recited it with her eyes shut.

CPL 628B.

She did not need to look above the radiator grille. Despite the dirt and the dark Stella knew what her dad had found:

A blue Ford, possibly an Anglia, was seen leaving Black Lion Lane at approximately eleven on Monday 27 July. Mrs

Hammond, an elderly widow aged 74, noticed it because her husband had owned the same model in the 1960s and it brought back memories. The last letter of the number plate might have been a 'B', but she couldn't swear. (Note: reliable witness, timing wrong.)

Mrs Hammond had seen the car an hour before Kate's supposed time of death around midday, so they had discounted her statement; the only definite sighting that day. After Terry found the photograph of Isabel Ramsay opening the Charbury Village Hall, the Ford Anglia gained new significance, but by then Mrs Hammond was dead.

Challoner had not driven the Ford Anglia since that day.

Stella straightened up and squeezed back along the gap. Sarah led the way back to the hall.

'That's the sitting room.' She jabbed the blade at a door beyond the foot of the stairs. To their left, brass stair rods were illuminated in the beam. At the top of the staircase was a portrait of a woman. The head seemed to turn when Stella shone her torch up. It was Katherine Rokesmith.

Sarah bumped into Stella; the blade sliced the air.

'You nearly had my ear off!'

'Sorry.'

Neither of them was whispering.

They heard a crack. It came from the sitting room. Keeping close, they flew to the doorway; Sarah swishing the blade like a sword. A fire was burning in the grate. It appeared to have just caught; flames flickered, whipping and licking around logs that hissed and crackled.

The room was empty.

A photograph of Kate Rokesmith lay upon the logs, just shy of the flames, warping and browning with the heat. Someone had stoked the fire: a poker lay on the hearth. Bright, white teeth between rosy parted lips, a pointed incisor to the left of the front teeth marring an otherwise even set, were crumpling amidst the smoke, the ink turning metallic blue.

'Jack!' Stella shouted. 'Come on.'

She rushed up the stairs two at a time and flung wide doors in the passage to check inside each room. Sarah caught up with her in the bedroom where sheets were heaped on the floor and the mattress was sagging off the bed's metal sprung frame. Make-up littered the floor and was scattered over the mattress. The mirrors on the dressing table were smashed, glass sparkling among lipsticks and foundation bottles in the torchlight.

The window frame blew to and fro, a rhythmic squeaking like stertorous breathing. The curtain twisted over the wood had half ripped from the hooks; it ballooned in and out with gusts of wind. Melted snow pooled on the sill and dripped to the floor with a steady put-put.

Stella raised the light; Sarah clutched her arm, staying her. Kate Rokesmith smiled at them from all corners.

For an instant, an absence pervaded the room – an absence stronger than the more temporal departure of the person who had ransacked it – and filled the cloying atmosphere with the irreversibility of death.

But after a moment Stella saw the bedroom was no more than bricks and mortar, mite-nibbled paper and moth-eaten bedclothes, damp walls pasted with photos and articles about a woman long dead.

She let herself breathe: there was no one there. Terry was dead. She would never talk to him again. Terry would never know she had followed in his footsteps. Her dad had gone.

'What an adventure, we'll have hot chocolate when we get home.'

'I know where they are.' Sarah ran out, finding her way easily along the corridor without the torch.

Sixty-Nine

Tuesday, 25 January 2011

It was Stella who found the bolt at the top of the door, stopping Sarah's clumsy struggle with the handle. She slid it across; the oiled mechanism gave at once.

Winding stone steps receded into darkness. Cool damp air laced with a clinical odour drifted up. Stella could smell Eau Savage Extreme; neither Ivan nor Jack wore it.

'It's hers.' Sarah's breath was hot in Stella's ear. 'The studio smelled of it after she had been for a sitting.'

They listened but heard nothing.

Logic came back to Stella: the door had been bolted on the outside so whoever was in the basement had been locked in.

'We're too late.'

She plunged down steep steps, catching herself with a rope slung through loops on the wall.

'There he is!' Sarah leapt the last three steps, jolting Stella, who lost her balance and dropped the torch, extinguishing the light.

'Challoner's dead.'

Stella thrashed about on all fours in the smothering darkness, flailing for the torch. The slate floor grazed her palms. She scrambled to her feet and at last found a switch. She knew it would not work, but habit made her flick it down.

The room was flooded with light.

Stella's first thought was that there was no blood. Next she saw her van keys on a step beneath a gigantic contraption of red leather beneath a cone of light. A figure lay supine, feet right up, a surgical mask strapped to its face, wrap-around sunglasses shielding the eyes. Thin plastic straps clamped the calves, waist and wrists. Challoner lay motionless, skin waxy in the remorseless glare.

'Antony!' Sarah darted forward and grabbed a wrist. 'I can feel a pulse.'

Stella ripped off the mask.

It was Jack.

'Pass me a scalpel. Quick!' Stella gesticulated at a jumble of surgical utensils on a worktop.

She eased the blade between Jack's skin and the plastic thongs, willing her hand not to slip, and released Jack's limbs. Only when she had finished did Stella think to remove the wrap-around sunglasses.

Jack stared through her with eyes like Terry's in the hospital, glassy and unseeing, the pupils dilated. She leant on the lever making the chair descend abruptly to a sitting position. Jack's head jerked to one side and a string of spittle swung from his mouth.

Sarah shut her eyes and, concentrating, tried his pulse again.

'There's a fluttering.'

'Are you sure?' Stella willed it to be true. She waved a hand over Jack's face but he stared impassively at something far away. 'Jack, wake up. What's the bastard done to you?' She gripped his shoulders, holding him to her, breathing in the familiar scent of detergent and damp wool.

'I think this might explain it.' Sarah held up an empty syringe. She pulled off the needle and sniffed the open end of the capsule. 'Lidocaine combined with adrenaline, judging by the size of his pupils.'

'How do you know?'

'I'm a dentist's sister, remember?' Sarah raised her eyebrows. 'It's a ten-millilitre syringe. One of these would be fine, the maximum safe dose is five hundred milligrams, which is five of these syringes. It depends how many times he's been injected.' She lifted Jack's arm and tugged up his sleeve. There were two red blotches on his arm.

'Three is OK, isn't it?' Stella demanded. 'That's three hundred.'

'Antony wouldn't overuse a site.' Sarah dragged Jack's shirt out of his trousers. There were three more areas of red on his stomach above the line of dark hairs from his navel. She fumbled with his other sleeve. 'Hmmm. Looks like he's had six hundred, with three jabs away from his heart, which gives him a chance. I can't say for sure – but too many, whatever. You can see he's suffering from visual disturbance.'

Stella stared at Jack. His gaze was unfocused and his lips working silently.

'He's trying to tell me something. Jack, how much did Challoner give you?' Jack blinked slowly and his tongue appeared between his teeth. 'It's no use. Call an ambulance!'

'There's no signal down here.'

'Go upstairs, then.'

'I don't have a mobile and there isn't a telephone. Antony got rid of it. Give me yours.'

'It's in the car!' Stella grabbed her keys and ran up the stairs. At the top she slammed into wood and, grabbing hold of the rope, only just stopped herself toppling back. The door was shut and there was no handle on the inside.

Challoner had locked them in. She kicked at the wood but it did not give. She raced down and wheeled impotently around the room, rattling instruments and banging the counter.

Sarah had somehow got Jack on to the floor in the recovery position and folded her jacket under his head. Dimly Stella considered she would not have thought of that.

There were no windows. No other doors. No way out.

'Help!' Stella yelled, her voice cracking.

'It's soundproofed. No one will hear us. Not even Antony.' Sarah swabbed Jack's mouth with a moistened pad. 'We won't suffocate – I can tell the air is fresh, but I don't know how long we can last without food. At least we have water.'

'I don't care about us. What about Jack? Is there something we can give him, to reverse it, neutralize the drug, anything?'

'I think there's an antidote but Antony won't have it here. He doesn't even keep oxygen down here. Jack needs supportive management –

his airway protected and cardiac monitoring.' Sarah Glyde's haphazard manner had vanished: she had turned into a medic.

Neither of them said the obvious: if they could not get Jack to a hospital within the next few hours, he would die.

'Did you tell your office where you were going?'

Stella shook her head. She had not told Jackie where she was going for days. 'Wouldn't Challoner's receptionist think of finding you here?'

'Mrs Willard wouldn't care, but if she did ask, he will tell her I'm away.'

Stella went over to the dentist's chair. Jack looked frightened. She stroked his fringe back from his face.

'We will get you help, Jack. I promise,' she whispered.

The counter took up one wall; apart from a sink and the instruments it was strewn with rubbish. And a mobile phone.

'He's left his phone!' Stella grabbed it and pressed the 'on' button. The screen lit up, accompanied by Nokia's tinkling signature tune, but then went blank. The battery was dead. Infuriated she slapped it against her palm and saw minute scratches on the casing. She tipped it towards the light.

'TCD'. Terence Christopher Darnell. It was Terry's phone. Final proof, had she needed it, that her dad had been here. Although she was convinced he had not seen Challoner's secret surgery. Challoner had found his phone and answered it when she rang the night of her dad's death.

The water fountain trickling into the ceramic bowl beside the leather dentist's chair filled the silence. *The murderer spends time dressed in white beneath the ground beside a bubbling fountain.* Not all psychics were crackpots.

Her dad had cleaned dirt off the Ford Anglia's registration plate. It would have been a strain in the tight space. He had not noticed his mobile fall out of his pocket.

Terry had told Martin Cashman he was going to ring his daughter and Stella had not believed it because he had not called. Terry could not ring because Ivan Challoner had his phone. Too tired to drive, he had slept in his car all night – in his clothes – and when he woke he'd parked near Broad Street and bought ham rolls in the Co-op. He was going to call her before he drove back to London and that was when he realized he did not have his phone. Upset by such a stupid mistake, his heart rate took off. Her dad had died in the street.

Sarah was talking: 'When I was a child – I must have been terribly young – I would be sent to find Antony at mealtimes. I'd get a chair and bolt the basement from the outside and then search the house. Bonkers really, it showed how much I hated him, but this was always the last place I looked, although it was where he would be. Eventually I'd pluck up the courage and sneak down the first few steps. The surgery was always empty with the light on and the rinsing fountain going. My mother would tell me off for trespassing because only Antony was allowed here.'

'This is hardly the time for a jaunt down memory lane,' Stella barked. 'We need to get Jack out of here.'

Jack groaned and, his eyes shut, moved his head towards the rubbish on the worktop and the images of Kate Rokesmith's childhood mouth.

'He doesn't want the light – he's probably getting tinnitus.' Sarah placed the sunglasses back on his face. 'My point is, having bolted him in, the only explanation for why Antony was not here when I came looking is that there is another way out.'

Fresh air. The door and window Stella had seen in the garden.

She put her dad's phone in her anorak pocket and this time paced the room purposefully, opening cupboards, poking in the space under the stairs. She found boxes of cotton-wool pads, swabs, syringes, plaster moulds, replicas of upper and lower sets of teeth, X-ray film: the equipment of a dentist working fifty years ago.

The music was faint at first, then swelled as if a door somewhere had opened.

'Beethoven's "Pathétique".' Sarah could have been introducing a recital.

Ivan Challoner was still here.

'Ivan told me this was his son's favourite music, his wife played it on the piano at bedtime while he read him Narnia stories.' Stella spotted the speakers, four tiny discs, inserted above overhead cupboards. 'I believed him.'

'It's all right, don't cry, we are going to solve this,' Sarah murmured to Jack. She rinsed out a glass on the counter and filled it with water. She gently inserted a straw between Jack's lips and held the glass. He sucked weakly on it but then gave up.

In a closet hung a row of dental coats, white faded to grey. The temperature was lower than in the room behind her. Stella dragged the coats off the rail and flung them on the floor. She felt the panel at the back, tracing the patina of the wood. A button was fitted into the panel. Stella pressed it, pulled it, pushed it, but it did not give. She twisted it and fell forward into the cupboard as the wall gave way. Threads of fog drifted into the room and cold air seared her cheeks. She was by the stone steps where Sarah had found her.

Ivan had used a secret exit.

Stella shouted back into the room: 'I'll get help.'

'I told you he'd do this, but you wouldn't believe me. You spoil that boy. Now look what he has made me do.' Ivan Challoner unhooked the poker from the carousel of hanging fireplace tools and stirred the embers noisily. He could not drown out his stepfather:

'Children have to learn the hard way, that's how they get backbone, Antony's like a girl. I'm keeping my study locked from now on. Antony doesn't know what to do with that steam engine, he doesn't play with it properly. I've confiscated it. He has his own room, I've told him to keep to it. We have to have rules. Children prefer them.'

If he fumbled over a sentence, Ivan Challoner repeated it, the next time getting the words right:

'When we move to London you'll have a bedroom all of your own at the top and must keep to it. There will be strict bedtimes and no answering back and crying. I've told you, your father is dead and now you answer to me. We have to have rules. You will never be my son, you have no backbone and I already have a daughter.'

Eventually Ivan had become word perfect, but by then Mr Glyde too was dead.

The fire had nearly died. Ivan held a sheet of newspaper over the aperture until it sucked inwards and glowed orange.

'Now look what he's done. When we move he stays in his room. We have to have rules…'

A flame popped up behind a log and he fed it kindling and blew hard. Another flame darted out and vanished. Then another, and soon the flames joined up. When the fire had taken hold he laid the picture of his Cathy just out of reach of the flames.

'You spoilt our son because you are spoilt, sullied, corrupted,' he told Cathy.

'He's not your son. He is nothing to do with you.'

He put the flat of his fingers to his lips, kissed them and tipped his hand away towards the fire. Cathy was smiling. Heathcliff smiled back.

'Go well, my darling. It's for the best. I told you I knew what was best for you.'

There was a sound. He knew all the sounds in this house. It was the kitchen door. Whoever it was imagined they were opening it quietly. He had planned properly and long before they arrived had cut the power and prepared everything.

'Sweet dreams, little Jonny. Sleep tight, don't let the bugs bite.' He knew what to say to children. 'Shut your eyes and count to ten. When a person dies they wake up. That is all dying is. We wake up somewhere else.

'We'll give them time, Cathy. Sarah will know where I am, but will put off looking. She is such a daddy's girl, while Stella Darnell is used to nosing in lives that are not her own. Sarah is not a proper sister; she does not understand loyalty.'

He heard footsteps in the passage. They would go upstairs, then to the garage and then they would go to his father's surgery. He hid in the passage and once they were on the basement stairs, he ran across the hall and drew the bolt across. He returned to the sitting room and, aware of the value of precise timing, waited a further five minutes.

He rested the needle on the record and when the music began gradually turned up the volume. Cathy played the 'Pathétique' beautifully; it always put the boy to sleep.

The cold air winded Ivan when he opened the back door.

The garden gate was still padlocked – he had expected to find the chain cut. He hurried along the gravel path, past the buttress, around the church and paused outside the porch to tie up his shoelace. The fog was clearing and the headstones were like carious teeth against the diminishing white. Ivan felt a stirring of dread. The snow was melting and the thaw was coming.

He pulled the knot tight and became aware of an infinitesimal creaking close to his ear. It was persistent; gathering force, it grew to a rushing climax with a thump. He whipped around. Behind him in the shadowy porch the great studded door was closed. It had not come from there. Then sounds were all around him. A slab of snow slid off the roof and exploded on the ground in chips of ice.

Ivan's shoes tightly laced, he was ready to pay his respects, but was mesmerized by the dripping and plashing so that when he heard the splitting of an icicle high above his head, he paid no attention.

Ivan Challoner was conscious long enough to feel the infinitely sharp object drive deep into the base of his neck. The pain was over before it had begun.

Stella used the church tower to get her bearings and sprinted over the lawn to the gate she had seen when she and Jack came to his mother's grave. The mist was clearing, the sliver of moon bright. The ground where the snow had melted was dark like craters in the strange light: one of these caught her eye.

Ivan Challoner lay face-down on the path, a stain spreading out from his head. Stella looked around. The churchyard was still, the wind had died down, and the quiet was broken only by branches shedding snow. Walls, graves, mausoleums were gradually exposed as snow melted.

Ivan's blood was soaking into the gravel. Stella bent down: he had been stabbed in the back of the neck.

Jack had found Ivan after all.

She stepped back, her hands away from her; this was a crime scene.

She aimed the remote control at Terry's car. Her phone was where she had left it between the seats. Stella dialled 999.

'Which service would you like?'

'Ambulance, two please.' Stella took a breath and heard herself say: 'We need the police.' She gave the address and rang off.

She gathered herself; Jack had been unconscious when they found him. Sarah would have been able to tell if he was faking the symptoms. Someone had bolted the door from the outside. Jack had not killed Ivan. Who had?

Sarah Glyde.

Stella jumped when the church clock chimed four times. Although it was the dead of night, it was not entirely dark and she could see the silhouette of the weathervane on the top of the spire. She wished that it could be her dad who answered her call.

She took out his phone from her pocket and climbed into his car, locking the doors. She turned on the engine and, uncoiling the car charger in his glove box, plugged it in. This time when she switched it on, it stayed on. She chose Dialled Calls.

She did not scroll down far before she found 'Stella mob'. The phone had been used to call her old number the afternoon before he died. Her dad did not have her new mobile number. She had not bothered to give it to him.

The headlights of the emergency services cut through the trees, making them seem to dance and swoop as if inhabited by Jack's phantoms. Stella got out of Terry's car and walked towards the lights.

Perhaps if she had given her dad her new number, he would have told her about the Rokesmith case. She would have agreed to work with him. She could have helped. Perhaps if she had answered his call, it would have changed the ending and they would be waiting by the church for the ambulance and the police together.

Perhaps.

Seventy

Stella parked her dad's car facing the River Thames. The wind was blowing and the water was choppy as gusts ruffled the surface. The snow had gone. Equating Challoner with the White Witch in *The Lion, the Witch and the Wardrobe*, Jack was convinced the thaw had heralded his death. Like the reign of Queen Jadis, he had declared, Ivan's time was over: Aslan was coming. The gravel sweep outside the crematorium was crowded. Stella had not expected so many. She sat in her dad's old Toyota, the engine idling, and contemplated leaving. No one had seen her.

There was a rap on the window.

It was Jack.

She let down the glass.

'Are you coming?'

'I never go to funerals.'

'You do now.'

Stella had fetched Jack from the hospital in Eastbourne a week ago. She had not seen him since. His near-death experience appeared to have done him good: he had colour in his cheeks.

He opened the door for her. When she got out, he took her arm. Stella did not object.

'Have you given up smoking?'

'Yes.'

'Thought so.'

They walked around the hedge that screened the car park from the crematorium. This was a single-storey brick building with a drive-through porch around which were clustered at least four hundred people, mostly in police uniform. Stella faltered.

'Keep moving.' Jack had her arm. 'It's going to last an hour, then we go to the reception in a place called Imber Court and then you can go home. I will drive you.'

'What's Jackie doing here?' Stella did not acknowledge him but as Jack had intended the schedule had reassured her. 'Who's minding the office?'

'It's closed. A tribute to Terry.'

A man in a black suit standing apart from the crowd raised his eyebrows in slight acknowledgement. Stella nodded in response although she didn't recognize him. She did know the woman a few feet from him.

'There's Sarah Glyde.'

Sarah Glyde looked more wispy than ever, trailing ribbons and layers of silks and bright wools. She stood out like a blousy bloom amid the sea of blue. She tipped a tentative hand to Stella and Stella smiled in acknowledgement. Forensics had cleared Sarah Glyde; an icicle had severed Ivan Challoner's spinal cord. Sarah had not stabbed her brother, although Stella was certain that had they found him alive Sarah would have done. The police had broken into Ivan's bedroom on the top floor of the Hammersmith house and found the room entirely free of dust and completely empty.

A few more steps and she saw that the man in the black suit was Dariusz Adomek from the mini mart below her office; she had only ever seen him in his shop uniform.

A man crossed the turning circle to meet them. It was D. I. Martin Cashman.

'All right, Stella?' He wiped his hand down his face: 'We've got a bit of a problem.'

'What kind of problem?' Cashman looked as trussed up and ill at ease in his suit as she did in hers. Perhaps Imber Court, the venue for major police events in West London, had become unavailable? That was not a problem.

'One of the pall-bearers is ill.'

'Surely there's someone one else who can do it?' Jack was stern.

'Not that simple.' Martin continued to look at Stella. 'It's about height. Everyone's got to be the same height or it goes wrong. Believe it or not, there is not a single person here who is six foot.'

'I thought you had to be six foot to get into the police?' Jack had Stella's arm tight. His mandatory outfit of black coat and trousers and black brogues suited the occasion perfectly.

'Not any more. So far the guys that have volunteered are either around five-ten or a couple of inches over the six. No one is bang on. Should be a uniformed officer. Janet is trying to rustle someone up so it's not a huge deal. It means we have a small delay. Nothing to worry about.' Cashman seemed to notice Jack for the first time. 'How tall are you, mate?'

'Six foot and half an inch.'

'Would you do it? That coat will blend in.'

'Sure, OK.'

'Here's my dad.' Stella moved forward and stopped.

A hearse turned in at the gate and made its way slowly along the drive. The sleek black vehicle was magisterial against the drab greys and greens of the landscaped garden. It came to a halt just short of the car park, waiting its turn.

Stella could see the light wood coffin through the glass panel. The chrome fender and radiator grille gleamed in the harsh winter light. The hearse looked different to any she had ever seen.

No other hearse had contained her dad's coffin.

Her dad should have been milling around with the rest of his team on the pavement, underdressed for the weather, rubbing his hands to keep warm, new shoes hurting his feet, his hair in need of a cut, but washed and brushed. Six foot himself, he would have stepped up to carry the coffin. If it had been Stella's coffin, her dad would have been one of the pall-bearers. The other five would have had to match him.

'I'll do it.'

'What?' Martin Cashman was signalling to a member of the funeral staff.

'I am the right height. Tell them I will do it.'

'I didn't mean that you had—'

'I will carry my dad's coffin.' She was firm.

Stella approached the porch, dimly aware of mourners falling silent, some looking at their feet, the crowd imperceptibly shuffling to make way. Martin Cashman had assembled the other bearers: police officers all the same height as herself, the same height as her dad. Like him, they were broad-shouldered, square-jowled, with an air of capability and spruced attention. Hands clasped before them, they had formed a huddle, but broke ranks to admit Terry Darnell's daughter.

There was more scraping of shoe leather, clearing of throats. Stella looked around for Jack but could not see him. The hearse rolled forward, led into the porch by a slow-stepping police officer, holding Terry's police cap balanced on a cushion. It glided to a stop and the funeral staff came forward and drew out the flag-draped coffin on its runners.

A man touched Stella's elbow.

'We will lower it on to your shoulder. Don't make any sudden movements, keep in step with the man in front and the man to your left and you will be fine.' He held her gaze, a slight smile lifting the corners of his mouth.

'We'll take it in turns. I'll carry it until we get across the road, then you can have the conkers when we get to the other side, I promise. I know you're a strong girl.'

Stella would not have a tantrum if he kept hold of the conkers all the way, but she would mind. She needed to prove herself. The basket bumped against her legs and he could see it was too much for her, but no way was she giving up.

It was getting light when they reached the house. She carried it all the way.

'That's my girl.' He gave her a quick smile.

The wood was unremitting; the pressure immense, crushing her. Stella clasped the underside of the coffin with her left hand; her right gripped the handle to keep it steady. She had to summon all her strength; the coffin grew heavier with every step.

The aisle was long. Pew after pew passed; she was in step with the other bearers, their feet in unison with slow and certain tread. The man who had helped her receive the coffin was again by her side; slipping into place in front of her he lowered the coffin on to the catafalque. With the others, Stella bowed her head to the coffin and then she stepped into the front pew where she sat alone.

> 'The Lord's my shepherd, I'll not want.
> He maketh me down to lie...'

'You're going to live in a brand new home with Mummy. You'll come here at weekends. We will have adventures same as ever. You and me, we'll be the best detectives ever.'

He gave her a bit of a push to get her going down the path so she didn't see his face. Stella was a clever little thing. She knew as well as he did that nothing would ever be the same.

> '...In pastures green; he leadeth me
> The quiet waters by...'

Stella and her mother had gone to live in a flat by Barons Court station in West London. From that day, she had made herself forget her dad. He had lied to her about it making no difference and she told herself she would not forgive him.

Stella laid two roses – one red and the other white – on his coffin. Jack had told her that the combination signified unity. Her lips moved silently: *May you rest in peace.*

> '...My soul He doth restore again
> And me to walk doth make
> Within the paths of righteousness,
> E'en for His own name's sake.'

She got up to leave and was flanked by someone either side of her; Jack and Jackie walked with her out of the church.

Behind them Terry Darnell's coffin trundled off the catafalque into the committal room and the curtains closed.

Seventy-One

Monday, 10 January 2011

Terry blundered into the cover of the trees. With so few graves in this part of the churchyard, there was nowhere to hide. He ran heavily, the change in his trousers jingling; he clutched his pockets. He tried to vault over the low wall, but his muscles would not work and he lost his footing. The drop on the other side was greater and he landed awkwardly, ripping his jacket on barbed wire. He lay on his back, staring up at the sky, waiting for a face to appear over the wall. In the silence he became aware of the call of rooks. He rolled on to all fours and clambered back to the wall, grabbing tufts of grass for meagre purchase. He counted to ten and peeped over the jagged flint.

Ivan Challoner knelt at the foot of the grave. He had a longish package wrapped in paper. He had changed his clothes; when he had left his surgery three hours before he was wearing a brown suit and a raincoat, every inch the sociable dentist, nodding to a passer-by as he unlocked his car. Now in baggy corduroys, a shirt and buttoned-up cardigan under a tweed jacket with leather elbow patches, he had become a country gentleman. Familiar with village routine, Challoner knew precisely when to bring his flowers so as to avoid meeting anyone.

Terry raised his camera. The light was thinning but he could not risk flash. He steadied himself on the wall and fired off some long shots; then he zoomed in as Challoner rested the flowers against the headstone, unfurling the paper. The images would be good enough to connect Challoner to the flowers.

Challoner had bought them from a florist's by Kew station that afternoon. Tomorrow Terry would show Challoner's picture to the woman behind the counter. She would remember him. Terry would build the case brick by brick; Challoner would not escape.

Challoner was muttering, but Terry was too far away to hear the words. He was just feet from the man who had blighted his own life. Terry wanted to accost him but Challoner would have a plausible story. Some photographs and the hunch of a jaded ex-detective was not enough to get a conviction. Terry needed cogent evidence.

He heard a rasping and looked about him before understanding that Challoner was making the noise. For twenty minutes, loose locks of thick grey hair tumbling forward, the man scratched at the inscription with what looked like a screwdriver, all the while talking in a soothing tone.

Terry was cold and his limbs were stiffening, but he dare not shift. He was relieved when Challoner stood up and, retrieving the discarded bouquet, stepped up the slope. Terry waited until he had gone and then clambered over the wall, ripping his shirt, and hastened after him.

He was in time to see Challoner stick the dead flowers in a bin by the gate. Terry let him pass behind the eastern buttress of the church and skirting the path by the beech hedge ducked between the mausoleums. Challoner was fiddling with the chain on the gate. He heard Challoner push it open and close it behind him, replacing the chain.

Terry scrabbled up, his back against cold stone, stretching his legs, bringing them one at a time up to his chest and down again in sketchy imitation of the exercise given to him by the physiotherapist. It eased the tightening in his chest.

On a nearby headstone was the name Edward Challoner: he had died in 1890, his wife Emily ten years later. Terry scrambled to his feet. A son, George, had died twenty years after his mother in 1920 and a Simon Challoner, only son of George in 1957, aged forty-one, 'his plane lost over the English Channel'. It sounded as if the man had died in action; Terry knew he had been to the races at Deauville and was Ivan Challoner's father. Although Ivan was Kate Rokesmith's dentist, he had not been on their radar because they had not needed dental records to identify her. The police did not connect that a Simon Challoner had treated her at his home in Bishopstone when she was three and an Ivan Challoner twenty years later in Kew. Had they done so, a lot else would have fallen into place.

Terry had posted Janet by the lych gate and joined the mourners by the grave. From her vantage point Janet would not have seen Challoner and Terry had missed him completely. Challoner had his own gate and after the funeral had slipped away. But for one photograph Terry would not have known he was there.

While supposedly keeping an open mind, as procedure dictated, the investigation was scaled down: Hugh Rokesmith was the killer and they would prove it.

Within this paradigm Challoner had free rein.

The fluorescent hands on Terry's watch said it was seconds before five, confirmed by tolls of the church clock as he traipsed up to the lych gate.

He sat in the front passenger seat of his car and scrolled through his photographs. Without downloading them he could not tell if they were in focus, but they appeared to be better than he could have hoped. It was clearly Ivan Challoner by the grave. Terry tucked the camera in behind a toilet roll in the top compartment: in this sleepy hamlet, thieves could operate with impunity.

He got out again. In London, the street lighting made it seem dark, but in this valley in the South Downs, the even light was enough to see where he was going. Terry adopted a stroll, ready to bid a hearty goodnight to anyone he encountered and say that he and his late wife had courted here if he got chatting.

He deliberately went past Challoner's house and then sneaked back out of view of the windows. If someone did come, he would hide in the garden and pray Challoner would not see him. Hardly ideal, but he had no choice.

A light burned in a downstairs room where Challoner had left the curtains open. Terry could see a green sofa, an ornate wall lamp from which the light came and a mirror in a gold frame above a mantelpiece. There was no sign of Challoner.

He risked a few steps into the front garden, treading on grass patches amongst the gravel to avoid making a sound. The building's symmetry was upset by a lean-to garage; Challoner had not put his car away. Terry was about to look through the sitting-room window when Challoner appeared. He shrank into the hedge but Challoner pulled shut the curtains without looking out.

Terry returned to the lane. Light from a lamp-post near the church did not penetrate this far and darkness enveloped him. Stars were pinpricks of light in the velvet sky. Terry congratulated himself for remembering his torch. Two dustbins stood by Challoner's drive. He squatted behind them, his jacket, which had hung heavy on him all day – he flushed with the slightest effort – offered scant warmth, but, huffing, he pulled it around him. He had put on weight and could not do it up.

Terry had the patience if not the stamina for a long wait.

After half an hour the front door clicked, the car's indicator lights blinked and the locking system bleeped. Challoner was returning to London for work in the morning.

Headlights swept over Terry's hiding place, raking the bins a fraction from where he crouched. Challoner reversed, a red glow picking out dew on the grass like droplets of blood. The BMW accelerated away.

Terry kissed his palm at the receding car. Challoner had handed him an opportunity. Everyone gets one lucky break in their career; his had been a long time coming.

He brushed himself down and hobbled back to the lane and in through the lych gate. Here he dared use his torch and, keeping to the path by the beech hedge, found the Challoners' gate. As he had seen, a chain linked around the latch was fastened with a padlock – but the intricately wrought fleurs-de-lis provided ideal footholds. As a younger man Terry would have scaled it like a monkey; in his sixties it took momentous effort to pull himself up and propel himself over. He did not jump down – he could not afford an injury – but gingerly descended on to the lawn where, mopping his face with his handkerchief, he tried to get his breath.

The shadows of the yew flitted over the grass through which the church tower was stark against night sky, its perky cockerel now dark and menacing.

He worked his way along flagstones slippery with icy moss, relying on an incipient ghostly moonlight to see, and tested the windows; all were locked with catches and limiters to prevent the sashes being lifted. A burglar alarm box from a company in Seaford was prominent above the back door but there was no obvious connection. When Challoner had left, Terry had not heard him set an alarm; in the countryside silence he would have heard the keypad bleep. He gambled that it was off. His hands slick with sweat, Terry fished in his pocket for surgical gloves and snapped them on. He still had no idea how he would break in but as he turned the kitchen door handle, to his astonishment it opened. No alarm.

Immediately he tripped over a pair of wellington boots beside a washing machine. He righted them and shone a light on hooks with waxed jackets, stiff from lack of wax, and sagging yellow waterproofs. He was in the utility room. Just in time he avoided a mop in a metal bucket.

Terry's rubber-soled shoes made no sound on the stone floor, his torch illuminated a passage going in two directions. He chose right and found himself in a kitchen. Given how immaculate Challoner was, how sleek and clean was his car, and according to his website how state of the art his surgery, this room had not been decorated for decades. Pans hung from a wall of crumbling plaster; dishes were stacked on shelves by an Aga on which was a kettle and a pressure cooker. The stove gave off a dying heat welcome to Terry after his vigil in the cold. A couple of plates and a pan stood on a wooden draining rack. Challoner was no interior designer, but he was clean and he too would not leave dishes unwashed. At this moment his own house was spotless and sparkling, and thinking this Terry imagined getting Stella over. She knew about finishing off jobs. She would finish this job with him.

He froze: the table was set for breakfast, a packet of Cornflakes, a jar of marmalade, a butter dish along with plates, mugs and cutlery. For two. Challoner's sister had given him the impression Ivan lived alone. She had not spoken kindly of her brother so it could not be her. A wave of tiredness engulfed him, making his legs ache. He was losing his grip: besides telling him that another person was in the house or was expected, what the breakfast table mostly indicated was that Challoner was coming back.

His heart was like a piston against his ribs. He should leave, except if he did then Challoner would have won. For the first time since Stella was a little girl, Terry felt alive.

A fire door lined with green baize gave a sigh when he pushed it. He was in a spacious hall with mosaic flooring stretching to the front door and a staircase to his left. Terry braced himself and climbed the stairs.

A carpeted corridor the length of the house had two windows offering a watery light. There were five doors in a row.

Outside a wind was getting up, its rising moan like a wounded animal; somewhere a casement rattled. There was a constant creaking; Terry held his breath trying to pinpoint the source of the sound. The house was adjusting to his presence and the diminishing heat from the Aga.

He switched off the torch, mindful of the lane and thankful that the moonlight was sufficient.

The first room was a bathroom with white ceramic walls that had the look of a morgue. He resisted the need to use the toilet and nudged the second door, which swung inwards. He shut it behind him and shone the torch: the room was crammed with cupboards, boxes, an upended bedstead, a roll of carpet; typical domestic junk. Terry stifled a sneeze; everything was choked with dust. He beat a retreat.

In contrast, the next room was sparsely furnished with a single bed and a wardrobe resembling a coffin. A wooden chair draped with clothes was beside the bed. He lifted up a man's shirt and sniffed, grimacing at the sickly aftershave. Beneath this was a pair of trousers, folded along the front seam. Was this spartan bedroom, more like a monk's cell, where Challoner slept?

He saw a movement and, wheeling around, stifled an exclamation. A quilt had slithered off the bed. Sweat broke out on his body again, which at least offset the cold.

He rummaged for a stick of gum in his trouser pocket and folded it into his mouth; the chewing calmed him. In the corridor, Terry turned off the torch before attempting the third door.

The gum did not stop his teeth chattering; he had rarely experienced fear like this. He had relied on the shots of adrenalin that pumped around his body while he counted down to raid a drug dealer's house, or faced a posse of journalists ready to annihilate him. The reality of coming here without a warrant, without proof, without even being a police officer hit him.

Headlines. Photographers. Disgrace. Failure to solve the Rokesmith case would be nothing compared to being caught breaking and entering.

Bang. Bang. You're dead.

He pictured the little boy aiming two fingers at him with dark, accusing eyes.

He was doing this for the boy and for his father.

Hugh Rokesmith had been a man of few words; his short marriage had blighted his entire life. Terry had been wrong and wished that he could tell him. He felt for the thin, slightly stooped figure whose drawling manner had done him no favours. When Rokesmith died Terry had been angry that he had evaded prison, but now Terry was sorry he could never make amends. At least he could present Jonathan Rokesmith with his mother's killer and exonerate his father. The prize was within his reach.

The door jolted on its hinges with a thump and Terry was bathed in orange light.

Brown eyes and shoulder-length hair. Eau Savage Extreme: she preferred aftershave to perfume. She didn't care what people thought.

From such clues as these had the detectives built up a profile of the dead woman, as if knowing her better would tell them how she had come to be murdered.

A pair of trousers and a blouse like those she had been wearing when her body was found were hanging from the wardrobe. It was like meeting long-lost friends. Isabel Ramsay could not describe Kate's clothes to the police because she had not seen her. A splash of green from the scarf to match the lemon patterned blouse; Terry did not know about clothes, but knew what he liked. His ex-wife had worn the same blouse until discovering it was the taste of a murder victim.

Under a chair, toes pointing out, the scent of perfume acceding to mothballs and damp, were her shoes.

A trickle of sweat ran into his eyes; he blinked and with a punch his chest constricted. Terry had no words to express the sight, yet words were everywhere; newspaper articles, the type small, large, black, white, were fitted around picture after picture: Kate Rokesmith's image was plastered over the walls.

A book lay on a wooden nightstand: *Wuthering Heights*. He made out an inert lump in the bed.

The second place at breakfast.

Wheels crunched on the drive. Crashing into the door jamb, he plunged along the passage, just remembering to switch off his torch. He stopped at one of the windows: Challoner was getting out of his car, younger, fitter and more agile than Terry, whose muscles were draining strength as if a plug had been pulled.

Terry was trapped. No one knew he was here; he had not told Stella.

He fumbled blindly with a cupboard door, grabbed the handle and found himself at the head of a staircase like the one at the other end of the passage. *Symmetry*. He felt a surge of love for the architect.

At the bottom, the silence told him he had not woken the person in the bed. If there had been a person at all; nothing in this bloody place was what it seemed.

Terry identified domestic sounds: the fridge door opening and closing, drawers slamming, a tap splashing which set pipes clanking. The roar of a boiling kettle, a rising whistle that subsided, water pouring into a mug, two mugs; comforting noises that offered him no comfort. With the scrape of a chair a shadow fell across the passage: Challoner was coming. Terry had no time to go back upstairs.

There was a door.

He tumbled down a step, twisting his ankle. He bit on his hand as hot pain seared up his calf, retaining enough presence of mind to pull the door shut after him.

Challoner must know he had an intruder; the sound of his heels clicking on the stone passage was close. He could have seen Terry's car, or maybe knew his back door was unlocked. Terry scrambled behind a shelf unit that would not shield him if Challoner put on the light. He curled into a ball and on a childish impulse hid his head in his hands to increase his invisibility.

A strip of light missed his hiding place by inches. He heard a chink of glass and peeped through his fingers. Challoner was lifting a bottle of whisky out from a wooden case stuffed with straw. He left and closed the door, but Terry did not move; he might be calling the police. Then he considered what he had seen: a shrine to a murdered woman. Calling the police was one action Challoner would not take. He got up and rolled his shoulders to encourage circulation.

Between him and the external doors was a shape shrouded in stiff tarpaulin. Wedged in tight, between it and the wall, Terry tugged ineffectively at one of the cords holding the tarpaulin; it was tightly knotted. He tried to undo it, but it would not budge. He laid the torch on the concrete floor and pulled his keys out of his trouser pocket. He sawed the cord between the teeth of the mortice key; old and frayed, it gave way and he snatched and tugged at the canvas until he had created enough slack to lift it free.

In the feeble light of the failing torch he knew what he was looking at. He pulled at the canvas until he could poke his torch beneath.

There were newspapers on the floor. He tore off a scrap and scribbled the number down.

He heard footsteps above.

The person might see the quilt on the bedroom floor and realize they had an intruder.

The garage doors were locked with two rusted bolts, top and bottom; after one desperate tug, the top one released with a bang like a gunshot. Terry went to work on the lower bolt and grazed his hand before he eventually wrenched it out of the floor. The door shuddered loudly when he opened it enough to squeeze through. He closed it behind him. In the throes of another flush, the cold air was welcome; he mopped his face with his handkerchief. He had pulled his shoulder at some point and it ached. His strained ankle hurt and his breathing was like sucking on a blowtorch. He was out of condition; when this was over – how extraordinary that he could think of the Rokesmith case as over – he would follow doctor's orders and get fit.

This time Terry risked jumping down from the gate into the churchyard. He executed a perfect landing on the tiled path and wished Stella had been there to see it.

Terry was woken by a pain in his cheek where the armrest had been digging into him. The papers had dropped from his hand and were scattered in the well beneath the front passenger seat. He gathered them up and, trying to stretch, hit his shin on the window. Terry was in the habit of taking documents from the case files when he left the house, hoping to spot something new. He smoothed out on his lap the psychiatrist's reports on the boy in the weeks after the murder. He had attended all the meetings, desperate that Jonathan would speak and describe his mother's killer.

He climbed out of the car, his damp shirt sticking to his skin. Seven forty-five and it was barely light. He had slept over eight hours, yet he did not feel better for it.

His bladder was full. He looked up and down the road; his was the only car parked in the seaside bays. Opposite was a recreation ground and in the distance there were already lorries on the A259. Out of sight, below a bank of pebbles, came the wash and hush of the tide. He clambered over a wall separating the beach from the road, crossed a concreted walkway and took jumping strides, his feet sinking into the shingle, down to the shoreline. Dark-grey sky merged with iron-grey sea. He laid the papers down, weighing them with a chunk of bleached wood, and peed. He swayed as he did up his zip. His head was a mush as if he had been drinking. Last night had been the first night for weeks when he had not had a drink and nor had he eaten.

Far off he made out a yellow dot. The Newhaven–Dieppe Ferry returning to Britain. Tucking in his shirt and doing up his cuffs, this sight cheered Terry. He would invite Stella to France, they would go for the day because she wouldn't be able to spare much time. Like him, her work came first.

Stella scampered over the beach when the water receded and waited, hands on hips. She bellowed at the sea: her words got lost in the rush of shingle dragged by the water, but he knew what they were.

'I'm not scared of you!'

The water rushed at her; Stella belted off pell-mell, squealing when froth lapped at her heels catching her sandals.

Terry swept her up into his arms high above the sea.

'Come on, Stell, let's get an ice cream,' he shouted. She scrubbed at his hair, her legs encrusted with sand. Maybe he'd buy himself one too.

A burst of wind buffeted him and shifted the wood. The pages flew into the air. Terry snatched at them, but they whirled towards the surf, fluttering like birds in the dawn sky. Helpless, he gazed out to sea; he did not need the reports, he could practically recite them word for word.

It was a steep climb up the shingle and twice, his balance poor, he stumbled on to his knees.

He fell into the front seat, shivering, his neck stiff from sleeping awkwardly. His jacket pulled at his shoulders, somehow making his chest ache. These days he had pain somewhere all the time. He was too old to camp out in a car. Yet this morning nothing could dampen his spirits.

He unscrewed the lid from his flask. He could have done with coffee last night but had forgotten it. Too exhausted to drive to London, he had told himself he had no deadline to meet, no press conference to attend. Ivan Challoner had no idea; he could take his time.

Terry had solved the case that had haunted him for decades.

Instead of going home he had found his way to the sea and, scrunched up on the back seat, covered with a skimpy picnic rug tainted with de-icer fluid, his jacket a pillow, had fallen into a thick sleep, dreaming of Jonathan Rokesmith and his bear named Walker.

Ivan Challoner would provide a plausible reason for the flowers; he would claim they were a tribute to Kate's years in Bishopstone where his family had lived for over a century. He would not be able to explain the stuff in the house. He would finally pay for his crime.

It was tempting to call the station, but Stella must be the first to know. He would show her police work in action. She was like him, she was thorough and methodical: together they would bring Ivan Challoner to justice.

He poured coffee and balanced the cup on the dashboard while he did up the flask. Steam clouded the windscreen. The liquid tasted of plastic.

He would buy breakfast in Seaford and call Stella. They would make a plan.

Terry spelled out his daughter's name in the steam on the glass with a forefinger. He flopped back in the seat, catching a whiff of himself: sweat and greasy hair. He puckered his nose and scratched his unshaven cheek with distaste. A clean and fastidious man, he disliked being unkempt. He would shower and shave before he saw Stella. He wanted to look good. He undid another button on his shirt – torn now – to ease the pressure on his chest. He checked to see if absently he had clicked on the safety belt and found that he had not. He shifted to release his jacket, which had rucked up behind and pain came like a stitch. He had drunk the coffee too fast. Terry felt every day of his sixty-eight years.

The sky was lightening towards the west. The steam had evaporated, and where he had written 'Stella' were vague finger dabs. He took out his handkerchief to blow his nose and the slip of newspaper with the registration plate fell out. He slotted it above the sun visor while he rubbed his chest to mitigate the cramps.

Terry followed signs in Broad Street and found a car park behind the Co-op. He paid for half an hour – the shortest period; at the outside he would be fifteen minutes – and displayed the ticket.

Seaford was a retirement town. This early on a parky January morning there were few locals about. It was too quiet. Terry could not imagine growing old here. This thought was contradicted by a derisive cry of seagulls above him. He retreated into the heated supermarket where he snatched up a ham roll from the chiller cabinet, hesitated, then made it two; he had missed supper. He grabbed a can of Coke. He broke into another sweat and, swaying, put out a staying hand. He needed to eat, that was all.

He waited in the queue, pressing the cool can to his cheek; only one checkout was open and the cashier was slow, examining each item as if it was foreign to her. Jonathan had thrown away the green crayon because he had not wanted the colour in the box. He had drawn Challoner's house in black and white. Terry cast around for another cashier. He ached; the food in his arms was heavy; the can was like lead.

He was being watched.

A small girl was by the counter, leaning back on it, a teddy bear clamped to her nose.

THE DETECTIVE'S DAUGHTER

Stella.

He would not wait until he was in the car, he would ring Stella outside the shop before her day got under way. Terry winked at the little girl and quick as a flash she vanished behind the wire baskets and peered at him through the holes.

[J. J. Rokesmith, 13 September 1981]

When Jonathan returned, Walker the teddy bear was on the detective's knee. He saw this immediately because Walker is his benign witness. Before he begins an activity he turns the bear to face where he has decided to be so that he is observed by him.

In this final session I began by giving Jonathan a task, one I have broached before. The adults: the detective and female sergeant, the female social worker and father were silent while I reiterated how Jonathan might help catch the bad person. If he had not seen anything, he could not help. He must not make up stories to please the police or me. He did not speak.

There was five minutes left when Jonathan came in from the garden. He hesitated on the threshold, apparently considering removing Walker from the detective, who remained neutral. He did not smile in case Jonathan interpreted this as triumph and decided he had 'captured' the toy. Nor was he stern, which might imply he had removed the bear as punishment. The impression given was that Walker had chosen his lap. Jonathan would see that if Walker was 'in the detective's corner' then D. I. Darnell must be a good man. He returned to his table and sat still. The questions resumed in a light voice – Walker was doing the talking:

Did you see a man talking to your mummy?

No answer.

Were you there when the man hurt your mummy?

463

No answer.

What colour hair did the man have?

No answer.

At the end of the session the boy trotted over to the detective and put his face close to Walker's face, glaring at him, implying betrayal. Then he collected him and left.

This time he did not shoot the detective.

Terry patted his jacket. He had left his wallet in the car. He felt himself redden; his breathing hurt – there was no air in the shop. The little girl had gone. Behind him the queue had backed up to the drinks aisle. Terry was about to abandon his breakfast when he found his wallet. He had forgotten his new jacket had inside pockets but was too tired to explain and handed over a ten-pound note. Always prepared, he had been to the cashpoint before staking out Challoner's surgery.

Terry lifted the carrier bag and nodded to the cashier. He wanted in some oblique way to share his buoyant mood, to say his daughter had bought his wallet and that he was this far from catching a murderer. A woman jolted him; he was in the way, so he left.

Janet, his colleague, had gone to the car but Terry had been finishing his notes, grabbing some peace. It was a sweltering afternoon; the air in the consulting room deadened even with the garden door open. He was exhausted then too. Terry had been invisible to the boy, being either a detective or in this session a bear, and Jonathan had stayed mute, so that was that: dead end. The case was cold.

The boy appeared, holding his bear by the ear.

'All right, Jonny?' Without thinking, he spoke to the boy as he would his daughter.

Terry had never heard the voice before.

'You have to know a very important thing.' The boy was confidential.

'Yes?' Terry kept still; he did not call for a witness. Walker the bear stared at him with button eyes.

'It's important that you know.'

'What should I know?'

'My mummy is dead.'

Terry Darnell faltered by the trolleys in the supermarket entrance. Until then he had been too preoccupied with catching Kate Rokesmith's killer to remember this bald fact.

In the search for his wallet he had not come across his phone. It was in the car. No, it was not in the car. It had been in his pocket when he was in Challoner's garage. He had mistaken it for his torch. He still had the torch but not the phone. Where was it?

He had dropped it in the garage. Challoner would know the police were on to him.

He could not call Stella.

The street was busier: sunlight suffused the mist, cars had parked along the kerb and pedestrians jostled on the pavements, wheelie shopping baskets rumbling, motorized buggies clearing a path.

Darkness squeezed him from the sides. The carrier bag was too heavy.

'My mummy is dead.'

Darkness pushed from above.

Stella!

And then from below.

A woman coming out of the Co-op knocked into the elderly man who had dawdled in the queue. She tutted and then exclaimed when he fell down in front of her.

Later she would tell police how the gentleman had toppled over like a toy soldier. She had shouted into the shop for someone to call an ambulance. She was a nurse and had tried to resuscitate him, but had established before the paramedics arrived that he was dead.

Epilogue

Mrs Ramsay's house had been empty for weeks. Stella caught a whiff of lavender in the air. Her feet clattered in the hall, the rug and hat stand had gone, dust had settled on the glazing bars and fine cobwebs occupied cornices. It needed another clean, but she would not say or Gina Cross would think she was touting for more work.

Gina Cross had not visited the house, nor had her brother and sister. Stella was used to the vagaries of families: she not been able to deal with her dad's house. Nonetheless, it saddened her: when she wasn't railing against their carelessness, Mrs Ramsay had spoken fondly of her children; for some reason they did not feel the same way about her.

In the kitchen the gathering dust had made less impression. The sink still gleamed, the draining board was immaculate. The 1960s décor was too shabby to have retro value, though; new owners would strip it out. She wandered through to the dining room and, resting a foot on the radiator beneath the window sill, gazed out beyond the yew hedge to St Peter's Square and read the postcard again: '11 a.m.'

The address side of the card was blank, the italicized message in turquoise ink confident and bold. The card depicted Hammersmith Bridge from the Barnes end and, going by the cars, the image might be 1970s; a red Routemaster bus – number 33 – gave nothing away. Kate Rokesmith wrote cards to Ivan Challoner, summoning his presence. She had not sent this one. Stella had received it that morning with nothing else in the envelope. There did not need to be.

She looked at her wrist: Terry's watch was three minutes fast, meaning it was ten forty-seven. Unlike the hot Monday in 1981, on this colder sunny day St Peter's Square was not deserted. Children played on the lawns and two mothers perambulated babies in buggies around the perimeter paths.

Stella was there to give Mrs Ramsay's house one last check. She would never come again. She returned to the hall and looked out of the back door at the garden. The lawn, a lush green, had survived the snow. She slapped her cheek, feeling a tickle; her fingers were wet. That morning she had put the box of toys that Terry got ready for her visits back in her old bedroom.

Stella heaved on her rucksack and went out on to the porch. She shut the front door and as per Gina Cross's instructions dropped the keys through the letterbox. She went down the steps, turned right and passed the house where Detective Superintendent Terence Christopher Darnell had lived for over forty years, walking on past the church. Jack said when a person was walking they were in no place at all, it was like death. No one had seen Kate walking. The clock in the tower showed ten fifty-six. Stella continued past the statue of the Leaning Woman and into the subway.

From the Bell Steps there did not appear to be anyone on the beach. Then she saw Jack Harmon coming up from the shoreline. His name was really Jonathan Justin Rokesmith. Stella would always call him Jack.

'You came.' Jack leant against the wall beneath Sarah Glyde's garden. The beach was a suntrap; out of the breeze it was warm. The tide had ebbed; the mud was viscous, the air heavy with its stench.

'Of course.' Stella rested the rucksack on a slab of concrete jutting out of the ground. She pulled out a maroon carrier of fake canvas and placed it next to it. Inside was a large tin.

Jack held out his hands to take the tin. She shook her head.

'It's OK.' She clasped it to her and stumbled over scatterings of bricks and glass, stepping from stone to stone, heedless of the rim of green slime around her loafers. A plank of wood, slippery and glistening in the sunshine, lay across the shingle, half in the shallows the red painted letters flaking:

'KE P TO TH RI HT'.

When Stella shuffled to the middle, it see-sawed with her weight. She prised the lid off the tin and handed it to Jack. Coarse grey-white grit sent a puff of dust into the air. The smell was not of ordinary ash, it was the smell of a body burned at an intense temperature for just over an hour in the Mortlake Crematorium: a smell unfamiliar to Stella. In a tin lined with plastic lay all that was left of her dad.

'Do you want to say something? Make a speech?'

Stella shook her head and crouched down; the plank tipped and steadied.

The ash made a brushing sound as first it trickled, then poured out on to the mud. Water lapped around it, drawing it out to a pale blurred shape. Stella replenished it with more ash and again the tide swelled around it until all the ash floated on its surface like the glitter she had used at Terry's for making Christmas cards.

'Make a wish and blow out the candle. Keep it secret. No, don't say what it is, not even to me. Blow really hard. That's all right. Have another go. One, two, three. Blow! Good girl! Your wish will come true. I promise.'

Stella stretched out as far over the water as she could, and tipped the tin upside down, shaking out the last of the grit. Jack held her shoulder. She dipped the tin in the river, sluiced it around and rinsed it out. The current was dispersing Terry's ashes and sending them downstream to the sea.

She handed Jack the postcard.

The message was meant for Ivan and Jack had neutralized it by sending it to Stella; they had met at the time Kate always specified.

With a flick of his wrist Jack sent the card sailing into the air. It twisted and fluttered in the mild breeze and, alighting on the river, caught an eddy. It swirled around before vanishing and reappearing; it was lost in the bright morning light.

'You hold the stone like this. Keep your wrist flat, hold steady. Flick it and keep your eye on the water. Imagine what will happen when you let it go. Like this.'

Her dad sent the stone out on to the water. It skimmed the surface and bounced five times. He never did less than five. Sometimes he made six but she knew his record was seven. She had a go, but the stone sank. Dad made her stand properly and she did it again. It sank. She knew he thought she would give up, but she hunted about and found the right shapes and soon had a massive pile. She took her time, 'gauging the throw' as he told her: the stone whipped the top of the water over and over and over. Four! After that she never got more than three. Dad said he wished he could bottle that moment. He said he wished her mum had come. She knew that was because he hoped her mum would change her mind about leaving and Stella could stay with him.

Jack and Stella stood on the spot where Ivan Challoner had murdered Kate Rokesmith because she would not leave her husband for him.

St Peter's Church clock struck quarter past eleven when they climbed the Bell Steps. They passed Sarah Glyde's house on Hammersmith Terrace and the Ram Inn on Black Lion Lane. They descended into the subway; the return journey that Kate never made. On the north side of the Great West Road they strolled up the ramp and between the bushes to the Leaning Woman. Sunlight through the trees splashed over her pitted surface, making the lines that represented the butcher's jointing invisible.

The earth around the plinth was soft from the rain, and Jack scrabbled at it, his hands quickly muddy. He made little headway. Stella found a beer can amongst leaf mould under the hedge; crushed in the middle it might work as a trowel.

'Use this.'

Jack flung off his coat and a tattered paperback fell to the ground. Stella gathered it up. It was his London street atlas. She flicked through: every page had been scrawled with ballpoint.

'Did you write these letters?'

'They're not letters, they're journeys. I told you, they helped me find Challoner.'

'What do they spell?' Stella wished Jack would not be like this and fanned the pages, the letters flashing by.

Jack cleared loose soil from his hole.

'This is a "C" and that's an "I" in front and again after. This could be a lower case "e". She leafed back three pages. 'That's an "L". Lice. Add this "A" and it's "Alice". She shut the book. She was getting carried away with Jack's signs. Much of Jack was a mystery and really she should not encourage him.

'Why are you digging?' She had put off asking.

'I'm bequeathing my amulet to the Woman for good luck.'

'Why don't *you* keep it?'

'The Woman needs luck more than me, that's how it works.' Jack pushed earth back into the hole covering the lump of green glass, working quickly, tamping it down with his palms. He jumped up and jigged about on the patch, stamping on it.

'Mine or yours for hot milk with honey?' He did a skip. 'Tea for you.'

'Mine's nearer.'

Kate Rokesmith's son and Terry Darnell's daughter walked in companionable silence between the budding cherry trees to the end terrace house in Rose Gardens North. Stella rubbed mud off her shoes on the squirrel scraper and slipped her key in the lock. Tugging on the letter box, she opened the front door.